Tidy Killing

Tidy Killing
a novel

by

Vera Mont

Published by Montland Books

ISBN-13: 978-0-9959174-1-5

Cover Photo by:
© Penywise | Dreamstime.com
© Pongphan Ruengchai | Dreamstime.com

CHAPTER 1

Though all the industrial plazas on Birchmount Road looked much alike, Alec Sims had no trouble recognising Ac-Me Plastics; it was awash with strobe-lights at nine in the morning. Half a dozen cruisers were scattered about the parking lot; a fire-truck just pulling out; an ambulance parked by the main entrance, its driver and attendant lounging against the near wall, chatting up a pretty young woman. Paramedics have seen it all, a dozen times over, and learned how to take their minds off it.

A large and solemn constable blocking the glass doors gave a curt nod over Sims' badge and directed him down a corridor. Sims registered faces as he passed them, familiar by the pale, dazed, wary look of people close to a death. The dead, he mused, fascinate, repel, and make us vaguely guilty, as if we owed them something we can never repay. The policeman guarding the last room before the fire exit was as large as the other, but on him, solemnity sat precariously.

"Constable DiMarco," Sims greeted him.

"Detective-sergeant Sims," the man replied, with the merest hint of condescension.

"What have we got?"

"*You've* got a stiff," said DiMarco, lowering his voice out of deference to the sensibilities of laymen present. "And no big case, either, by the look of it. Coroner's been called - is on his way, if you believe old Benson moving so quick."

"Is the st-- victim identified?"

"Sure. All those people," DiMarco raised his massive chin slightly in the direction of the group farther up the hall, "know him. Half of them's been in tramping around. Name's Morley. PhD Chem. He ran their research department. Seems to've spent the weekend doing overtime. That nice little number," the chin zeroed in on the younger woman - Sims agreed privately with 'nice', had reservations about 'little', and positively winced at 'number' - "came in this morning and fell over him."

Sims entered the room, stopping just inside the door, which softly closed of its own accord. A bright, very clean laboratory, with benches arranged in the form of an F, the vertical stroke under four tall windows facing north. To his right, a tidy, empty desk, with a telephone on its near outside corner. To the left, a coatrack, and beyond that, another desk, this one with books, pencils, sheets of paper in no obvious system. There was nothing on the bench-tops, except a Bunsen burner on the short arm of the F, lying in a pool of something yellowish-green and frothy. Stepping toward it, Sims had his first sight of the dead man - or at least part of him; a foot in grey sock and brown suede loafer, and the lower end of a grey pant-leg. No skin showing.

The right-side wall had two doors cut into it; the body lay near one of these. His right leg and left arm were hidden underneath; the right arm flung up over the head, palm down, fingers slightly curled, all but touching an overturned wooden stool; left leg stretched out. He looked relaxed in this awkward position. The face was averted, so that Sims could make nothing of its expression. On an otherwise clean white lab-coat lay a few blobs of the foamy green muck. A great deal more of it was on the floor, and in a large flask, from which it appeared to be flowing. Sims put a tentative finger to the edge of the puddle; it was solid; frozen in mid-ooze. It made him want to leave. There was something vile about the stuff, noxious - it seemed animate, somehow - as the man did not. Sims conceived the notion, both compelling and irrational, that the green ooze had killed the man - deliberately. He wished he hadn't touched it with his bare hand.

The dead man wore surgical gloves. Only the back of the right one could be seen; taut rubber, through which the hairy hand showed dark, with a small triangular tear just below the rolled cuff. Sims fished out his own latex gloves – a recent improvement, in deference to AIDS – on the cotton ones he had been accustomed to wearing at crime scenes. Hardly taking his eyes off the corpse, he tore open the paper pouch, shook out, inflated and pulled on the left glove, then the right, folded and pocketed the empty sac, absently, all the motions made automatic by repetition. Then he paused, looked at his own hands, peeled off the gloves and slowly pulled them on again. Funny. Once more he tried it, pulling them by the back of the cuff.

Yes, you could do it that way - but would you? A dandy might: had he not seen such affected donning of gloves in late-night movies? Yet, this man did not look the part: under the rucked-up lab-coat sleeve was the cuff-end of a brown jacket, but not of a shirt. While Sims might wear a short-sleeved shirt with a sport jacket; none of his well-dressed acquaintances would. Gingerly, making sure of a clear section of floor, he knelt beside the body. He'd like a look at the palm, and perhaps at the man's face...

"Don't. I repeat, Do Not Tamper with the deceased."

Sims started - managed, just, not to jump - like a kid caught with the cookie-jar. Dr. Benson had that effect on people, even when not purposely sneaking up on them. Dr. Benson was broad, florid, self-important; he had the air, cultivated by headmasters and televangelists, of being, by definition, always in the right. Sims disliked him, for no valid reason, which only increased Dr. Benson's right to be so. In this case, more-over, he was. The detective stifled the excuse that sprang to his lips, and settled for a too-hearty greeting.

"Morning," said Dr. Benson. "Far too early in the morning, if I had anything to say about it. I'd not even arrived at my place of work yet, and here work is already."

"I was about to remark how promptly you came," said Sims, in a tone commendably devoid of sarcasm.

"Yes, well, let's get this over with."

The coroner sank to one knee, not without effort, on the other side of the dead man. "Help me roll him over."

Sims did, and saw revealed a quite unmemorable face, but for its expression of mild surprise, and the dark-light pattern of lividity. So he had been dead for some while - at least a day. It was the face of a man in middle age, perhaps a little fuller than the national ideal, a little heavy in the jowls, clean-shaven, allowing for a faint stubble, receding of hairline, greying. A not-unpleasant face... Sims caught himself stealing a glance at Dr. Benson's veined, fleshy nose and small dark eyes beneath heavily corrugated brows.

The coroner startled him once again by saying, "One of us. Oh, not you and me - you're young and muscular, Sergeant...?"

"Detective-sergeant Sims," he answered smartly, turning

the instinctive beginnings of attention-stance into a nearly rude shrug - which was just as bad. Worse? He could do nothing right, around Dr. Benson.

"Sims. Yes, I think we've met."

Only a dozen times, you pompous old buzzard, Sims thought, and you insist on forgetting my name every time. But the coroner had resumed his examination of the body. He was thorough and efficient - even his worst detractors had to give him that: Benson made very few mistakes.

"No sign of violence, no indication of a struggle. I'm not about to undress him here and now, but I'll venture a guess that lividity is consistent with the present position... rather, with the position in which he was found." He looked up sharply at Sims, "I take it you'd not moved him?"

"Of course not."

"Hm. All right. Well, naturally, there will have to be a post-mortem, but the purplish tinge points to congestive heart failure. He looks to me like a prime candidate: working too hard, having too much to eat, too much to drink - smoking too much... Of course, that's redundant; any smoking is too much."

"How do you know?" asked Sims.

"I've seen their lungs."

"I mean, how do you know that this man was a smoker?"

"Look at his hand," said Dr. Benson, holding out the dead man's now bare left. The nails of the first two fingers were stained a dull yellowish colour. "These days, with good soaps and excellent toothpastes, the discoloration is not so obvious as it once used to be... However, you can't wash out your lungs."

The stony glare which accompanied this last remark told Sims that the coroner remembered him perfectly well, warts and all.

"That's what killed him; cigarettes and stress. Our vices get all of us in the end - unless our occupations do. This poor fellow probably thought he was getting a jump on all the ambitious young know-it-alls nipping after his job. All he got was a coronary. Still, there are worse ways to go."

"So, you don't think it could be homicide?"

Dr. Benson gave another of his well-practised sharp looks, "Do you?"

"I don't know yet."

"Well, nothing like that is going in my scene report. It looks very like a case of natural causes, and that - unless and until someone convinces me otherwise - is what I am writing."

In fact, Sims had nothing but a bad feeling in the back of his throat. Dr. Benson would put that down to smoking too much - any being too much.

"Could I check his pockets before the body is removed?" he asked.

"Do whatever your morbid suspicion drives you to," said the coroner. "I'm finished here. When you're finished, let the ambulance know."

Sims experienced a childish satisfaction; the proper hostile mood was re-established. For a brief moment, he had been tempted to feel sympathy for Dr. Benson - an emotion difficult to reconcile with deep-seated dislike. Sims did not enjoy having inconsistent emotions, a state in which he found himself far too often.

When Dr. Benson had departed, he catalogued the contents of Dr. Morley's pockets. Lab-coat, right: packet of tissues, light blue disposable lighter. Left: nothing. Upper: black marker, two blue pens and one red. Jacket, right: one package Player's filtered cigarettes, unopened. Left: nothing. Upper outside: nothing. Inside: wallet, chequebook, pen. Open-collared blue sport shirt, front pocket: nothing. Trousers, right: loose change amounting to $2.45, one plain key-ring; house and car keys, and two small ones, such as might open a desk, trunk or cupboard. Trousers, left: more tissues in a neatly-folded square. Hip-pocket: nothing.

Before putting them into a plastic bag with signed label, Sims tried the small keys on the nearest desk; they did not fit. However, none of the drawers was locked, and he made a brief, not strictly legal, survey of the desk. Its neatness irritated yet intrigued him. Blotter, unscribbled, pristine green; along its top edge, all in a straight line: a calendar, showing Friday, May 11, 1986; a green-and-white ceramic pen holder; white coffee mug turned upside-down on a precisely folded paper towel, clean glass ashtray... This was consistent with unopened cigarettes. So, what was wrong? Only the telephone was wrong: a good ten inches out of alignment, and askew. Of course: the emergency call must have come from here. The center drawer held notebooks, dated at the upper right corner of each page - he flipped through to check; yes, every page - the last entry being May 11, headed: 'W-7/p.prod.' Gibberish, of no earthly use to Sims. Other drawers contained pencils, all sharpened, of course; another blue lighter, blank paper, new notebooks, cellotape, order forms, chemical catalogues... nothing of any interest - and all, all in military order. What kind of person keeps everything so tidy?

He wandered over to the other desk. Now, this was more like something a normal human being would have used. None of the drawers was locked. Just as well; otherwise he'd have to open and reseal the evidence bag - and then explain why. Which might have been a small price to pay for learning that this was the victim's desk. It was friendly: it had clutter, unfinished business, more notes in scientese - but messy, the way gibberish ought to be. No ashtray, so it couldn't be Dr. Morley's, after all. And are you disappointed that the man you like more is not dead? Or the girl... Lady? Woman? Who is there to object to what you call female personnel inside your own head? Only it would be nice to get it straight once and for all, so that you're never caught using the wrong term out loud.
Closing the last drawer, Sims recalled his wandering mind. What had he not seen yet? Doors. The first, beyond the right-hand, compulsive - presumably the vicitm's - desk, swung open to a store-room. Glassware on one side, all neatly shelved; on the other, chemicals in brown jars, arranged in ranks, from aluminium ammonium sulphate to zinc oxide. Nothing out of place, nothing upset; no gaps. Could anyone be such a perfectionist as to put back even the materials he was using, before he started work?
The other door, near the body, which Sims walked around carefully, led into a small room; this one had a window onto the back lawn and was bright with mid-morning sun. It contained a laboratory bench, cupboards and two fume hoods, side by side. Sims remembered using one at college: you cook things in there, that would otherwise kill you. So, why had Dr.

Morley not? They were empty and clean. On hooks on the near wall hung a row of bug-eyed faces - gas masks - each with a name on white adhesive tape: 'MORLEY', in black felt pen; 'Jones', in round, clear print; 'DUMONT'; 'Frayne', in red script, and 'P.F.A', in green ballpoint. Five Halloween faces; five people in the hall - one on the floor.

In the wastebasket, he found the wrapper from a pair of surgical gloves, size ten. They had come from a drawer Sims opened after glancing at stainless-steel instruments, filter paper and thermometers. Arranged by size from six - the nice little number? - to eleven - the fair stocky man, or the tall gawky boy? The sink in this room had a water-stain in its bottom; the one in the main lab was sparkling clean. Sims was becoming depressed by all this cleanliness and order.

Even the corpse looked tidy now, arms and legs straightened out, eyes (hazel) staring at the ceiling. The only flaw on him, now that the splashes of greenish ooze were not visible, was a long smear of something greasy on the right arm of his white coat, close to the shoulder. And a brown jacket with grey slacks. Why wear a jacket? The weather had been warm until Sunday afternoon. And Sunday afternoon was much too late for time of death: rigor had already passed off.

The back of Sims's throat scratched abominably.

CHAPTER 2

Voices, notably DiMarco's rumble, outside the door alerted him to the arrival of the scenes-of-crime team. He knew them well: John "Flash" Jackson and Simon Woo, affectionately known at Toronto's 43 Division as the odd couple. Jackson was young, unkempt, laconic; his partner, small, owlish and very nearly silent. If those two communicated at all, it must be by telepathy. Yet they were good - and at least, nobody had ever heard them bicker, as most teams did most of the time.

"Hey, Sims,"

"Hey, Flash," to Simon Woo, you just nod, if you notice him at all.

"You took your time."

Jackson shrugged, began unloading cameras and equipment cases onto a patch of pristine floor just inside the door, the smallest possible patch that would contain them. "Big deal?"

"I don't know. I think so - Dr. Benson doesn't, yet."

"So?"

Translating this correctly as "What do you want done?", Sims showed him the body, indicating the position in which it had been found. "I hate this," he remarked while arranging the victim's left leg. "You have to be a ghoul to do this."

Stepping back, out of the photographs, he continued to explain. "I'd like that muck analyzed, and get some scraping from the floor there, see the scuffmarks?"

Simon Woo cast him a venomous look. You don't tell ident men their business. "Well, okay, of course you saw it. Check for prints on the doors, the phone, desk, maybe that gas-tap - Wait a minute! The gas-tap is closed. He might have finished with it..." In any case, Sims made a note in his rapidly-filling book. "Could we have him taken away now?"

"Sure," said Jackson, "make room." He was already taking rapid shots of the laboratory.

Sims went into the hall. More people had collected, naturally. It would be awkward to have the stretcher carried past such a multitude concentrated in the narrow space. Perhaps the ambulance could come round to the fire exit.

He told DiMarco as much, but decided to check for himself. The heavy metal door yielded with silent ease; he found himself on a narrow paved walk with a bed of gold tulips dividing it from a lawn on one side; on the other was the parking lot. Quite nice grounds, surrounded by a tall hedge. A little way from the single step down, half under some of the flowers, lay a wooden triangle, well-worn across the middle. He left it there.

Meanwhile, the fire door had closed itself; he would have to knock and look foolish, or walk around to the front, as if that had been his intention all along. He walked, taking a survey of the parking lot. Only two cruisers remained, now joined by a number of other cars and little knots of pedestrians speculating among themselves, no doubt spreading the usual amount of misinformation. The ambulance-men had struck it rich - the original girl was gone, but they had cornered three new ones. He told the driver where to pick up his cargo, it was unnecessary to say where to deliver it.

He asked the policeman on the front door, "Do you know which is the victim's car?"

That worthy indicated the only vehicle on the lot guarded by a uniformed constable - Sims should have noticed that.

"Thanks. And I think you can go now."

The vehicle in question was a maroon, mid-sized four-door sedan, perfectly clean - what did you expect? - but for some rain-spotting on the windows. That would be yesterday afternoon; no windshield wiper tracks. The car was locked; he had to peer inside. No mud on the floormats, no litter, no nothing. Of course. This was the cleanest damned case he'd ever investigated.

It was time to start questioning people. He strolled down the long corridor to the research wing. It was all alone, he noted, well separated from a large, nearly windowless block which would be the factory, and beyond the offices, at the end of the wing. There wouldn't be many potential witnesses going back and forth. Among the faces lining his way, he picked out one with authority written on it; a slight, balding man in his late sixties.

He showed the man his badge and introduced himself.

"Charles Quick," said the other, "general manager."

"The man in charge, I assume?"

A little smile stole across the creased face. "Sometimes. Not that I relish the distinction at this moment," he added hastily. "Mr. Meyer should be arriving soon. I telephoned him, of course, but he lives out in King City. Mr. Meyer doesn't usually do Mondays and Fridays - not all that many Tuesdays and Thursdays, come to that. He is what you might call semi-retired."

"And Mr. Meyer's position?"

"He's the Me in Ac-Me; the president. One of the original partners and major stockholder. Mr. Acton passed away some five years ago." He sighed. "And now Edward. Soon I'll be the only one left."

"Edward was the given name of the deceased?"

"Yes. I'm sorry, of course you've only just arrived. You will want some information. We might just step into my office?"

Sims followed the little man into a pleasant room, well lighted by two more of the tall windows looking out onto the back lawn. Through several gaps in the hedge a street of small brick houses could be glimpsed.

"Do sit," Mr. Quick invited. "I suppose you will want to know the... layout? Personnel? "

"Both, yes," replied Sims gratefully. "And perhaps some background on Dr. Morley. He had been in what position here, and for how long?"

"He was the original chemist - the only one, for some time - since Ac-Me began, in 1965. We were small potatoes in those days; I, with one little typist - she may be a grandmother by now, I wonder where? - I was nearly the entire administrative end. With the partners, of course. We've done very nicely, don't you think?" He glanced up at Sims with shy pride. A nice little man, but interviewing him could take some time.

Better get back on tracks. "So you have known Dr. Morley for twenty years?" Please, God, he doesn't want to tell me about it day by day.

"Oh yes. Edward left a very promising research position in Montreal to join us. He was only 30, 32 - and already had quite a reputation. What a terrible waste... Well, here we have been, ever since. In fact, I may presume to consider myself his closest friend. Insofar as Edward allowed himself friendships. Ac-Me was virtually his whole social life. Bridge, you know... lunches... Christmas party at Mr. Acton's house. Mr. Meyer hasn't kept that up; pity - but he's Jewish, so I don't suppose he should be expected to. He has been very generous with contributions to the little festivities we hold every year, right here. Tinsel and a nice big tree in the lobby, and turkey dinner for the staff, of course... Oh, dear, I shall miss Edward."

Thankful not to have to interrupt again, the detective seized this opportunity. "And the present research department consists of?"

"Yes. Yes, indeed. I was wandering off the subject. This is really so upsetting - one becomes nostalgic. The present research department. Yes. Doctor Morley is - was - the senior man. I suppose it will be young Jones now. Not so very young as he was, either - I suppose he will do well enough. Not as decisive or experienced as Edward, of course, but still. Dr. Jones has been with us for almost ten years. A reliable man. Then we have Eve Dumont. She's a lovely person, poor thing. She found Edward, you see... a terrible shock for the girl. Eve has been with Ac-Me for, let me see... almost as long as young Jones, eight or nine years. And then, after we built the new wing - all this section is new, you see - that would be '82 - we instituted what they call an intern program. Our most recent staff members are graduates trained right here. Isn't that something? Mr. Acton initiated it - I only wish he could have lived to see the results. Frayne, his name is, David Frayne, our very first intern. And there is a new one now, name of... Arnott, Paul Arnott. Time was, I knew every employee by name and sight... Growth is very nice, but you do lose a sense of family, don't you? It's sad, really."

Sims thought, if I don't ask some questions, fast and furious, I could spend the rest of my life reminiscing about a company I'd never heard of before this morning. "About this new wing. What does it accommodate?"

"Well, it was primarily built for the laboratory. Rather cleverly designed, if I may take credit - of course, Edward had a great deal to say about it. Do you see where the main block ends? The offices are on this side, the cafeteria is behind there," he waved a thin, brown-speckled hand.

"But then there is storage space, archives, and the washing-up room. Thus, the laboratory is effectively isolated from the main building. Where most of the people are, you understand. Beyond that door, each room, or the whole section, can be sealed off - in case, God forbid, anything should happen. You can't be too careful..."

"What sort of thing might happen?"

"Oh dear me!" sighed Mr. Quick. "What might not! Fire, explosion, poison gas... Fortunately, and thanks in large part to Edward, nothing ever has. Of course, the laboratory wing has its own exit, as does each section. Mr. Burgess is in charge of emergency drills... Do you know, we can evacuate the building in seven and a half minutes?"

"I didn't know," Sims admitted. "And, naturally, you have the usual sprinklers and so forth?"

"Of course, of course. Well, in fact, we have something rather better. We have - only in the factory and laboratory, mind you - a really wonderful new safety system, especially designed for noxious fumes. If the device senses a certain concentration of anything dangerous, it automatically shuts off all electricity and gas to the section, and activates the pumps. At least, I think they're pumps. Or is it fans? Both, I should think. In any case, the bad air is sucked out and good air is sent in. Ingenious, don't you think?" Sims nodded agreement, preparatory to moving on, but Mr. Quick wasn't finished. "We've timed that, too. The laboratory is cleared in ten to twenty minutes, depending on the concentration and type of gas, I'm told; the whole section takes a few minutes longer."

"And where does the gas go?"

"Oh, I'm glad you asked," said Mr. Quick. "That is the best part. We don't send nasty air out into the neighbourhood, oh no. It all goes into a frightfully complicated filtering system. The manufacturer assures us that it can neutralize eighteen different toxic fumes. Isn't that amazing? In the old days, we simply took our chances. We didn't know any better, you see."

"Is there any possibility that the system was not working, over this past weekend?"

The older man suddenly looked stricken. "You don't think...? Oh, no, I'm sure not. The safety devices are inspected every three months. But I shall call the company today, to make quite certain." He seemed to become lost in unpleasant conjecture, from which Sims recalled him with some difficulty.

"Would you be so kind as to introduce me to the research staff? I must speak to as many people as possible before I go to the morgue."

"The morgue! Oh, dear! I have to go there too. I understand from the constable.... I can't recall whether he told me his name. He must have, though; policemen are always so polite, don't you find? Of course you do, being one. I understand that there has to be a formal identification?"

"Yes, that's true. And you were asked to make it?"

"Well, you know, it isn't something one can ask a lady to do, is it? Poor Amanda! She will be quite upset enough when she hears - I mean, she can't be expected to go... there."

"Amanda?"

"Mrs. Morley. Edward's wife, of course. Poor woman."

"She has not been notified?"

"Well, really, I don't know... the constable may have... This isn't something one can tell a person over the telephone... at least, well, I certainly could not..."

The old man cast down his eyes in shame - unjustified, Sims thought: volunteering to make the identification was heroic enough. Probably, a uniformed man had, indeed, been dispatched to inform the widow.

"I believe," he told Mr. Quick gently, "that Dr. Morley's been taken away. Would you prefer to go in one of the police cars, or on your own?"

"A ride would be convenient, thank you. I don't know where... that is, I've never had to...But," he sparked up briefly, "I've never ridden in a police car. It will be like an adventure. It might be the only part of this whole business about which I can tell my little grandson. Well, then," - this was the most decisive he had been thus far - "we'd both better get on. If you will come with me?"

Sims was introduced to members of Ac-Me staff in order of their proximity to the office. "This is my secretary... er, assistant, rather, Miss Hillyard. Detective Sims. The officer will almost certainly require some files and so forth... Please assist him in any way you can."

Miss Hillyard gave a curt nod, but also a rather sweet, slow smile that could be meant for him personally. She was an attractive blonde in her late twenties who might be worth investigating, primary investigation permitting.

Miss Valentine, he had already noticed, outside. A coffee-coloured beauty with immense round black eyes from which a smile seemed never far away, and skin the texture of some very, very expensive fabric that you long to touch, yet dare not. Unfortunately, she looked only about seventeen. "Miss Valentine assists Mrs. Benz, who takes care of our laboratory... glassware, equipment and so forth." Mrs. Benz was plump, motherly - like other people's mothers, not in any way like Mrs. Sims, who aptly called herself 'a dry old stick' - though probably just as stern on the subject of shoes in the house, or elbows on the table.

At last they came to a knot of people nearest the lab door. They were drinking coffee and conversing among themselves in subdued voices: the body must be gone, thought Sims; a weight's been lifted from them.

"Dr. Jones, our senior chemist," blushed furiously from his shirt collar to his freckled, high forehead and right up among the roots of thin sandy hair. What a way to hear about your promotion! Quick was no less flustered, only in his usual flustered manner, it was less evident. "Well, what I mean is, you know, the senior person present..."

They moved right along. "And this is Mrs. Dumont. I'm afraid the officer will have to put you through the whole thing again, my dear. I'm terribly sorry, have I said? Afterwards, perhaps you would like to go home? Someone could call the doctor?"

Nice little number, indeed! Eve Dumont was at least five foot seven, broad-shouldered and square-boned. A bit angular for Sims's taste, but he was more than willing to overlook want of flesh for so singular a face. The woman positively radiated intelligence. Her eyes, dark brown, the same shade as her hair, were clear, wide and alert; her lips, not overly full, but exquisitely carved, set now in an expectant near-smile; nose, a fraction more prominent than the norm, strongly aquiline; square chin - everything in that face was clear, definite - a face that God had finished to His satisfaction and was proud to display; an original.

And you're staring, Sims told himself, like a booby. Oh, well, she'd be used to men staring at her. Anyone would want to know a great deal more about what's behind a face like that. And someone does; she's wearing a wedding ring. Damn. It figures, but damn, anyway.

"I'm perfectly all right, Charles," she said. Oh, Lord, the voice fits! I could be in serious trouble.

"I understand you discovered the body, is that correct?" he took refuge in officialese, thinking, 'remind me to give you one really good kick, Sims, when we have time.'

"Correct," she answered.

Mr. Quick had two more introductions to make. The tall handsome boy was Paul Arnott, (presumably P.F.A.; must ask him what the middle initial stands for, since he obviously sets great store by it) and he was the current intern. The other young man, whom Sims had not noticed earlier, was the junior chemist, David Frayne. Mr. Quick, senile or not, was able to remember all the names, and to differentiate ranks - apparently quite clear in his own mind - by the subtle stratagem of calling some people by their full names. This did not seem to apply to ladies, however, who were Miss or Mrs., regardless of age or station. A gentleman of the old school.

As soon as all introductions had been performed, the old man seemed to fade back into his vague and flustered persona. Sims wondered fleetingly whether he might not be putting it on at will. DiMarco was requested to find him a ride to the morgue.

"Now," said Sims, biting off a 'then'; he must not speak like Mr. Quick if he could possibly help it. "I wonder if there is a convenient, somewhat more private place, where I might speak to each of you?" No, he couldn't help it, but it would wear off soon.

Mrs. Benz stepped forward. "You can use my room." She had a slight accent, very much suited to her appearance, and a sweet, well-modulated voice.

The place indicated was a room next to the laboratory. Much of the floor-space was taken up by a huge dish-washing machine - fortunately not in operation yet - and deep, wide sinks. There was a window, and below this had been placed a small table and four ill-assorted chairs, left over from different stages of office refurbishing. On the counter nearby was a coffeemaker, even now dispensing the black gold of wakefulness. Mrs. Benz poured him a mug without asking, and he accepted gratefully. Are there no women in this place you couldn't fall in love with?

As she was already here, and as it was her domain, why not begin? "Did you know Dr. Morley well, Mrs. Benz?"

"Sit," she said, and noticing his glance at the ashtray - empty and clean, like everything else - "It is all right. Yes and no," she addressed the question, as he made himself comfortable and lit up for the first time that day. Pretty good, considering. "Yes, we have worked together for many years, next door here. And yet, also, I did not know this man."

At his enquiring look, she continued. "I have worked in this same place since I came to this country; it is 15, 16 years now, and he was here already. I have learned much of my English from Dr. Morley. He speaks - did speak - very nicely. Always he was polite, always a gentleman. All this time, I have taken care of the laboratory, the glassware. He liked things done properly, and myself, I like to do things so. We understand each other in that way. But no more. He never speaks about himself, personally. I also... either? Good morning, good night, it is cold outside. Even with the others, in there, he talks only about the work, not private things. That is how he was."

"And when did you last see him?"

"On Friday afternoon. It was past five o'clock, when everyone leaves. I went in to see that things were put away. Dr. Morley was going home also. We said good-night, and that is all."

"You put things away every evening?"

"Oh, no," she said. "The girls, they collect glassware to wash. I say girls, when there is only one, because it is always a different girl. They are students who help me, and they go away soon. Little Val, I would like her to stay longer; she is very neat. Myself, I check only on the second Friday, when the cleaner comes."

"Tell me about the cleaner."

"We have a young man who sweeps the floors and

20

empties the baskets, always. And also, one Friday every month, he does the big cleaning. For this, everything has to be put off from the benches, away from the floor. Then all is washed and polished."

"Even the doors?"

"Yes, he is quite good. The doors are cleaned and oil is put on them, and the floor is waxed, and the sinks are scrubbed."

At least the unnatural cleanliness of the laboratory was explained. "And this happens the second Friday of every month?"

"That is right. The other people in there, sometimes they forget to put away, so I look."

"Now, if you could tell me something about the research department. For instance, did they all get along well? Did his colleagues like Dr. Morley?"

She gave him a sharp appraising look. "Gossip?"

"Well, yes, that might help."

"I will tell you that Dr. Morley was respected; I cannot say that he was very much liked. There was no trouble. The others, they like their work, like each other, I think. They get coffee here, sometimes they talk a little; they do not stay long."

She was not going to pass along any gossip.

"Thank you very much, Mrs. Benz. And for the coffee."

She stood. "I will leave now. You wish to see poor Eve, I think. Be kind; she has had a bad morning." She stood, raising her generous form as gracefully as a woman half her size and age. "I will ask her to come."

CHAPTER 3

Sims had every intention of being considerate; he offered Mrs. Dumont the least uncomfortable chair, and to fetch her coffee, but she quickly put an end to this: "Please stop fussing," she said. "Everyone's been treating me like an invalid. The experience was unpleasant, yes, but I'm not traumatized for life. Please, just let's get this done." She sat down neatly, feet together, smoothing the brown wool skirt over her knees. That still left plenty to look at.

Sims nodded, "All right. Tell me, in your own words, what happened this morning."

She took a deep breath. "I came in a little early today, about half past eight, because it's my husband's week for the car. He dropped me off on the way to the hospital. I saw Edward's - Dr. Morley's - car in the lot."

"Was this unusual, his being here early?"

"Unusual, yes, not unheard-of. If I thought anything, it was that he's eager to begin a new project. We had finished with the Walters container; it would be something fresh - perhaps more interesting. It occurred to me that he might already have made coffee, and I wouldn't have to."

"Go on,"

"This room was closed. I went into the lab. I didn't see Edward, but there was something on his bench... the Bunsen burner... a retort stand, lying on its side. And then I noticed..." Sims waited for her to pull herself together. This was the literal term; she went through an exercise of arranging limbs and features in straight parallel lines, even to laying both hands on the table, palms down. Nice hands, well-kept and capable-looking, at least size seven. "Then I noticed...him," she resumed, "on the floor."

"Did you touch him?"

"No! No. There was no doubt in my mind that he was past helping. I'm not sure how I knew, exactly..?"

"I think," Sims assured her, "that it was evident. Did you telephone the police right away?"

"No... In fact, I never phoned. Martin did. I mean Martin Jones."

"He was already here?"

"Not then, no. I was alone with... with Edward. I left the

room. Walked back to the front... I was looking for someone - anyone - alive. The building was so silent, I felt there might be nobody else left in the world..." She shuddered slightly, through her whole frame, as if blown by a cold wind. "And then Martin got here. I told him what happened. He went in - I stayed behind, in the hall. A minute later he came back and called 911."

"From where did Dr. Jones place that call?"

"From the receptionist's desk, in the lobby."

"Not the lab? Are you certain?"

She was. "I stood right next to him. And then other people started to arrive."

More to keep her mind busy than because he needed the information, he asked, "In what order? Can you recall?"

"Mrs. Benz, Mr. Quick... He looked in the lab, then he went off, to phone Mr. Meyer. The firemen came, then Ferdy - Mr. Arnott, along with the police."

Sims thought: Precise and concise. This lady doesn't miss much. "In the laboratory, did you handle anything?"

She reflected. "No, I don't think so."

"You didn't, for instance, consider using the telephone, and change your mind?"

She shook her head definitely. "No. I only thought of finding help. Is it important?"

"I don't know," he said honestly. "I can't tell what's important, yet. Did you notice anything odd – about the counter, or in the apparatus?"

"The retort was knocked over. And there was a flask on the floor. I think that's all."

"Anything seem strange about the room itself?"

"No.... Officer, is there something... suspicious?"

Sims had an almost overwhelming impulse to confide in her. But he controlled it, saying truthfully, "The coroner thinks it was a heart attack. Could you shed any light on the state of Dr. Morley's health?"

"Nothing useful," she said. "He seemed well on Friday. Quite normal."

"Is that when you last saw him alive?"

"Yes, at about 4:30. Edward never left early, but the rest of us did, when work was slack. I was anxious to pick up my husband."

"You didn't happen, at that time, to discuss plans for the weekend?"

She thought a minute. Whereas, for most people, thinking requires, at the very least, facial exertion, for her it appeared to be a rest: from the effort of rigid self-control to mere thinking was almost the exact reverse of the pulling-together exercise. "I must have mentioned Martin's dinner party; we were invited. He may have said he would be home alone. His son Brian is away at university - not doing very well. But I can't be certain it was last Friday - I may be recalling past conversations."

Sims thanked her and asked her to send in Dr. Jones. Alone, he gave himself a warm pat on the back: he had behaved admirably. He had not treated her like the fine porcelain her skin resembled; had kept to officialese, refrained from asking whether she was happily married - of course, her two gratuitous references to a husband helped there - and never once even came close to touching her. He rewarded himself with a second coffee, double sugar, double cream, and a cigarette.

The man who entered was far less collected than either Sims or his previous witness; Martin Jones looked decidedly put-about, as Mr. Quick would describe it.

"This is an awful business, Sergeant. I don't know how things are supposed to go on now." He let himself down into the chair recently vacated by his more attractive co-worker. "Must you do that?" he added peevishly.

"Sorry." Sims put out the half-smoked cigarette, and conceived a prejudice against the man, in that very second. "I didn't realize it would bother you, given your late colleague's habit."

"Of course it bothered me, but he was my boss. Anyway, we had a kind of understanding; we never went to coffee or lunch together."

"I see," said the detective. "And in the laboratory?"

Jones shrugged minutely; a slight lifting and letting-fall of heavy round shoulders. He was a big man, about six feet tall, and stocky, though not fat. His hands, large, square and pink - almost certainly the size eleven glove - lay close together on the tabletop. "He kept to his desk and I kept to mine. Edward wasn't a sloppy smoker... I mean,

24

he'd never smoke at the bench, during an experiment - only at his desk, after washing his hands. And the ventilation system is pretty good. Well, I mean it has to be, given the substances we work with."

"I have the impression that Dr. Morley wasn't sloppy in general. Would this be accurate?"

The round, fair head bobbed up and down three times, slightly displacing horn-rimmed glasses on too small a nose; Jones carefully readjusted them with both hands. Sims, who had subconsciously classified him as a bridge-jabber, suspected that here was someone born with a proclivity to large gestures who had trained himself to subdue them.

"Edward was the most methodical person I have ever known. Compulsive, some people would say. Some people would even make fun of him. But he was right, you know: chemistry cannot be an approximate science. More: science cannot be approximate." This sounded as if it had been learned by rote. There briefly passed before Sims' inner eye, the spectre of Professor Jorgens, his most detested and feared teacher, holding forth on exactitude. Sims had lasted two terms in that course, and had never missed an intimate knowledge of chemistry, until today.

"Now, take your time and tell me what happened when you came to work this morning."

"It was a quarter to nine," the witness began. "I came in the front door. I met Eve in the lobby." He looked up from under pale lashes, to check how he was doing; Sims nodded encouragement. "She was upset. She told me Edward was in the lab, dead. So I went to look, and he was. Is." The big man shuddered. "There was some stuff on the floor... he must have knocked it over when he fell."

"Did you recognise this - stuff?"

"No. Well, I mean, I didn't get a close look at it, and... I just didn't think about it."

"I understand that Dr. Morley kept notes on all the activities of the research department."

"Yes, it all went into a day-book. A little spiral job," Jones clarified, "about yea big." He measured out an oblong with forefingers and thumbs, five by seven inches, much like the ones in the dead man's desk. "Black."

Sims nodded. "Can you tell me about your current project?"

"There isn't one. What I mean is, we just wrapped up W-7 - that is, a new container for hair dye, for a company owned by the Walters Group. It's supposed to go into production now. Edward hadn't decided what the next one should be - or maybe Charlie Quick couldn't make up his mind, I'm not sure which."

"Are there many to choose from?"

Another three fast, small nods - what he lacked in magnitude, he would make up in quantity - business with glasses. "We all have our pet project, sort of. I mean, everybody would like his little invention or modification to be next up... But, if any decision had been made, Edward wasn't telling."

"Do you have a pet project?"

Again, the scaled-down shrug; this fellow seemed to have a very small repertoire of gestures. A result of self-discipline, or lack of imagination? "I do have one or two ideas - in early stages yet... It wouldn't be fair, though, to push one of them, seeing as the Walters thing was mine." A faint blush began to creep up his neck and cheeks, but faded before it reached the hairline. Sims thought, he's getting used to the idea of being in charge pretty fast. "It will be up to Mr. Quick and Mr. Meyer. I guess, whatever they think would be most worthwhile."

"You say the others have inventions, too?"

"I don't think Eve - Mrs. Dumont - does, just now. Dave Frayne certainly has, and Ferdy will get all worked up about that, of course."

"Did Dr. Morley have a project of his own?"

For the first time, Jones left off inspecting his hands as if they had been something of vast scientific moment, and looked Sims full in the eye. A sort of dawn was breaking on his broad freckled face, giving him the expression of an overgrown three-year-old, full of wonder at the world - and incidentally wiping out the last of his interlocutor's antipathy. "I didn't know. Well, I mean, except for something kind of far-fetched he's been pottering with... But he must've had, right?"

He blinked several times in rapid succession, and then shook his head, rather in puzzlement than negation,

"I can't imagine him not saying a word about it. Especially if it was a go, and with all of us hanging there. Edward was not a warm person, if you know what I mean, but he was never inconsiderate. Unless..."

"Yes?"

"...unless it *wasn't* a go. Maybe something he'd been kicking around with the bosses, and he wanted to see if it could work... That might explain what he was up to."

"You mean that it was not usual for Dr. Morley to work alone? Or outside of regular hours?"

"Both. No. It was not usual. He didn't approve of hot-dogging; he took team-work seriously. Except, none of us was all that excited about his clean plastic. I don't think it's possible, frankly."

"So, when you last saw him, on..."

"Friday. Friday quitting time. No, I'm lying, I left a few minutes early."

"...he didn't mention planning to work over the weekend?"

"No. I can't remember what we said, but nothing like that."

"About this day-book," Sims changed the subject, carefully avoiding a change in tone or emphasis. "Could you show it to me?"

Jones, who had relaxed visibly in the past minutes, now reverted to his initial wary nervousness. "It would be on his desk," he said in a voice devoid of inflection.

"Did you notice it there, this morning?"

"I don't think so, no. To be honest, I didn't notice much, except... you know..."

"But," the detective persisted, "with your keen sense of smell, you must have detected gas, or something in the air."

Jones considered, wrinkling his brow and nose. Regretfully, he admitted, "No, I can't recall anything. But then," he brightened, "there wouldn't be. The fan would have come on, and everything turned off, lights and gas, I mean, as soon as that stuff boiled over."

"A good safety system, is it?"

"The best Edward and Charlie could find. Besides," he added, putting his glasses straight, "I wasn't in the room all that long."

"Just long enough to make a phonecall?"

Jones looked up in alarm. "Not from there! I mean, the phone is on his desk... No, I called from the lobby."

"Did you touch anything?"

"No. The door, I guess. Then I went looking for Eve... didn't like to leave her alone... She was pretty shook up."

Right, thought Sims, and you were Mr. Cool. Gently, he said, "He's not there anymore. And you will have to go back in, sometime. I understand you are to be the new chief."

"Yeah." Jones sighed and gave his whole torso a slight shake. "I can't figure out how to feel about that."

They were interrupted by Flash Jackson in search of a large paper carton, in which to carry away the remnants of Edward Morley's last experiment. There, Sims thought, that proves the Odd Couple are telepaths - how else could he have timed his entrance so perfectly? It was an excuse to dismiss Jones and return to the scene and confer with the ident team.

In the second aim, he was thwarted by P. F. Arnott, who, picking up his trail, was also in the room before anyone could stop him. His eyes were riveted on the far right corner where the only current attraction was Simon Woo with a scraper, loading greenish goo into plastic bags.

"Get lost," remarked Flash in a moderately friendly tone.

"Aw, come on, guys! I just want to see the police in action. I won't touch anything, honest."

This kid is about twelve years old, Sims decided.

CHAPTER 4

On closer examination, he might be twenty. He was tall, slim, vaguely athletic-looking. His dark brown hair was cut more conservatively than the fashion for his age-group; his clothes were expensive, a touch too consciously coordinated for Sims' taste. Trying to appear older, more serious? Trying to fit in?

"Mr. Arnott," Sims asked, "have you any material information to contribute?"

"Not really," said Paul Arnott, "just rubbernecking, kind of. What is that stuff?"

"I should have thought you'd know more about that than we would."

"Well, it sure doesn't look like anything we ever made in here before... Say, what was the old man up to? You think somebody offed him?"

"Do you?"

Arnott frowned. "I wouldn't have - but then, what are you all doing here?"

"Our job," Sims replied testily. The kid was starting to get on his nerves, and he didn't much care about alienating a witness, "which is more than I can say for you."

Alienating Arnott wouldn't be quite that easy: he laughed. "But I work here. Right over there." He indicated the far left corner of the room, "Between David Frayne and Eve Dumont - can you say as much?"

Sims imagined tossing him bodily out of the room, but desisted. The ident men had finished packing their equipment and took their leave. He supposed he might as well get this interview over, for what it was worth. Keeping it terse: "When was the last time you saw Dr. Morley alive?"

"Friday. That would be May 11."

"What time on Friday?"

"Five... no, that's wrong - I must have left about 4:30, 4:45. I had a heavy date." He winked.

"Did you have any conversation at that time, or at any previous time, concerning the victim's plans for the weekend?"

"Aha! You said victim - so he *was* murdered."

"Mr. Arnott, you watch too much television. Could you just answer the question?"

"Oh, sure. No."

This was better. "No, what?"

"No, we didn't converse. We never actually did, what you call, converse. The old man would tell me what to do - better yet, he'd tell Marty to tell me what to do - and I shut up and did it."

Sims couldn't quite suppress a smile. "I find half of that statement hard to credit."

The kid laughed again. "You didn't know the old man. For him, I shut up. See, you're not a bit scary."

"Right. So he didn't confide in you."

Paul Arnott spread his arms, "Me and everybody else. He wasn't big on confiding."

"Therefore, you had no idea whether he planned to come back later that evening, or the next day, to work on a new project."

"Course not. Anyway, *what* project? Far as I know, there wasn't one - thought we'd be goofing off for a while, tossing the bull, arguing about SuperFoam... In the end Dave would get through to the movers and shakers, and then we'd really be cooking. Looks like the old man had something up his sleeve - anything, I guess, just so it wasn't SuperFoam."

Sims ignored - or, rather, put aside for later decoding, most of this. "What is Superfoam?"

"It's only the biggest breakthrough in aircraft insulation, that's all. Dave's baby - he's been working on it, off and on, for a year. The old man was determined to squash it... Maybe he was jealous... maybe he just couldn't see it. He was a cheap old... didn't like spending money."

"Surely it wasn't his money?"

"His, the company's - same difference. He was a stickler for budgets. Hell, he was a stickler about *everything*."

"And this Superfoam would be expensive to make?"

"Not to make, I don't think, once it goes into production. We just need time to get the bugs out."

"As an expert, then, you believe the substance is perfectible."

"As an expert," Ferdy Arnott smiled wryly, "I don't know piss-all. Dave's the brain. No," he added earnestly, "I mean it. The old man knew his stuff - in the stone age. Marty Jones is pretty competent, but no imagination. Eve's smart as a whip, only she's not here half the time - I mean, her mind's on other things. The hot-shot surgeon comes first, second and the next ten... She's letting her career go to hell. Kind of a shame, but more for us, eh?" Sims found his speech remarkably easy not to ape: it was already aping someone - or everyone - else's. The boy finished, "David Frayne is a solid gold, honest-to-God genius. He's going to be famous one of these days."

"I see," said Sims, who was beginning to. "And this substance that was spilled, it didn't look familiar to you."

Ferdy Arnott shook his sleek young head, shrugged dramatically. "Looked pretty deadly, though. Naw... if it'd been dangerous, he'd have used the hoods, right? Course I'm right. One thing you have to know about the old man - he wasn't careless."

"That was the impression I had, yes," said Sims dryly. "Is there anything you can add that I haven't heard yet?"

"Who, me? I'm the original mushroom. You know, the one they keep in the dark and..."

Sims cut him off, "In that case, why don't we both get back to work?"

The kid said, "I can't, but that's okay. You want to see Dave in here, or in the washup room?"

Sims didn't want to see Dave, the solid gold genius, anywhere, but supposed he better had. "Send him in here, if you would, Mr. Arnott."

That, at least, rid him of this one. The other one - he was beginning to think of the young chemists as a matched set. There was a physical resemblance, as well as the blatant hero-worship. Had he not disliked them on sight, he would want to know more about their relationship. The other one sauntered in. Utterly self-possessed, Frayne gave only the briefest glance to the area by now known throughout the building as the place where the body was found.

"You wanted to see me Inspector?"

"Detective Sergeant."

David Frayne tried to cock an eyebrow, managed to raise the right marginally higher than the left. Sims refrained from telling him to keep practising. This young man looked as if he spent some very satisfying time in front of mirrors. Well, he had plenty to work with; tall, chiselled, dark-haired, he was handsome in the way of late-night movie heroes, and he obviously cultivated the style. He wore cream-coloured slacks with a matching silk shirt, topped by a sport jacket of moss green; his tie was striped in green and ivory. Too sartorially perfect for words - not to mention its total unsuitability for a laboratory.

He now sat down in Martin Jones's desk chair, swivelled it around to face Sims. There was no other chair nearby. Sims wondered if this was a deliberate ploy, forcing him to stand, thus putting him at a disadvantage. Not himself of meagre stature, and with a few pounds on the other man, he walked over slowly, to lean on the corner of the desk; too close, so that Frayne had not only to turn his chair, but move it backwards. Point for Sims.

"Yes, Sergeant," he said smoothly, "what can I tell you?"

"Whatever you know that might shed some light on Dr. Morley's death."

"I wasn't actually present. By the time I got here, there were police all over the building."

"All right then, let's just go through the routine questions. When did you last see the deceased?"

"Last Friday afternoon."

"Did you and he have any conversation?"

"No."

"What had the staff been working on?"

An expression of weary tolerance passed across the handsome features. "Containers for hair-dye."

"And what would you be working on next?"

"That's up to management."

"Superfoam, for example?"

David Frayne smiled indulgently - a practised smile. "Well, after all, it's not impossible. But, given the attitude in the front office, it may be some time coming."

"Would you like to tell me about this Superfoam?"

"No, Sergeant, I would not. The technical details are complex, and I doubt it's relevant to your investigation."

32

Point for Frayne. Sims paused as if deep in thought. "Could there be any secret projects going on?"

"If you mean, do we keep our formulas to ourselves, yes. But, no, there is no other project going on at the moment. Unless it's a secret from me."

"Except, of course, the one Dr. Morley started over the weekend."

"If he had, it's the first I've heard of it."

Sims was aware of being at least two down, if he'd kept score, which would have been childish. The fellow was intelligent, and very, very cool. "Did you and Dr. Morley get along well?"

Both eyebrows went up. "He was the chief; he never let anyone forget it. I was an Indian - I have no problem with that."

Sims did not think there was anything useful to be gleaned here. He ought to close the interview while he had the upper hand. "Mr. Frayne, do you have any relevant information? On *any* subject?"

"It doesn't seem likely."

"In that case, I'll waste no more of your time."

With that, turning to leave, Sims awarded himself another point. On sober reflection, though, the round had gone to Frayne. Did that matter? It shouldn't. Only, something about the man - his bland non-reaction to the tragedy, or perhaps the oh so perfect appearance, irritated him. And something else, too: Frayne's attitude - not his words or gestures, exactly, but the too relaxed stance and lazy lowering of eyelids - suggested more than a reciprocal antipathy. Had Sims brought that on himself? He must try to be more careful; must try not to reveal his personal reactions to witnesses.

CHAPTER 5

Sims approached the quiet residential neighbourhood with trepidation. "Why me?" he had asked, and been answered, "Why not?" Normally, Inspector MacDonald would have sent a policewoman; such were his prejudices that even Venables, hardly the soul of tact, might do in a pinch. But Venables was still in hospital. In any case, DiMarco made better company.

Flowering chestnuts lined the street. The houses were old, self-contained behind hedges, tulip trees; here and there, an island of flowering shrubs. Few people were about: a plump young woman, setting out impatiens in a garden, watched by an even plumper orange cat; two ladies of advanced age, in little round hats, making their cautious way toward the shops on Avenue Road. A small black dog ambled along, marking the fence and lamp-posts. 39 Linette Avenue was a tall brick house, set well back from ancient pines flanking the driveway, behind a tidy lawn. The drive curved off into a thicket of lilac bushes on the verge of bloom, to the double garage. Though a handsome and well-kept building, it was given a brooding air by evergreen shade. The front door, too, was painted dark green. Taking one deep breath, he knocked on it.

And knocked again, before noticing the bell-button, disguised as a lady-bug in a cluster of brass flowers. Hoping DiMarco behind him on the porch steps, hadn't seen, he rang it surreptitiously, waited, then knocked again. It seemed to him an age, standing there; it was two or three minutes.

A woman in jeans and sweatshirt opened the door. "Yes?"

She was middle-aged; her short brown hair had some silver in it; just a woman, not very tall or large, yet with something decisive and confident in her manner, which made her a little formidable. Sims introduced himself, reaching half-heartedly for his ID folder. "And this is Constable DiMarco. May we come in for a moment?"

"Why?" she asked bluntly.

"Mrs. Morley?"

"Yes."

"It's about your husband..."

A series of wild conjectures flitted across her face, and Sims, knowing he must confirm the worst of them, had to fight the temptation to turn around and run. He very much didn't want to be here. She said nothing; merely stood aside, closed the door as soon as they were in the hall - a generously proportioned entry hall, which suddenly seemed an awfully confining space, in part due to DiMarco's fidgeting bulk. So he's no more comfortable in this role than I am, Sims realized gratefully, even though he's been on traffic long enough to have done this more than once before. Both policemen would have preferred to stay near the exit, but Mrs. Morley was preceding them into the living room. It was a pleasant room, in which dark blue and light grey predominated; the furniture was old-fashioned, undistinguished and serviceable.

She indicated a couch and armchair. Sims accepted the chair; DiMarco hung back and perched himself on another, closer to the door. Mrs Morley took the couch. "What about my husband?"

Phrases from the movies presented themselves to Sims - phrases meant to break the news gently - only to be rejected. When he couldn't endure the silence any longer, he blurted out "He's dead."

"I see." she said. "Where?"

Now, there was no going back. "In his laboratory. He was found this morning by a colleague."

"This morning," she repeated in a flat tone. "I see. What happened?"

"We don't know for certain yet," Sims said, "the coroner thinks it was a heart attack... Had he any history of heart problems?"

"No," said Mrs. Morley in the same matter-of-fact voice. "I understand these things often come suddenly. Where is he now?"

This was another inevitable part of the interview he had dreaded. "Well, you see, there will have to be an... a post-mortem examination. He's at the... Forensic Sciences Building." Having imagined that its full title would carry more dignity than 'city morgue', he heard it sounding instead more threatening. He hastened to explain, wondering why this was so much harder on him than it seemed to be on her. She was a very cool customer, indeed. "That's just routine... any unattended... er... anybody who dies, well, not in hospital or something like that..."

She cut him off; "I know what unattended means. Of course an autopsy has to be done. Do they need consent?"

"Well," he began to explain about it being automatic, but didn't get time to finish. Mrs. Morley sprang out of her seat with a half-stifled exclamation, and ran from the room. Sims, without thinking, followed her; DiMarco took a second more to decide, lumbering along behind. She had disappeared through a door which opened onto basement stairs, and was already down them. At the near end of a short corridor, she entered another door; Sims followed, feeling stupid.

It was a small, well-appointed darkroom, no more than eight feet square, and every surface used. She was unwinding a spool of film from one of the tanks, holding it up to the dim light. "Damn!" she said. "They're ruined. They're all ruined... Damn, damn, *damn!*"

Tears ran down her cheeks, a flood of them, unchecked and unnoticed. "Oh, damn it to hell," she added more softly, almost conversationally, and leaned against the detective, who stood in the doorway like a post. Of course, he put his arms around her. Her head came just to his shoulder, where she continued to weep silently for some time. He didn't have to do anything, say anything; he simply held her and waited. At last she pulled away, and looked up, her face rather the worse for wear. The flood had abated; only a few last tears were coursing down her cheek.

"I'm sorry," she said, in something like her normal, competent voice, swiped a sleeve across her face, didn't wait for Sims to make the meaningless noises he felt he ought to. "Let's get back upstairs."

They did, preceded by DiMarco, who had waited outside all this time. In the living room, Mrs. Morley said. "If you'll excuse me while I wash my face, we'll have some coffee and then, I'd like to hear the whole story."

Sims began to demur, "We don't have to do that right now,"

"I want to get it all over with at once, not bit by bit. Like docking a dog's tail, you know?"

She was gone only a few minutes; wash her face was exactly all she must have done, and perhaps run a comb through her hair: there was no makeup to repair. She looked fine, if a little pale.

"I've put the kettle on. Is it coffee you gentlemen would like? Or tea? I may have beer..."

They both agreed to coffee and she disappeared again to prepare it. DiMarco looked pointedly at his watch and made some dumb-show of driving away. Sims shook his head definitively.

"Now," said Mrs. Morley, resuming her seat, and passing cups, "Tell me what happened to Edward."

"Well, it seems that he was doing some overtime on the weekend," Sims began.

"On the weekend? I thought you said this morning."

"He was found this morning. Excuse me, but you must know when he left for the lab?"

"No," she said. "I didn't get home till two hours ago. There was a storm last night, so I returned early this morning."

"May I ask where you were?"

Her quizzical look made him suspect he had phrased it wrongly, but she answered readily enough. "We have a cottage on Sculpin Lake. I spent the weekend there, hunting waterfowl. I had some good shots, too. I meant to print them this morning... Well, they're a write-off, now." She looked as if she might begin to cry again, but didn't.

"When did you last see your husband, Ma'am?"

"On Friday morning, when he went to work. I left before he came home. And please don't call me ma'am."

So she'd be no help in pinpointing the time of death. He might as well simply tell his story and retreat. "Sorry, Mrs. Morley; it's habit. It seems Dr. Morley was working on an experiment, sometime over the weekend, and suddenly, well, collapsed. That is the truth, by the way; it was very sudden."

She nodded acknowledgement. "When can I see him?"

Taken by surprise, Sims told the truth. "The autopsy is scheduled for 1:30... there isn't much time. Are you sure you want to?"

"Yes."

"Would you like me to take you, Ma... Mrs. Morley?"

"That would be kind. Finish your coffee while I change."

They dropped DiMarco at 43 Division. On the way downtown, Sims wondered if he ought to warn her about the appearance of the body, didn't know how to bring it up, and decided she could cope. She could probably cope fairly well, in any situation. He had questions, but they could wait.

However, she had a question. "Why did they send a detective?"

In the face of her forthrightness, Sims found himself strangely hesitant, yet compelled to be frank. "In these cases - I mean, in cases where a person is found dead, we have to make sure there was no foul play."

"Foul play," she repeated. "I see."

"We have to rule that out first. Then we have to consider accident and suicide, too."

"But this wasn't any of those." she said. Then she gave him a very shrewd glance, which made him uncomfortable. "Was it?"

"The coroner thinks not."

"That's the second time you've quoted the coroner," she pointed out. "Do you agree with the coroner?"

"Well," Sims defended, "he's an expert. And, of course, the pathologist will have the last word. I'll be talking to him, after... I could give you a call, and tell you what he thinks..."

"I see," she said again. "You're a kind man, Sergeant Sims, and you don't want to tell me what you, as an expert, think."

He couldn't help a fleeting smile. "No, I'd rather not. Since nobody else thinks it, I'm probably wrong."

"Foul play? Edward? Yes, you're probably wrong."

She had recovered her calm matter-of-factness; there was no trace of the weeping woman from the basement. Was she really so unmoved by her husband's death, or merely very good at controlling her feelings? Sims didn't seriously entertain the possibility that she had killed him, but would nevertheless have to check on her movements.

Once he had narrowed down the relevant time.

The morgue visit, to which Sims had not been looking forward, went smoothly. Mrs. Morley spent only a minute, viewing the remains, thanked the attendant, made no comment, then or afterward, though she appeared somehow smaller and frailer on the return journey. Then she thanked him, too.

"It's none of my business," he said, "but is there someone you could stay with for a while? It's not a good idea to be alone."

She nodded. "Actually, I would prefer to be alone. But I must call my daughter... she has to be told. I expect she'll come over. I have to call my son, too... He'll have to come home. Arrangements to make... The man said they'll be through with the... with Edward's body... You know," she added wonderingly, "it's Edward, but it isn't. Anyway, I'll be busy."

Not knowing quite how to offer to stay with her till reinforcements arrived, Sims was inspired with a perfect excuse. "I wonder, would it be all right for me to see your husband's room?"

"Which, his bedroom or his study? And why?"

"We still have only the most approximate idea of the time. I thought there might be some indication when he left the house."

"Yes, all right. Oh, wait," she added, "I may be able to help. Before I left, I prepared Edward's meals for Friday evening and Saturday. I'll check now, if you like."

Sims followed her to the kitchen. "See," she said, "there is the casserole and a plate in the dish-rack... Edward was always tidy... he couldn't stand dirty things around him. That was a chicken and rice casserole, with green beans and almonds... one of his favourites. For Saturday, I made pork-chops." She seemed to be talking to herself, as if having forgotten his presence; putting away the dishes, going to the refrigerator, and returning with a plate wrapped in tinfoil. Now she uncovered it: two chops, three potatoes, some green peas, all of which she scraped deftly into the garbage pail under the sink. She took a few seconds to turn around.

The detective said, "This means Dr. Morley must have been at home for dinner on Friday."

She nodded. "Well, then, I'll show you Edward's rooms."

These were upstairs, on either side of a spacious hallway. One, a small bedroom, furnished in heavy dark wood - as tidy as if nobody had ever lived in it. Of course. The bed was neatly made; the curtains drawn, a closed book on the bedside table: 'A Perfect Spy', a brand new hardcover edition. Sims checked the bookmark: less than two thirds of the way through, and subconsciously eliminated the probability of suicide. Behind him, Mrs. Morley opened the door across the hall and withdrew to make her unenviable telephone calls.

A fine layer of dust covered everything. In the closet, jackets and trousers, all in brown or grey, hung like executed soldiers. The shirts were white and long-sleeved, or pale blue, pale grey, beige - one adventurous pale yellow stuck out like a sore thumb - and short-sleeved; to go with the grey, blue and brown slacks. Of course. Could such a man have enjoyed spy stories? Why not? Just as conceivably, he might have been working his way through popular literature as a chore. There were other books in a low glass-fronted cabinet: Freddy Goes to Florida, Charlotte's Web, half a dozen other children's classics, including a very tattered Winnie the Pooh. He had two children. It was a little surprising that he should have kept their old books in his bedroom.

Howard Fast, Galsworthy, Gibbon, Golding, Harrison... a varied and interesting selection. Several volumes of poetry, a whole shelf of novels and poems in French. Had not Mr. Quick mentioned his having come from Montreal? Only, the bookcase didn't look at all like the closet. Or rather, it resembled the closet in its neatness, not in the taste it reflected. Sims found himself unexpectedly confronted with a three-dimensional man - a *person*, not 'a stiff'.

In the adjoining bathroom - a one-man bathroom, bearing no trace of feminine occupancy - he experienced a strong reluctance to go through the laundry hamper. This was invasion of privacy, even as examination of the actual body had not been. But he persevered. One white shirt, underwear, socks, towel. So we're still at Friday evening. Not that any of this, including the casserole and plate, couldn't have been arranged afterwards, a part of his detective mind noted. The medicine cabinet gave away little beyond the dead man's orderly cast of mind: cap on the toothpaste; razor free of hairs; toothbrush and cup the same shade of red. Nothing stronger than aspirin and vitamin pills.

The study across the hall was, naturally, tidy. The bookshelves were mainly occupied by scientific material. The calendar said May 12: Saturday. Now, would he change it in the morning, or the evening before? That was no help. The ashtray had two butts in it; a half pack of Players' and a light blue disposable lighter sat on the desk. In the middle drawer, as expected, were fresh writing pads and pens. In the right hand drawer, bills with red felt pen dates of payment on - all current. In the lower one, documents - he scanned through them quickly. Insurance policies, tax returns, correspondence from the University of British Columbia, report cards of both children, going back to first grade. Methodical or sentimental? Letters. Maybe for later scrutiny, if necessary. In the left upper drawer, date-books, very like those in the laboratory, but the contents appeared to relate to family and personal matters. In the lower left side, a bottle of scotch - or what was left of it: not much - and a tumbler. Oh? Yes, but who knows how long it had been there, how long it had taken to deplete, and in what company? One tumbler?

He closed the drawer and returned to its neighbour. He took out the stack of diaries and placed it on the desk, nudging aside the cigarette package. It caught his eye. Well, sure. Dr. Morley had forgotten to put them in his pocket when he went out, so he'd bought new ones. All you have to do is trace his route to the lab; he must have stopped off at some convenience store on the way. He could be a regular customer, someone might recall seeing him. Sure.

Happy to be back in the realm of police leg-work, Sims decided to leave the books for now. They might be relevant, or not: this was more to the point. A quick glance in the waste-basket revealed a cellophane wrapping, probably off this same cigarette package, and two crumpled sheets of writing paper. "Dear Brian," one began, and the other: "Son, I know how much you dislike lectures..." Both were headed with Friday's date. Looking at them made him feel as he had looking in the laundry hamper - like a peeping tom. Nowhere did he find anything like a suicide note. Of course, that, too, can be removed - and very often is.

Ah, well, at least he had something concrete, and less personal, to go on with. He closed all the doors before returning downstairs.

Mrs. Morley was sitting in her living room, perfectly still. He made some noise as he entered, to avoid any appearance of sneaking around. He asked her not to clear out her husband's things just yet, "It's unlikely we'll have to come back, but you never know." She agreed. She seemed uninterested, as if she had forgotten who he was or why he was still there, and didn't really care. Their conversation felt stilted, more wrong somehow, than the earlier and more delicate one. He felt like a guest hanging on past the hour of decent departure.

"Well," he mumbled, "I'll be in touch."

"Yes," she replied, not looking up.

Sims took his leave. Sometime, he would have to question her, and the daughter as well, and perhaps the son - although out of town, he evidently corresponded with Dr. Morley. He'd have to be in touch, like it or not. On the whole, he minded only the reason for this, not the fact.

CHAPTER 6

The written report didn't look like much. The typed and signed statements from witnesses had not yet arrived, and what Sims had in his own notes was all negative. Still, there were the discrepancies in the scene; no known history of illness; no previous mention to anyone that the deceased meant to work over the weekend: the negatives seemed to him a pretty fair circumstantial case. The pathologist, in his verbal report, had only added more negatives: no heart disease, not more than the expected amount of atherosclerosis, mild liver damage - not enough of anything to account for sudden death.

"Bit of a tippler, was he?" Dr. Cates had asked. Sims could not answer with any degree of certainty; it was possible.

"Virtually certain," the doctor had replied, "but, I think, not to fatal degree. Tissue sections will be done by the weekend, though I don't expect to see anything new. We've taken samples for a standard tox screen - usual drugs and poisons - should be back in a few days. I put a rush on the cyanide test." At Sims' enquiring look, he added: "I thought there was a little extra tint to the lividity, maybe a whiff of something in the viscera. The blood-alcohol will take a bit longer." Sims knew this; the labs were always a couple of weeks behind on alcohol tests; there were simply too many. "Anyhow," the pathologist had gone on, "we're also having the stomach contents analyzed... Maybe it was something he et?"

Sims had asked, as tactfully as possible, for time of death. "Now, that's a poser. I can't tell you any more than you probably guessed already: sometime between late Friday night and Saturday evening... midnight to midnight, roughly. Not more than three hours after his last meal, if that's any use."

With that, and an assurance that he would be notified as soon as any lab results were back, Sims had to be satisfied.

"You think foul play, Benson thinks natural causes," Dr. Cates had mused. "I'd like to see the old so-and-so eat crow, just once. I'll do what I can for you."

He had gone next door to the forensic science labs to submit an official request to test for cyanide the plastic material they had collected from Dr. Morley's bench, and to be told it was in the works already, informally. They knew their business.

"Skimpy," was what Inspector MacDonald called it. "Look. You get what you can... on your own; I'm three men short as it is. Well, two and a half," he snorted into his second chin. Sims wondered idly how Mrs. MacDonald could put up with so many irritating mannerisms for so many years. Not to mention the plain physical fact of the man. Sims resolved, as he did every time he saw the inspector, to diet seriously, before it was too late. He deemed it polite to enquire after Venables and Petersen.

"She's so-so," the inspector said. "Mending, but not real sweet company, I'm told. And him, he's shittin bricks, waiting for a hearing. Oh, well. Whole thing should be over in a couple weeks. Anyhoo," - another irritant to the sergeant's ears - "you get on with it, see what dirt you can dig up, and we'll talk some more. But," he added very firmly, as Sims was about to leave, "if it doesn't come up better than this horse manure," he waved a huge and furry hand over Sims's report, "I close the case. No ifs ands or buts. Capiche? Good."

Sims didn't get home till after seven. Lancelot charged at him with rather more than the joy of reunion; had no time for affection, in fact, until he'd been taken outside for urgent dog-business. Odd: Mrs. Field would usually let him out during the day... Oh, Lord, he hadn't been digging? Through winter, the problem had been on hold; now, with flowerbeds in preparation, he would have to do something about it. But not tonight; he was too tired.

Having filled the dog's water dish, he turned his energies, such as they remained, to feeding them both. No easy task, since Lancelot, lying full-length, cradling his empty dish, filled the kitchen from doorway to refrigerator, only thumping his tail as Sims stepped over him. The fridge contained half a carton of milk, five slices of stale bread, peanut butter, something in tinfoil he couldn't recall putting there and was reluctant to investigate, limp celery, dry cheese...nothing he would want to eat. The scrap of cheese disappeared inside Lance in under a second, eliciting a copious Pavlovian reaction. There was kibble, but no canned dog-food.

"Never mind - we'll go to MacDonalds for some...."

In Lancelot's vocabulary, there was no room for 'Down', 'Stay', or 'Drop it', but MacDonald, in a way exactly opposite to Sims's own association, had a magic akin 'Walk' and 'Car': he was at the door before the sentence ended. "But you *have* to eat the bun. And keep quiet, for Heaven's sake - I'm not up to discussing you with Mrs. Field today." Amazingly, Lance fell silent; he padded softly up the back stairs. Just as well, too, for as he pulled off the parking apron, Sims caught a flap of light at the front window. The landlady would be watching for him now... the Serious Talk About That Animal couldn't be postponed indefinitely.

In the deserted park they shared their meal, the dog fastidiously licking every trace of mayonnaise from the bun, which he then nosed under the bench, and shoved a little dirt after it for good measure. Sims let him off the leash, automatically warning, "Don't chase anything," and thoughtfully sipped at his milkshake.

What did he have? A man dead at his place of work. Not unusual. Only, by all accounts, a very careful man, skilled at his job, supposedly messing around with what could be a poisonous compound - outside the fume hood with no precautions. Supposedly having set up equipment, brought jars of chemicals out of storage, opened and used them, then put all away again, even the measuring implements. Without touching anything else. Wearing rubber gloves, yes - that could be seen as a precaution. But they were one size too big for him. No recipe, formula or notes. No butts in the ashtray. A jacket under a lab coat, on a warm day - besides, he'd had the Bunsen burner on.

Sims set half of his milkshake on the bench, for later enjoyment, and lit a cigarette. He'd been good today, only half a dozen or so... to be honest, simply because he'd had little opportunity. "Lance! I said no chasing!" Apparently in obedience, really, Sims knew, from purely selfish motives, the dog returned to his side. The side where the milkshake stood; his long black nose was nudging the container hopefully. "It's strawberry. You hate strawberry." The dog denied this vehemently, kept begging till Sims gave in and put the cup down on the ground, where Lance gave it two tentative laps and then rolled it under the bench next to the rejected bread. "I told you."

Lance was pushing imaginary earth on top of the pink puddle. Sims picked up the bun and threw it into the bushes, whereupon the dog, who had never fetched anything on command, brought it back to drop at his feet. They did this until the bun was too sodden to handle: birds would find it in the morning. He tossed the milkshake carton for a while. When Lance grew bored and took off after some inaudible noise, his master virtuously carried the paper cup to the nearest trash can.

Okay, so he's not likely to poison himself accidentally. How about setting up a suicide to look accidental? That might explain the jacket: some suicides get undressed first, some dress up: Morley would certainly fit the second category. But if he were staging this, would he not take the same care with his costume that had been taken with the props? Would he wear grey slacks with soiled cuffs and casual shirt? Would he not have a last drink, a last cigarette? Well, perhaps he'd done that at home, alone, late at night, brooding on his life...

Perhaps he'd planned a car-crash, then, thinking on the messiness of it, had gone on to the most familiar place... Would you clean your car before crashing it? Yes, Edward Morley would. In the middle of a Le Carre novel? Sims had read that book, all of it, in one night and half the next day. Of course, Morley might not have liked the story. Only, he was the kind of person who finished things anyway, from a sense of order, if nothing else.

No. All sorts of things are possible; too many are unlikely. Somebody else killed him. More; somebody planned it, stage-set it, cleaned up the evidence... Somebody cool and competent had done it. Why? Why would tell you who; who would tell you why - Dr. Cates would soon tell you how. And you have a probable means of finding out when. That, obviously, was the next step.

There was nothing more to be done about it tonight, however. He collected his dog, not without difficulty, and went home. While Mrs. Field was still awake, he realized, too late. He swore by everything he could think of, to break Lancelot of the digging habit.

"I doubt that," said the landlady. "You haven't managed to teach it anything yet. I can't imagine what possessed you to bring that animal here, in the first place. I do know you ought to get rid of it."

Mrs. Field was a nice woman, really; until recently, she had been an ideal landlady. The rent was reasonable; she would take telephone messages sometimes; occasionally, she used to stop by for a chat on Sims's day off, with a welcome offering of food. He had not known until last fall, when he brought Lancelot home, that she thought and spoke of animals as things - a habit Sims found repugnant. After all, there are only two sexes; what does it cost to remember which applies? At first, in spite of her prejudice, she had been willing to let the dog out when Sims worked long hours. Then the trouble with the garden had started. This was no joke, Sims admitted; Lance could do serious damage, and had done, more than once.

Mrs. Field concluded, "Anyway, until you do, it's not setting foot in my yard." That was her final word on the subject; he knew there would be no appeal. Also, that relations between himself and the landlady would never again be cordial, unless he gave Lancelot away - which, in fact, meant never.

"You're more trouble than you're worth," he told the dog. "Come to think of it, you're not worth anything. You eat too much, scratch too much, and you chase squirrels... Don't deny it, you chase everything. Thank Heaven you're too clumsy to catch them."

The apartment was a mess. He moved two soiled shirts from the sofa to the chair - they'd be happier with their own kind; tossed a lone sock after them - all his socks were identical; it was never a problem matching them. He stretched out, pulled the ashtray closer and turned on the news. Dr. Morley's death was mentioned briefly. "Dear Brian, Son I know how much you dislike lectures" must have been informed by now. Must be feeling guiltier than hell. Must be on his way home. I've got to think about something else, Sims told himself. Like the fact that I didn't buy any groceries. He wrote himself a note and put it in his shirt pocket. Later, he took off the shirt, and collecting other scattered laundry, alertly fishing out two socks that Lance had buried between the sofa cushions, pushed it into a sack. On Saturday, he would launder the note, a five-dollar bill, and the inevitable tissue.

On Saturday, he would open all the windows, put all the books back on the shelves, vacuum the carpet, wipe the sticky rings off the tables. It was only Monday night; by Saturday, he could possibly have a date - not with Mr. Quick's secretary, whose name he had momentarily forgotten, but whose hair and smile he recalled with perfect clarity. She would think he was only after privileged information...and indeed, he *would* be tempted to find out more about Ac-Me Plastics.

However, he might take Lance to the vet, and he *might* finally get up the nerve to ask her out. It hadn't happened on the last three occasions he'd invented ailments for the dog. Dr. Litton, so gentle with animals - so unexpectedly and gratifyingly gentle even with an animal as ungainly as Lancelot ("He's just a big baby," she had said) - was a lot more approachable in fantasy than in real life. Besides, she probably regarded Sims as whatever the pet-owner equivalent is of a hypochondriac.

He fell asleep on the couch, unopened, without a blanket, and dreamed about finding inexplicably dead men, in suits and ties, in a snowdrift, and trying to get Lance to bury them again, knowing he would be blamed if their wives saw them. As soon as he managed to conceal one body, another appeared - each with blue and yellow lividity on a slightly jowly but not unpleasant face. One of the corpses could possibly have been Dr. Benson; there was a relatively thin and benign version of Inspector MacDonald... one was almost certainly a woman, and that scared him awake, because it resembled both Mrs. Field and Gloria Venables.

It was 5:30 in the morning. Unwilling to go back to sleep, lest the nightmare resume, Sims decided to take Lance for a proper walk. This might turn into another long day... Besides, he thought, spreading a critical hand over what could be described as an incipient paunch, they both needed the exercise.

CHAPTER 7

The most reliable means of establishing time of death is a witness. Dr. Morley had been at home and gone back to Ac-Me Plastics: someone must have seen him, somewhere. Sims needed a photograph.

The victim's possessions were kept under lock and guard, in the police station basement. 43 Division adhered strictly to the book on continuity - at least, it had done, since the time a vital piece of physical evidence was lost, and with it their entire case against a master forger. Eventually, the embarrassment would be forgotten; vigilance would relax; properties would go missing...

The clerk opened the locker; Sims wrote date, time and case number in the ledger, and signed it. Then he spread the contents of Dr. Morley's pockets and desk out on the long table provided: they were never to leave the room. His own tags were still on the plastic bags, and where the seals had been broken, they were replaced by new ones, initialled and dated by Flash Jackson. What he had wanted was a copy of the driver's license, but the photograph on it was as bad as the usual ID photo. Reluctantly, he replaced it, resealed and initialled the bag. As long as he was here, though, he might as well re-examine the notebook which had so intrigued him.

It began, dated March 8, with a note to call Bio-Tech for repairs to a fume hood. March 9: "meet with C & A (Charles Quick? Sims had yet to encounter any A. except for Paul Arnott, and he didn't seem likely to attend a meeting with management). about SF 21: Hold till after W". March 11: "Bio-Tech repairman, 2 hours!" March 15: "W 2 - friable; change proportions HC 50+?". March 20: "W3 - still too brittle; -- T?". March 22: "ED absent, again - 3rd day this month... find out problem. W4 to DF?" March 27: "W4 - OK; ED - OK; Let DF proceed with SF???". Apr.3: "Call Bio-Tech; hood 2 drawing < 85%. Tell C. withhold payment". Apr. 5: "Lunch with C, Walters VP - wants results by end of month. Twit. Could do by mid-May. Get C. hold him off". Apr 8: "Meet C, A, Thurs.2:30" So it went, with events and comments, notes to himself to get things done. The mixing machine was due for regular service;

technician's visit, report; recommendation to investigate a replacement model. Lunch dates, staff meetings becoming more frequent, the later ones including ED (Why? There had been no mention of her working on this project.) and someone called BW, until May 11: "W7 - start prod. C happy - no more Walters VP! TG. Monday, meet C, A, MJ, - has idea worth trying."

It told Sims little enough, but he had it photocopied anyway. Then under the watchful eye of the young female clerk, he carefully resealed the bag and put everything back in its box.

Much as he would like to see how she was holding up, he was reluctant to approach Mrs. Morley so soon. Had not Mr. Quick mentioned employee files? And that he should ask Miss...? Having forgotten her name made this undesirable, but that's the price one pays for taking incomplete case-notes. Anyway, he should look into all the relevant backgrounds.

It came to him as he entered the office: "Good morning, Miss Hillyard!" he said with the extra heartiness of relief.

"Good morning Sergeant," she replied. It's nice, thought Sims, to have a rank or title; you need never know who forgets your name. Nonetheless, he wondered if she had.

While going through the documents she obligingly fetched for him, Sims gave Miss Hillyard a surreptitious once-over. Several times, over selected parts. Her hair was really magnificent: a warm honey-blond, silky and thick and alive. Frank, open smile; graceful hands. Her legs were hidden beneath the desk, but he'd made a note while she'd walked out of the office and back. Her face, he wasn't quite sure about: pretty, but disguised by too much makeup, in colours too vivid; this suggested she might be younger than his first estimate.

There was no photograph of the victim, or anyone else. He did find out how much money they all received in compensation. In Dr. Morley's case, over $100,000, well over, in some years, with patent royalties and profit-sharing. More than adequate to support his life-style, or what Sims had seen of it, and nearly twice what his second-in-command was making. The others fell into the expected hierarchy below Jones. Nothing startling there.

Jones held a patent several years old, that had not resulted in big dividends, but the most recent product was credited to him and he would become eligible for shares in his tenth year. Too, there would be a substantial raise in salary now. Eve Dumont had two patents, both over three years old, modestly successful. Frayne had none: he had only been with the company three years. Was this useful information? If the motive were financial, yes; otherwise, he was prolonging his stay under false pretences.

When Miss Hillyard offered coffee, he accepted, and as she was also taking her break and seemed inclined to socialize, he stopped reading.

"Your work must be more exciting than this, usually," she ventured.

"Not really," he said. "This is most of it. Three hours of dull routine for every minute of action."

He realized belatedly that he'd left little conversational room, so he added, "I imagine it's the same with any occupation. Do you find it so?"

The girl shrugged. "It's a job. I'm not gonna do it for my whole life."

"Oh, you have other plans," he invited.

"Yeah," she said, sipping coffee, almost without touching the rim of her mug, so as to preserve her lipstick. "I'm quitting as soon as I get married. Or, anyway, as soon as I have a baby. It's important for a mother to stay home, don't you think?"

Mrs. Sims had been both at home and not, with her six children. Between the preparation of meals, she'd spent most of her time keeping the books and ordering supplies, cleaning the store, stocking the shelves and a hundred other chores. Had she been less busy, her son might have received more discipline - a terrifying thought. He reflected on his friends and colleagues. Some of their mothers had worked outside the home, some had not, and he could discern no pattern in how the children fared. He said this to Miss Hillyard, whose response was: "Well, I think so," which closed that topic.

He turned to something less general. "In a place like this, I suppose everybody gets to know one-another quite well?"

She shrugged again, daintily; a cultivated habit, he guessed, and took another year off the age he'd assigned her: down to about 23 now, and he'd begun, in any case, to lose interest. "Just the staff in accounting and sales, mostly," she said. "We never see them from the factory, except in lunchtime. Except the foreman, Ernie, he comes in a lot. He's kind of a sweet old guy."

"How about the people from the lab?" he pursued. "What are they like?"

"Well," she said, conspiratorially lowering her voice and leaning a little toward him. "That David Frayne is really cute. Too bad," her bright red lips turned down in a fetching pout. Sims, unfairly, he realized, could not abide a fetching pout. It reminded him of Marie, and that always put him in a bad mood. "Turns out, he's engaged. To the girl that used to have this job before me. Talk about being in the right place at the right time!"

"Mr. Arnott is quite handsome," Sims prompted, but elicited only another dainty shrug.

"Oh, Ferdy. Yeah, he's a nice enough kid."

"And what did you think of Dr. Morley?"

Miss Hillyard giggled and then remembered the recent tragedy. "Oh, I couldn't say. Well, I mean, the poor guy's dead." Her blue eyes grew big and round with the drama of it. "Did he get murdered?"

"Would it surprise you?"

"Oh yeah," she said. "I mean, he wasn't the nicest person in the world, you know, but he didn't do anything real bad, did he?"

"I don't know," Sims replied, "did he?"

"Oh well," she said, composing herself to speak ill of the dead, "he was kind of mean sometimes. Especially to Dave and Ferdy. Maybe he was jealous - of Dave, I mean, not Ferdy."

"Any special reason he should be? Jealous of Mr. Frayne, I mean?"

"Oh, no *special* reason," she said. "Just, like, the usual. Dave is so smart and attractive and a real go-getter, you know? And women like him. All that."

"Women didn't like Dr. Morley?"

Miss Hillyard giggled without reservation this time. "Mrs. Benz, maybe... Anyway, I heard he got along real well with *somebody* at Ac-Me. No, it couldn't of been her, though. Maybe it's not true... just some old talk, before I was here, even."

"And how long is that?"

"Almost two years," she said. "With the company, I mean. I only got this job a couple of months ago, after what's-her-name left. Seems like a long time."

"Why?" asked Sims. Having found a copious source of gossip, he wasn't about to let it dry up. "Is Mr. Quick difficult to work for?"

"Oh,no! He's an old pussycat. Well, I mean, he's kind of formal, you know, like Dr. Morley was, but that's okay; he treats you like a lady. He likes everything just so - spelling and things. Throws a fit when you put one of those little whatd'yacallems in the wrong s's." Sims groaned inwardly: this is a girl who not only apostrophizes plurals, but knows not what they're called. "But he's a doll, really. And you get used to the funny smells around here after a while. Just, it's kind of boring."

That line of questioning didn't get him very far, and he could not easily return to personalities. Miss Hillyard didn't seem to know very much about very much. He glanced at her file: 28 years old? His first guess had been the most accurate. Good to know, but no longer important. Besides, he had used up a great deal of time. After jotting down a few relevant facts from the files, he returned them, thanked her, and left the office.

Because the parking lot was full, he had left his car on the fringe beyond the laboratory wing. It seemed more natural to walk down the corridor than around the building. Abreast of the wash-up room, he was surprised by young Mr. Arnott, in the act of negotiating three coffee mugs through the swing door.

"I'll be with you in a minute," that young man said.

Sims opened the laboratory door and stood aside, wondering how he would have managed alone; this door, like the fire exit, swung only outward. Ask to be admitted by whoever he was bringing refreshments for. (For whomever he was, etc...) Though he hadn't intended to seek an interview, Sims thought it civil to wait until the other divested himself of his burden and returned.

"So, what's shakin', what's breakin'? Have you come to make an arrest?"

"I'm afraid nothing so exciting. By the way, do you always open doors with your shoulder?"

This put the young man off-balance for the blink of an eye, which he performed. "Yeah, I guess. When my hands are full, anyway. Everybody does. That's why they make swing doors, isn't it?"

"Could you do it for me again?"

"Sure." They stepped into the wash-up room. Since his hands were empty, Arnott first approached the exit with left hand out, palm forward. Realizing that this was not what was wanted, he checked, stepped back, clasped some air in front of his midriff and approached the door again - sideways, pushing with his upper arm. "Like so?"

"Yes, thank you."

Ferdy Arnott grinned happily. "Next time I'll show you how to turn on a light switch, and then, if you're very good, we can do advanced stuff, like, say, water-taps."

Sims couldn't help smiling. The little smart-ass was impossible to dislike. "If you can do it with your nose," he said. "Anyway, thanks."

"You coming in to talk to the gang?"

This seemed a good idea, if only to prevent too much personal significance being attached to the little demonstration he'd just held. All the staff was present, apparently not busy. They looked less different in their white coats; more like a team. David Frayne was assembling some glass apparatus in the far corner, but Eve Dumont and Martin Jones were sipping coffee at the latter's desk, conversing in low voices.

"The sergeant was just passing by," Ferdy announced. Sims greeted each of the occupants, his gaze lingering only the polite length of time on Mrs. Dumont, and addressed himself to Dr. Jones.

"I wonder if you could show me around."

"Sure, why not?" Jones stood, leading the way. "This is the store-room," he pulled open the heavy door with his right hand and reached around the jamb to backhand the light-switch on. "In here we keep supplies: chemicals on that side, portable equipment and glassware on this."

Sims looked around the shelves he'd seen before, pointed out a large flask like the one now at the forensic lab. "Could you bring that, and a jar... any one..." He scanned the shelf for potassium cyanide, saw none, settled for potassium chloride, took down a random jar from the S section and stepped aside for Jones to precede him. The man, now with his hands full, pushed the door open, as expected, with his left upper arm and shoulder.

"Reenacting the crime?" he asked, as they both placed things on Dr. Morley's desk. "I don't know what you mean to produce, but I can tell you it'll be salty."

Sarcasm? From timid Dr. Jones?

He had a quick look around the fume room, again noting that Jones, empty-handed on the way out, used both palms on the panic bar. The other chemists had gathered in close, meanwhile. He asked, "Would you please put these things away... I don't know where they belong." It sounded as lame to him as it must have to them, but they complied.

Mrs. Dumont sashayed past him and picked up the flask. Boy-o-boy, is that lady trouble! Exiting, she theatrically and unnecessarily leaned the full length of her back against the door and swung it slowly, sensuously outward, to enthusiastic applause from young Arnott. Frayne followed with the brown jars, opened the door abruptly with his elbow and marched back to his bench, all without a word.

Sims thanked them and left with the feeling that he had just convinced four more people that he wasn't quite right in the head. Don't you believe it, he told himself; these are intelligent people; they know what you were up to.

He was surprised to find the Morley household full of activity. The young woman who answered his ring had evidently been busy in the kitchen, and returned there after the most perfunctory of introductions. She was Louise Whitlock, the Morleys' elder child. In the living room, under the harassed supervision of Mrs. Morley, was a very small Whitlock of indeterminate gender, hastening across the carpet on all fours, and an even smaller one in a carrying cot. As Sims began to make his explanations, there entered a young man whom he recognised as son Brian before he was told. The resemblance to his father was startling: stature, colouring, eyes, even the line of his jaw was similar, allowing for the next thirty years.

"Brian just arrived," his mother explained. "Isn't it amazing?"

"I was pretty lucky," said the young man, "to get a seat on the first flight out. First class, too. You know they serve breakfast on china plates? Too bad I can't eat at five a.m."

Though he would have preferred a quiet word with Mrs. Morley, Sims was glad to see her surrounded by family. He asked Brian Morley whether he had been in touch with his father in the past week, and receiving a negative answer, decided that a proper interview could wait a day or so. Then he asked for a photograph of the deceased.

"I'm afraid I don't have a recent one," said Mrs. Morley, "but I did make a few portraits - oh, three , four years ago, when I first became interested in photography. He hadn't changed very much in that time."

She led him to a pleasant, spacious room at the back of the house, looking out onto the garden. Unlike her husband's study, this room was all light and colour, with a chintz-covered sofa and leaf-green walls - what could be seen of them between bookcases and framed photographs of the family, of birds and wildflowers. She took a folder from a folio marked 'People, 80 - 85' and laid it open on the pine table under the window. There was a series of studies: Brian as a gawky adolescent; Louise as a young bride, somewhat thinner than the woman he had seen minutes ago. And of Edward Morley... it took him a second or two to realize this: the man in the photographs was handsome, in an imposing, serious way. One picture, he found especially arresting; it was a bust portrait, like the others, but the subject's expression told of sorrow, disappointment and reconciliation. It was the face of a man making the brave best of painful circumstance. Mrs. Morley noticed him studying at it.

"Don't take that one," she said quietly.

He hadn't wanted to; it was too personal. It made him feel almost as if he had overheard something he should not know. He chose the most neutral of the pictures - the least successful, from a photographer's point of view, adding, "You're very talented."

56

Why should a simple, rather bland compliment make her eyes cloud over, when seeing the face of her late husband had not?

"I know it's selfish," she explained, "but I just now realized how much easier it will be, now, to work on the book."

"Book?"

"The grebe book," she said, and as he still stared at her in incomprehension: "A friend of mine - Jonas Thompson, you may have seen his work. No? He's quite well-known. He lives at Sculpin Lake, where he also teaches photography. When we discovered a small flock - well, really only three pairs - of red-necked grebe at our lake... they're extremely rare this far east..." Her face had taken on a light, not unlike that of religious fervour. "Grebes used to nest all across Northern Ontario, and we think maybe they're coming back! His publisher asked Jonas to do a book - oh, not just pictures of the grebe, but their habitat, neighbours, predators, life cycle... It would be especially valuable to document their success, if they were re-established. The publicity would be useful, to get them some help from the government. If the book sells, the publisher has pledged half the profits to a grebe rehabilitation fund. Isn't that wonderful? Jonas is committed to another project, so he suggested I do it... You don't know what that meant to me."

"A professional start?"

She nodded emphatically. "Professional!"

"And why could you not have done it before?"

"Oh, I could. I was... until I spoiled the shots from last weekend... But, you see, now I can spend more time at the lake. I can even follow my birds on migration."

A quick perusal of the city map gave Sims the most likely route from Don Mills to Ac-Me Plastics. This would take all afternoon, unless he found a way to narrow down the possibilities. Okay, when is likely? The man came home, changed, maybe watered the lawn. What time? Six, seven in the evening? He started to write a letter... then what? Heated his dinner. Did some calculations? Had an idea? Became depressed? Time passed - three hours after he ate, by the pathologist's guess. Most drugstores would have closed by then, also supermarkets... except the 24-hour one at the mall. If Dr. Morley had bought his cigarettes there, he had more than half an hour to drive... Would he not have opened the pack? Maybe... some people don't smoke while driving. Sims would leave the supermarket till last.

He started with the immediate neighbours. Knocking on doors and explaining his business to housewives was a tedious occupation, but it didn't take long. In the four homes with reasonably unobstructed view of the Morleys' front yard, nobody had any recollection of seeing Dr. Morley outside, at any time during the weekend past. Nor, one elderly man pointed out, did they spend their time watching one another.

He was beginning to think it a wasted afternoon; most of the milk and variety stores along the route were staffed by different people during the day and evening - something he should have thought of. He showed the picture anyway, with uniformly negative results, until he was almost at Ac-Me Plastics. And there, not two long industrial blocks from the plant, was a small suburban plaza: one drycleaner, one drugstore, a Chinese restaurant, a photo-finisher and a milk store. The young man behind the counter recognised Dr. Morley at first glance.

"Sure, he comes in all the time. Lunch-time, mostly - I guess he works around here."

"Could you recall," asked Sims hopefully, "whether this man came in last Friday, fairly late?"

The boy shook his head. "Wouldn't know. I'm full time... Don't work evenings or weekends."

Sims asked him who might have been present and received two names. "Leroy will be here at five," the boy added, "but Patti only comes in weekends. I got her phone number here, someplace." To have covered all bases, Sims took it down and planned to return in the evening.

Unless he could think of something more relevant to do, there went a whole day, with nothing to show for it. He wouldn't put in for overtime, unless the interview with the student, Leroy, produced results.

CHAPTER 8

Pending real progress, Sims decided to discharge a duty long put off, and visited Gloria Venables in the hospital. He bought flowers, as his mother had taught him - that was his second mistake.

"Lose the roses," she greeted him. "I'm allergic."

He took the offending bouquet to the nurses' station and asked to have it given to some other patient. "How is Sergeant Venables doing, by the way?" he asked.

The nurse frowned. "I wish she were better. I'm afraid she'll be here another week or, maybe more." The last word sounded like a moan.

Determined to put in the mandatory ten minutes, he offered to bring books or magazines from the gift shop; listened politely to her complaints about the care she was receiving.

"Here," she said, "I'll show you," and pressed the buzzer. "See, they take forever." When the young woman whom he had seen earlier came into the room, she demanded to have the foot of her bed raised; as soon as the nurse was gone, she told him to lower it again.

"So!" Gloria changed topic abruptly, "have they kicked Petersen out yet?"

"The hearing is tentatively scheduled for the 19th. I think," Sims added, "they want to be sure you're strong enough to attend."

"Oh, I wouldn't miss it. The bastard should be strung up by the balls for what he did to me. Look at this goddam cast! Plus which, I got internal injuries. And *he* waltzes away without a scratch."

"I never really heard what happened," admitted Sims. "You were returning from a weekend seminar, and went off the road, that's all anyone told me."

"*I* didn't go off the road - *he* did. Stupid bastard was driving, like always. Thinks he's the only one that can."

"It was late at night, I understand," Sims prompted diplomatically. The lectures must have ended no later than five p.m., and London to Toronto is a two-hour trip.

"Yeah," she said, "pretty late. There was this farewell

party, after. Bastard was pissed. And pissed off, too. Real bad news."

This was much as Sims had conjectured, and knew he wasn't the only one. Chances were also good that Venables herself had been in no better condition to drive than her boyfriend. "Still - something must have gone wrong with the car. It wasn't raining,"

"No. Not so much traffic, either. He didn't watch the road, that's all."

Sims decided not to pursue the matter: it would come out at the hearing.

"So, anyways," she said, "looks like I'll need a new partner. How 'bout it?"

"Well," Sims prevaricated, "it's hardly up to me. I suppose there will be some reassignments."

"Ask anyways," she commanded. "That'll count some. I'll put in a formal request, too... They owe me for this," she brushed the tips of her fingers across her bruised face. "So! Big Mac set up the Drug Bust of The Decade yet? Wanna go on a stakeout with Little Gloria... hmm?" This last was accompanied by a leer so cloying, he barely refrained from a physical recoil.

"I haven't heard any new developments. I believe he's working on it," Sims said neutrally. In fact, he was fairly sure that the plan was complete and would proceed with all speed. And fervently hoped he could somehow get out of the detail: it would certainly be a fiasco. The entire city already seemed to know about it.

As Gloria Venables didn't open another topic within ten seconds, Sims judged it not overtly rude to take his leave, "Well, I am on duty, so..."

"Come again," she said. "In the evening. It's so goddam *boring* here."

He nodded and smiled, but was able to escape without a verbal commitment.

Division switchboard had a message from the forensic pathologist. Rather than telephone, and as there was no more pressing work, he would drive down to the morgue and talk to Dr. Cates in person.

The secretary, whom he had seen on his last visit, and

whose name he had not asked at the time, was new, very young, and full of enthusiasm. "He's on the phone right now," she told him, "arguing with somebody in Winnipeg. It shouldn't take too long. Get some coffee."

He did, putting a quarter in the tin, even though nobody was looking, and wandered back to the desk.

"Which case are you on?" asked the girl, who seemed to have nothing else to do. He told her. "Oh, then you're Sergeant Sims."

He acknowledged this, adding diffidently, "I'm afraid I don't know your name."

"It's Pamela," she said. "Isn't that gross? That's why everybody calls me Pebbles. That's silly, too, I guess, but it's better than Pa-am."

She might have continued in this vein with very little encouragement, were she not interrupted by the emergence of her boss from his office. Dr. Cates' face was a darker shade of red than usual, but was not scowling: he had obviously won the argument. He held up one rough-skinned hand at Sims. "Pebbles, cancel that court appearance in Winnipeg. I'm not about to lose two days and eat airline food, for a routine ten-minute testimony. They'll have to make do with a deposition. Get out the Whittaker file. Now," he turned to Sims. "Eager little beaver, ain't you?"

Dr. Cates went into the small lunchroom where the coffee machine lived. Sims didn't miss his glance into the money tin and the minute satisfied nod at the lone quarter reposing there. Policemen often forget to contribute... policemen often don't get the cooperation they hope for. A little good faith goes a long way. "Got a verbal report from toxicology today. Amazing, innit?" Sims nodded; it really was fast. "We've got cyanide confirmed. Not a lot, mind you... it's elusive stuff. Nothing in the stomach contents, which doesn't rule out ingestion, some hours before. Just about three hours, by the way, as I guessed. Find out when the guy had his supper, and you've got time of death, plus or minus a half hour." He slanted bushy eyebrows up at Sims. "Any chance?"

"I doubt it," said the detective. "He seems to have been alone. But it would be late Friday night. I'm working on a lead on that, by the way."

"Good. As to the poison: the speed of death - no vomiting, no convulsions... I would say - not under oath, mind you - I'd say, in food or drink, the dose would have to have been big enough to leave some trace. Inhalation is your likely method. They haven't found any in that huge lot of disgusting muck you collected, but that doesn't mean anything: it burns off." He paused to light his pipe; Sims knew better than to interrupt. "So, why is this guy, who must know his stuff, messing with a cyanide compound outside a fume hood? Two possibilities. One: he was drunk... it's going to be a while before we get an answer to that. Or, two - just between you, me and the lamppost, this is my idea - he meant to. My gut feeling is, a nicely staged suicide. Any evidence?"

"None," Sims shook his head. "No suicide note. Mail wouldn't have reached its destination yet - we'll check with his lawyer in a day or two. He may have written a letter to his son. But I don't think it was that kind of letter."

"Good. If nothing turns up, we don't have to make an issue of it. I hate the vengeful suicides, the kind that make a bloody mess of the nuptial bed or land on a passing car. But if a fellow goes to some trouble to spare his family, I don't mind giving him a hand."

"He had a full pack of cigarettes in his pocket," Sims mentioned. "Unopened."

Dr. Cates, busy with his pipe and fifth match, understood. "Hm. All right. Maybe he doesn't want to give himself time to change his mind. That happens. For legal purposes, it's probably an accident. Unless he got some help, of course."

"That, just between us lampposts, is *my* belief."

"Almonds in the green beans. Hmmm. Jealous wife? Greedy kids?"

Sims shrugged. "Jealous colleague, greedy boss, angry girlfriend? I don't know, but I'm working on it."

"Well, best of luck to you."

Sims thanked, and left him puffing thoughtfully over his second coffee. It had to be the green frothy substance - had to be. Edward Morley had not concocted that stuff; somebody else had set it up.

He stopped by Division, just to be seen filling out forms, then went home in time to prevent an accident.

Lance would enjoy riding along when Sims returned to the milk store.

Leroy was a surprise of two kinds. The first was a child's round, blue-eyed, fair head on the body of a weightlifter... with fine manners and a well-modulated voice. The second, and less welcome surprise was that, though he recognised Dr. Morley as someone who had been in the store occasionally, he denied seeing him on the previous weekend.

"I don't believe this man has been in here, at least, during my shift, in two months or more."

"You're sure?"

"I'm positive. I haven't missed any hours."

"And nobody else works here, say, very late on Friday?"

"I'm the only one."

Patti Robinson was not at home, but her mother expected her back from the library in an hour or so. "Would you like to drop in then?" She gave him the address, not far from Ac-Me Plastics.

That gave Sims and Lancelot time for a long, delirious romp in the ravine. It really wasn't fair, he knew, to keep such a large and dynamic beast locked up in a small basement apartment, so much of the time. He ought to take him out more often. He ought to think about moving to some place with an accessible yard... At least, Lance was better off than he had been before Sims acquired him, and obviously happier.

Patti Robinson was a diminutive redhead with feline green eyes, freckles all over a pixie face and a smile to match. An apprentice heart-breaker, Sims thought, momentarily assailed by a fear that he might be harbouring a tendency to paedophilia. Wasting no time, he showed her the photograph of Dr. Morley.

"Sure, I've seen him. In the store. He didn't seem like the type to be in trouble with the cops. Sorry - police. You just can't tell, can you?"

Sims told her that it was nothing like that. "The problem is, he's dead. It was on the news, didn't you hear?"

Why should she have? Even if teenaged girls take an interest in the day's events, Dr. Morley had been a very minor news item, with no accompanying picture - important only to those who had known him, or who had become involved since his death.

"No," replied the girl, "I never heard his name. People don't introduce themselves to cashiers, you know. If anyone did, though, he would have... I don't think I ever had another customer with such nice manners. He'd always say please and thank you, and he'd look right at you, like you were a real person, not some kind of vending machine or something, you know what I mean? It's too bad." She sighed deeply. "What did you want to know?"

"I very much hope you remember the last time you saw this man."

"Oh, that's easy," she said. "Saturday. About 9:30 in the morning, because I hadn't been there very long, and nobody much came in. Saturday morning is slow, you know - that's when I get my homework done. Anyway," she continued without prompting, "I was surprised, because I never saw him at all since I got switched to weekends. The manager said it'd be safer to have Leroy in, evenings. How come somebody's holding up a milk store, like every week, practically?"

"I guess, because it seems easy," the detective said. "Your manager had the right idea. Can you recall when this change was made?"

"Of course I can recall, what a silly question! It was in March, right after that girl got beaten up at the Mac's store. That really scared us, you know? My dad wanted me to quit, but I sure can use the money, so I was glad they put Leroy on nights."

"If it makes you feel any better, we did catch the man."

"Yeah, I heard. But there's so many of them."

"We try," said Sims, "and we mostly succeed."

"Oh well," the girl shrugged. "It's okay. I don't waste a lot of time on being scared."

He returned to the original topic. "You haven't seen Dr. Morley in the last two months, then he suddenly showed up on Saturday. And you're quite sure about the time?"

"Give or take ten minutes, yeah."

"What did he come in for?"

"Cancer-sticks, like always. I used to tell him they'd kill him one day... But it wasn't the smokes, or you wouldn't be

64

here, right?"

"Right. Could you be a little more specific?"

"Oh, sure. He always bought a large pack Player's filters. A Mars bar, now and then. And sometimes a lighter - blue, to match the box. He was fussy like that. Last weekend, though, just the cigarettes."

"Now, think hard," Sims told her. "Did you notice anything about him that was different?"

"Yeah, now you mention it. I don't know if it means much, but he wasn't dressed as nice as usual. I used to notice that... He was always neat, kind of old-fashioned, not flashy, you know, but formal, everything matched. That time, he didn't have a tie on, and he wore a sport jacket - brown, I think - with grey cotton slacks. Dorky. That's a word my mom uses. I guess because it was the weekend... People dress more casual for Saturday than for going to work."

"That's very observant," Sims approved. "Anything else? For example, did he seem more or less happy than usual? More or less bothered? In any way odd in his manner or mood?"

"Well, I don't know. Maybe in kind of a hurry. Maybe a little bit grumpy. Except, that wasn't so unusual - he never was the life of the party type... Real polite, but not, you know, jokey, like some guys. Some of them can be real jerks, you know? This guy never did that. I guess there wasn't anything all that different."

"One last question. When Dr. Morley left your store, did you notice which way he went?"

"I wouldn't know that. He got into his car - it was parked right outside the door - and backed up. That's about all you can see from behind the counter. Half the parking lot, a little bit of street, the bus shelter and the newspaper boxes. I know, because I spend a lot of time there."

Though not what he had expected, it was important information. He would now have to re-think the whole scenario of Dr. Morley's death. Not Friday night, but Saturday morning. What then, of having eaten less than three hours before? Sims tried to bring forward the picture in his mind of the Morleys' kitchen. In the drying rack next to the sink: one casserole dish, one plate, glass, knife and fork. No breakfast things. Well then, suppose he hadn't eaten the night before - or had gone out for dinner? There is no law against chicken casserole for breakfast...

Saturday morning, a man wakes up, heats his prepared food rather than make breakfast; cleans up after himself. While watering his lawn has a bright idea... jumps into his car, goes to the lab to try it out... without any precautions... and dies - by accident. Okay, that might be believed. But *not* of Edward Morley.

He waters his garden, puts everything away, comes into the house. Sits around smoking, gets depressed, decides to kill himself... Maybe late at night, but not on a sunny May morning... Unless he had decided already, and was carrying out a plan, deliberately, step by step...

Then, why not have a last cigarette? No. He didn't plan this; somebody else did. How could someone know that Edward Morley would be in the lab? He or she would make certain of it.

Man wakes early, gets up, eats, starts does his chores, becomes preoccupied....belatedly remembers an appointment, rushes off. Or: the phone rings; it's a colleague with a problem. He hurries out, realizes along the way that he's left his cigarettes behind, stops to buy some, gets to the lab. He's not surprised an experiment is already set up; unwary, he walks right into the trap. Before he can do anything, he's overcome by fumes...

If the cyanide was in the green muck, it's already in the room. In which case the other person has to be wearing a gas-mask. That would alert the intended victim... Or, the killer had the cyanide ready; overpowered him, if only for a second. Which would mean somebody stronger than the victim. Not Charles Quick, nor any woman, probably. He reluctantly left Eve Dumont on the list of possibles. Upon reflection, he put Mrs. Morley back on the list, too, though why she would want to do it there...?

To remove suspicion from her own environment, that's why; to make it look like an accident. Jones, Arnott, Frayne were all big enough, strong enough. Whoever and why-ever, something like this must have happened. The cyanide would be in some easily-vaporized form. Does it come that way? What sort of container? How big? What material? Whom to ask?

At almost seven in the evening, the forensic labs were

closed. The one person he trusted there, Dr. Cates, was notoriously protective of his privacy: he could not be reached at home, except through one of two absolutely reliable assistants, both of whom would judge the nature of the emergency accurately: i.e., negatively. It could wait till morning. Sims would have to wait until morning.

Sims, in any case, was tired and hungry, and the dog must be ravenous. Eat out - again? Or stop at some late-hours grocery store and make a proper dinner? He opted for the second, buying the second most expensive dog-food as a special treat, and stocking up, while he was there, on staples. Bread and milk, onions, ground beef and tomato paste. One of these days, he would cook spaghetti sauce again... One day, fairly soon, he ought to invite Marjory and Scott; he'd eaten at their house four times, since last he'd had them over, and single or not, that didn't seem fair. Sisters are not for exploiting - especially kind, understanding sisters, like Marj. He added some mushrooms, oregano, clove garlic - that would force him to do it soon.

A trunkful of fresh, wholesome food gave him a sense of all being right with the world. How primitive we are, really, he thought: bringing home groceries is one of the touchstones of life - important, pleasant, imbued with warmth and security. He'd used to feel that way after the weekly shopping with Marie; it was a sort of ritual, reaffirming their bond. We bring home the food together; therefore, we belong to a privileged unity. Progress, my foot: we're all cavemen at heart. Maybe too much of the caveman for Marie. He sighed. Well, he thought, I hope she has found someone better. As for me and my canine companion, we shall feast royally, a privileged unit.

Had Edward and Amanda Morley felt that way? They had separate quarters, spent weekends apart. Sometime, though, they must have: they had made two handsome children, and stayed together, longer than a lot of people - we know who we are. What had gone wrong? Never mind. She didn't do it. It would be a good idea, as well as correct procedure, to find out whether she had actually gone to Sculpin Lake. Her reaction to the news of her husband's death had been as genuine and unrehearsed as any he'd ever seen.

Sims could not avoid a twinge of guilt for having caused the spoilage of that film. Now, there was no physical proof of her weekend activity. Grebes - he'd have to look it up, but was pretty sure it's some kind of duck - if, indeed, there were grebes on that overdeveloped film - couldn't be called as witnesses. Still, if she had been there, someone must have seen her, spoken to her; someone should remember.

CHAPTER 9

It was Wednesday morning, after he'd telephoned Dr. Cates, and been told: "What you want is a wee glass capsule, something the size that gelatine comes in - have you never had soft fingernails? Say, two centimetres by one, made of thin glass. Sealed, you understand: for one-time use. Break it, and it's all over. Literally. Small quantity, possibly half a gramme. It would be a white crystalline substance. You'd have to burn or dissolve it to get the gas. Instantly deadly, and it would dissipate without a trace."

Here, Dr. Cates had added a cautionary note. "If he did that himself, I wish you'd let it lay. There is no way on God's green earth that a chemist would attempt such a thing without a dozen precautions. Fume hood, gas mask, fans going to beat the band. That could not possibly be an accident. If someone else did it, maybe... Tell you what. I'll have the gentlemen next door to look for glass fragments. Fair enough?"

" More than fair," responded Sims. "Thank you."

Then he had spoken to young Brian Morley, who seemed uneasy.

"Well, yeah," he said, "every Friday, he called me, or I was supposed to phone him, collect. Only, I didn't..."

"What time did he call you last Friday?" The detective persisted.

"Well, he didn't, either. I guess he might've, only I wasn't there. I mean, Dad was so punctual all the time, you know? So, when he didn't call by seven, I went out. To a party. That makes me sound pretty awful, I know,"

"I don't see anything wrong with that," Sims remarked.

"Yeah. Except, I left, like one second after seven. And then I kind of, not exactly forgot to try calling later."

"Did you have a reason?"

"A stupid reason, yeah. Dad would have asked about my biology exam, and I could never lie to him, but I didn't want to tell him the truth. The truth is, I blew it, and I blew it cause I didn't study and I didn't study cause I hate biology, nearly as much as I hate physics and chemistry. God never meant me to be a scientist, but Dad wouldn't believe that. So, anyway, I just didn't need the aggravation right then. I was going to tell him, sometime. The truth is, I *did* mean to tell him, but I never quite got up the nerve... I'm not going back," he blurted out in a rush of words.

"That's something you'll have to square with your mother, now," Sims told him gently. "It's none of my business. And it's not relevant to my investigation - so, relax. All I want to know about is the last time you actually spoke to Dr. Morley."

"Oh. That was the Friday before last. He bawled me out for not working hard enough. Pretty much par for the course."

"At that time, was there anything in your conversation to indicate a change of some kind? How shall I put this? Did he seem especially unhappy? Worried? Preoccupied? Did he have anything on his mind, besides your poor performance in school?"

"No. Not that I noticed, anyway. If you're driving at what I think you might be, the answer is no. My father was *not* suicidal. Besides being a sin, it's a chicken-shit thing to do. If there is one thing my Dad wasn't, it's a coward. Not like me. I put things off, try to pretend they don't exist. Not Dad; he faced things."

"Including your inability or unwillingness to learn sciences?"

"I meant his own problems, not other people. But, yeah, I guess he did know but wouldn't accept it. That's not cowardice; that's stubbornness - there's a difference."

The detective smiled. "Yes, you're right. Well then, what *do* you think about his death? Off the record, I mean. An accident?"

"No way. He wasn't a coward, and even a lot more than that, he wasn't careless. No way would he make that kind of mistake."

"Not even if - this might sound harsh, I'm sorry - not even if he had been drinking?"

The boy paled, squared his jaw - and faced it. "Yeah, that is kind of cold. Okay, so he drank some. Who doesn't? But get this straight. My father liked his whisky, maybe more than other guys do - and maybe he had some reason to. Not that we meant to disappoint him, just that he was... I don't know... demanding, kind of. Like he wanted *more* from people, maybe more from life, than they could give him, and he had an awful hard time accepting it. So, anyway, I know he hit the bottle once in a while, but he only hurt himself. He never, never once, raised a hand to me, or my sister; he never threatened... You know what? He never even swore, that I recall. Freaky, huh?"

"Thank you," said Sims. "You didn't have to tell me all that. And I probably won't need to use any of it. Okay?"

Brian nodded. "Yeah. Okay." He took a deep breath. "So what we're saying is, if my father didn't kill himself - and he didn't - somebody ...murdered him."

Sims nodded soberly. "Any ideas?"

The boy thought hard for nearly a minute. "No. I mean, he didn't make a lot of friends, but he didn't make enemies, either. He was so... so proper all the time. Straight with people. Honest - you know? Decent. Who could possibly hate him enough to... kill?"

Sims noticed that he hesitated each time before using the words for kill; only a fraction of a second, time enough to balk, then to reject a euphemism. He respected that in a man, especially in such a young one. Too, for people who had not seen eye to eye, there must have been a great deal of love and respect between Brian and his father - and a surprising insight in the son.

He asked, "Who benefits?"

"Who benefits?" the boy repeated, half-belligerently, but then subsided into thought. "I guess, Mom and I do, in a way. Me, because he isn't going to give me a hard time about school anymore." He noticed Sims' minimal head-shake. "Not exactly a motive for murder. But, for all I told you, it could have been worse than I said. Knowing Dad, there's likely to be money, too. Not that he was ever cheap about stuff we needed, but he didn't throw it around. So Mom or I have to go right out and find a job. I guess you could figure she's got a motive, but you'd be wrong."

"With all due respect, I'm not sure you would know all there is to know about that."

"Wouldn't I? No, maybe not, since I've been away. But kids know a lot more about their parents than they're told. And I'm not a kid anymore."

"True enough. What is it you want to tell me about your parents?"

For the first time, Brian looked long and hard at him. "You don't have to warn me - I may be a dud at science, but I'm not dumb. All I meant was, whatever you might have heard from other people, my parents would never hurt each other. They were always true friends. You know what that means?"

Sims nodded, "I think so, yes. Which leaves me pretty much at square one, doesn't it?"

"I guess. Well, then somebody at his job..."

"I'm looking into it."

That, except for necessary courtesies, wound up the interview. Sims felt that young Brian had been more than cooperative; had he known anything relevant, he would have told it. Unless he knew something to implicate Mrs. Morley - did he protest too much? - in which case no amount of questioning would get it out of him. The kid was certainly not dumb. Nor cowardly.

Having most of a day still ahead, and a strong reluctance to return to Division, he decided to check Amanda Morley's alibi. There was no telephone line, as yet, to the Sculpin Lake cottages; Jonas Thompson could be reached by letter to the village of Sculpin Falls, or in person. Actually, that was stretching the truth just a bit: on police business, Sims could have arranged for an OPP cruiser in Sculpin pick Thompson up and bring him to the nearest telephone... But it was a fine, sunny day in May, and anyone caught at 43 Division might be recruited for the Great Drug Bust.

"I wonder," he asked Mrs. Morley, "do you have anything pressing to do today?"

"I was to meet with our lawyer this afternoon... It's hardly pressing, though - it can wait. Why?"

"I thought I'd go up to Sculpin Lake - please don't be offended - to check on your movements of the past weekend. It would set my mind at rest. I wonder if you'd like to come along and show me the way."

She gazed at him in conjecture. "Would there be time for me to go out on the lake - on my own - for a while?"

"Well, I have to talk to Mr. - Thompson, is it? If you tell me where to find him, I'd be all right on my own, after that. I do feel badly about spoiling those photographs the other day. Is it too late for you to take more?"

"That is a fine idea," she said. "I'll get my gear."

"One more thing. I'd like to bring my dog."

"As long as he doesn't chase waterfowl."

"He doesn't even like water."

Half an hour later, they were en route.

"I've never seen a dog like that before," she remarked, with admirable composure. "What breed is he?"

"I usually tell people he's a Carpathian Wolfhound. Actually, there never has been a dog like this before. The vet guesses Great Dane, Doberman, Labrador and some wire-haired terrier..."

She tore her eyes away from the back-seat passenger - who evidently enjoyed being discussed - to stare at him, "...how?"

Sims burst out laughing. "Nobody knows."

Indeed, Lancelot was a strange-looking animal: immensely long and tall, with a square body, narrow head, small, close-set yellowish eyes, short pointed ears - half-erect, so that they stood away from his head and could rotate in any direction, like antennae. His fur was black and coarse, forming a bristly fringe around his upper lip. Sims had stopped, some time ago, thinking of him as ugly, but now, seeing him again through the eyes of a new acquaintance, he had to admit it.

"You would think," said Mrs. Morley, "that a dog so - how shall I put it, not to hurt his feelings? unprepossessing? - would be frightening. But he has such a sweet face, he couldn't scare a rabbit."

That does it, thought Sims, she's innocent. And I'll probably fall in love. Lance, too - for, though his vocabulary didn't extend to five-syllable words, he could certainly understand the sentiment: his tail was threatening to beat the back seat apart.

"Where in the world did you find him?"

While making good time northward, because it was a week-day and traffic was thin, and because beside him was not another cop, so that he could get away with a bit of conservative speeding, Sims recounted the saga of Lancelot.

"It's the only time in my life - I swear, the *only* time - I ever cheated at cards. I wasn't very good at it, and I'm pretty sure the other players noticed - helped, maybe: who in his right mind would want to win an ugly dog that eats its own weight in money every week? But I had to."

She didn't ask why; she said, "Yes, I see. Like that Hardy novel, Mayor of Casterbridge." As the reference was lost on Sims, she explained. "A man got drunk and auctioned off his wife. If someone is willing to gamble away his dog, the dog deserves a better master."

"I don't suppose that man's wife had much of a life with him, either. As to Lance, it's taken eight months to make him stop cowering. I had no idea how to go about it, at first. We had dogs at home, but none of them had reason to be afraid of us. It used to drive me crazy."

It occurred to him that Mrs. Morley was putting up with a great deal of his pet subject - not bad, as puns go, yet he refrained from using it - and he ought not to strain her good manners; he would drop the Lancelot topic and try to find something he could ask her about, that didn't sound like interrogation. Grebes, perhaps.

She didn't give him the opportunity. "Go on. How *do* you break a dog of cowering?"

She was genuinely interested. How about that! "Well, you obviously can't punish him - that's how the habit was established in the first place. And you can't reward him, because that would reinforce the behaviour you don't want. Actually, our veterinarian was a big help. She said the first owner must have confused him with contradictory commands and arbitrary punishment: he was constantly apologising, in effect, for being himself."

"What a rotten thing to do!" she burst out. "You know, people do that to children, sometimes. Not because they mean to - just because they're confused themselves, about what they expect. Was your friend like that?"

"He's not my friend; I only have to work with him. Yes, he's something like that. He seemed to want a tough, mean dog... and also a doormat."

"No wonder, then. This fellow couldn't be mean if his life depended on it... so he did his best as a doormat. Poor baby," she turned in her seat to pat the bristly muzzle, which rewarded her with copious lickings. "And so, how did you straighten him out?"

"The trick is to keep telling him that he's all right, while maintaining consistent rules and discipline. I'm afraid I haven't been very effective on the second part - that's still to come. What you do is, you give him orders he can easily understand and obey, and then praise him like mad. If he gets it wrong, you ignore it. If he grovels, you ignore him - just walk away."

"I see. You use every opportunity to praise, and try to avoid situations where you have to punish. That makes sense. And, of course, you give lots of affection for no reason at all. That wouldn't be too hard."

"It's not all that easy, either. He has some pretty bad habits. There have been times... The reason he's here today is that I try to get him out of the apartment as much as possible: we're in trouble with the landlady."

"You live in an apartment? With *him*?"

"Well, yes. In the basement of a house, though, not a high-rise. It was ideal for me, before. I should have cleared it with Mrs. Field, getting a dog... only, it was a spur-of-the-moment decision. Once I'd won him, I had to bring him home - cold, as it were. Imagine her shock. She was very good about it, though, till he started digging up her garden."

"Yes, I can see that might be a problem. Well, you'll simply have to break him of it."

Easier said than done, he thought; nevertheless, she was right.

In the two and a half hours drive to Sculpin Lake (He made a note of it: the trip could possibly be done, traffic permitting, in two hours; certainly no less.) they talked about many things. The subject of dog-training had quite naturally given way to the raising of children: she had; he had not. Which led to Sims' own history - or, rather, the history of his four-year relationship with Marie. No intimate details, of course; only why he had never married. Which took them to the Morleys' twenty-six year marriage. He had been careful, at first, not to ask probing questions, but found that he was interested, apart from the investigation. She spoke frankly about her husband, and kindly.

"Edward was a brilliant student... in many areas. He was not a narrow specialist, like most science majors: he also did well in the humanities. Nineteenth century French poetry was a particular hobby of his at one time. He was on the debating team, two years running. He studied music, too." She sighed. "He played the flute beautifully. I was so sad when he gave it up."

"Why did he?"

"Because he felt he wasn't good enough. He had reached a certain level and couldn't improve further, and so he said, that's finished. There was, for him, no point in pursuing something one cannot perfect. 'Know your limits,' he used to say... His worst fear, I suppose, was looking foolish. For Edward, nothing was worth doing just for the fun of it. Even at games, he was less interested in winning than in playing every hand as well as it could be played... though, Bridge isn't really a game, is it? They all seem to take it so deadly seriously. That's why I was hopeless - I couldn't think of it as anything more than a game. After trying to teach me, oh, ever so patiently, for a few years, Edward finally gave up. Charlie Quick was a far better partner for him."

"It doesn't sound," said Sims diffidently, "as if you had very much in common."

"No, we didn't. At first, there was romance; dreams, the adventure of youth... He was handsome and clever, a graduate student - and not so confident as he seemed. Perhaps he needed someone to admire him, and of course, I was flattered by his interest. I wasn't much of anything in those days; just another sophomore in general arts, with no particular talent or ambition. I went to university because my parents thought I should, and did my best, because I owed it to them. Edward had ambition enough for both of us. And we were happy, in those first years: everything was new and exciting. The differences in attitude, in character, only became a problem later on.

"By then, we had moved here and had two children, the house, a career which was increasingly important to Edward, as his horizons narrowed. He kept reaching his limit in old fields of interest, and not opening new ones. I often wonder if we didn't make a mistake, staying together... A stronger woman might have... I don't know... brought him out more. But, we were comfortable; we got along well... The thought of separating, taking a chance, starting over, was too threatening for both of us.

"Of course, until quite recently, we also had a child still at home. It looks as if we - I - have him back again. Do you know -" she suddenly turned to him, as if remembering that he was there, "what Brian wants to do?"

"He mentioned leaving school,"

"That, yes. I doesn't surprise me, given his record there. But he's thinking of becoming a minister."

"That doesn't sound bad to me," Sims remarked.

"Not bad, of course not. Only unexpected. We're nominally Anglican, but we haven't been church-goers since... since I left home, in fact. Edward was - well, naturally - a rationalist; he didn't quite approve of religion. And I don't know the first thing about studying to be a minister... I don't know how to help him."

Sims thought for a moment. "Maybe I can. I have a good friend who is a priest and used to advising kids. In fact, that's how I know him: he counsels some of the young offenders. Perhaps your son would like to consult him?"

There was a short silence. He glanced over to see if she was still with him. "You know," she finally said, "I've never had anything to do with the police before - well, aside from the odd traffic ticket, and they're always so polite, as if they were intruding, when actually, you're the one who's done something wrong. I didn't have many preconceived ideas - and yet, you keep surprising me. You're not typical, are you?"

Again, he had to laugh aloud. "I guess not. I'm not very effective, either."

There were houses scattered along the road; difficult to say how many, for all the lots were thickly-treed, predominantly with large conifers, but the village of Sculpin Falls appeared to consist of a corner gas-station. Attached to it were a diner, a small general store, a bait and tackle shop and the inevitable video-rental, all in one sprawling, casual structure.

"This is where we buy our groceries, if we haven't been wise enough to bring them. I only do in an emergency, because their selection is poor and their prices, high."

Less than a kilometre past the intersection, she directed him down a near-invisible dirt road that wound up and down among huge trees. Here and there, a cottage could be seen - empty at this time of year, with no smoke rising from any of the chimneys, but one.

"Here we are. Turn right. The next house is Jonas'."

The shaded drive led to the back of a small log house. The front faced the lake, which could be reached by a rough, precipitous stony path. The view was magnificent: placid, dark blue water opening out and out; a few small rocky or treed islands to break up the expanse, and in the distance, cool pine-covered hills.

"You see why I'm so fond of coming here."

"I see," he said. "Well, we both have work to do, and not much time... Would it be all right to meet back here at, say, three o'clock? Is that long enough?"

"It will have to be. Actually, I know exactly where to go this time, so it'll be quicker."

She unloaded her camera case and tripod from the trunk while Sims held tight to Lancelot's leash. They watched her make her confident way down to the shore and launch the canoe which was kept there.

"No, you idiot," Sims told the fretting dog, "she doesn't need rescuing. She doesn't need you at all. Or me, for that matter. Come on, we'll go for a run in the woods up there. I bet it's full of squirrels."

CHAPTER 10

Even after his need for relief and exercise were amply satisfied, Lance begged piteously not to be left in the car. "All right – but you *must* be civilized." Sims led him along on foot to Mr. Thompson's place.

He had done some research, if one could call it that: he'd stopped by the library and looked through Jonas Thompson's half dozen collections of nature photography. Good stuff, beautiful images, though he found one much the same as another. The important thing was not to be altogether ignorant. And it helped to recognise the man who answered his knock.

"Mr. Thompson? I'm Sergeant Sims of Toronto 43 Division." The man nodded minutely and remained silent. "I'm investigating the death of your neighbour, Edward Morley." Still no comment. "I wonder if I could talk to you?"

"Haven't got much to say," the other answered after due consideration. "Haven't seen him in three, four years."

He wasn't going to make it easy. "Well, all right. Have you seen Amanda Morley recently?"

"Sure."

"How recently, please?"

"Twenty minutes ago," said Thompson, "out on the lake."

Sims felt ridiculous, standing in the doorway, holding Lance with difficulty on a tight leash, lest he insist on trying to make friends with this unfriendly man. "Yes, I'm aware of that - I brought her. Look, Mr. Thompson, I don't know what you think. What I'm trying to do is solve a murder. I don't suspect Mrs. Morley, but neither can I definitely take her off the suspect list, until I account for her movements at the critical time. Can you help?"

"That's different," said Jonas Thompson. "That animal housebroken?" Sims assured him, yes. "Better bring him in, then. Scare off the grebe if you leave him loose. Scare off anything," he added after regarding Lance for another second or two. "Ugly beast."

The inside of the cabin was comfortable; raw timber and worn furniture covered with hooked rugs and crocheted blankets; coloured photographs of forest and lake decorated the walls - not one of which Sims recalled from the books. In the main, they were standard, pleasing depictions of nature; a few were arresting - seemed somehow more animate, if not as technically perfect as trademark Thompson photographs.

"I see you like the pictures. Students' work. This," he indicated a close-up of a mysterious fungoid entity, "was one of Amanda's early assignments. You can see the talent right off." He chuckled. "Anyway, I could. Some of the others are all right," he waved his arm along the wall, "but all the really good ones are hers."

For some reason unrelated to logic, Sims felt a little glow of pride. That had been his own opinion - who'd have thought he was right? Meanwhile, having worked his nose along the perimeter of the room, Lancelot came back and dropped at his feet with a huge sigh.

"Want a beer?" asked his host.

He gratefully accepted, reflecting on the sudden about-face. No question whose side Jonas Thompson was on. Was there more to the relationship than teacher-student friendship? They were not so far apart in age, and obviously had something important in common... and this Jonas Thompson was certainly attractive, of a type - lean, wiry body, wind-burned face, thick grey hair, eyes the colour of an overcast day - of a type, let's face it, that most women like. It couldn't hurt that he was successful, and supportive.

"Now," said his host, settling into the other couch and sipping beer from the bottle - he had brought a glass for Sims, who ignored it. "What d'you want to know?"

"Not much, really. I understand Mrs. Morley was here - I mean, at the lake - last weekend. I'd like to know if you saw her, spoke to her - and if so, when?"

"Well, sure I did. She got here about four, four-thirty on Friday. Had a couple hours of good light. Came over for dinner and stuck around to talk about the book... You know about the grebe book? Good. So, she went back to her place, maybe ten. Wanted an early start."

Sims nodded. "That accounts for Friday evening. And then?"

"Didn't see her most of Saturday – she was out in the reeds all day, hunting nests; I had a pile of scripts to review. Talked a few minutes, just down by the shore there, when she stowed the canoe. That'd be at sunset... eight o'clock or there'bouts. She went into her house. Said she got some good shots, that should be some kind of proof where she was all day. *Are* they good?"

Sims was forced to admit that the pictures were spoiled. Internally, he had also to admit that he could not be certain they ever existed. In the back of his mind, a little policeman began wondering whether there was a missed avenue of investigation. "They don't prove anything."

"Damn shame," said Jonas Thompson. "All the eggs'll be hatched by the end of the week. If she can't get good enough replacement today, there'll be an important chunk missing from the story."

"Is there any possibility," asked Sims, to satisfy the little nagging voice, "that she took similar pictures in the weeks before?"

"None. It's a short season. Besides, she wasn't up, the week before. Not much going on – hens just sitting."

Well, as far as Sims was concerned, that cleared her. The forensic lab ought to be able to make *something* out on overdeveloped film, and an unbiased expert could surely be found, to say when the birds did whatever they were doing on the film. Unless she'd thrown it out.

"And then?"

"Then what? Oh, Sunday. She was on the lake again, all morning, half the afternoon. And then it started raining. Hard. She got back, soaked to the skin. Storm getting worse, I persuaded her not to drive home. She made a batch of stir-fry and we spent Sunday evening, discussing layout and griping about deadlines. Okay?"

"Great. I think the lady has a solid alibi."

Jonas Thompson leaned back. "You neglected to say what the crucial time was."

"I know the time," Sims nodded. "I don't know the nature of your relationship."

The older man laughed. "Friends. That's all. I'd lie for her, if I knew the right lie, and if I thought she needed it. She might even do the same for me. But I don't think she needs it. Amanda wouldn't so much as inconvenience her husband, or hurt his pride - never mind kill him."

"That's what I thought. Anyway, in case it is needed, you're only half the alibi, I'm hoping those famous grebes will supply the clincher."

"Appropriate," said Thompson.

There was plenty of time to be thorough, even after rewarding Lance with another romp among the flowering wild strawberries and get lost a couple of times. The drive back to Sculpin Falls was easy. Under cover of buying lunch - two hamburgers so greasy and wilted, only Lance could possibly enjoy them, and thick, bitter coffee, which he sipped for appearances - he asked the young girl behind the counter about local folk. She knew Jonas Thompson all right, and was not surprised at interest in the resident celebrity. She knew who Mrs. Morley was, too, but she had not been in lately. Getting an overpriced fill-up, which he would charge to the department, Sims went through a similar routine with the teenaged boy at the gas pump. And, again, in the store section, with a wispy, colourless woman who bore a strong resemblance to both young people. This was a family operation. None of them had seen Mrs. Morley for three or four weeks.

None of this was of any use at all, but left him in possession of milk, sliced bread and peanut butter he didn't particularly want. By three o'clock, he was back at the cottage. At three-fifteen, Amanda Morley hove into view, paddling swiftly. He helped pull the canoe well up on the shore and flip it over.

"Any luck?" he asked.

"Oh, yes, four good rolls, at least. And you?"

He explained his conjecture about the ruined film. "You haven't thrown it away?"

She thought. "No, I can't have. I haven't been in the darkroom, since... Monday morning."

That was all right. Not exactly air-tight... on the other hand, a murderer would have tried harder to be seen a long way from the crime; would have stopped to chat at the gas-station or somewhere.

"I wish," she said, "I could stay ... get some dusk and dawn shots. Grebe aren't very active at mid-day. They just sleep." She shook her head. "I'm being unreasonable again. Never mind. I'll come back another day."

"I have some provisions," he said. "If you could put me and Lance up for the night, we might return to the city early

82

tomorrow. Would that help?"

"If you did that for me, I'd let you have the bedroom. And cook dinner. I'll even sew on that missing button you're trying to hide under your tie."

Sims had to make yet another trip to Sculpin Falls to use the pay-phone, which fortunately had a private booth. It was time for some creative fiction.

"It's nothing too serious," he told the constable on desk duty, "just a brake lining. They can't fix it today, but they'll get on it first thing in the morning. I should be back by noon or soon after. Don't bother Inspector MacDonald with it, unless he's looking for me."

Well, so what? At the moment, there was nothing very urgent in town that he could go ahead with. This seemed the more important place to be. More pleasant, too. Having locked Lancelot in the cottage, Sims took the bow position in the canoe and discovered that, after twenty years behind the wheel of a car, paddling is hard work. Yet Mrs. Morley thought nothing of doing it alone; a strong lady, this. And he finally saw the famous grebe in all their breeding plumage. He was fascinated by the nests floating among the reeds, and by the birds' unlikely wailing call to one another. He had to keep these impressions to himself, though, until the sun set, and they headed ashore.

There were three at dinner, for Jonas Thompson invited himself and supplied the fish, caught that morning. The mood was not in the least funereal. That would come on Friday; he suspected that the widow was deliberately shutting the reality away, for this little while. She was different here, in this setting; almost another, much younger woman. They did not speak of Edward Morley, by mutual consent.

He took Lance for still another run - this day ought to hold him for quite a while... unless it had the opposite effect, and made him more than ever restless. Sims was so tired and so much at peace, that by ten-thirty when Thompson went home, he, too, was ready to fall into bed. He slept more soundly than he had in months, and was troubled by no dreams at all.

On Thursday, he was not so lucky. Having dropped his passengers at their respective homes, and changed into fresh clothes, Sims went to the station to update his report. His visit there was calculated to coincide with lunch-hour, so as to be seen by the fewest possible colleagues. Unfortunately, and not by accident, the inspector was one of these.

"Well, well. Sims. Wasn't sure you're still on the payroll. So, tell me what you've got."

In the telling, it was less than he'd fondly imagined.

"All you've said is, the wife probably didn't poison him - but you can't be sure; she didn't need to be there. Fine. You still haven't convinced me the guy didn't poison himself - and if he did, it's none of our business. If you haven't got anything better by this time tomorrow, the case is going on hold till after the inquest."

Sims had been expecting something like this. But worse was to come.

"By the way, starting Monday, you've got a partner again. Great news, huh?" Inspector MacDonald glared out of slitted eyes. "Say it's great news."

"It's great news," he obediently repeated. "May I ask who?"

"Petersen."

"Petersen?"

"Yup. Boy's been re-in-stated. Wonderful, ain' it?"

"But..?"

"The department does not see fit to pursue the matter at this time," his boss recited. "Too goddamn embarrassing, and they figure nobody knows; nobody needs to know. Cover-up. So, what else is new?"

"But... Petersen?"

"Come on, now. Aside from a bit of drunk driving, he's a pretty good cop. It couldof been worse. Guess who put in a formal request to be teamed up with you?"

Sims groaned. "Gloria Venables."

"Right. Anyhoo, you had it all your own way for weeks - time you got back in routine. Hey, look on the bright side. If this little case of yours don't turn into a full-scale murder investigation, you get to be in on the biggest drug bust of the decade. It's 95 percent sure, for next week."

"I don't know how to thank you, sir." Sims replied flatly. Inspector MacDonald walked away, chuckling. "What have I ever done to him?"

"I heard that, boy."

If he had only today to turn the case into a full-scale murder investigation, he'd better get something, *fast.* Where? First, call the forensic lab. The chief technician also served as spokesman, lest the able-bodied help be kept so busy on the phone with policemen that they'd never get any work done.

"You probably heard already," he told Sims. "Your vic died of cyanide poisoning. No trace in the stomach contents, so we figure, most likely inhalation. We also checked out that grunge your ident guys saw fit to bring in toto - my God, there was a lot of it! - and there wasn't anything in there - not for sure. Wouldn't be, if it was boiled off. What we did find, because Dr. Cates told us to look for it, is little bitty fragments - too small to do anything with, so don't get excited – flakes of glass, not from the flask, which is intact.

"Want hairs and fibres? Well, there aren't many. His own, as far we can tell. Oh yeah, some woollen fuzz on the inside and outside of the lab-coat, matches his jacket - or any good quality brown wool garment. What else? Oil smear on right upper arm, consistent with sample from door... Say, this sounds like you guys are trying to make something of nothing... well, no skin off my arse. Plastic stuff on back of pants and coat matches substance in flask. Stain on pant-cuffs and socks - tapwater, household detergent. Soil on shoes: soil. Plain old garden dirt. No further analysis requisitioned.

"You really want me to read the whole damn report over the phone? Oh, all right. Scuffs on floor: rubber, consistent with shoe-soles worn by deceased. Here's something! Stain in fume-room sink: tapwater. Can you beat that? Okay, okay. Fingerprints. There's, like, about four in the whole damn place, but you knew that. Clear ones on door and bench are the victim's and a couple belonging to somebody identified as Jones. A couple more, overlapping previously described, one Charles Quick. Cute name. A few - door, bench, gas-tap, match with Dumont - a female. And that's it. Man, this is the feeblest collection of physical evidence I've seen all week!"

"And the car?"

"Oh, the car - a real goldmine! It's been released, by

the way, if the owner wants to pick it up. The car is clean. I mean, *squeaky*. Probably washed just before. Waxed, polished, inside and out. Except it's been rained-on. Doesn't it always rain after you wash your car? It's a law of nature, which even death breaks not. Yeah, okay, don't get your knickers in a twist. Fingerprints of deceased on driver's door handle, seat, steering wheel, gear shift, signal lever. Nothing else, no place. If we can be of any further assistance… ? Well, bring it in. Of course we can tell what was on overdeveloped film; we are highly trained specialists."

In spite of the sarcasm, Sims thanked him nicely. He even managed a little banter - it's important to stay in the forensic lab's good books.

In order to disturb everyone's work again, he'd need an excuse - or, anyway, more than he'd had on the last occasion. What had he learned since? The time and means of death. He knew something they didn't know he knew. How best to go about it? The most politic approach would be through Charles Quick. Remember, he cautioned himself, the less you give away, the better. Act on your convictions. As if this were the full-scale murder investigation you want it to be.

"I wonder," he asked Mr. Quick, "if you have a calendar or day-book or something, like Dr. Morley's."

"Oh, you mean the ubiquitous little black book? Oh, no," he said, "I never actually felt the need. You see, Edward was a perfectionist in all things; he simply could not rely upon memory alone. Not that there was anything wrong with his memory, mind you - only that he could not bear to be caught out in an oversight or error."

"Well, then, perhaps you can recall one or two events of the last months." Sims consulted the copy he had made of Dr. Morley's book. "For example, there was a problem with one of the fume hoods?"

"Oh, yes, I do recall that," Mr. Quick said. "They had to come and fix it twice - the first time didn't take. Edward made a point of rejecting that bill."

"Can you tell me when the second call was?"

"Oh, sometime in March, I suppose. Why?"

"Would there be an order form or something, with the

date on it?"

"I don't see that it matters, since it was certainly working before the accident... but, if you'll tell me why you need it, I'll ask Miss Hillyard to find the document."

"Well," Sims explained, "I find it odd that Dr. Morley should note the first, unsuccessful service, and not the second, satisfactory one."

Mr. Quick's usually vague expression focussed. "You think Edward was forgetting things? There may have been something wrong with him? "

"That's one possibility," Sims allowed.

"I should have noticed, if that were the case... Well, I'll just see to the invoice." He lifted the intercom, stopped half-way. "Is there anything else, while she's about it?"

"Perhaps. I'd like to know whether you and Mr. Meyer had a meeting with Dr. Morley on April 11."

"I know there was one about then... there is, every month, though we keep the dates flexible - in deference to Mr. Meyer, you see; he has other commitments. Well, that's one thing that *would* be on my calendar." He punched the button and proceeded to instruct his secretary, carefully repeating everything in slightly different words, Sims noted. An idiosyncrasy of the old man, or an estimate of Miss Hillyard's comperhension?

Whichever, the girl appeared remarkably fast with the information. The service invoices - $478 for less than two hours! - were dated March 11 (this one had a note in red pen across its top: HOLD) and April 4, stamped 'paid'.

Mr. Quick's appointment calendar confirmed the date of their meeting. "What was discussed? In general terms."

"Well now, let me see... The Walters project was coming along; we must have talked about that... production time and so forth... estimates of cost, precautions to take. Of course, the final meeting was only just last Thursday... it seems so very long ago... strange."

"Can you think of anything else Dr. Morley might have brought up at that meeting?"

The old man stared into space, as if hoping to read the minutes there. "Other projects, I think... trying to decide what next to work on."

"Staff problems?"

"No... nothing like that. But, wait, there was a product

young Frayne was terribly keen on, and Edward opposed...
I believe it was decided to leave it out of our immediate line
of endeavour."

"Was this a unanimous decision? No argument?"

Mr. Quick gave a breathy little laugh. "Argument? That's
unthinkable. Gentle persuasion, at most. No, you see,
Edward was our - what do the young people call it? Our
guru. Neither Mr. Meyer nor myself know the first thing
about chemistry... Mr. Acton now, he was a true
Renaissance man, he knew a little about everything... In
the old days, he could give even Edward a smart riposte
once in a while. But not we, I'm afraid. No, no. If Edward
said a thing was worth doing, we would consider doing it -
financial prospects being favourable, naturally. If he said
no, the thing is too costly to perfect, unstable, unsafe or
unmarketable - why then, we wouldn't touch it with the
proverbial barge-pole."

Sims knew that he had let himself in for this. And then
again, what had he to lose? Suppose, in his meandering
fashion, the old man should reveal something of import.

"The substance under consideration, was it likely to be
unmarketable?'

"SuperFoam," Quick produced the laugh again. "Sounds
pretentious, doesn't it? Oh no, potentially, it might be quite
marketable indeed. Very, oh yes. The trouble is that it has
a long way to go... Edward believed, a long and most
expensive way. And then there was no guarantee that it
actually would work, you see; that it would not break down
under extreme conditions..."

"Excuse me, but what exactly is Superfoam?"

"Oh, it's supposed to be a very light, very effective
insulator, for use in aircraft... even," he leaned
confidentially across the desk, put his palm alongside his
mouth, and stage-whispered, "even, possibly, spacecraft."
He settled back again, with a self-satisfied air.

"Do you realize what that would mean? Government
contract! Or, rather, sub-contract to a much bigger
corporation. Large quantities of money..." His face
relapsed into gloomy folds and creases. "And with that,
probably, a great deal more interference than one would
care to accommodate. However, if it were only to be used
on ordinary aeroplanes, the company could still realize

considerable profit... The trouble, of course, is that if the material were really not all that it should be, the company could as easily sustain considerable damage, financial and - and, well, there is one's reputation to consider. Were it not totally stable; were it, for example, to be involved in some accident and burn, or otherwise break down, the components thus released could pose an ecological hazard. Not to mention what it might do to any surviving passengers. Oh, yes, so Edward assured us.

"Therefore, you see, it is a proposition fraught with peril." He sighed. "That's how it is: to reap great benefit, one must take risks. I myself am too old, too set in my ways, for such adventuring. So is Mr. Meyer. And so, in fact, was Edward Morley - though it was not always true - of any of us. I don't really expect young Frayne to understand... But then, he too, must weather his share of frustration, in order to earn his future success. Is it not so of everyone?"

Sims allowed that, in his limited experience, it was.

"But I have been monopolising you," Mr. Quick said. "Is there anything else I can do? Anyone else you wish to question?"

Gratefully, he asked for the man who cleans the laboratory.

"Oh, I'm afraid he doesn't work the day shift. He is a student, you see. Except for the supervisor, the entire cleaning crew are students. That was one of Mr. Acton's policies, to give as much employment as possible to young people... Over the years we have been able to recruit some quite talented graduates. You can get the measure of a man in his performance of a menial task; if he is conscientious there, he will be responsible in any position. You see, it's an arrangement beneficial to both parties. Isn't that clever?"

Sims agreed, but really wanted to avoid further discussion of the redoubtable Mr. Acton. He said he would wait for the janitor.

"The cleaning crew arrives at half past five. Unless, of course, you would like Miss Hillyard to give you their home addresses?"

"That won't be necessary. Five-thirty will be fine, thank you." It was now past three. "In the meantime, perhaps I can interview the laboratory staff again."

"Certainly. Shall I come along?"

"No!" Sims replied too vehemently; tried to soften the discourtesy. "No need, I assure you, Mr. Quick. I've already taken up far too much of your time. You have been very helpful."

A little too helpful, perhaps? Too eager to please?

CHAPTER 11

He wandered down the long corridor toward the lab; finding the door of the wash-up room open, he stopped to greet Mrs. Benz and her assistant. The former offered him coffee, which he accepted; the latter went off about her business, though not without one or two backward glances.

"Is there any news, Sergeant?" his hostess shouted over the glass-washing machine. "Have you found out who killed Dr. Morley?"

He shook his head. Indicating the machine in the background, he asked: "Does this mean the lab is back in operation?" It abruptly stopped in the middle of the sentence, so that he was yelling into silence.

"Oh yes," she said, in a normal voice. "They are making many things. They are using glassware and glassware... very busy, all different."

He lit a cigarette, leaned back in the old chair. "Do you remember last time, when I asked for some gossip concerning Dr. Morley?"

Mrs. Benz clasped her plump hands under her chin and nodded tightly, warily.

"Well, I'd like to ask again, in a more specific way. I heard a rumour that you and he were friendly. Perhaps more than friendly..." He broke off, his words drowned by her laughter.

"Do you ask me if I had a... a love-affaire? With Dr. Morley?" she managed to ask between gusts of irrepressible hilarity.

"I'll take that as a no, shall I?" He affected dignity: though inclined to join in the laughter, it would have been insulting to do so.

"Please do. It is no. It is also very foolish." She had regained control by now, but her pink, round face still shone with amusement. "Who says such a thing?"

"I wouldn't like to name the source... it might embarrass them. Anyway," he continued, "they didn't say it was so, only that the possibility was rumoured at one time. There were other candidates mentioned," he lied. He was now serious again, and coherent. "You see, if the man did have some extra-marital involvement, it would be useful for me to know."

"Ah," she nodded wisely. "You are looking for a crime of passion. It is difficult to imagine... But, there, people are surprising sometimes. Do you wish me to say I heard such rumours?"

"Only if you have."

"Yes."

"And do you believe there was something in them?"

She hesitated, reflecting on the propriety of exploring this line of country, then sat down opposite him, glancing around. "All right. Because the poor man is killed, this becomes important, yes?" It was Sims' turn to nod soberly. "Then I will tell. Yes, I believe there has been... involvement, as you say. But it is a long time ago. I do not believe it was so very improper. Also, there can be no bad feelings, after such a time. Two years, perhaps even more, that it is finished."

"Someone in the company?"

She nodded minutely. "There was no - how should I say? - upset, no drama. It is a very little thing; I do not believe you will find a cause for murder there."

"May I know the woman's name?"

"Not from my mouth," said Mrs. Benz, so firmly and finally, that he knew it was true. "I do not think you will find an answer there, and so I shall not call names."

With that he had to be content.

"Sergeant," she added, "Valentine has been with us only a short time. She knows nothing of this." It was a warning, to keep his information from the young, possibly indiscreet, and he would heed it.

There was, indeed, much activity in the laboratory. All the staff were present, and each seemed to be carrying out a different experiment. He noted the bleak emptiness of Dr. Morley's station, and the placement of Ferdy Arnott between Eve Dumont and David Frayne. The fourth place also had equipment laid out, but he could not see Martin Jones; assumed he must be close by, perhaps at his desk. Some amusing by-play passed between the young man and the woman in the far corner; she smiled fondly at him and he was practically wagging his tail. Sims knocked on

92

the open door as he entered.

"Is it all right to come in?" he asked the room at large.

Everyone froze. This should have been gratifying, but somehow wasn't. Anyway, it didn't last.

"Hey," Ferdy Arnott exclaimed, "it's our friendly neighbourhood gumshoe! If you want us to practice opening windows, you're out of luck - they're sealed. We'd be more than happy to show you cupboard doors..,"

He was definitely getting tired of this boy, but put on a good-sport face. "Maybe another time," he told Ferdy. "Today, I'm interested in gas-taps."

"Oh, wow! Advanced stuff!"

During this lame-brained exchange, the others had drawn near; now Jones remembered his role. "Gas-taps, you say, Sergeant? Please clarify."

Sims approached an outlet on the only unoccupied bench - he didn't know if this was conducive to his purpose or contrary; the choice of the victim's station was made for him.

"Here," he said, "is a tap turned off. I would like each of you to demonstrate turning it on and off again."

They looked at him suspiciously, but complied: lined up like schoolchildren at the water fountain, in order of seniority. As Jones went through the motions, on and immediately off again, the little metal handle disappeared in his palm. Then Eve Dumont reached out with three fingers and thumb, rotating the tap delicately, right and left again. As she did so, a puzzled expression crossed her lovely face - but it was gone by the time she stepped away from the bench. Frayne came next, twisting forcefully, angrily, with full palm, and Arnott made what was almost certainly a deliberate imitation of his defiant gesture.

Frayne, who had not before spoken to him voluntarily, asked: "And what's all this supposed to prove?"

"I'm not at all sure it proves anything," Sims told him. "Just something I was curious about."

"Oh, feel free to come here any time and disrupt our work, to satisfy your curiosity."

Sims ignored the sarcasm. But they were all looking expectant, as if he owed them more than this little bit of stage business. "I do have some questions... but you all seem busy."

"There isn't as much going on as you might think," said Jones. "I can leave the accounts without suffering much pain. And I'm sure the others can leave what they're doing, given a few minutes..." He glanced around at the company and received reluctant nods, except from Arnott, who couldn't let it pass without a wise-crack.

"Do you want to stick around and watch us turn all the equipment off?"

Once Jones swung the door shut, the hallway was reasonably private. They perched on the wide windowsill.

"What do you want to know?"

Just as directly, Sims told him. "I'd like to know where each of you was on the weekend. For the record."

"Oh. I see. Okay." Jones adjusted his glasses, straightened his tie, laid both palms flat on his knees. Composed, he began to recite. "On Friday afternoon, I went straight home. No, I stopped off to buy some wine. I got home about 5:30. I gave the children an early dinner and kept them busy while my wife prepared for company. Our guests arrived sometime after six. The Dumonts were first, another couple named Ferris - Jill and Dan - showed up a few minutes later. They left after eleven - I don't know the exact time. We cleaned up, checked on the kids, and went to bed. That was at 12:24 a.m. - I set the alarm."

"That's really excellent, Dr. Jones. You're the kind of witness policemen dream of. Go on."

For a second, Jones seemed uncertain of the compliment, then decided to accept it at face value. He smiled faintly, inclined his head fractionally, and continued. "On Saturday morning, I woke at 7:00, but felt tired, so I stayed in bed an extra half hour. Then we had breakfast - the children were already up. Then my wife took them to their classes - Justin has karate and Courtney takes dance lessons. Meanwhile, I mowed the lawn and trimmed the hedge."

"You were alone during this time?" Sims interrupted.

"If you can be alone when everyone on the street is doing the same thing."

"So, people saw you, mowing your lawn,"

Jones looked startled. "Of course, people saw me. It's not something you can do in secret. Besides, I didn't kill anybody."

94

"I'm not suggesting you did, Dr. Jones. I'm only trying to get a complete account."

The witness sighed, performed his concentration ritual of subdued gestures: glasses, tie, hands. "At about noon, my wife and daughter returned. Then I went to collect my son. In the afternoon, we all went shopping for grosheries," Sims winced, but decided to forgive him, pending more serious faults, "came home and had a cookout. Hamburgers, if you want to know, barbecued outside. In the evening, we played Monopoly, let the children watch one hour of TV and sent them to bed. We stayed up no later than ten. On Sunday, we slept in, lazed around the house, did some chores. It rained all afternoon; couldn't do outside work, or go to the park or biking. I helped my wife fix dinner. We watched Disney with the children. I was with my family the whole weekend. And that's all there is." He heaved a regular sigh, not his usual miniature.

"Thank you very much," the detective said. "You have been precise and concise - I appreciate that. On the off-chance that some corroboration should prove necessary, may I assume you have no objection?"

"You mean, ask my wife when I loaded the dishwasher?"

"That sort of thing, yes."

"Why should I care? Besides, she won't have noticed."

"Well, thanks, anyway."

"Sure." Jones stood, pressed his palms to the small of his back and began to stretch, but stopped himself. He dropped the offending hands by either side and held them a little away from his body - disowned. "Listen," he turned, "you just fishing here, or are you on to something?"

"Just fishing," the detective said. "Or, rather, filling in all the blanks I can. I'll wait," he added. "Whenever someone has a few minutes, ask them to come out, would you?"

Before anyone else emerged, Miss Valentine happened by, with a push-cart full of shining clean flasks and beakers. She stopped to say hello - and, as it turned out, a little more.

"Do you want to know something about the dead person, Sergeant? I think he drank. Yes," she nodded her glorious halo of tight curls. "Everybody knows about it, but nobody wants to say. Maybe it's important. Maybe that's why he had the accident."

"I have heard something of the kind," he told her gravely. "Thank you for confirming that. I take it this isn't just rumour?"

"Oh, no! I wouldn't say, if that's all it was. I've seen him myself, at the Christmas party."

"Drunk, was he?"

"Oh, man! He didn't act like himself at all - he'd get all excited - even..." she hesitated, ducked her head in a coy little gesture, and, Sims could have sworn, in spite of her dark complexion, blushed, "...fresh. Made a pass at me. Well, kind of... Not really a pass, like the boys do. Nothing rough – only talkin at you, like."

"Just that one time, or were there other occasions?"

"Me? Just the one time. But," her eyes grew round and earnest, "I did hear about other times, other women. I don't know," she added. "I think that was just talk, about him having a... an affair with somebody... On'y time he ever went near us was when he was pi... intoxicated. I know it inn nice to say, but he *was*, every party, far as I know."

Did he imagine it, or was Miss Valentine's college-girl English slipping into a Caribbean cadence? If that were to happen, he'd have to be very careful: he found it the most contagious of all speech patterns. "Who, in particular?"

"Oh," she shrugged, "it don matter... just any girl that happen to be round. There's some would come round on purpose, you know, to tease him. For the devil of it. See, reason I wanted to tell you bout that - I guess that old rumour got started from nothing - cause nothin ever come of it. He din' go touchin, or grabbin - just lecture at you to save the worl'. See, I din like the man all that much, but I don want to hear bad talk bout nobody that can't defend his self, bein dead."

He would have asked more, probably, had not Eve Dumont stepped out of the lab at that moment. Miss Valentine, flustered as if she had been caught at something illicit, rejoined her cart and ducked in through the door.

"Mrs. Dumont, I 'preciate you makin time for me." Sims looked around for a chair to offer, which he knew wasn't there, hoping the moment's delay would cover his lapse in elocution.

96

She gave him a quick, bright smile. "I understand why you're here," she said. "I *did* turn off the gas-tap at Dr. Morley's bench. When I told you I hadn't touched anything, it wasn't a lie... I truly didn't remember doing it, until just then, when I stood in the same spot."

Sims, who had been about to ask something of the sort, and casting about in his mind for a way to ask it, tried to look intelligent and purposeful. "I assumed as much, since your fingerprints were found on that tap. Do you now recall exactly when you turned it off?"

"Why, right after I had found him. I went around the bench, to... well, to put something between me and... him. It seems - I don't know, exactly - rude? unfeeling?... to run away..."

"There is nothing wrong with being afraid of death," Sims assured her. "It's all right to run away. So, you withdrew to another section, and?"

"And I must have noticed the gas being on, with no flame. I don't recall noticing it, but this becomes a sort of reflex, when you work with Bunsen burners. That's the only excuse I have."

"But you didn't notice any smell? "

"No. There was no gas. The safety system must have shut it off at the main."

"You have known this to happen before?"

"Oh, many times," she smiled again - with an effect, at such close range, not unlike a flash-bulb going off in one's face. "It could be annoying. The sensor doesn't know the difference between dangerous fumes and the normal by-products of making plastics; if there is a high enough concentration of anything unnatural in the air, it seals the room, turns off the gas, and starts the fans. Then everything stops dead, till it's reset."

"Who could reset it?"

"Anybody... at least, any of us, or Mrs. Benz, or Mr. Burgess, the maintenance supervisor."

"Obviously, on this occasion, it hadn't been done,"

"Obviously. There was no-one to do it - or care." She tried to hide her face, but made a tactical error in averting her face toward the window, where sunshine caught and back-lit the single tear on her cheek. She finished very softly: "He was all alone, even then."

Sims tried, with an inconspicuous cough, to shake loose whatever had got hold of his throat. "Could I bring you a cup of coffee? Or something?"

Eve Dumont turned to face him. She succeeded in arranging her features in severe angular lines, not in making them any less attractive. "I think you wanted to ask something else?"

"Yes." He wanted to ask a lot of things, most of them improper in the circumstances, all of them irrelevant to the investigation. He finally managed, "Yes, of course. I meant to ask how you spent the weekend." Without, he'd have liked to add, too many references to the admirable doctor.

"Oh. Certainly. On Friday evening, my husband and I had dinner with Martin and Beverly Jones. The Ferrises were there, too - old friends of Martin's. On Saturday morning, Yves had an emergency call, so I went back to bed, had a late breakfast, and then I did some chores. In the afternoon, we looked at houses. They're terribly expensive - we may have to consider going to the suburbs. On Sunday, we stayed at home."

Short, sweet and imprecise. He had expected better. He had hoped for an estrangement, a fight... At the very least, the man might have stayed home - but, no, he has to go off on some emergency that's easy to confirm, just when he should be keeping an eye on his wife. Why are you so annoyed? he asked himself. She's not a suspect - what does she want an alibi for? Because, a little, ugly voice whispered, I think she's the mystery woman. Why do you think that? Because nobody else has shed a tear for Edward Morley - except his wife, if she was crying for him and not for her pictures. And because... because you're jealous, the little voice persisted. No, just a little envious. What he said was: "I don't suppose you could fill in some times? Like, what time you got home on Friday night?"

"Oh, certainly," she said - composed, now that she'd got him flustered. "Close to midnight. And Yves left at about eight on Saturday morning, without any breakfast. He phoned at 11:20 to say he'd have a bite in the cafeteria while waiting for me to pick him up. We drove straight to the realtor's office; she took us to three homes. We returned close to supper time... I think 5:30, 5:45. I still have the realtor's card in my handbag, if you want it."

"That won't be necessary," he said, more curtly than he need have. "Thank you."

She stood up, evidently puzzled by his change of manner. "If there's nothing else?"

"Thank you." Sims repeated lamely. And forgive me, he added silently, for what I've been thinking, as well as my bad manners.

She gave him a brief, formal handshake before disappearing into the lab. Well, if Edward Morley had to run around... Run? He couldn't picture it. If he had to have an illicit relationship with anyone... But what could she have seen in him? It's a puzzlement, said the little voice, not nearly as ugly as before.

He had not long to worry it, for David Frayne joined him. They were doing this, too, formally, by seniority.

"All right. You want to know where I was and what I did all weekend." Frayne checked the windowsill for dirt, lowered himself upon it gingerly, carefully pulling up the creases of immaculate navy trousers. The shirt under his labcoat was white; the tie, patterned in navy and dark red sprigs... when he went home today, it would almost certainly be in a maroon blazer.

"Yes." Two can be blunt.

Frayne interlaced long, well-kept fingers, fixed an unwavering, faintly supercilious gaze on Sims' face. "On Friday after work, I went home, ate some microwaved food and called my fiance. That would be around seven to 7:30. I did a little theoretical work on my invention - we've mentioned it before. Then I watched the news and went to bed. At half past eleven. On Saturday morning, I rose at eight and worked out till 10:45." To Sims' raised eyebrow, he added: "There is a gym in my building. I find Saturday morning a convenient time to use it, as most people sleep late and I have the equipment to myself. As it happens, the place was deserted last weekend. I didn't see anyone but the towel-boy." He paused to check if Sims was taking this down. He was. "Then I showered, changed, and went to my fiancé's apartment, as we'd arranged to go shopping for bedroom furniture.

"We visited no less than half a dozen stores, downtown, without finding anything we agreed on. I then took her home, stayed to watch the early news. We were to have dinner, but I didn't feel well - some kind of virus. I went home and straight to bed. This would be around seven. On Sunday, I was properly sick, all day. My fiance came over, but I needed rest, rather than nursing, so I persuaded her to go out with a friend. And that is all: I spent Sunday alone, in bed, miserably. Anything else?"

"Just one thing: the name and address of your fiance."

"Roberta Farrell, 134 Copernicus Crescent. All right?"

"All right," said Sims. "Fine. Thank you."

He had no intention of saying an unnecessary word to this man. Why? Because he was too cool, too smooth, too good-looking - and anyone with that many o's shouldn't be trusted. Not a rational reason. But then, it's all right to be irrational in one's likes and dislikes, as long as one remains fair and truthful. Nevertheless, he would speak to the girlfriend, and the towel-boy.

Next and last, came Ferdy Arnott, to join him companionably on the windowsill. "Listen," he began, "I'm sorry about razzing you, back there. I didn't mean any harm, okay?"

Sims nodded curtly, not yet ready to forgive. "All I want," he said, "is as complete as possible an account of where you spent the weekend."

"Yeah, I heard. Collecting alibis. That's okay, because I've got one. I mean, I've got *some.* What time?"

"I'd like the whole weekend," said Sims.

"Oh? You still don't know? Or you just won't tell me? Okay." He took a deep breath, hitched up his pant-legs, intertwined his fingers in front of his stomach and stared into space. "Friday. Date with a girl, right from work; 4:30. Maybe you noticed her around – Ruby Valentine? Now there's a name to conjure with, eh?" He gave Sims a sidewise wink before resuming his studied witness stance. "We had some pizza and went to a movie. 'Kerblooey!' Have you seen it? It's a riot. See, there's this absent-minded professor and..."

He paused to measure the degree of calcification on Sims' face. "Okay, so you don't want to hear it. I took her home before midnight - had to; her parents are *strict*! Then I went home. I live with my parents, too, but they're pretty cool. Maybe they heard me come in, maybe not. So, anyway, Saturday, I was up at the crack of noon, because my mom woke me. Oh, nothing obvious, like banging on the door and yelling 'Get your ass out of bed!' What she does is, she vacuums. Right in front of your room. For, like, an hour. Mean, huh?"

Still getting no sympathetic response, he continued. "Ate food. Cleaned yard. Went with parents to sister's house. Had boring time, good meatloaf. Home by ten. Watched 'Dallas' with the folks. Bed. Sunday. Up at I don't know - 11? Supposed to go to Center Island with friend and friend's friend, but friend gets flu. I guess you know I mean Dave. So, anyway, he asked me to take Bobbie anyway - get her off his case; she's being Florence Nightingale all over the place and wearing him out. So I did.

"I mean, would have, except it started raining, so only got as far as Ontario Place. Stood in line for sick-making movie, got wet, played arcade games. Had fun. With poor old Dave alone in his bed of pain. Are we monsters? No. He's better off, sleeping. Proof: Monday, he's back to work, bright-eyed and bushy-tailed. I told her it'd be okay, and it was. There." He folded his arms and gave a triumphant little nod.

"Fine," said the detective.

"Fine? Is that it? I twist my poor brain into a pretzel to deliver an exhaustive, comprehensive, positively picture perfect report of every single minute of an entire weekend for you, and all you can say is 'fine'? Well, *fine*, then."

Having hit his stride half-way through, and delivered this last bit in a creditable Aunt Polly voice, sniffed loudly, which made him cough, which turned into a laugh.

Sims, contrary to the resolution he had made only ten minutes before, joined him. "I'm sure you do great bird imitations, as well. But please don't."

Ferdy rolled his eyes and held shaking hands out before him. "Sorry... sorry... I don't know what comes over me sometimes..." He caught the drop-dead look; said in a normal voice: "Sorry."

Sims acknowledged that "Thanks for the statement. It's certainly comprehensive; I hope it's factual."

Ferdy nodded energetically. "I might make fun of the fuzz, but I was brought up never to lie to them. Now, if we're through, it's just about quitting-time, so..." He made a deep stage bow and backed away toward the lab door. Less than half-way, however, he bumped, hard, into Martin Jones coming out. Serves him right, Sims thought.

Politely, he said good-night to each departing chemist. He stopped Mrs. Benz and asked her to stay till the maintenance man should arrive, to make the introductions, but Miss Valentine, also among those present, protested.

"Mrs. Benz has to go home, to look after Mr. Benz, don't you, Honey? But I'm not rushin off anyplace."

CHAPTER 12

Thus it happened that Sims met Victor Sturac. Miss
Valentine took some persuading to leave - moreover,
young Sturac, with his warm glances and friendly banter,
was no help in persuading her. Twenty-one or -two years
of age, that was all he had in common with Ferdy Arnott:
none of the other boy's pretty self-consciousness. He
carried his large, rough-hewn frame with the confidence of
a young man secure in his identity. He was intelligent and
likable; to Sims' mind, a far better match for this
extraordinarily attractive, vital girl. However, all Sims had
any business to ask for was an account of cleaning the
laboratory last Friday.

"Yeah, that's the second-Friday clean sweep. They
really take it seriously, too. Everything has to be done - the
whole works."

"And you did everything?"

"Right, right," said Victor. "Waxed the floor, polished the
hardware, oiled the doors, wiped down every blessed
surface and object."

"Even the telephone?"

"Oh, sure. Fingerprints all ov... Hey! I wasn't destroying
evidence, was I?"

"No," Sims assured him. "On the contrary; you may
have created an extra problem for the killer."

"So, it's true, then."

Sims nodded, "I think so. Where was the telephone?"

"On the desk, of course..." Victor cast down his eyes,
hesitated, then bravely continued. "On the desk. Except I
did something... a kind of joke. See, the boss in there has
his stuff arranged in straight lines, all square. When I clean
his desk, I often put one thing in the wrong place, just to
bug him. This time, it was the phone. I meant no harm..."

Well, that's one mystery solved; nobody had to make
any calls from the lab. "That's all right," said Sims. "Now,
what I really want to know is, did you see the wedge that
goes under the back door?"

"The wedge? Well, sure," said the young man. "I had the
door open the whole time... it was a nice day. So the
wedge was under the door, right up to when I finished the
lab and got ready to wash the hall floor."

"And then?"

"And then I took it out and put it where I always put it, on the windowsill, right there."

"Are you sure?"

"Of course I'm sure. That's where the wedge is kept."

"It's not there now," Sims pointed out.

"I can't help that - it's," his thumb fingers surreptitiously touched fingertips, "five days since I put it there."

"You couldn't possibly have kicked it or knocked it out and forgotten to pick it up?" Sims persisted.

"No," Victor was adamant. "I pulled it out - with my hand - no kicking - lifted it up and put it right. There." He jabbed at the spot. "What's the big deal, anyway? If the wedge is lost, I can make a new one."

Sims explained that it wasn't lost, so much as displaced. "I found it, on Monday morning," he paused to let the significance sink in, "outside, in a flowerbed."

"Oh. Well, all I can tell you is where I left it Friday evening. If somebody moved it later on... Oh, I see. Sorry I can't help."

"But you *have* helped," Sims told him. "It would be a piece of luck if you happened to have seen anybody hanging around...?"

Victor shook his head. "Fraid not. I was all alone."

"One more thing... no, two. Was there anything left out on the benches when you arrived, at..?"

"Five-thirty. Maybe a few minutes later - I emptied the wastepaper baskets in the offices first. No, there never is anything left around; Mrs. Benz makes sure of that."

Sims nodded. "And what time did you leave?"

"Hm... let's see... It takes a good couple, three hours. I guess, after eight."

"Thank you. You may be called to testify at the inquest. Is that a problem?"

"If it is, I've solved bigger," said the young man cheerfully.

Therefore, sometime after eight p.m. Friday - that would let out the Joneses and Dumonts - and before 9:30 a.m. Saturday - this could be any of them - somebody let himself (or herself, of course, but he didn't choose to think that) in. With a key. That would have to be by the front door, clearly visible from the street. After dark, when the area was deserted, would suit the killer. Or would it? The entryway was well lit. Someone familiar might not be noticed in daytime. Would he take a chance on coming twice, once to set things up and again to do the murder? In fact, setting up couldn't have taken very long; a few minutes, perhaps. If only somebody could tell Sims how long it took for that evil-looking substance to cook! Would he come early, so as to be seen by the fewest possible people, or late, so as to spend the least possible time? Would anyone have been around the factory?

"Would anyone have been around the factory on Saturday morning?" he asked Mr. Quick.

"Why, of course," replied that worthy. "You see, we had already begun to manufacture the Walters' containers. Once the decision is made, we move along at a fair clip, you understand... and the client, in this case, was rather impatient. There would have been a full shift present... that is, I assume so. The foreman would be aware of any absentees... You may consult with him. Mr. Draper, that is. I believe he is on the premises, even as we speak. Shall I ask him to join us here?"

Is it likely that anyone wants to be this cooperative? Perhaps not, in the detective's usual working environment - but then, he had not often dealt with people, in any situation, with Mr. Quick's old-fashioned good manners.

"Thank you," Sims answered in kind, "but there is no need for that. If I may go to him..?"

"Of course, of course, this way," Mr. Quick bustled around his acre or so of mahogany desk, covered at the moment with file-folders, and out the door. "This will be a little break for the workers, a little excitement. I know it always makes a pleasant flutter when we have visitors in the factory."

This was a part - in fact, by far the largest part - of the building, which Sims had hardly noticed. From the outside front, it was a tall, blank wall, with only one strip of window, high under the eaves. Entered from the main lobby, however, it was revealed as an enormous room, with lofts on three sides and supply racks along the fourth. The floor-space below was occupied by a frightening number and variety of huge covered vats, conveyer belts and other, more esoteric machinery, humming busily. Busy people in blue or white overalls scurried about in their shadows - figurative, of course, since the lighting was an even soft yellow: no headache-causing fluorescent fixtures here. The loft on the near wall was divided into glass-fronted cubicles, accessible from a sort of steel balcony with a flight of stairs at either end. Up one of these, Sims followed Mr. Quick, and into Ernest Draper's office. (E.D. Of course; Eve Dumont had not been at those meetings mentioned so cryptically by Dr. Morley; Ernest Draper had.) Polite introductions were made. Mr. Draper had also been on duty all day Saturday, but seen nothing out of the ordinary.

"Which isn't surprising, since I never left the plant, from eight to 4:30. Had lunch in the cafeteria - in back of the offices, over there. So did most of us."

"And there was no car in the parking lot, when you arrived and when you left?"

"Well, sure, there were lots of cars... like I said, we had a full shift in, from eight."

This was something Sims had not counted on. But he had another idea. "When you go to the cafeteria, you cross the front lobby. I wonder if anyone noticed the fire door at the far end of the hall?"

"What about it?"

"Was it open?"

"Not that I saw. The near end door to the hall was closed, which is normal. You'd pretty much have to walk right up to that and look down the hall to the other end. Maybe someone did, but why should they?"

It wasn't worth following up: lunch-time was far too late; the fire door would have closed long before. "You might just ask if any of the personnel saw anyone before lunch-time... anyone who isn't on your shift - either in the halls or elsewhere on the premises."

"Sure, why not?" Mr. Draper pushed a button on his complicated telephone and spoke into the receiver: "Attention, everybody. We have a policeman here who wants to know if you saw anybody hanging around the place, inside or outside, on Saturday. Before lunch, he says. Saturday morning." He glanced enquiringly at Sims for anything to add, but the detective was looking down at the factory floor, where most activity had ceased and

106

curious faces turned toward the loft. He felt like an exhibit in a glass case.

Mr. Draper concluded his announcement. "If any of you can remember seeing somebody - besides the kids - come on up, as soon as you can safely leave your station, and tell the man about it. Now, don't get to nattering among yourselves, and don't forget about those vats, okay? Over and out." He replaced the phone.

The three men in the office watched with interest, as below, knots of people formed, exchanged words, and broke up again. Gradually, work resumed along the production line. Only one pair stood talking, possibly arguing, for their discourse was accompanied by conflicting gestures. Presently these two, a man and a woman, turned and approached the stairway. Mr. Draper groaned, but did not offer an explanation. What he said was: "The girl's name is Marcie. You let me talk to her."

The man entered first, with the reluctant step of one who expects to be chastised. "Uh, Ernie, don't get sore..."

"Later, Franco," the foreman stopped him. "Just tell the policeman whatever you have to say."

"Well, see," the man faced Sims, after a sideways glance at Mr. Quick, "Marcie an me, we was outside Sat'day... just for, like a little walk, you know... around maybe ten, in our coffee break, see?"

Sims nodded encouragingly. "Yes?"

"An so, Marcie says to me, there is a guy there, an' I din pay no tention, cause there's all the time, kids n stuff cuttin across the back fence there... I mean, like, it's not a fence, it's only kinda like bushes, see, an there's holes where the kids in back there take a shortcut, like, alla time..."

"Yes?"

"Get on with it," put in the foreman.

"So, anyways," Franco continued, "she says, no, it's a grownup man, so I looks. But I din see nothin, really. Just, like some guy's backside, an he already got out, and then he was gone. So, I din think nothin of it... just some guy takin a shortcut."

"This was at ten a.m., you say?"

"Somethin like, or a bit later. Like I said, we take our break at ten, so id be a few minutes after. An that's all I seen."

"But your friend - Marcie - saw the man?"

The witness shrugged.

Mr. Draper addressed the girl - a slight, pale creature with the distracted air of a small child who has broken a rule she does not understand. "Marcie, it's all right. I'm not mad at you. Nobody is mad at you." This was delivered in soothing tones, followed by a look at Franco which clearly said: it does not apply to you. "This nice policeman would like to hear all about the man you saw. Last Saturday. You went for a walk with Franco, right?"

She nodded. "We just went for a walk. Franco said, it's such a nice day, we should have our break outside." She aimed a glance of sweet appeal at the man, Franco, who cast down his eyes.

"That's right, Marcie," said the foreman. "It *was* a nice day. So, you were outside. Walking. And you looked at the hedge. That way," he waved a hand toward the back of the building, on his left, "or that way?" he indicated the wall behind him.

"That way." Marcie raised her own right hand. "At the back. Yes."

"And you saw a man." The girl nodded enthusiastically, too caught up in the game to be frightened any longer. "What was the man doing?"

"Nothing," she said, disappointed. "The man was just walking. Cause it was a nice day," she added.

"Was he walking fast or slow, Marcie?"

She pondered this. "He was walking fast. Yes, I think so. Walking real fast."

"Running, maybe?"

"No, he wasn't running."

"Good girl. Now, think hard. Was the man walking fast toward you, or away from you?"

"That way," she waved her whole arm at the rear of the building. "He was walking fast, away."

"Did you see the man's face?" Mr. Draper asked in a very serious tone, to show that it was important.

Once again, the girl began to look frightened. "I'm sorry, Ernie, I didn't see his face."

"That's all right," the foreman soothed, "it's not your fault. We only want you to tell the truth. You're doing fine. So you saw a man walking away, fast, and you saw his back."

"I did," she agreed. "I did see his back."

"What colour was it?"

"It was brown!" she answered, as if she had only now discovered colour. "It was all brown. The man had brown hair and brown coat and brown pants. He was an all-brown man." She appeared quite delighted by this fact.

"And then the brown man went through the bushes, right?"

"Yes. Through the bushes. Franco saw him too."

"And you didn't see the man do anything else at all."

"Yes, I did," she contradicted. "I did, too. I saw the man put his hankie away. Like this." She held an imaginary object before her face with her left hand, removed it and stuffed it into a non-existent pocket, higher than those on her overalls, and a little way out from the body: the side pocket of a suit jacket.

"But," Mr. Draper argued gently, "how could you see him do that, if his back was turned?"

Marcie was not intimidated this time; truth was on her side. She turned her back to the company and repeated the gesture. "I did, too, see the man put his hankie away. So there."

The foreman assured her that she was believed, and praised her lavishly. Sims added his own kudos, as did Mr. Quick. When Mr. Draper told her that she might return to work, the girl positively glowed with accomplishment. "Well, you've made her whole week," Mr. Draper told Sims.

"I'm not sure she hasn't made mine." the detective replied. "May I ask...?"

Draper sighed. "Drug overdose. Attempted suicide, four, five years ago. She was seventeen. They found her too soon, one way of looking at it... But she does a decent day's work, and she finds a lot more to be happy about than she did before. So there," he echoed Marcie. "As for this... this specimen... Franco, I'll deal with you later. Now, get back to work." He watched the young man down the steps, then added, "I don't know. He isn't that much brighter than Marcie. If they get married someday, that's all right... But if he's just messing around with her, I'll wring his scrawny neck." He returned abruptly to the present. "Sorry about that. Well, I don't suppose it was much help, but it's about all we seem to have."

"On the contrary," Sims assured him, "it was a lot of help. I believe that young lady may have seen our killer leaving the scene. Even if she can't identify him, she's told me to look for a man in brown, and she's given me the exact time."

"What do you mean, even if? Of course she can't identify him; she never saw his face. Anyway, you can't get Marcie into court."

"I could, you know," Sims contradicted again. "But," he added hastily, seeing the big man's face fill with storm-clouds, "I don't want to. Still, if it became absolutely necessary, the judge would make sure she was cross-examined with all due consideration."

Draper nodded grudgingly. "Yeah, okay. Maybe I'm a bit over-protective. I've got kind of a soft spot for that little girl."

"We won't hurt Marcie, Mr. Draper."

CHAPTER 13

As they left the factory, it occurred to Sims that loquacious Mr. Quick had been curiously silent all this time. Now, he made up for it. "Marcie's not the only one he has a soft spot for," he confided with a breathy laugh. "Ernie has a dog with three legs, an epileptic cat, and an endless succession of injured birds. He always appears so competent - well, he *is* competent, of course - I think I mean tough. People never cease to amaze one, do they? Do you know, in spite of company policy - set by Mr. Acton, oh, years and years ago, before anybody thought of putting it into law - I had reservations about hiring Marcie. You see, I was afraid that, with her limitations, she might be prone to injury... This can be dangerous work, no matter how many precautions one takes. But Ernie insisted. He said, you have to give people a chance to take their own chances. Rather neatly put, I thought; I've found it useful to remember... and, really, I knew it would be all right, the way he runs things. I never interfere in the factory side of the operation, you know, and neither does Mr. Meyer. At least, not since Ernie Draper took charge."

None of this was relevant to the murder investigation, nor, Sims couldn't help thinking, was it any of his business - yet he didn't mind hearing. Believing was a different matter. It all - everything about Ac-Me Plastics, especially the legendary Mr. Acton - seemed too good to be true. If this were indeed the workers' paradise, the one big happy family, that Mr. Quick made it sound, how did murder fit in?

He told Mr. Quick, "I've asked everyone in the research department for an account of how they spent the weekend. Would you mind completing my notes?"

The old man stopped short, wheezed out a small laugh. "I must confess I have been a little miffed that you didn't want my alibi... One hates to think one is too old - or feeble, or innocuous - to be counted a suspect. As it happens, however, I do have an alibi of sorts. I visited my daughter in Elmvale. Do you know it? Oh well, no reason you should; it's a little place, near Midland. She's married to Conrad Smith - an attorney. I visit them every other weekend or so. I drive, which takes less than two hours for most people - two and a half for me... I'm the old codger you see pottering along below the speed limit, with whom all the other drivers are so cross. Well, in order to arrive for luncheon, I have to leave no later than 9:30. In point of fact, I set out shortly after nine."

Somewhat daunted by this overflow of information, Sims took a moment to recover. "On which day was this?"

"Why, on Saturday, of course. Did you not just now tell us that Saturday morning is the crucial time? So, you see, Marcie could not have seen me - " he broke off for a spontaneous bout of laughter. "I'm terribly sorry. I realize this is not a subject of mirth. Only, it has been such a long time since I even considered crawling through hedges... I might give it a try, if only I could be quite certain that no-one is looking."

Caught out, Sims elected to abandon this line of enquiry, except to caution: "We can't be absolutely certain it was the killer Marcie saw. The murder may have taken place earlier, maybe even," he fixed Mr. Quick with what he hoped was a hard look, "before you set out for Elmvale."

"Then I can still be a suspect?" The old man's innocent gratification abruptly gave way to chagrin. "Oh dear," he mumbled, "I didn't mean to make light of..."

"Well, then," Sims began briskly, to cover the other's lapse, "it's getting late. By the way," it suddenly occurred to him, "what are you doing here at this hour? Besides being exceptionally helpful?"

"I should think that were sufficient reason," said Mr. Quick, fully recovered and dignified. "Actually, I had been going over laboratory notes for the past year or so. You see, we simply cannot have the research department stand idle very much longer - the operating cost alone is prohibitive - and I must choose a project to recommend to Mr. Meyer at our meeting next week. I'm afraid there is very little of any promise... In the end, I may be forced to reconsider Young Frayne's insulating foam, after all." He looked distressed. "Edward, rest his soul, would be terribly cross with me, even for thinking of it."

"I'm sure he'd understand," Sims told him. "I suppose you have been understanding of his - weaknesses - in the past." This was a shot in the dark, and he was sure that his companion knew it.

112

"Certainly not in matters pertaining to his work."

They had been standing for the past minutes in front of Mr. Quick's office door, both shuffling a bit, eager to get back to their respective tasks. Yet something in the tone of the reproof - or, rather, in what it did not exclude - gave Sims a glimmer of hope for more background. "In personal matters, then?"

"I'm not sure that is an appropriate topic," said Mr. Quick, in his second uncharacteristically terse statement of the day.

Sims decided on a direct appeal. "Sir, I do realize that it must be distasteful to you to discuss the private life of a dead friend. But you must also see that I need to learn everything I can, and sort out later, what is and what is not relevant. If I learn something irrelevant and personal, I shall not broadcast it about. It is not part of my mandate to damage reputations. So, if you know something, tell me now, in confidence... otherwise I shall have to continue digging for it, disturbing, perhaps, matters that need not be disturbed."

Mr. Quick regarded him intently; there was perception, and possibly a touch of amusement in his eyes - certainly no least hint of his usual vagueness. "Well said, sir! You speak my language, after all." This was meant as a compliment, Sims believed, but it struck him a light blow in the ego: he had taken much pride in resisting Mr. Quick's mode of speech, through quite long conversations. Oh well, it could not be helped.

"All right, then. I understand that you have been asking everyone on my staff about Edward's little peccadilloes. If it will convince you to desist, I'll tell you what I know. It really isn't much. Over the past few years - five or six, I would say - Edward has been dissatisfied with his life, restless - oh, I don't know why, really... Perhaps he had wanted to achieve more... Perhaps it was not a good decision for him and Amanda to remain together..." He heaved a sigh twice his own size and gazed into the distance. "I don't know. Suffice it to say that he sometimes took refuge in oblivion - drank to excess. Now, you must realize that this was not a regular habit, not at all. An occasional, and one could guess, quite deliberate, indulgence." Sims nodded intelligently to show that he followed and understood.

"There were occasions, in his cups, when he seemed intent upon subjecting himself to a kind of test. He would make advances - oh, very mild ones, by today's standards - to any young lady the circumstances happened to present. These were doomed to failure, as he was certainly aware - one might even suggest that failure was the object of the exercise..."

"...except once?" Sims put in gently.

"Yes," said Mr. Quick with deep resignation. Then, after a short pause for thought, took it back. "No. No, that was a different matter, actually. That was something rather more like a friendship. You see, they had much in common at the time; it does not seem so very odd."

"Eve Dumont?"

"Yes. Well, you were bound to find out, I suppose. Only, at the time, she was Eve Langtry... not yet married to her young doctor. Eve comes from Montreal, as did Edward... French-Canadian anglophones. That was one bond between them. Unhappiness was another. In any case," the old man surfaced from his reverie and became brisk, "that was two years ago. It passed; she married; Edward resumed his solitary ways. The working relationship between them seems to have suffered no reversals. There were no repercussions, no reason to suppose that the matter has any bearing on present events. And there you have it."

"Thank you," Sims told him solemnly. "I expect you're right about it being irrelevant. I shall stop probing."

At last, and with considerable mutual respect, they said good-night; Mr. Quick to return to his office, the detective to stroll out the fire door at the laboratory end, and across the grounds.

There were, in fact, several gaps in the hedge, which had obviously been used for some time. The street behind the Ac-Me grounds was a modest residential one: it would be convenient for the younger residents to cut across on their way to Birchmount Road, rather than walk around the block. However, there was little to be seen - because four days had passed, two of them wet days, and because the sun was already setting. All that Sims was able to establish was that a man could easily squeeze through at least one of the gaps. And that, if the murderer had left his car in this street, it could not be seen from the Ac-Me property. It would almost certainly not be remarked at all, as the whole length of the roadway was lined with parked cars.

"I know what happened," he told a moderately attentive Lancelot that evening. "I know how. I know when. At least, I'm pretty sure I know all those things. Hey, don't tell me you've got fleas again!" The dog immediately left off chewing a spot on his shoulder and resumed gazing raptly at his master's face. The little yellow eyes, looking slightly myopic - which, come to think of it, might be the case, and might account for his failure ever to catch the squirrels he persisted in chasing - were fixed on him in innocent puzzlement. "Don't make me laugh, now. This is important stuff." Lance rearranged some of his limbs in order to lay his long snout on Sims' knee, sighed, and continued gazing.

"All right. Here's the story. Edward Morley is at home Saturday morning. He's had breakfast - casserole that he was supposed to eat the night before, and didn't... because he was upset about not reaching his son, and his wife was away, and maybe he got to thinking about everything that was wrong with his life - in any case, he tied one on maybe, and forgot to eat. So, in the morning, he's a bit hung-over, but functioning normally. Washes the dishes, washes his car - I know because nobody uses detergent on the lawn - all neat and tidy.

"Then he gets the phone-call. This is about nine o'clock. Whoever it is, calls from some other place - doesn't go to the lab, till he knows his victim is coming. No mystery about the phone on his desk; the cleaner did that. He leaves in a hurry - doesn't change, just throws on a jacket and goes. Realizes that he's forgotten his cigarettes. If you moved a fraction of an inch, I could reach mine right now. That's better, thanks. So he stops at the convenience store to buy some. He arrives at the lab, around a quarter to ten. Parks and enters by the front door - the lot is full of cars, because the factory's in operation, but all the workers are inside and nobody sees him.

"He goes down the hall. He has no reason to be afraid or suspicious. The back door is propped open, which isn't strange, since it's a warm, sunny morning. He walks into the lab. There is some paraphernalia set up, on his own bench, which might make him angry, but wouldn't scare him off. Probably stuff already cooking away in that big flask. He doesn't see anyone, because the killer is hiding in the fume room. He approaches the bench. The killer jumps him from behind, breaks a cyanide capsule and drops it into the boiling plastic. In a matter of seconds, Edward Morley is either dead or unconscious - it doesn't matter which, because it'll take the safety system ten minutes or more, to clear the poison fumes from the room. The killer is wearing a gas-mask. And rubber gloves, and Dr. Morley's lab-coat. I don't suppose you'd pass me that beer? I didn't think so. What good are you?" He twisted around on the couch carefully, so as not to dislodge the dozing animal's head, and helped himself.

"Where was I? Oh, yes. The killer takes off his gloves and puts them on the corpse - it's not that easy, pulling surgical gloves on an inert hand," Sims shuddered as he imagined the procedure, causing Lance to open one eye questioningly. "so he rips it a bit. That's my first clue: when you pull on gloves, you hold the inside of the cuff, not the outside - you see that? Then he does the same thing with the lab-coat. Again, not easy. He should have taken the victim's jacket off first, but maybe he's in a hurry now, anxious to get away. Planning a murder is simple - doing it is quite another thing. Maybe he's scared, even a little sickened, and not thinking straight.

"He lets the body fall back in a natural position, more or less, and knocks over the retort on the bench - maybe on purpose. We know it didn't fall over before, because the stuff in the flask dripped on top of the body. Then he goes into the fume room, whips off the gas-mask, and runs out the back door, kicking the wedge away. He's holding a handkerchief in front of his nose...

"No, he isn't! Stain in the sink... It was wet paper towel from the fume room. Sure. He stuffs it into his pocket and then ducks though the hedge, seen by Marcie, but he doesn't know that. I hope. His car is parked on the back street. He drives away. It's a little after ten. And, now, I'm afraid I'll have to trouble you to shift your bulk, because I need my notebook.

"I know when and I know how. But why? And who? The killer must be strong enough to hold a well-nourished middle-aged man; there was no struggle to speak of. And he had to be at least as tall as the victim... or clever enough to make higher rub-marks on the swinging door, to make it look as if Dr. Morley himself had opened it... Is any of them as subtle as that? Probably. Their combined IQ has to be in the thousands - a damn clever bunch of people. Is any of them as cool and calculating as that? Again, probably: they're all disciplined and self-possessed, with the possible exception of young Arnott, and even he has shown plenty of mental agility."

They all, with the exception of Eve Dumont, had an alibi for the critical time, some more air-tight than others. Sims would have to go through the laborious process of checking with family and neighbours. He would start on that tomorrow, right after the funeral. And hope that at least some of the four - all right, the six - just because simple Marcie said she had seen a man, and he was reasonably convinced that it was, indeed, the murderer Marcie had seen - she could be wrong. It could have been a woman wearing brown pants and a jacket. Not very likely, though; let's stick with the men. They all have brown hair - except Mr. Quick, whose hair is well-salted, what there is of it. Of course, there is nothing to stop a killer disguising himself, with a wig, say - or men's clothing? - just in case he (or she... see how objective I am?) were seen by some of the workers, who would recognise him...

But why, why, *why*? What had Edward Morley done to any of them? In what way did he threaten them? Stand in their way? What did he have that any of them wanted? Money, freedom - Amanda Morley. Top job, more money - Martin Jones. He'd nixed a potentially very profitable project - Charles Quick. Which was dear to the heart, the ambition, of - David Frayne. Or even Mr. Meyer, whom he had not before considered; whom he had yet to meet, and whose given name he did not even know. Yes, he did; he'd seen it on a closed office door: Abraham.

"What else? A past affaire, with a woman who was now to all appearances happily married, and who possibly didn't want her husband - a hot-blooded Frenchman; perhaps jealous? - to find out? Well, what *about* the jealous husband, then? Suppose he had found out? Revenge - Yves Dumont. Hey! We're trying to shorten this list, not keep adding to it. Anyway, the Dumont situation was two years in the past. Paul Ferdinand Arnott? Nothing. All right, then, let's make it Jones, Quick, Meyer, Frayne, and, whether we like it or not, Mrs. Morley. We don't like it one bit. And when did we start using the royal 'we'? In this case, perhaps we can pass it off as an editorial 'we'.

Sims wondered if he'd had too much beer, but there were only two empties on the coffee table. It must be fatigue that was making him punchy. He took care of Lancelot's basic needs - short walk, water, kibble - and then his own, and then watched the 11 o'clock news from bed.

CHAPTER 14

Of course it rained. It was bound to, if only symbolically. A woebegone light drizzle had thoroughly wet the young grass and made a layer of mud on the mound of freshly turned earth. Sims, having felt he might be out of place at the service, joined the mourners here. Besides the family - including a presentable but colourless young man, with his arm around Louise, minus babies - all the senior staff from Ac-Me Plastics was present. (Given time off work through a long-standing policy of Mr. Acton's, no doubt.) Charles Quick in a venerable black suit, drawn and genuinely unhappy; Mr. Draper, Mrs. Benz, Miss Valentine in a respectable black, so loosely attached to her slight frame as to suggest a more comfortably endowed female relative. The research department, all in a cluster, yet separated by attitude. Martin Jones looked like a man repressing some pain; Ferdy Arnott, alert and fidgety; David Frayne, with the studied solemnity of a stage priest... and Eve Dumont, pale and still as a statue.

There were three men somewhat past middle age, whom he had never seen before. The one in a suit like Sims' own might be Mr. Burgess of Maintenance. The distinguished one with silver hair and wearing, at a conservative guess, a thousand dollars worth of virgin wool, had to be Mr. Meyer. He looked resolute, self-possessed... and also, one had to admit, mournful. The third was half-way between them in outward show of prosperity, rather more flamboyantly dressed then either - sales manager or chief accountant?

The proceedings were brief. An Anglican minister made the usual recommendations, heedless of the fact that God had already had six days, post mortem, to review Edward Morley's application for admittance to heaven. Louise wept openly; Brian, less so - but, to his credit, made little effort to hide it; Amanda was stoically dry-eyed. The moisture on Eve Dumont's chiselled face, unshielded by a hat, might have been rain. The family cast clods upon the coffin and tried to be discreet in wiping their hands. Mr. Quick and Mr. Meyer followed suit, and so, as awkwardly as an adolescent, did Ernest Draper. Whatever his shortcomings in life, Dr. Morley still had the respect of his peers.

Directly it was finished, and the assemblage began to drift away, Amanda Morley came over to Sims. Almost timidly, she asked, "Will you join us at the house, Sergeant?" He was casting about in a blank mind for some graceful demur, when she added: "It seems odd, somehow, to keep calling you that. You must have a given name..?"

"It's Alastair," he replied automatically, "Alec."

"Your people are from Scotland? So are mine. At least, some of them..."

This was acutely uncomfortable. Sims thought she was as relieved as he, when he said: "I can't. I'm supposed to be at the station. It was just... I thought I ought to come."

"That was gallant of you," she said softly. Then she rejoined her children, and was gone.

Everyone was gone. In the muffled distance, a car engine turned over reluctantly. Sims could not recall ever having been more alone. And he was standing; unlike the other, he still had options. He picked up a handful of damp earth and threw it into the grave. "You made a fine mess of your life, Edward Morley. And then again, who knows? You might have salvaged something, given a bit more time... Nobody had a right to steal that time."

"Ain't it the truth!"

Sims didn't jump two feet into the air - at least he hoped not. But the back of his head felt as if none of the hairs on it would ever lie down again. It was only a burly grave-digger, come to do his part. The theatrical effect of his sudden appearance was somewhat spoiled by the hard hat he wore and the large yellow earth-moving machine on which he was leaning. He smiled benignly as Sims bade him good-day.

If he went back now, it would still be with empty hands. He had a story - a coherent enough story, to be sure - about what must, or might, have happened, but nothing like tangible evidence. A stop by the office of the dead man's lawyer added little of relevance: Dr. Morley had been comfortably off; had left his family comfortable. No vast sums of cash, but there was valuable, unencumbered real estate, patent royalties amounting to several thousand a year, a life insurance policy, standard for all Ac-Me employees, and a trust fund for Brian's education. Similar funds had been started, but did not yet amount to much, for the Whitlock children - both boys, he noted: Andrew and Edward. (At least he had lived to know a small namesake.) They were not precisely wealthy, but no surviving Morley would have to rush right out and find a job. Of course, this had been true the week before. The only one who would benefit substantially - if one considers independence beneficial to a nineteen-year-old - was Brian: the only one with an airtight alibi. He had been three thousand miles away when his father died.

Sims remembered the promise he had made; upon arriving at Division, his first call was to Father Mike. And the first thing Father Mike asked, after being apprised of the situation, was: "Is the boy getting any counselling now?"

"Counselling?"

"You just told me," the priest explained patiently, "that he is nineteen, an only son, and that he has lost a father with whom he has been at odds for some time. Have you no memory?"

This was a telling, and not entirely fair, shot. Sims had been thirty-three, established in his career and a relationship he had supposed permanent, when his own father died. Yet, it had taken him a year, with considerable help from this same meddlesome priest, to make peace with the fact. He *had* made peace with it; the occasional dream in which the elder Sims appeared now, was not in a class with the sweat- and guilt- soaked nightmares of the first few months.

"Yes, that's all true," he said. "When can you see him?"

"The sooner the better," replied Father Mike. "Tomorrow morning, if you can get him here. I have nothing on from – let's see - ten to noon."

That, pending Brian's response, settled, Sims felt a little better. He took out his case-notes, earlier reports, the forensic lab findings which had arrived that morning, the autopsy report, and the copy he had made of Dr. Morley's day-book. He had yet to decide what to do with it all, but his desk was covered deep enough in paper to convince anyone passing by of his busyness. He picked up the day-book pages. Many of the entries were in Chemistrese, which meant nothing to him. Initials referring to staff members no longer presented any problem; dates of meetings and equipment repairs held no mystery... except the ones that were not there. Had Dr. Morley been growing absent-minded? Had he been preoccupied, under some stress...?

Staring at one of the pages intently, willing it to yield some kind of answer, he brushed at a hair on the lower inside corner. It wouldn't go away. He looked again: it was not a hair, after all, but a line, faint and jagged. The way a photocopier renders a ripped edge of paper. Well, of course. How dense can you be? When somebody - a murderer, say - tears out a leaf, a fragment may be left behind. He hadn't noticed any when handling the book, but he would go now and look again.

"Day-dreaming on Metro's time?"

From Inspector MacDonald, the rebuke was so mild as to be startling in itself - aside from its having broken into his reverie. The inspector had just returned from lunch, and therefore in his best mood of the day.

"I was going over the case, sir," Sims told him.

"What case is that, boy?"

"The Morley homicide." Sims was about to launch into an account of what he had learned and conjectured, but MacDonald stopped him with both palms.

"I been reading your reports all morning," he rumbled. "Goddamn boring crap." He scratched idly at a gap between shirt buttons. "You got a suspect since yesterday? You got an eye witness?"

"As a matter of fact, the killer was seen leaving the scene. Or at least, the premises."

"Yeah? Who?"

"I don't know who. But the time fits, and he was holding a wad of paper towel, or something like it, to his face."

"Hm." MacDonald inclined his massive head, insofar as the chins allowed. "Running from the room?"

"Walking fast, and ducking through a hedge."

The scratching resumed in a hypnotic circular motion. Sims had difficulty tearing his eyes away and looking up at the man's face. "Was this person unknown seen anywheres near the body?"

"No," he admitted.

"How do you know it was the killer?"

"I know."

MacDonald nodded sagely. "Right. Shelve it."

"Pardon?"

"You heard me, boy. Shelve it. Inquest, Tuesday next, one p.m. If the coroner says so, we pick it up. Meantime, put that junk away and see me about an assignment."

Before Sims could begin to protest, the inspector's ponderous back was disappearing around the corner. Not that protest would do any good. I don't like that man, he thought. I don't like that man even a little bit. But he's doing a job as best he can. A job, one might add, that I should be doing by this age, and probably never will - had never even been strongly inclined to apply for.

Slowly packing his papers into a file box for storage, he wondered what it was he really wanted to do. Right now, solve this murder, yes. And after that? And next year? Would it really satisfy him to become an old detective sergeant? There were cases he cared about, people he grew to care about, yes. And then there was most of the work... I would be happy, he answered, if only I could pick my cases. But no cop has that privilege.

As a tiny act of defiance, he delivered the material to Records in person, and took a side-trip to Properties. He asked for the box containing Dr. Morley's possessions. The clerk brought it promptly and slid it across the table with a fetching smile. "You're really involved with this case, huh?"

"Yes, I suppose," he said absently. He was already opening the box.

"I admire dedication," the clerk, whose name he did not know, ventured.

"Sure," he said, laying the contents out on the table.

"It must be exciting, being out there, with the real crime..."

"Exciting?" he looked up at her in puzzlement.

"Well, sure. Look at me. I'm supposed to be a cop, too. But I'm really just a file clerk. I could do the same work for a corporation and get better pay. Wear nicer clothes, too."

Sims, who had never noticed the girl before, did now. Truly, the uniform was unflattering; he tried to imagine her in a dress - a pink flowered dress, to complement her fair complexion and pale blond hair. The image did not set off any bells. "Why aren't you?"

"Why?" she shrugged prettily, "I have this thing for policemen..."

"Oh," replied the vegetable in Sims' clothing. "Well, there are plenty around here."

The girl went and sat on her tall stool by the doorway, without another word. You clod! he reprimanded himself. That was about as sensitive as a MacDonald response. Well, the other half defended, what was I supposed to do? A little pleasant conversation wouldn't kill you, the first voice scolded. She's about twenty-one, for heaven's sake - and none too bright. So what? She's a woman - they're not exactly beating down your door these days. You could maybe ask her out. I don't even know her name. Wouldn't be that hard to find out. All right, he settled the argument, I'll find out - tomorrow.

There was no scrap of paper in the little black book. If pages had been torn out, it had been done neatly. Well, why not? Everything about this murder had been done neatly. But he shook out the plastic bag before returning it... and a tiny fragment of white paper, straight-cut on two sides, concave on one, and ragged on the fourth, fluttered onto the table. It fit perfectly with the outline on the copy.

And this proves? This, the dominant Sims answered triumphantly, proves that at least one page has been torn out of this book. And that proves that, since all the notes in the book refer to the research department of Ac-Me Plastics and its work, the killer is one of his colleagues. Moreover, one whom Dr. Morley's notes threatened in some way.

Unless, of course, the victim himself had ripped out a page, to - oh, I don't know - to copy down a phone number, or directions to somebody's house. On the page next to an incomplete note? Unlikely; not impossible. Sherlock Holmes would tell you: once you've eliminated the impossible, what is left, however improbable, is the solution. Sims had conducted much of his career on the obverse: when you've eliminated the improbable, what's left is impossible only until you know the facts. He put the fragment into a tiny plastic bag all its own, signed and sealed it.

On the way out, he apologised to the clerk, "I didn't mean to be snarky, you know. It's just this case - frustrating." She forgave him. She smiled sweetly. She was very young, quite receptive and physically attractive. The improbable remained possible - for tomorrow.

"You're on call, okay?" Inspector MacDonald leaned back in his oversized swivel chair and stretched. A three-beer lunch had mellowed him almost to the point of jocularity. "The cases we got - the real cases - are pretty much under control; those guys don't need your help. But we're kinda short on calls. Anyhoo, stick around. Something comes in, grab a constable, right?"

"Can I have DiMarco?"

MacDonald dropped his feet back onto the floor and consulted a ledger. "Nope."

"Why not?"

"DiMarco's off a couple days. Cramming. Take one of the guys that's around."

Sims was momentarily crippled with guilt. He had completely forgotten about Constable DiMarco's exam - had not even wished him luck. Well, that, at least, could be rectified before Monday morning... And there was a bright side: if - when, he corrected loyally - DiMarco passed, there would be a new detective on the roster - one Sims would be glad to have for a partner.

"On call. Right," he said. "Anything else?"

"Nope. That's pretty much it," said the inspector, about to embark on another stretch. "Be at your desk, boy. And no daydreaming; I still haven't seen a follow-up report on that milk store holdup - last Thursday, was it? A week late, is it? Sez here you got Sat'dy night - that oughta keep you on the streets."

He sat disconsolately at his desk. Report on the robbery finished - two teenaged boys arrested at their home, an hour after the crime, counting money - he really had nothing to do. He phoned DiMarco. Then he looked at the duty roster for uniformed personnel, and found the blonde girl's name: Stephanie Foster. He tidied some drawers and he smoked.

At 4:21, he set off in a police cruiser, with an

uncommunicative constable named Burnside, to run some children out of a factory warehouse, and to warn them, very sternly, about the many ways they could get hurt - or killed - in there. One of them, a rosy-cheeked ten-year-old, swore so colourfully, he was tempted to bring the kid in, to conduct a seminar for policemen. Report on this incident also finished, at 5:30, he signed out and went home.

CHAPTER 15

At 6:30, he dialled the Morleys' number.

"A couple of things," he told the widow, after brief preliminaries. "Remember that friend I mentioned, the priest? His name is Michael O'Connor - Father Mike, to his friends, which includes almost everybody. He would like to see Brian tomorrow, if that's convenient..."

"Yes, it is," said Amanda. "Well, more than convenient; it's wonderful... I've been concerned about him."

"If anyone understands young people, Mike does. He'll be at his office between ten and twelve," said Sims. "I'll give you directions. The other thing is: I'd like to take that roll of film - the one you developed on Monday morning? - to the forensic lab."

"Fine. Will you pick it up? When?" Sims told her tonight, any time, would be good, and she asked: "Have you eaten yet?"

"No, "

"Then, come for dinner. It's only the two of us now, all the people are gone, and... I haven't had time to prepare anything special... just meatloaf. But it's a good meatloaf." Sims would have hesitated longer; might have protested that he was terrible company, had she not added: "And please bring Lancelot. I'd love for Brian to meet him."

He was at 39 Linnette in less than half an hour. His lecture on proper canine behaviour went to waste as soon as Lance saw Mrs. Morley: he hurled himself out of the car and into her arms in one leap. His master was a full two seconds behind with the leash.

"Sit!" he shouted. The dog rolled over on his back. "Stop that. Come on, now, sit up." Sims told him more calmly.

Lance, contrary to expectation, sat up, yet managed to get in two more wet swipes at Amanda Morley's hand. "It may be my conceit," she said, patting the reptilian head, "but I think this dog likes me."

"I think this dog is your slave for life," Sims replied. Did he feel a touch of jealousy? Yes, but only a light touch; it would pass.

Brian did not make quite so easy a conquest of the dog. There was no hostility: Lance had been trained early and

127

well to reverence Man, but there was a marked wariness on both sides. A few minutes and a few cookies, however, resolved the situation. "He'll be all right now," Amanda said, "won't you, Sweetie? He was only nervous." When Sims took a proffered chair, the dog lay down at his feet, heaved and enormous sigh, and settled his head on both outstretched front legs. "There, that's settled."

During the course of the evening, the presence of Lancelot bridged more than one conversational rough spot: he was something they all could look at, fuss over, accompany for a romp in the back yard, talk about. He did nothing disgraceful, to Sims' relief, and was sometimes amusing. Brian warmed to him, admitting candidly that animals made him nervous. "It's not that I'm scared of them - it's more, kind of, not knowing the rules. I never had a pet... You don't want to make an ass of yourself, not even in front of a dog, you know?"

The meal, though unpretentious, was better than anything Sims had eaten in weeks. They shared a bottle of wine with it: "I've been legal for two months now," Brian remarked, "the novelty's worn off." Though somewhat guarded, he did expand upon his interest in the religious life. Sims told him, perhaps a shade too enthusiastically, about Father Mike. There was general talk concerning the nature of vocations - for example, how one decides to become a minister, a photographer, or a policeman... Sims liked the boy for his honesty: he did not try to impress, or pretend to be more sophisticated than his years. Any specific reference to cases, however - to the case in hand - was avoided by tacit agreement.

At nine o'clock, Brian excused himself on the grounds of fatigue, and said a courteous good night.

"You must be worn out, too," Sims told Mrs. Morley.

"In a way," she conceded. "I always find people in large numbers tiring. Yet, I was reluctant... even a little bit afraid, to be alone tonight. I'm glad you agreed to come over, though we weren't very good company."

"You both have been charming," contradicted Sims. "I'm a zombie; I've had a rotten day... Now, that was a remarkably stupid thing to say! After the day you've had."

She brushed away the implied apology. "Is there any progress?"

128

He was forced to tell the truth, without going into detail. "So, there won't be any, officially, till after the inquest."

Amanda nodded in understanding, resignation. "Do you know, this morning, at the service, at the cemetery, I was perfectly aware what it was all about. And yet, I had no sense of Edward being there. That was how I felt in the morgue, too. But then, when everyone had finally gone and I didn't have to put on a brave face anymore, I thought: well, that's over; now we can get back to normal. It was t then that I realized there is no normal anymore. I think this afternoon is the first time I actually believed that Edward won't ever again come out of his study, to ask if supper is ready, to lecture Brian on his study habits, to leave for a bridge game..."

Sims felt very much as he had on that first morning he'd met her: fervently longing to be elsewhere, and to offer some comfort, both at the same time - unable to do either.

"I'm sorry," she said. "This must be terribly awkward for you." He made some unconvincing noise, which she ignored. "It's just that there isn't anyone else I can talk to."

"Jonas Thompson?" he asked tentatively.

"Not about this; he and Edward never liked each other. And we aren't that close." She blushed, realizing where this put Sims. "Well, you're part of the circumstances: you became, sort of, my last link with Edward, when you brought me the news of his death. See? I can say it now. The children have been strong, at least on the outside, but I mustn't add to their burden."

"Sometimes," he suggested, "it's good to have burdens. To feel needed..."

She smiled, "I suppose... Louise has made some attempts at mothering me and I'm afraid I don't quite know how to accept or reject it... It's foreign to the relationship she and I always had. Louise was her father's child, his one-girl fan club and confidante. Andrew and the children are a great comfort to her, but nothing can replace that first, special bond...Of course, since she married and moved out, they haven't been as close, but Edward has kept all the books he used to read to her as a child... He took such pleasure in watching her grow! She was a charming little girl, pretty and sweet... Being an only child himself, I think Edward didn't really want another baby."

129

She gazed off into space with a soft smile, perhaps watching some tender scene in her mind. Sims held his tongue, but the little policeman in its separate compartment, made a note to question Louise about any problems or conflicts in her father's life. "I insisted. Brian was mine... I wonder if that was a mistake. I've never thought to question it before: it was so when I was growing up. My sister was my mother's child; I was my father's. It seemed an equitable arrangement. Is it like that every family? Was it, in yours?"

"In a way, I suppose," he said slowly. "There were six of us, though, which makes it a lot more complicated. My eldest sister, Mary, was Mother's, I think. Eileen was nobody's - ever since I can remember, Eileen went her own way. She was the most adventuresome - " he broke off, chuckling, "her own free person... a little bit wild - nobody ever knew where she was, and nobody knows yet. She's a journalist; the last we heard, somewhere in the Middle East. Shows up, out of the blue, once or twice a year, and tells fantastic stories. Eileen was my earliest hero - I think she may be, still."

"Not your father?"

"No. Well, that's the difficulty. You see, I was the only boy, and as such, slated to be Father's: his namesake, heir, disciple... But I made the mistake of coming along quite late - there is only one younger sister, Marjory - of course, she became Mother's baby - and Faith's favourite dress-up doll - and my own playmate and best friend, naturally.

"Also, I was all wrong for the part. Penny should have been Father's child - she has his temperament, his head for figures - his eyes and jaw, even. But, try as she might, there was no way she could be the son Father wanted. Still, I believe - and he concealed it as well as only a hide-bound, taciturn Scotsman can - I believe Penny always knew that Father loved her best."

"Are your parents..." she was going to say, living, but changed it to: "in this country?"

"My mother is, and three of my sisters. My father died some years ago."

"I see. That's why you've been so good at finding just the right tone with Brian. Because you do know how he's feeling right now. It's awful for him... He and Edward have never understood each other - at least, not since Brian was about twelve, when he became his own man... That sounds a bit portentous, applied to a skinny little boy with angelic eyelashes... but he was stubborn. Not noisy and rebellious, like most boys... Let's just say he developed passive resistance into an art-form... That's what is most like Edward in him, that solidity. He knows exactly what he is, what he wants, and nothing, nobody will deflect him from a course he's chosen. I admire that quality, perhaps more than any other... I've always been a reed in the wind myself... Where is your mother now?"

"Mother and Penny are in Hearst. We were all born there, because Norris has no hospital. My father owned the hardware store there. When the CNR terminated service on that line, he closed up and moved us to Hearst. When he died, Penny took over the business. It had been obvious all along that she would be the one, not I, and yet he never stopped showing his disappointment."

"Funny, isn't it?" she remarked, still in a dreamy, far-away voice. "This nonsense of gender... Edward was perfectly happy to accept Louise, just as she was. He didn't expect her to study science or to share any of his interests - which she did, in a casual sort of way. And he didn't especially long for a son. Yet, once Brian was here, he had a sort of obligation thrust upon him, to carry on... Where are your other sisters? What do they do?"

"Eileen was off as soon as she finished school. Faith married and moved out west - she has four children, two in university now. The youngest, Eric Alexander, my god-son, may have been a classmate of Brian's. Marjory lives here in Toronto, with her husband. Scott is a contractor; Marjory is his draftsman - person."

"And Mary?"

"Mary is gone."

"Dead?"

"We don't know. She just left one day. A long time ago."

In the silence, Lancelot opened one eye, then the other, snorted, stretched, yawned and clambered to his feet. "He's right," said Sims, "it's time we were going."

"I'll get those films," she said.

In the doorway, he thanked her for dinner, gave her one

of his cards, and held on to the hand that reached for it. "If you need to talk about - it - or anything, call me. Brian will be all right. And so will you. For what it's worth, I don't see you as a reed in the wind."

He was home by half past ten; not too late to call Marjory. After catching up with the latest on family life, he extended an invitation to her and Scott for Sunday evening. Then, still not inclined to sleep after the day's events, he sat down and wrote a letter - in longhand, because Mrs. Field would certainly object to the sound of a typewriter at this hour - to his sister Penelope, and Mrs. Sims. He would call Faith tomorrow. He would fly out to see her on his vacation. He would keep in closer touch with them all...

When he finally slept, Mary, almost grown up and very beautiful in the eyes of four-year-old Alec, came to tuck him in. "It's all right, Darling," she said, smoothing back his hair, "Father is hard sometimes, but he loves us all, really."

CHAPTER 16

There followed three days of inexpressibly tedious routine, broken only by a convivial evening with Marjory and Scott. Possibly because it was unexpected, they praised his meatloaf unstintingly - till he had to confess the source of the recipe. Amanda had been glad to give it, and incidentally report that Brian was most impressed with Father Mike, and would be seeing the priest again. So that was all right. Best of all, from the co-host's point of view, they brought along Ginger, their Golden Retriever. Mrs. Field had some well-chosen words concerning the pleasure these two dogs took in each other's company, but that couldn't be helped. Mrs. Field was becoming an irritant - and the irritation was mutual. Very soon, he would have to look for another place to live.

On Sunday night, he worked - if it could be called work, to sit in the office, listening to other policemen complain about their wives, children and neighbours. Sims had nothing to contribute, and the conversation made him feel acutely lonely. How could Whistler be so peevish about his fine, healthy infant son? Why couldn't Pappas appreciate the woman who always packed a napkin with his lunch? He half suspected that much of the grousing was really bragging in disguise.

Still on night duty, Sims had Monday to sleep late and catch up on chores. Somehow, he found both options resistible. He would take Lance to the park - there was no rule about which park; why not Toogood Pond? If it happened to be near the Unionville subdivision where Martin Jones lived, that wasn't his fault. And if he should happen to drop in for a chat with Mrs. Jones, well, he hadn't been forbidden to.

The lots were not small; they only appeared so because the houses - Tudor, Georgian, Colonial; Tudor, Georgian, Colonial - were so large, and because the vista was not cluttered with old trees, tall fences, or anything with character. The Joneses had a young forsythia hedge around their front yard, which would have been in full golden bloom now, had it not been pruned within an inch of its life. The lawn, too, was close-cropped; the kidney-shaped flower-bed in its centre was planted all in yellow tulips. The house was dense-looking; pale grey, with two tall pillars on its front, unnecessary support for a shallow portico. Sims parked in the wide driveway paved with silver grey interlocking brick.

The woman who answered the door had on a yellow and white dress of crisp linen. Her hair was a classy muted blonde and perfectly combed. Her unchipped nail polish matched the pink of her lipstick. She was pretty, in a magazine-picture sort of way, and very gracious.

"Yes, Officer, I'm Beverly Jones. How can I help you?"

He told her the nature of his business and she made all the appropriate comments on the tragedy. But she remained firmly planted between him and the interior, with one hand resting lightly on the door. That is, until a stout mature lady emerged from the house next door and became absorbed in weeding her flowering border nearest the hedge. Then she asked him in. Sims accepted a chair in the gold, green and white living room. He would have refused refreshment, had she offered any.

"All I need," he said, "is to fill in a few blanks in the movements, last Saturday, of everyone involved."

"Well, I certainly wasn't - involved. I hardly knew the man." But then she volunteered: "He seemed nice enough."

"It's your husband I'm really interested in," he said. "I understand he was at home all that day."

"Well, yes," said Mrs. Jones, "except to pick up Justin after his karate lesson. I'm afraid I was out most of the morning, though. Martin cut the grass," she added.

Looking around the perfectly-proportioned, beautifully decorated, totally barren room, and at the perfectly groomed woman, Sims revised his opinion of married life. Perhaps it would not suit him, after all. Money ought to help: everything here was costly, down to the bone china bowl full off tulips on the antique coffee table - and yet, it held no charm. "Lovely room," he said.

"Thank you. It was done by Ridley's. They're really quite good, aren't they?"

They ought to be, Sims thought; it was a firm of interior decorators so much in vogue that even he had heard of them. As a necessary corollary, they must also be expensive. "Did you have them decorate the whole

134

house?"

"Why, yes." Her impatience to be rid of him struggled briefly with her pride of ownership. The second won. "Would you like to see it?"

His real purpose in coming here had now to contend with anxiety to have a word with that neighbour. "Yes, thanks, if you have the time."

There was much white, much yellow; white marble tile in the three bathrooms, pale yellow satin in the master bedroom. The boy's room ("Pardon the mess; he's only eight, you see." She replaced the two stuffed animals out of rank on the bed.) was wallpapered in blue, with a border of stylized toy soldiers. The little girl had unicorns on hers, and a pink canopy over her bed. She was currently at French-immersion nursery school, he learned. Martin's study was done in leather, glass and chrome – in no way reminiscent of the man he had met. Sims found it all profoundly depressing. "Very, very impressive," he said, upon returning to the foyer, where Mrs. Jones hovered hopefully. "Well, I won't take up any more of your time." Though I can't imagine what you do with it, he added in his mind; those hands certainly don't keep all these windows clean... there must be someone else to do it.

The neighbour had not gone inside; she was still busily weeding, with one eye on the Joneses' door. Now... if he got in the car, he would have to stop and get out again, ten feet down the street, thus drawing attention to himself. But if he walked over to the hedge, Mrs. Jones must see him from the window; it would seem rude. On reflection, he didn't very much care what Beverly Jones might think of him. He crossed the perfect lawn.

"Good morning," he called over the crippled shrubbery.

"Hello," replied the lady, getting to her feet with some difficulty. "Lovely day."

He agreed. He asked one or two foolish questions about horticulture. Then he gave his name.

She seemed delighted. "Of course! I should have guessed. You'll be investigating about Martin's boss who was murdered."

"What makes you think he was murdered?" he asked.

"Why else would there be a plainclothesman nosing around?" she answered with magnificent circular logic.

"Martin didn't do it," she added.

"How do you know?"

"He couldn't hurt a fly, that's how I know. Why, he never even hits that boy of his - and let me tell you, he'd have plenty of reason. That Justin is a brat."

Sims wasn't deeply interested in the behaviour of the Jones kids, though privately, he made an excuse for young Justin - having to spend one's formative years in a room 'done' by Ridley's might unhinge anyone. "What I'd like to know," he told the neighbour - Mrs. Butterworth, he learned in due course - "is whether you can recall anything about last Saturday? Not this one past, but the one before."

"Let me think... It was a fine day, wasn't it? The rain came on Sunday. Not that I minded, the flowers are all the better for it. Yes, Saturday was fine. That was when I set out the borders."

"So, you were outside, here, in the morning?"

"Was it morning?" she wondered. "Yes, because in the afternoon, we had my daughter and her family. Now, her little boy, Christopher, he's younger than the Jones boy, he'll be seven next month, but he already knows how to behave. A dear child, Christopher. Even if he does look like his father. Now Jennifer, she's a little doll, the very image of my Bonnie at that age."

"And so," the detective steered patiently, "you saw Martin Jones cutting his lawn."

"Of course I did," said Mrs. Butterworth. "He mows every Saturday morning. You could set your watch by him, not like some others I could mention. That's what I tell Mr. Butterworth. He likes to stay abed of a Saturday morning. Of course, he can't do it on the Sunday, for going to church, you see. Well, I've put up with it for forty-five years, I don't expect to change him at this late date. I'm an early riser myself, always have been."

"And trimming the hedge." Sims added. Why should she have the monopoly on non-sequiturs?

"Yes, that's right. Though I did tell him, I said, leave them alone for another two weeks, or you won't get any blooms, but he said, it looks so untidy. There should be something a little bit untidy in a garden, I always thought."

"So," he persisted, as Marcie flashed before his mind's eye. "Mr. Jones was in his yard all the morning."

"Why, yes. Except for when he went to buy fertilizer. Lawn food, he calls it. Personally, I don't think it needs all the food he feeds it, and I told him so."

"He went out? What time?"

"Well, I don't know," she said. "After that wife of his left with the children... They take every kind of lesson under the sun, those children. Yes, I do, too, know. He said, the nursery will be open by now, so it must have been nine o'clock."

"Did you see him return?"

"No, I went inside to make Mr. Butterworth his breakfast. Brunch, I suppose that Mrs. Jones would call it, and I wouldn't be surprised if she served something French. Of course, she has help. I always fix a good solid breakfast of ham and eggs, even if it is after ten o'clock. Which it was. He's not a lazy man, Mr. Butterworth, he just likes his lie-in once a week."

"And so," the plainclothesman plugged away, "Dr. Jones was gone from sometime after nine till after ten, and you didn't see him again that morning?"

"He's not really a doctor," Mrs. Butterworth corrected. "He does something with plastic. And I did see him again, because we had a barbecue, and the Joneses were out in their back garden, too, half the afternoon. The children played together. I don't care for that boy of theirs, he's a bully. But little Courtney is quite sweet – and she adores the baby."

"Only one more thing," he said, with a slight emphasis on 'one'. "The place Martin Jones buys his fertilizer. Do you know where it is?"

"Of course I do. We get all our plants and things there. It's called A Summer Place - like the film. Quite a reliable garden supply, that's why we don't mind paying a little more. It's on Kennedy and... now let me see, near Helen, I think, or is it Highglen? Mr. Butterworth has to come along because I'm not allowed to lift heavy things, and he always drives, being the man. It takes about ten minutes... I'm sure you'll have no trouble finding it."

"I'm sure I won't," Sims told her and quickly added thanks and farewell, all in a breath, to escape further information.

He did pass a nursery and garden supply store on the

way to Ac-Me. It was called The Summer Place and occupied the north-east corner of Kennedy Road and Denison Avenue. Twenty-two minutes from the Jones house. Martin Jones could have made it to Ac-Me and back in the loose hour suggested by Mrs. Butterworth's accuracy, even including a brief stop for lawn food, if he actually bought any. It would have been difficult - but possible.

Since Lancelot was not best pleased with the proportion of travel to frolic, Sims stopped at the ravine before returning home. And now, he was sleepy - the laundry could wait.

They spent the first half of Monday night, cruising a seedy stretch of the main drag, as a courtesy to the understaffed 12th. "Man, I missed this!" Petersen stretched luxuriously in the passenger seat. "I was goin nuts. Two whole weeks, sittin around the house. The old lady was ready to put a dust-sheet on me. But tonight," he added hopefully, "tonight, we could maybe have a good time."

"We're patrolling Yonge street," said Sims mildly.

"Yeah!" his new partner misunderstood. "Sodom and Gammara! Pick up a couple hookers - watch it, though, don't go for the real young chicks, we could get in trouble. I'll tell you when I spot the right babes."

"What's the point of arresting prostitutes?" Sims objected. "They'll be back on the street in a day. And we can't arrest the customers, unless we catch them in the act of handing over money - which isn't likely,"

"Man, are you for real? Or what?" Petersen explained patiently: "We arrest 'em, but we take our sweet time gettin to the station. And, who knows, before we get there, we might hafta lettem go for lack of evidence or whatever."

Sims kept his eyes on the road. There was plenty of activity; though well past midnight, the lights over bars, massage parlours and adult bookstores were bright as day. Pedestrian traffic featured the young and flamboyant, for want of a better word, and the cars tended to move sluggishly. It was not his favourite time or place. Petersen, unperturbed, kept entertaining him.

"It's too bad about Gloria. For a cop, she's a terrific lay. But then, she was getting to be a pain in the ass, so I

138

guess it's all for the best. You ever been married?"

"No," said Sims, more or less truthfully.

"Lucky you. I been married. Course, I was too young to know any better. Lasted a big six months. So then I hadda move back home, or I'd've starved to death... I gotto give my mom credit, she cooks pretty good. Price I got to pay, though, don't know if it's worth it. She won't leave me alone. Why can't you pick up your stuff? Why don't you go out with some nice girl? I know the kinda girl she means. Women! Can't live without em, but you sure as hell can't live with 'em. Y'know, there's only two kinds of women in this world - the fun kind and the ball-an-chain kind. Gloria, now, she was fun, to begin with, she really was fun. But lately, she got all ball and chain crazy, y'know what I mean?"

Sims grunted noncommittally. It was enough. "Yeah, Little Gloria wants t'get married. C'n you see it? Her, as somebody's wife? Not mine, I tell you that for nothin! If I ever do that again, and I might, y'know. Truth. Well, see, I'll be twenty-eight next birthday, and the ol' biological clock like they call it is tickin away. So I guess I'll prob'ly find some nice little chick, like maybe eighteen, y'know? The old lady'd like that. And me, I don't want no second-hand goods. Cause it'd be nice to have kids. You got any kids?"

"No," said Sims. He pulled over to the curb suddenly. "That looks like a problem."

Two women, one young and slim and definitely under-dressed for a cool night in May, the other of indeterminate age, with flaming red hair, were evidently at odds with a middle-aged man in overcoat and hat. The contretemps had already attracted some helpful passers-by, offering advice and moral support to one or another party.

"Forget it," said Petersen. "Let a cruiser handle it."

There was no police car in sight. "Someone could get hurt," he said, stepping onto the sidewalk.

As soon as he asked what the trouble seemed to be, there wasn't any: all participants disclaimed having any problem at all. The onlookers melted into the night. The detective got back in his car.

"Hey, come on," his partner said, "that was crow-bait. Okay, the little chick was cute, but we need two, remember? Keep truckin, man."

Sims kept. With judicious avoidance of knots of people where violence was not evident or imminent, and a resolute refusal to pull over at any time Petersen recommended it, he was able to get through the night, just trucking. At seven in the morning, he was able to sign out, with no incident sheets to file. "Well, g'night," Petersen called after him. "See you tonight. Isn't it lucky, how good we get along?"

"Why," he asked Lancelot, "do I not own a dart-board? I gave you nice things for Christmas, didn't I? I gave you dog biscuits and that horrible rawhide bone you threw up all over Mrs. Field's rug. How come you didn't buy me a dart-board?"

The dog began to crawl forward on his belly, for which the kitchen was really too small. "All right, I'm sorry. You're a good dog. It's not your fault."

Reassured, Lance went back to his breakfast... supper... whatever meal comes between work and sleep. For the dog, it was all the same: something brown and hard in the shape of large pellets; he seemed to like it. Of course, he liked foam rubber and dirty socks. For Sims, on this occasion, it was meatloaf on toast. He made three sandwiches in order to have two for himself, and ate one and a half, standing up, without a plate or cutlery to wash.

"Martin Jones," he explained between bites, "is spending an awful lot of money. He did not inherit any, though Beverly may have. And he is not earning an awful lot. Or, he wasn't. The promotion will help, and so will the royalties from this Walters project... Don't even suggest," he warned, tossing a piece of sandwich to his friend - who, as usual, let it bounce off his nose and split into three portions, and then was too busy, searching for the middle one, to make any suggestion, "going to his bank, because bank people are more secretive than doctors. I'd need a warrant. And I can't get a warrant, because, not only is he not a suspect, but there isn't even a case for him to be a suspect in. You follow, so far?" Lance gazed intently at his hand, rather than at his face. "Anyway, I don't like him as a suspect. I think Mrs. Butterworth is right. I just don't see him being cold-blooded enough to go through with it.

140

Unless his wife were coaching him... I can see her as Lady Macbeth.

"You're right, that is unlikely. And besides, the gain isn't so dramatic as to justify the risk. It's all gone, can't you see? No more. Eat your own food. Unless being in charge gives him a crack at something big... No, I don't like Jones as a suspect. Of course, that's partly because I like him as a person - or, at least feel sorry for him... You should have seen that house. The man is presumably paying for it, yet I bet you couldn't pick up his scent in the place."

CHAPTER 17

Inspector MacDonald came in, exceptionally, with the night shift, to brief them in person. The roster had been rearranged - mangled, some would say, and did, but only under their breath - so that a full complement of officers in uniform as well as those in plain clothes, would be present.

"This," MacDonald told them, "is the biggest operation we've mounted all year. When it's over, we'll have busted the city's worst crime ring. These guys are not just pushing drugs, not just smuggling." He looked hard at each man in the front row. "They're responsible for at least two homicides this year alone. These guys are dangerous." He proceeded in this solemn vein, using his Sunday English, and periodically fixing them each with significant stares, to explain what most of them had known for the past month or more.

He carefully reiterated the various points of information gleaned from undercover agents' reports. He traced their appointed routes and stations on a large-scale map of the area. He named leaders to groups of four vehicles each. Sims was less flattered than he should have been, to lead one such group. He and Petersen, with three squad cars to back them up, would cover the most probable line of retreat... They would, in fact, spend much of the night parked in an alley behind a restaurant, and were forbidden to leave the car for so much as a cup of coffee. "Not even a piss. Got that?"

It was as long a night as he had ever lived through. By 11:30, Petersen was well launched on a treatise on women. Sims was able to stanch the flow from time to time by checking with his back-up units on the radio. Hearing DiMarco's sane voice every twenty minutes; knowing that Pappas, Handleman, Whistler, Burnside and Peebles were somewhere in the darkness, thinking decent thoughts, in spite of their boredom and general discontent, helped him to control his own homicidal urges.

"You're too goddam conscientious," his partner remarked. "You know they're out there. Where they gonna go? So, anyways, this little chick in the pay office, she's got a face on her like dessert - like a cherry pie, ha, ha. But she's got an okay body - you can always turn off the lights, right? So, she's been comin on to me for months, y'know, and I'd've buttered her bread before, except Little Gloria kept me pretty busy, if y'know what I mean - talk bout demanding! So, anyways, I'm in there the other day, they screwed me around with this suspension crap, so I hadda go in there to fill out all these forms, and she's helpin... she gets nice an close an' just kinda makes sure to brush up against my arm, like - real cute, so I tell her I'm on the loose, an' I give her a little encouragement, you know, like just a friendly little squeeze, and you know what she does? She freaks! Man, that little bitch suddenly starts actin all innocent, like she don't know thing one, and I'm some kind of rapist or somethin! An' she starts in givin me all this crap about how she's gonna report me, so I says to her, look, Honey.... Hey, you're not callin all the squads again?"

But, call as often as he might, they had nothing new to report. In direct defiance of orders, he even tried raising the assault squad (two detectives and six constables, armed with three rifles among them, whose assignment was to rush the front door of the target building, as soon as all of the suspects had entered). The leaders didn't answer, presumably being out of their car. On foot, they would be in touch only with Inspector MacDonald, who would, in turn, alert the back-up units. "They don't answer," he informed Petersen unnecessarily. "That means they must be about to go in."

"Yeah, right," replied his partner.

No word from MacDonald.

By one a.m., Petersen had covered every aspect of sexual politics in the work-place, and was well away on the fringe benefits of law enforcement. "Y'ever get involved with a case? I mean like lay the star witness, or the accused's wife? Now, that stuff can get you in some heavy shit. I remember one time..."

Sims, although he had never actually studied the technique of self-hypnosis, was able to drift clear. He mentally reviewed every clue, every statement, every conjecture in the case of Edward Morley. By the time he tuned in again, Petersen was winding down on the subject of involvement with suspects and witnesses. His definition was different from Sims', of course - but the dangers were equally real, whether the police officer made sexual advances or shared confidences. "I suppose so," he said.

"Huh? Man, I could use a leak. And something to eat. What time is it, anyways?"

It was two-thirty in the morning. He radioed every team he could locate. Nobody knew anything, except how tired and fed up and hungry and uncomfortable they were. At 3:25, MacDonald came on the air to all cars. "We can't wait any longer," he said. "We're going in. Stand by." They stood. At 3:35, the same voice, somewhat less forceful, told them to stand down. At 3:51, it dismissed them. The target building had been duly entered, searched, and found to harbour neither criminals nor illicit drugs; neither guns nor corpses. It had been cleaned out, stripped of everything but a few sticks of furniture the Goodwill would reject, and abandoned. Thus, to no-one's surprise, ended The Great MacDonald Drug Bust.

The nights were not overwhelmingly busy; what made them tiring was the constant, the inexorable, the un-silenceable, Petersen. Sims had tried everything from ignoring him to outright rudeness - nothing made the slightest impression; it was as if the man had no ears, was all mouth. And what a mouth! As he became accustomed to Sims in the next seat, he grew more trusting; was more willing to confide the ups and downs of his personal life, in such exhaustive and graphic detail that Sims was convinced he returned home every morning with noticeably more white in his hair.

On the other hand, time spent at Division with other officers, was scarcely more congenial: Inspector MacDonald was in a bad mood. This meant, besides the occasional profane outburst at anyone who happened to be between him and the coffee machine, say, or missed a comma on an incident report, they were subjected to unremitting criticism. They were a sorry bunch; none of them could keep anything to himself; they might even be in the pay of organized crime. They dressed badly, spelt badly; sat, stood, walked, ate, breathed and probably excreted badly. Inspector MacDonald was not, at this time, a man taking pride in the units under his command.

Therefore, Sims was not unduly concerned about turning up for work half-asleep. If nights were to be a dead loss anyway, at least he would make use of the days. Doggedly, he followed up every alibi. Mr. Quick's daughter in Elmvale confirmed his by telephone: indeed, her father had arrived before noon on the Saturday in question and spent the afternoon with her, husband Conrad and their young son. He was known to be a slow and careful driver. He had seemed much as usual on that day.

Paul Ferdinand Arnott's parents were vague about his movements, but certain that he had been at home that night and that he usually slept late on the weekends. He had been around in the afternoon and all evening. Some creative subterfuge also revealed that Dr. Dumont had been on call that weekend, and had performed an unscheduled gastrectomy on the Saturday morning. Scratch one possible off the suspect list, gratefully. Which, of course, left Mrs. Dumont with no witness at all to her whereabouts. This was still nothing, but it was now properly documented nothing.

On Wednesday, he went to David Frayne's apartment building during working hours. He was not quite sure how to go about finding the towel boy (who must have a more dignified job title) so he approached the doorman. This was an individual of mature years and a well-developed sense of civic responsibility - and recall so nearly total as to be suspect.

"Not last Saturday, but the one before, sure. I saw Mr. Frayne twice that day. Around 8:30 in the morning, on his way downstairs. That door," he clarified, "goes to the storage rooms, laundry, the gym, and the garage, one more flight down. I knew he was going to the gym, on account of he had on a sweat-suit and carried a gym bag. A couple hours later, he came back again. Out that door and around the corner, to the elevators."

"That's remarkable," Sims told him. "It was almost two weeks ago. Do you remember everything so clearly?"

"It's a kind of trick I got," Mr. Edmundson confessed. "I just close my eyes and run a sort of movie, you know what I mean? Doesn't work all the time, but I can set it off if I bring up one odd fact. It could be the weather, or somebody wearing a funny hat... This time it's the way Mr. Frayne acted."

"What was odd about it?"

"Oh, not to say odd, really, just different. He said something both times he went by - just, like, good morning, how are you, nice day, sort of thing, but from him, that's pretty unusual. Must be in love or something," the old man chuckled.

"In a happy mood, was he?"

"Cheery, yes. Full of pep - anyway, the first time. On the way back, not so much. Probably overdoes it, like all these young executive types. Thinks, if some exercise is good, too much is better."

"You're very probably right," Sims agreed. "Though I understand Saturday morning is not a popular time for exercise,"

"That's true," Mr. Edmundson allowed. "Doesn't get real busy before noon. Mr. Frayne was just saying, that's what he likes about it."

"But there is an attendant?"

"There is a young fellow at the pool. Supposed to a be a lifeguard, but I guess they've got him doing all kinds of joe-jobs." The man looked at his watch. "He wouldn't be there yet - the pool's closed, week-days, till five."

"Is there any other staff downstairs?"

"The janitors come and go all the time - no telling where either of them is just this minute. And there is a fellow looks after the garage - so people don't steal stuff out of the cars - or worse. He's in a little kind of booth, on account it's cold in the winter. Also a security guard. Two, really, one in the daytime and another one, with a dog, at night. If you want, I'll get one of them to show you around. I can't leave my post, you understand."

Sims thanked him, complimenting him once more on his fine memory.

"Will I be a witness?" the old man asked.

"I don't know," said the detective. "You'd certainly be a good one."

"What he do, anyway, Mr. Frayne?"

"Probably nothing wrong. What you just told me goes some way toward clearing him."

"Too bad. Never liked the little snot. Thinks he's better'n everybody else."

The young security guard had been on duty on the Saturday morning. "Every second weekend" he stated. He

146

had not seen David Frayne. "But I saw his car. It's a metallic blue Trans-Am, the kind of car you notice. It was here all morning. And then, on my noon round - really, about a quarter to - I noticed it wasn't there anymore. Didn't come back in my shift, but it was there all day Sunday."

Sims dutifully made a round with him, incidentally learning a great deal he didn't really care to know about fast cars with minimal road-clearance. Once around the garage, the cement stairs leading up to the exercise room, pool and sauna; past the elevators to the storage lockers and laundry, a glance into the furnace and utility rooms, checking that the emergency exits on both underground levels were closed, took an hour, almost to the minute. His companion then embarked on the same journey, but in a different order, he proudly explained, "to fake them out."

The swimming pool attendant was another fresh-faced youngster, more muscular than the security guard, inside and out. Yes, he had been on duty last weekend, but he didn't know the tenants' names. Sims described David Frayne, with no better results.

"Half the guys that live here look like that."

Sims wondered how he could get a photograph of David Frayne without drawing attention to it. "Well, how many of these guys were in here last Saturday?"

"A couple, I guess," said the boy. "Saturday morning isn't that busy. 612 was in, like most weekends and 1723..."

"You mean you know the tenants by apartment number?"

"Well, yeah... I mean, just the members. See, they got lockers and keys and stuff with their numbers on. I give out the keys," he added proudly.

The detective sighed. "All right, good. Now, think back to last weekend - not the one just past, but the weekend before. In the morning. Were any tenants using the facilities then?"

"Yeah, but not a lot. Just a couple, like always."

"Was 1723 here?"

"Oh, sure. He always is. Comes down, eight, 8:30, leaves around 10:30, eleven."

"He never misses a Saturday?"

"Not since I been here. Quite a lot of guys like that, regular. That's how you should exercise, regular. Ladies, they come down any old time, most of 'em, just when they got nothing better to do."

"Good," Sims told him again. "So you're certain Mr. Frayne was here. What time?"

"Like I said, he always comes between eight and nine in the morning."

"And what did he do for two hours?"

The boy shrugged. "There's all kinds of equipment in the gym - bicycles and rowing machines and stuff. If he's smart, he does about twenty minutes on each."

"But you don't know?"

"How could I? I got to stay by the pool. All's I know is, he gets his key and a towel. When he's done, he gives me back the key. I do remember, he put the towel in the hamper. Yeah, he even said something about how a lot of people are sloppy about that kind of thing. Which was funny, cause 1723 is one of the slobs."

"And you remember what time this was?"

"Sure, it was quarter to eleven. Cause he asked, and the clock is right up there, over the door."

"Were there any other tenants in the gym at the time?"

"I dunno," said the attendant, "612 didn't show... There was 1402 and her boyfriend in the pool, foolin around... The couple in 505 were in the sauna. They're old. Long steam, short swim. That's about it, all morning."

Sims thanked him and left. He looked briefly into the well-equipped exercise room, the sauna, showers and the men's locker-room. All were, as yet, deserted, but in the passage from which the different basement sections opened, there was what amounted to a small crowd. When an elevator stopped, a man in shorts and tee-shirt and another in overalls got off; three people with grocery bags and briefcases took their place. Sims didn't get on board. He waited for the fitness club member to enter the door he had just exited, and for the janitor to disappear toward the utility area. Then he considered taking the stairs to the lobby and decided instead to leave by the one marked 'Garage'.

It was a busy place; home-comers hurried toward him from all directions; gasoline fumes were thick in the air.

148

Avoiding the booth which overlooked the car entrance, he made for the pedestrian exit in the far corner and took the two flights of stairs to the outside parking lot. Here he encountered and saluted the young security guard. Then he got into his car. Three minutes. Twenty-five more to drive to Ac-Me Plastics. Less on a Saturday morning, no doubt...

Yes, of course it was possible - easily. Except for one minor detail: Frayne's car had never left the garage. That still didn't make it impossible: there are other forms of transportation. Steeles Avenue was only a block away; a bus ran straight along it to the appropriate intersection. He made a note: get a transit schedule of weekend service. He copied the route number of a passing bus. Of course, that would take longer. So what? So, nothing. More well-documented nothing.

As it was, anyway, too late to sleep and too much fun, driving around in rush-hour traffic, he also followed the shortest route to the Arnotts' house. Nearly an hour, which would make it about forty minutes in better conditions. P.F.A. would have to have tiptoed out no later than 8:45 a.m. and returned at close to 11. Possible. In fact, his battered white Toyota was already parked in the street. Sims didn't stop; he made a note of the time.

"And this proves," he recounted to Lancelot between bites, tossed and eaten, of takeout fries, "that any of the four could have managed the trip and returned within the time-frame."

The dog regarded him with deep respect: he was holding food. "Eve Dumont doesn't have any kind of alibi. The others? Well, hardly air-tight. Mr. Quick could possibly have done it before he left - by the skin of his teeth. Frayne could have sneaked out of the gym and back again. Arnott could have left without his parents noticing. Jones did leave... and Jones lied about it. None of the others lied, that I know of. All right, all right, she forgot to mention the gas tap, but that's the sort of thing anyone could forget. What do you mean, Jones could have forgotten about the fertilizer? Whose side are you on, anyway? Go, run, I don't need you."

He sat on the bench, idly watching Lance chase his

tail. He kept snapping at it and missing; whenever he made a particularly energetic lunge and missed, he would fall down in a chaotic heap of limbs. Then he would roll on his back and kick ridiculous stick-legs in the air. Then clamber upright and start again after the tail. "That's just the way I feel," Sims told himself. "Wrong," he answered, "Lance does it for fun; you take no pleasure in chasing your own tail. Any of them could have been there. Only one was. Which? It's time you stopped flogging this dead horse, 'when', and dig up one convincing 'why'."

CHAPTER 18

On Thursday, donning a shirt he'd worn only a few hours in more prosperous times, Sims decided that laundry was his most urgent priority. He put all his clothes into a bag, tossed the bag into the trunk, ordered his dog into the back seat, and drove to King City.

There was no royalty here, and nothing like a city. There was a fine new shopping mall, however, spread out north, south and east of Islington Road, roofed in pale green glass. At one end was a huge shiny supermarket, where he bought essentials - mainly dog-food. There was a pet supply store, which he noticed too late, but bought another large bag of kibble anyway, because it cost half of the one he already had - it wouldn't go bad - and spent the difference on black and green dog biscuits, guaranteed to make Lancelot's breath sweet. There was a very bright new liquor store, where he bought some wine and, on impulse, a cognac so expensive that he wouldn't normally so much as glance at its shelf. There were boutiques, a hardware store featuring cedar lawn furniture; five restaurants, a health food store, a florist whose merchandise seemed to include nothing that had ever been in contact with soil and an ice cream parlour, decorated like a set of some '50's musical. There were four bank branches; he stopped at the money-dispenser to replenish dwindling cash in hand. There was a computer supply outlet, a video rental place the size of a city block, a shoe store and a toy store... but nothing even remotely like a laundromat. Well, there wouldn't be. But a major department store held down the south end. He bought one shirt, one pair of socks and a pack of three briefs. He found a wall of pay-phones and made arrangements.

The Meyer house was invisible from the road. He found it easily, however, by the rural mailbox, in the shape of an elegant little white house with red roof and trim. Though he didn't know it till two minutes later, it was a perfect replica of the big house at the end of the winding, chestnut-shaded drive. 'Big' was the operative word. Six bedrooms, at a wild guess, though bedrooms were not its main feature. Patios figured prominently on the outside, as did early climbing roses and fieldstone. The place would have smelled strongly of money, were it not for the heady scent of flowers.

Mrs. Meyer answered the door. She was a little Dresden china figurine of a woman, with rosy cheeks and fair skin, incongruously dressed in shorts and flapping tee-shirt. She had a soft, melodious voice. "Sergeant Sims, come in," she said. "My husband is expecting you. To tell the truth, he's been expecting you for over a week. "

"She led him, past the open double doors of a wood-panelled dining room in which the average wedding reception could fit comfortably, to the back of the house, to the doorway of a sun-room bigger than Mrs. Field's whole house. "Abie," she said, "Detective-sergeant Sims is here. I'll just bring you something to drink," and went off on dainty noiseless tennis shoes.

Mr. Meyer hurried over to shake his hand. He, too, was dressed for summer, but the knees of his pale blue cotton slacks and the front of his designer polo shirt were stained with earth. The space in which they stood was full of exotic flowers. "I've been pottering," Mr. Meyer explained.

"Very successfully, by the look of it," Sims remarked. "Are those orchids?"

"Oh yes," said Mr. Meyer, "all of them. There are up to 30,000 species of - oh, no, not here! I have only 124. My ambition is to grow two hundred species before I die. You may say that's a frivolous pursuit... but I do no harm, and I derive a great deal of pleasure from it. Not everyone can say that of his ambitions."

Much as Sims might have enjoyed being introduced to these fantastic flowers - not all of them beautiful, he was surprised to note - this was not the right time for it. Before he could find a way, however, to change the subject, Mr. Meyer did. "But you didn't come to hear about my hobby. Let's sit outside." He led the way to a sheltered patio, furnished with natural oak tables and armchairs. "The humidity in there is too much for some people. Now, how can I help you solve this terrible crime?"

"It's not officially a crime yet," Sims cautioned.

"I don't care what it officially is or isn't," his hitherto mild-mannered host snapped. More softly, he added: "There is no doubt in my mind that someone killed Edward." He regarded Sims with eyes of tempered steel.

"Is there, in yours?"

The detective replied just as levelly. "No." Then he asked: "What makes you so sure?"

"Simple. Natural causes, you would have dropped it a week ago. Suicide is not Edward's style and accident even less so. Now, have you a suspect?"

"I have several. Whom do *you* favour?"

Mr. Meyer dropped his gaze. "Nobody," he admitted. "I don't know the staff very well personally, but my impression of Dr. Jones is that he has neither the temperament nor the inclination for murder. I suspect he'd be horrified, even to hear me speak of it. Mrs. Dumont is a woman with class - what they used to call breeding - not to mention, very attractive - I could hardly suspect her. The two young men, I've barely spoken to - I can't say either struck me as particularly sympathetic."

"Brass and Crass, Charlie calls them. Charlie Quick, that is," he amended, just as Sims was wondering if he could possibly mean the only man named Charles so far introduced. Certainly that sort of humour had not been evident in any of his own conversations with Mr. Quick. This would have led him off into a contemplation of human character, had Mr. Meyer not recalled him in time. "As for Charlie, I've known him more than twenty years. He is out of the question. I'm inclined to say the same of Amanda Morley."

"So am I. But where does that leave us?"

"That leaves someone I don't know about. Someone outside the plant. A professional rival? A personal enemy? It seems far-fetched. But then, if anyone had asked me two weeks ago if I believed Edward a candidate for murder, I would have laughed in his face. It's not funny now."

Mrs. Meyer came out, carrying two tall glasses. "I forgot to ask, Sergeant, would you prefer a hot drink?" When he declined, the sullen boy in a white jacket who had stopped two paces behind her, deposited his burden on a low table near the two men. It was a wooden bucket full of crushed ice, in which reposed a variety of bottles: beer, soft drink, fruit juice and wine spritzer. Mr. Meyer selected one of these, twisted off the cap and took a long pull, disdaining the glass. Sims took a beer and followed suit. When the procession of two had disappeared through a screen door adjacent to the conservatory, he asked: "Is it a school holiday?"

"Robbie, you mean? No, he goes to school in the morning, works in the afternoon. Jared works mornings." Because Sims was still looking bewildered, he explained. "They're from the Second Chance program."

Of course, Father Mike's pet project. The city was full of kids, sixteen and under, who had left school, run away from home and been in some trouble with the law. Instead of juvenile detention, the Second Chance program placed as many as possible with employers who would send them to school part time and train them in some useful skill. Unless the kids had been involved in violent crime, they lived in supervised group housing.

"I had no idea any homes were so far out of the city."

"They aren't. Robbie and Jared live with us. We always have two boys or two girls in the house - one would be lonely, three could make too much mischief. They get some pocket money, but we put most of their wages in the bank, for later."

"How old is Robbie?"

"Fifteen. He'd been on the street for two years, can you imagine? When he first came here, he was too frightened to speak. And angry! Walked around all the time, all clenched up. You can't blame him... some of the things he's lived through. But he's coming along. Jared's done him a world of good. Phew! That's an even more terrifying story. His stepfather tried to kill him - probably more than once. That was over a year ago. Jared is almost thirteen, but he can pass for ten, he's been so undernourished. He'd hardly been inside a school his whole life. He stuttered so badly, no-one could understand him. Robbie had to translate... Ergo, Robbie had to speak.

"And you know what? That kid is reading now! Okay, so he's not reading Tolstoy, but Uncle Funny Bunny, he can read - aloud! In just a few months! That is a bright, bright kid. And good with plants? Born with green thumbs. If they let me keep Jared the full three years, I'll make such a gardener out of that boy! Robbie, he wants to be a truck driver... My wife won't let me promote him to the garage yet, thinks he's too young and needs mothering. She usually knows."

154

A sudden silence fell as, having paused, Mr. Meyer appeared to realize how much he'd been talking. Sims asked: "This isn't a policy of Mr. Acton's, is it?"

The other burst into a great booming laugh. "You've been talking to Charlie. As a matter of fact, no. But Mr. Acton would have approved... Approved? He'd have twenty kids swarming around his place. He'd *love* it."

"Have you had any - trouble?"

"Trouble? Oh, you mean *trouble*. Not really. These kids aren't violent; they mostly behave. We had one girl who stole everything that wasn't nailed down - passed it on to her boyfriend to sell for dope. Fifteen years old, can you believe it? We couldn't talk her out of it, couldn't bribe her, couldn't scare her... had to send her back, finally." He sighed. "That was awful. An awful waste. But she'd started to corrupt the other little girl and we couldn't have that." He sighed again, more deeply. "Oh well, they say you can't win 'em all. But," he sat up straight and reached for another cooler, "you didn't come here to listen to kid stories. You want to solve a murder. How can I help?"

Sims wasn't exactly clear on this himself. Frankly, he was bemused... and suspicious. He believed everything Mr. Meyer had been telling him about the street kids, but found it difficult to believe in Mr. Meyer. He had classified the late Mr. Acton as a folk-hero: it's all too easy to mythologize a dead person. The handsome man before him was very much alive, and rich, and powerful. It's not uncommon for the wealthy to give generously of time and money to worthy causes. But this generosity with heart and home was on a different order. Too good to be true? A cover for something? An expiation of guilt for... oh, some secret vice, or the means by which he had become so rich. The facade was so smooth, so flawless, it had to cover *something*. Is that you speaking, he asked himself, or Petersen? Why can't a man be both rich and decent? If anything, material comfort ought to make it easier to be good - God knows, poverty makes it much harder.

What he said was: "Tell me something about Ac-Me Plastics. Have you, for instance, any products that might be - sensitive?"

Meyer was right with him. "Military? No, we're too small for that. One or two products, though, that some of the big

155

companies would kill for... Oh, my God! I didn't mean that. There is industrial espionage, even on that level, I won't rule it out. But I'm not vain enough to put Ac-Me in that league. Besides, we haven't produced anything enviable in, probably years. I'm not saying I wouldn't *like* to," he added with a small, rueful smile.

"What about super foam?"

"Oh, that," Mr. Meyer dismissed it with a wave of his bottle. "That seems to exist mainly in the head of - what's his real name? - young Frayne. Edward advised against it."

"Did you always take his advice?"

"Yes, eventually." He sighed; a big, gusty sound. "I don't know what we'll do without him. Probably Martin Jones will grow into the job - Charlie seems to think so. But I don't imagine we'll ever have the same confidence... It's not really fair, I know; he's a competent chemist, from all I've heard. And yet, there can never be the trust, the sort of," he waved the bottle around a bit, as if trying to catch his meaning in it, "growing together, if you know what I mean. Edward was one of - of *us*, the nucleus, the company. Acton, Meyer, Quick and Morley... that worked. It worked," with his empty hand, he swept a half circle, including the house and gardens, "very well indeed. I suppose it doesn't matter if production slows down. Two of us are gone; Charlie and I aren't getting any younger - and anyway, we have everything we could possibly want. My sons are happy in other fields... And then, too, the whole industry is a kind of — what five-dollar word would Charlie use? Anachronism, that's it."

"How do you mean, anachronism?"

"Plastic is a dirty word anymore." Abe Meyer put down his empty bottle, interlaced his fingers in his lap, and stared at them. "In the days when we started, there was no question in any of our minds that we were doing mankind a favour. It was our idea, Bob's, mostly - Mr. Acton's - that it's still possible to make money and also do good. We would develop and produce materials, at a low cost, for safer containers, lighter shipping, better housing - better everything. We could pay our employees well, provide decent working conditions, keep them loyal, and still turn a profit. Well, we did that.

"We also contributed to an ecological nightmare. We

were, none of us, stupid men - only short-sighted. You know, sometimes I feel like a dinosaur... But then, there are the optimistic days, when I think maybe we can help turn things around. We haven't got much time, Charlie and I - but maybe we can set a reverse trend in motion and hand it on to younger men."

"Do you have a plan, a project, in mind?" Sims had a flash image of himself, with his little notebook and pencil, as an interviewer for some slick magazine. An inept one, for the dialogue was completely out of his control: he was here to provide counterpoint to Abraham Meyer's musings. He ought to steer the conversation back to murder, but was reluctant to stop the flow of confidences. Aside from the possibility of useful information, he was intrigued.

"I don't know, now. Yes, we'd got started recycling some materials, and Edward has - had - a pet notion that he could design biodegradable plastic. It was a side-line, you understand - no money in it, at least for some years. But, without him, I don't know."

"Is the rest of the research staff not involved?"

Abe Meyer shrugged largely. "Who knows? There is no money in it, like I said, for them or for the company. It's easy for me to forego profit, but how can I ask it of a young man, waiting to make his fortune? Still, there are some passionate young people - with brains, too - out there. If we can recruit some... Charlie and Edward hoped the Langtry girl would come along - she had such intelligence and – intensity? Is that what I mean?"

Sims, who knew he was referring to Eve Dumont, asked: "And she hasn't, now?"

"Oh well, she got married, you see. That changes everything."

"Why should it?" asked the liberated man, out of duty to his convictions, knowing all the while that it was true.

"Why? I don't know, exactly. Maybe, for some women it makes no difference. Look, when Gracie and I met, it was commonly accepted that a woman had either family or a job - mostly family, of course. I could - and did - divide my time unevenly between the company and my family. But I expected Gracie to make me and the kids the centre of her life. It's a sort of deal we made, without spelling it out: I give her everything that's in my power to make her happy, and she gives me all the attention I need. It's worked for us. She knew exactly what she was getting - knew about my ambition, knew that I'd be busy.

She hasn't been just a mother, or just a decorative hostess at the social functions that go with business - though she does both beautifully. She's also given me advice, encouraged me when things went wrong, believed in me... She's kept me honest and she's kept me sane. The business may not have been her choice; it came with the package. And she's a big, big part of my success. Okay, so it's an old-fashioned attitude. I'm old enough to get away with it.

"Social thinking has changed. So? That doesn't mean men and women have. I see attitudes much worse than mine - primitive attitudes - in the very young. I mean teenagers. Some of these boys treat their 'women' like medieval peasants - and the girls take it - ask for it, you might say. At least, in my day, there was an understanding that a man owed his wife protection and support - and courtesy. Girls have so much more choice now - and so many of them choose men – beasts - who treat them badly. The only way I can explain it is that human nature - the nature of relations between the sexes - hasn't changed all that much since we climbed down from the trees." He took a deep breath. "I can't believe I'm making speeches here, and you're letting me."

It had crossed Sims' mind that his host might be a little drunk. From two wine coolers? "So," he dropped into the little pool of reflection, "were you familiar with the notebooks Dr. Morley kept?"

"The famous little black book? Sure. What about it?"

"Well," said Sims, "the most recent one seems to be incomplete. I believe there is a meeting once a month, which you usually attend?"

"Not usually," said his host, "always. I know I haven't been at the office much lately, but I wouldn't miss the bull sessions."

"Can you recall - better yet, do you keep any record of - what was discussed at, say, the last two of these meetings?"

"Well now," Mr. Meyer said, groping in the ice bucket. Failing to find any more spritzer, he settled for a pineapple

158

juice. "Another beer? No? I don't take notes. The whole point is to talk freely about anything that's on any of our minds - we keep it pretty casual. What was discussed? Finances, mostly - whether we can afford some new equipment, expand, upgrade, that kind of thing. New projects we might start, how current projects are going..."

"Couldn't you be a little more specific, about the most recent one? It was only two weeks ago."

"Don't think I'm being secretive," said Mr. Meyer, with a charming lop-sided grin, "but I don't like to blurt out too much about my business. I can tell you that was the meeting in which we put the Waterman containers into production. I'm kind of proud of it: those bottles can be recycled almost indefinitely. Jones started it. So then, what else? Oh, yes, we shelved the superfoam nonsense, once and for good. Well, I mean, they'd been working on it for months, off and on - and I can tell you, in round figures, it cost a fortune - and it wasn't getting any better.

"Edward was convinced it never would be safe. He showed us formulas to prove it. We'd talked about it before. Brass actually came to me with the proposal... What gall! After he'd already gone to Charlie. Oh well," he chuckled indulgently, "he's young and ambitious, and he seems to think he's onto a great thing. So, I said, what the hell, give him another chance. I guess that would have been at last month's meeting. Then Edward nixed it, and that was that."

"You didn't decide on a new project this month?"

"Not positively. Edward wanted to push on with finding ways to re-use old plastics, and Charlie thought we should have a money-maker going at the same time, and I kind of sat on the fence, because nobody showed me anything I could get really worked up about."

"And so, you don't think Dr. Morley's death was related to his current work?"

Mr. Meyer spread his hands wide apart. "I don't see how it could be."

"Which leaves greed, jealousy and revenge."

"Right," said his host, with no trace of vagueness. "And I don't know anyone with any of those motives."

"No guesses?"

"None. I'd sort of expected you to ask where I was on

Saturday morning." At the detective's look of surprise, he explained, "I may not be in the office much, but I keep in touch. I was here. So was most of my family - sons, sons' wives, grandchildren - the whole zoo." He clasped his palms together. "Cast polymer resin. Water-tight."

"So it's okay if I cross you off the suspect list?" asked Sims, facetiously.

Abe Meyer raised his eyebrows. "I was never on it. Listen, if you insist, I'll tell Charlie to throw open the books, have an accountant translate - we're solvent. Only, promise to be a little bit discreet, don't broadcast our business all over the place. Okay?"

Sims nodded dumbly, imagining long afternoons spent with incomprehensible lists of figures. His first impulse had been to refuse, but he was curious to see how genuine the offer was - and also, one does not turn down any possible source of information. "Thank you. I'll let you know, if ever I have to resort to it."

Mrs. Meyer reappeared in time to conduct the visitor on the last leg of his journey, from the greenhouse to the front hall. It was almost as if the house were divided into his and her territories, like life, as described by Abe Meyer. If the lady was unhappy with this old-fashioned arrangement, it had left no visible mark on her.

To allay his own feelings of guilt and Lancelot's putative resentment at being left in the car so long (he was stretched along the back seat, snoring) Sims took him to the Kortright conservation area. They picnicked on groceries from the trunk and drank from the Humber river - one with the simple faith of ignorance; the other with a cautious optimism.

CHAPTER 19

On Friday, with no new leads and no ideas, he slept. In the evening, in the blissful knowledge that he would not be on duty, he accepted, for both himself and Lance, an invitation to the Morley house.

Brian was in a hurry to finish his dinner and get downtown: "Father Mike invited me to the Second Chance open house. You know about it?" he asked Sims, and receiving a nod, explained to his mother. "The city's full of kids with no homes. Can you imagine that? Sixteen, fifteen years old, even younger, with no place to go and nobody to care for them. What the program does is try to get them off the street and back into school. Every Friday night, there's this open house - well, it's just a storefront, really, and a different one practically every time - whatever space they can borrow - they're trying to raise money for a permanent place. Anyway, the idea is just to let the kids come in, give them something to eat and talk to them. Father Mike says I could be useful - first time anybody ever thought my age was an asset!"

When he had gone, Amanda gazed at the door for a while. "Well, that seems to be good for him."

"I saw Mr. Meyer yesterday," said Sims. "That's not a complete non sequitur; he has two of those kids from Second Chance at his house. He must be a good man," he added with a glance inviting comment.

"Yes," Amanda agreed, "I think he is. He and Gracie are very good people. Of course, it was always a policy of Mr. Acton's..."

They both burst out laughing. "But it's true," she continued, when seriousness had been restored, "The Actons, the Meyers, Charlie Quick, Mr. Draper, even my poor unsociable Edward, they all had, have, a strong sense of social obligation."

"Do you have much contact with them, now?"

"Charlie calls... to ask if I'm all right. I wish he wouldn't; we really don't know what to say to each other. Abe Meyer was at the funeral - but you saw him. Gracie sent a bouquet from her garden and a note. She couldn't come, because of some domestic crisis... They try to keep in touch, out of duty."

"But you don't especially like them. Why?"

"It's not that, exactly," she groped for the right tone. "It's not about liking one another. I was always made welcome at the bridge nights and the company parties - I just never fit in. They're so... so up to date and 'in touch'... so handsome and clever and well-dressed and...and confident. I always felt - I don't know... out of my depth, I suppose... a bit uncomfortable. You see, I'm not good with people. I could never bring home a brace of troubled adolescents - it was all I could manage seeing my own children through those years. I'm happier with my grebes – they're simple."

"Is that the only reason?" he persisted. "You never had any qualms about them – I mean Acton and Meyer - being on the level? For instance, the way the company is run... nothing odd about that?"

She gave him an uncharacteristically shrewd look. "What are you looking for?"

"Motive," he said simply. "If you noticed anything?"

"Yes, I believe it is on the level, as you say. For example, with all this new awareness of the environment, they've been working on - well, anyway, Edward has - on cleaner, safer products. He wasn't happy about the progress, complained that young people aren't interested, and it's about their future... But he always had the backing of management. He said Abe Meyer was very enthusiastic."

"He does seem to be. And Mr. Quick?"

"I'm not sure. I didn't hear of any opposition from him. Edward only complained about the youngsters."

"Does that include Martin Jones?"

"No... it should have done, I suppose: he must be within a year or two of profit-sharing, and this scheme would certainly cut profits. It was the others he had trouble with; the new one, what's his name?"

"Paul Arnott?"

"No, he's only a student or something. The one they secretly called Brass. Frayne, David Frayne."

Sims was all ears. "What about him?"

"Well, it seems, far from getting involved in the recycling projects, he'd come up with some potentially dangerous insulating material. Edward was opposed to pursuing

162

development on it, and this young man was apparently quite upset."

"How upset?"

She shook her head. "I wasn't there. I only know that Edward came home more than once, angry and bewildered. Finally, he said, he'd stopped the project - what was it called? Some kind of foam. He'd stopped it once and for all, and Frayne would just have to lump it."

"Did he say why he stopped it?"

"At interminable length," she smiled sadly, "I don't mean to be flippant, but he did go on. I didn't understand the technical details, of course - it was not my job to. The gist was that this stuff might break down in low pressure, and would definitely break down in a crash, and release some awful pollutants. Into the plane, and the atmosphere."

"But then, nobody would want to use it, would they?"

"Wouldn't they? It's supposed to be lighter and cheaper than anything they're using now."

"The Ac-Me management wouldn't touch it,"

"Well, I don't know. It seems they were fairly keen at first. It was hoped - anyway, from what I gathered, Charlie Quick was hoping - that it could be made safer. Edward disagreed. They had some, what for Edward anyway, were very emotional discussions on the subject."

"When?"

"When what?"

"The discussions!" he nearly shouted. "Try to remember."

"All right. It was recently. Early this month, and at least once, last month. Maybe twice. He didn't report on every meeting, you know."

Sims tried to calm down. He took three deep breaths. Then he explained. "These would be important meetings, from Edward's point of view, wouldn't they?" She nodded. "Well, then, he would note them in his book. The little black book. And there isn't a word. What there is - I think there is - at least one missing page. Somebody tore it out."

"I see," she said. "I see. You think Edward was killed for opposing a product?"

"For opposing a product that could make somebody an awful lot of money. Not just somebody, several people." He told her briefly about the alibis he had been collecting, and summed up: "How would you like to take a trip tomorrow? Unless you're busy with the grebes?"

"No," she said, "I was at the lake the last two days - I prefer to go during the week - less traffic. Where are we going?"

"Elmvale. I'll pick you up at 9:30... Oh, wait. Maybe that's not a good idea. I have to go to Ac-Me first..."

"Don't worry," she said, "I won't faint or cry or anything. I want to be in on this - I owe him something."

"I see," said Sims, and he did.

With coffee and the excellent cognac he had brought, their conversation turned to other matters. He was apprised of the grebe population's doings, and found himself genuinely interested. He especially admired the photographs of the new birds - two of the nests had hatched over the past week - trying the water for the first time. When she talked about waterfowl, she was not at all tongue-tied; her face took on an animation it normally lacked. Normally? he checked himself; he'd never seen her in normal circumstances. He'd met her in the worst possible moment, and since then, there had been nothing but grief and frustration. At least, he supposed it would be frustrating to have one's spouse murdered and the police come up with nothing, arrest nobody, in almost two weeks. In any case, when she talked about her birds, her lake, her pictures, Amanda Morley was very attractive.

It would be a long trip; Sims made sure Lance had eaten a good breakfast and taken care of business. On the way back, they could stop, but the drive to Elmvale had to be made all at one go. He filled the gas-tank. Amanda was ready, standing on the front steps, holding a carryall.

"What's that? Provisions for an army?"

"No," she said, "I thought, *we* could have lunch anywhere, but Lancelot might need his own water and bowl."

"A bowl! I could become very dependent on you."

He should not have said that - things sometimes fell out of his mouth when he wasn't paying attention. But she laughed, if perhaps a little nervously, so it was all right.

He drove past the factory at 9:57. There were cars in the parking lot, all clustered at the factory end, leaving the area near the fire exit empty. In the street abutting the Ac-Me property, he found a curb-side space and parked. There was little activity, besides children and the occasional dog. He would wait until the factory workers' break. Amanda glanced at the map once or twice, though they had both already memorized the shortest route to Elmvale. At last, Sims started the engine.

They cruised past Conrad and Christine Smith's restored century house with its authentic gingerbread trim, at exactly 11:56. He had done some calculated speeding, not enough to attract attention. A killer as cool and smart as the one he was after, wouldn't take a chance on highway speed-traps. Still, here they were, well in time for lunch. And, in fact, Charles Quick's enormous black car was in the driveway.

"Damn," he remarked, "I was hoping to talk to the daughter. Not that she's likely to say anything new," he added. "Anyway, Mr. Quick is not my favourite suspect. Unless he's much stronger than he looks, the method is impossible. Besides, if his motive were money; if his problem were the production of a dangerous and lucrative substance, surely he could simply have overruled Dr. Morley and produced it anyway..."

"Unless," she said slowly, "Edward threatened to quit and expose it... He might, you know."

For a moment he had forgotten who his passenger was. He began to apologize for his insensitivity, but she interrupted. "Look, Alec. I know what happened to my husband. I have good reason to want his murderer caught. I want to help. If you keep pussyfooting around, trying to protect my sensibilities, keeping things from me, I can't help, can I? So, stop it. All right?"

"All right," he said. "It's an unusual situation - so, bear with me if you can."

"That's fair," she agreed. "Now, I'm trying to keep an open mind, and I see that Charlie is possible. I don't believe it, though. Not because he's too frail... well, that too, but mostly I can't see him killing anyone, let alone his oldest and closest friend. They were together for twenty years. Nursing that company along at first; jubilating over its successes, and then, lately, worrying about the harm they have done. Caring. And I don't see money as a real motive: Charlie has enough. So does Abe Meyer. I've never known them to do anything dishonest, not even when they didn't know how to meet next month's invoices... I know Edward wouldn't have stayed otherwise. Who else is there?"

"Martin Jones," he said. "He lives higher on the hog than his salary can possibly support... Have you met his wife?"

"Yes," said Amanda, "a few times, at company functions."

"What was your impression?"

She hesitated. "You'll think I'm just being an old cat, because she's gorgeous and... well - poised."

"No, I won't. I've met her. Come on,"

"I don't like her. I think she's trying to be something she isn't - and worse. I think she's making Martin over in her fake image... Him, I rather like, by the way."

"Yes, so do I. Would you say she was pushing him?"

"Like a bulldozer."

"Demanding that he be more successful, buy more showy things, make more money?"

"Yes, I see. Would that be enough?"

"It's been known to happen." He proceeded to tell her all he knew about Jones' alibi. "So, he could just have got there and back. Like Mr. Quick - it would be tight, but possible."

"And he lied about - or forgot to mention - going to the garden supply place."

"That's right."

She sighed. "I see. Who else?"

"David Frayne. You know the motive. He appears to have been in the gym at his apartment building all morning. His car was in the garage, but he could have rented a car, taken a taxi, had a friend pick him up... A bus that runs past Ac-Me takes about forty minutes and stops two blocks from his door - say forty-five altogether. There is another exit from the garage. He was seen by the pool attendant, coming and going; he was seen by the doorman, coming and going - the question is, was he seen by anyone else, in between? I may have to question some fellow tenants."

"Could he get back in through the parking lot exit? Do tenants have keys? I assume it's kept locked, in the kind of place that has a doorman. What security?"

He told her, as he would have told a fellow detective on a case. It crossed his mind that this was unorthodox, if not precisely against the rules. But then, other than DiMarco, who was still awaiting the result of his exam, he had no colleague whom he trusted as he had come to trust Amanda Morley. Besides, as she had said, nobody else had her reason to want this case solved. As a suspect, he had been only half-hearted about her at the start - by now, having had word that her films "were full of ducks and weeds, no people", he had altogether dismissed her.

"So, it's not very likely he could get out and in again, without being noticed. It's too bad - I've only met him once or twice, but there is something about that boy I don't like."

"I feel the same way," said Sims. "And so does the doorman at his building. But unpopularity is not evidence."

"The doorman," she said softly. "We lived in apartments, in Montreal and when we first came here... The elevator goes down to the laundry room and lockers and things. Doesn't it, there?"

"Sure it does. Oh. Oh, I see. Why should he go through the lobby, you mean? To pick up his mail?"

"Both ways? And on a Saturday, when mail isn't delivered?"

"For the exercise?"

"True, some people run up and down stairs. But then, why not all the way from his apartment?"

"It could have been, at least in one direction," he said. "The stairwell to the apartments is on the far side of the elevators. There is a separate flight down to the facilities. I can't see anyone working out for over two hours and then climbing seventeen floors, though. Even for a fanatic, that's too much. Besides, the doorman says he looked tired."

"Then, what we have is another possible. Just barely possible. That's three. You said four."

Once again, he hesitated in a gentlemanly fashion, but she was looking at him so intently, he could neither lie nor keep silence. "Eve Dumont."

Amanda smiled. "I see you've heard the rumours. Well, of course you have."

"I believe it was more than just rumours," he said gently.

There was a different quality of silence, and then a long release of breath. "Maybe you'd better find a nice place to park. Lance needs a rest stop anyway."

Hearing his name, the dog was all ears and muzzle, hanging over the back of the seat, wetting Sims' shoulder. "Says he's all for it."

Attaching Lancelot's collar to the length of rope he always kept in the trunk, and the other end to a tree: "Sorry, kid, it's too close to the highway for you to run loose." He sat beside Amanda on a grassy slope. "I don't think my car is bugged," he told her, "but if you're more comfortable outside, all right. You have my undivided attention."

"I know about it. Not from gossip - I know, because Edward told me. We hadn't been close - to tell the truth, we were barely on speaking terms at the time. Lots of reasons, none of them relevant now. Anyway, he formed this... attachment. It wasn't as silly as it sounds; lots of men in their forties end up with women some years younger... and she wasn't a teenager. Oh, I know, she's beautiful and sexy and all that - but, actually, Edward wasn't so bad himself. He was terribly clever, urbane - he could be charming, too. They had things in common. French literature, music, chemistry... interests he could never share with me... and this new-found need to make amends to the world. Also, and I guess the most important thing, they were both... unhappy. Well, as I said, Edward and I had problems... and she broke up with her... her doctor... They had been living together for some time, I gathered. He accepted a residency in Quebec City. Anyway, she needed someone... And he was only human."

Amanda stared away over the trees. Lance was rolling in the grass with all his limbs in the air, clowning: Sims looked at him. What would I do, he asked himself, if a heart-broken Eve Dumont turned to me for comfort? Anything, he answered promptly. Even if I were married? Depends on the marriage, doesn't it? What if my wife were barely speaking to me? Depends on why. What would I have done to her, to deserve it? When something of the sort had actually happened in his life, he hadn't known exactly what he'd done to Marie. Now, he did: not being what she needed... Had it been his fault? Hers? Anyone's?

168

And, if, he asked himself, at that time, a heartbroken Eve Langtry turned to me for comfort, would I have dropped everything and run to her? Like a shot. Only human.

"Yes," he said to Amanda. "What happened then?"

She laughed briefly, bitterly. "He fell in love. Oh yes," she nodded emphatically, "like a sack of coal. For the first time in his life. It's all right, really. I knew by then that he had never been more than fond of me, and even that had worn down to habit. I was willing to let him go. Oh yes, he did ask. We were half way to settling the matter... amicably."

"And?"

"And then Dr. Dumont returned. Out of the blue. He'd changed his mind, come to his senses, was ready to settle down. And she went back to him. Of course she did. Any neutral observer could have seen *that* coming. And they lived happily ever after."

There was an even longer silence. Lance stopped rolling in the grass and began nosing around the base of his tree. A bird called shrilly, twice, somewhere among the foliage. Sims said, "And you didn't."

"We didn't. There was no point then, in a divorce... Anyway, we made a kind of peace. We lived in the same house, had the same children, took meals together more often than not... talked. We talked more than before... Got to know each other better, I think. Really, we weren't married, in anything but name, but we did become pretty good friends. It was convenient, and neither of us had anywhere to go. So, if you want to look at it that way, I had a motive - and she didn't. But two years have passed... I've actually been happier in the last two years than I was in the ten years before."

"You stopped going to the parties, stopped seeing the people at Ac-Me... I understand that. What I don't understand is, how they - I mean Eve and Edward," she winced slightly, but nodded for him to continue, "how they could go on working together, as if nothing had happened. He had a lot invested in the company - but she - why didn't she leave?"

Amanda shrugged. "People are strange sometimes. I suspect she never took the affaire as seriously as he did. Maybe she didn't even know... Edward was awfully good at covering his feelings. Most people think he didn't have any. I knew better - or should have, before it was too late. I know that sometimes he held himself together by sheer discipline."

"And alcohol?"

She removed her gaze from the treetops and transferred it to a dandelion near her foot. "Yes," she said faintly. And then, in a more conversational tone: "He'd done his share of social drinking before, and the odd after-dinner whisky or two at home... but it was then, after he lost... her... that it became a problem. Not," she added, with a quick level glance at Sims, "a problem for us - the children or myself. We knew, when he locked himself in the study all evening, that he had Mr. Walker for company. The next day, he would go to work as usual. Sometimes I almost thought it would be better if he'd made a scene; if he sang or laughed or shouted or something... I was kidding myself, of course: I wouldn't have preferred a scene, not really. That wasn't Edward's style, anyway. He simply made it clear that it was none of our business."

Sims kept quiet for a minute, to let the subject pass. Then he asked: "Does Brian know?"

"About the - about her? I don't think so. Louise wasn't told, either - but I'm fairly certain she guessed."

"Charles Quick knows. So does Mrs. Benz, the glass washing lady. No-one said anything to me until I cornered them. I hope they have the same reticence at the inquest."

Amanda looked at him sharply. "Why?"

"Because, to a lot of people, what you've just told me would seem a good argument for suicide." She began to protest, but he stopped her. "I'm convinced. You're convinced. We have at least three people with motive, means and opportunity. The scene, the victim's actions, cyanide, rubber gloves, someone seen ducking through a hedge. It adds up to homicide, all right, but it's all circumstantial. If I had just one solid thing - an object, a footprint, a witness - something to connect one of those people to the scene!"

"The notebook?" she asked timidly.

"Hm, yes. Mr. Quick has been so cooperative, and yet he couldn't - or wouldn't - tell me what should have been on those missing pages. Or, rather, the one page I can prove is missing."

"Did you check Edward's calendar? In his study?"

"Yes," he admitted, "first thing, after looking for a suicide note. It told me nothing. But I wouldn't mind having a look at Mr. Quick's calendar... All right," he said, brightening. "That's next on the agenda. Being on night shift has its advantages. In the meantime," he added, "it would be just as well to keep that... other matter... to ourselves."

"Good. We won't talk about it anymore."

They got back into the car, tugging a reluctant dog away from whatever he was trying to dig up among the roots. Soon after, they stopped at an attractive roadside diner and polished off enough fried chicken for any four people, plus a piece of chocolate cream pie each. I can afford to indulge, Sims told himself; I've had one decent meal all week. They talked about everything except murder, Ac-Me Plastics and the people who worked there. Edward Morley was not mentioned again that day.

CHAPTER 20

On Sunday, after a brisk walk with Lance, after a short and relatively friendly talk with Mrs. Field, after a morning of intensive cleaning of the apartment (How can one person, who is almost never at home, make so much mess?) Sims cooked dinner for Father Mike. Sims had no shame: before taking her home yesterday, he had asked Amanda Morley to accompany him to the supermarket, and questioned her extensively on the preparation of stir-fried beef with red peppers and celery. In fact, it was quite a simple dish, and turned out very well.

"So," his guest said, over a second helping liberal enough to make up for the cautious first one, "there is a new woman in your life."

"What makes you think that?"

"Elementary, my dear Sims," he counted the reasons off on stubby fingers: "This is not spaghetti, and yet it is eminently edible. Therefore, someone must have instructed you. Also, you spent anything up to ten dollars on a haircut in some establishment that does not use a lawnmower. Also, this apartment is cleaner than at any time since that very pretty nurse showed you the door. Am I right?"

"About one thing, yes," Sims admitted. "I did get the recipe from a friend. A woman friend, not a girlfriend. But you're wrong about everything else. It so happens that the barber I've always gone to has a new assistant, who may have a lighter hand than the old man, but doesn't charge any more. And," he counted off the second finger, "I always clean up for company - even if it's only you. Amanda hasn't even been here. And, furthermore," he added the last finger, "Jody didn't 'show me the door' as you so charmingly put it; I stopped calling her. Therefore, Sherlock, don't give up your day job."

The priest laughed, "I wish it were! It's more of a day and night and morning and noon job. Still, it has its moments. Who is Amanda?"

"Brian Morley's mother."

"Ah!" Father Mike put down his fork, the better to attend this interesting subject. "Light begins to dawn. Had any luck with the investigation?"

"Not really. I've found out some things... But it's all circumstantial. Lots of little bricks that don't add up to a wall. I still have three suspects, maybe four."

"Mrs. Morley isn't one of them, I take it? Good," he added when Sims shook his head, "the boy has enough problems. And suicide isn't a possibility?"

"No. I'm sure he was murdered."

"Again, good. I think Brian is afraid of that possibility - he denies it so vehemently. He's a nice boy, Alec. Very unhappy and confused, understandably enough. Once the reason for his father's death is resolved, he can get on with his life - not before."

"I'm doing my best," Sims told him. "Do you think Brian will make a good clergyman?"

"Now, that's a question. In fact, that's two questions. One, will he become a clergyman? And two, would he be good at it? The second answer is easy: yes. The boy has intelligence and conviction: whatever he chooses to do, he will do well. The first," he shrugged, "who can tell? Right now, his faith in his father is a bit shaken. This faith has never been examined; it was a given, a pillar of his life. So, he's defending it, if only against his own doubts. Now, that's all tied up with faith in Our Father, you see - in Brian's emotional life, though he may not be aware of it. Imagine two ropes, twined around each other. If one seems to be fraying, you cling all the harder to the remaining rope. That's not a bad thing - faith is a wonderful thing - but it's not a vocation. Until he's sorted out his feelings and beliefs, we won't know whether he has a vocation.

"What he does have," Father Mike leaned back in his chair, "is a way with my street kids. I want to recruit him as a counsellor. I'd like him to take the summer course at St. Bartholomew in Chicago. Do you think his mother could spare him for six weeks?"

"If it's what Brian wants, Amanda won't oppose it."

"I'll sign him up then. Whatever he decides to do with his life, I want to keep him as a volunteer. Besides, the atmosphere at St. Bart's will do him good. The course doesn't start till the end of June... by then, you'll have all this other mess cleared up."

"You're right," said Sims, "faith is a wonderful thing. I

wish you'd lend me some."

They had banana cream pie for dessert, two hefty wedges for Father Mike, who said, "I'll do penance for this tomorrow. Mrs. Morley is an excellent teacher."

"Father, I cannot tell a lie. I did not bake this - I defrosted it."

They had coffee and cigarettes, but no cognac, because Sims had balked at replacing the one he'd left at Amanda's. He did find, however, two inches of scotch in a forgotten bottle. While drinking it, they talked about the rewards and frustrations of their occupations. Sims enjoyed the opportunity to grouse about his new partner to someone familiar with the workings of the police department. Father Mike enjoyed any and every chance to hold forth on his youth programs.

"Do you know an Abraham Meyer?" Sims asked him.

"Meyer? I know a Gracie Meyer... oh, that would be her husband. They've been a great help."

"I understand they have a couple of your kids living with them."

"Oh, yes," said the priest. "These are the kind of people we need more of - the kind who put their money where their mouth is - not to mention their time, their home, their - for want of a better expression - parenting skills. Do you know, in the past four years, they've had eight - no, nine - kids, and only sent back one." He shook his head sadly. "A hard case, that little girl. We lost her, finally."

"She died?"

"Oh, no! She went to prison. What a terrible waste! On the other hand, I don't know," he said, spreading his hands, first one then the other, palm upward, weighing, "At least it separates her from a very destructive young man. You can't always be sure what's best for people. Why are you interested in the Meyers?"

Sims told him: "He's president of the plastics company where Edward Morley worked, and was killed. I've talked to him... Frankly, I think he's too good to be true."

"Is he a suspect? No? That's a relief - I'd hate to lose him. I don't know about his business practices, but as a supporter of Second Chance, he's literally a God-send. Besides, there is no such thing as too good." The priest settled back comfortably and sighed. "I suppose, in your

174

job, it becomes a habit to expect the worst of people. It doesn't give you pleasure, though, does it?

"Alec, have you ever considered changing jobs?" At Sims' look of alarm, he continued in a more conciliatory tone. "It's not just this... I've wondered for some time. Heaven knows, a policemen with your - how shall I put this, not to sound like a wuss, as the kids say? You have a sense of fairness, an open mind, a... well, a gentleness that I, for one, don't see in cops as often as I'd like. But," he held up his palm to prevent interruption, "I don't think you're as happy as you should be. I suspect you don't have a vocation." He blew air out through his considerable nose. "There, I've said it. I've been wanting to, and now I have. If I'm wrong, just tell me to butt out, and I'll never mention it again."

Sims was taken aback. Stunned would not be putting it too strongly. But, after all, no harm had been done. He simply had to explain. "I've always wanted to be a policeman, since I was a kid. I never seriously considered anything else."

"What *did* you consider - unseriously?"

"Oh, well," the detective smiled, "I once decided to be a trick-rider in the rodeo - I must have been all of four, when my dad took me to see one. Seems I drove my parents crazy, pestering them to buy me a horse. And then there was an essay contest... grade six, I think. I won the county finals and had my picture in Le Nord and a mention in the Kapuskasing Times. So, for about three weeks, I was going to be a famous writer. I've outgrown that, too."

Father Mike looked at him thoughtfully, while he refilled their glasses. Then he asked, "Why a policeman?"

"Because of the OPP, I guess. You know in the small communities provincial police do a lot more than chase speeders. They were admirable men. I'm convinced most of them still are. They check on fire permits, find stray children and cattle, rescue people in a snowstorms, control the rowdies on a Friday night... You know; protect the community, in a very direct, personal sort of way.

"And then, of course," his gaze drifted off into the distance, along with his thoughts, "the time our store was robbed. Dad was upset - almost incoherent with rage... Now, I think it was more a question of pride than anything else - I think he felt belittled in the sight of his family, his neighbours... Alastair Sims let himself be robbed! I've since wondered if his decision to move to Hearst, a year or so later, was more from shame than good business sense. Of course, nobody else saw it that way. There were two young, armed thugs. Nobody expected him to get killed for a few dollars and some portable stock. Anyway," Sims focused once more on his listener, "the OPP officers were great. One was Constable Saunders. Pete knew just how to talk to Dad. Calmed him down, got a good description out of him, reassured the rest of us. And, of course, caught the robbers in a couple of days. Not all that difficult - we didn't have a lot of criminal types in the area, and these boys were stupid. They kept four boxes of shotgun shells for their own use... At the time, though, it seemed to me a feat of heroic proportions. That's the kind of hero I wanted to be."

"And are you?" asked the priest very softly.

"Sometimes. Yes," Sims amplified, "some cases do give me that kind of satisfaction. And some don't. I imagine Pete Saunders felt the same way; he had his share of domestic disputes and people burning down their own barns for the insurance. In any case, he left soon after - whether promoted, transferred or resigned, I don't know."

"How old were you?"

"Ten, just about."

"An impressionable age," the priest said thoughtfully, then added with a small laugh: "As if all ages weren't impressionable, given the right circumstances! But then, why are you on the big city force?"

"Oh, that was mainly to please my parents. They insisted I go to college. I guess I became more ambitious - the reasoning was something like: if a uniformed policeman is good, a detective must be better. And there's television: Dragnet is more exciting than Andy Williams."

Father Mike nodded. "So, now you're in the big time. Big crime, big heroics, no regrets, no dissatisfaction."

"I wouldn't go quite that far... As you know, some of what we do is tedious - some of what we have to deal with is petty, or disgusting - some of the people we have to deal with would make the most hardened criminal in Hearst sick to his stomach... or the most hardened law-man, for that matter. As far as I know, Pete Saunders never had a single child-abuse case in his career."

"You knew this officer quite well?"

"Fairly well - he was courting my oldest sister for a while."

"And?"

"And, nothing. My dad didn't approve. I wasn't privy to the details, of course, but I gather the Saunderses were not quite respectable... something like that. Anyway, after he left the area, we never heard of him again."

The whisky was gone and the hour late; soon, Father Mike took his departure. Sims, accompanied by Lancelot, walked him to his car, and then kept going around the block, twice. "That will have to do you, kid. I'm back on days tomorrow."

After washing the dishes and emptying the ashtray, filling the dog's water-dish and making up his couch for its night duty, Sims found himself standing a long time in front of the mirror. The man facing him, fresh haircut and trimmed moustache notwithstanding, didn't look that great. Not ugly, no; that would at least have been interesting. Not so old and worn as he sometimes felt: a little grey in the hair, the odd crow's foot around the eyes lent his face some character, though he could do without the vertical lines on either side of the mouth. Do I frown that much? he asked himself. All in all, given a few pounds' leeway, not that bad, either.

He didn't look happy, that was true. "Damn the priest," he said aloud, but immediately recanted. "No, don't. Well, curb him a bit; hold his tongue once in a while, and make him, if possible, without reducing the good he does, a bit less astute." He laughed without mirth: he'd just said what amounted to his first prayer in years, and it was wishy-washy, equivocal. He stared at his reflection again while brushing his teeth - better: this time the image amused him - finished his ablutions and went to bed.

That he should dream of Norris was no surprise. Nor that his father, as victim of a crime, should figure in the dream. That Alastair Sims should resemble Edward Morley, and that the policeman calming and helping him, should be seven feet tall, with a neatly trimmed salt-and-pepper moustache, was odd; in fact, Pete

Saunders had been fair and smooth of face, not much over the minimum size requirement, and quite a lot younger than the present Sims. But that, half way through, the victim should turn on the cop, berate him for his unsanctified relations with Marie and reduce him to tears, was disturbing enough to wake him in a sweat.

"Get off me, you beast!" he shoved Lancelot's head roughly from his chest, "I can't breathe." Of course, when the animal, startled out of a sound sleep, sidled into a dark corner, he repented of his harshness. "I'm sorry, kid, but you're just too big. Come on back here, and sleep on the rug."

CHAPTER 21

Duty did not require Sims to remain in the office all day. Having answered one false alarm and taken routine statements in a B&E that had occurred during the night and been adequately reported by the uniformed team on the scene, he and Petersen agreed to split up for an hour. Sims would have been reluctant to suggest this himself but when Petersen did, he jumped at the opportunity. Since Petersen needed the car, he asked to be dropped off at Birchmount and Denison.

"Into gardening all of a sudden?" his partner asked.

"Yeah," Sims told him, "I'm thinking of it. Pick me up here when you're finished."

In fact, he had come to interview a secretary named Roberta Farrell. He had seen, and at the time thought nothing about, a letter of reference in the Ac-Me personnel files, addressed to Summer Place Nurseries. His badge got him into the office with a minimum of fuss, though not without some curious stares. And there she was: dark, petite, short curly brown hair brushed off her forehead, bright-eyed and very young.

"Just routine," he assured the girl. "Of course, you know about the death of Dr. Morley." She nodded, looking puzzled. "We need to document the movements of all the people associated with the deceased, at the critical time." Officious enough? It should have been 'movements, at the critical time, of all the people', but she didn't seem to notice; nodded again. "Well then," Sims continued, "I understand you are engaged to David Frayne."

"Yes," she said warily.

"And I understand that you and he spent Saturday, the twelfth, together."

"Yes," she said.

"What part of the day would this be?"

"All afternoon," she said.

"Could you tell me a little more about it?" asked Sims, trying to keep the exasperation out of his voice.

"Yes," said the girl. "David came over to my place at around 11:30. We had lunch. Then we went out shopping. Then we got back to my place around dinner time, and soon after that, he went home."

He wasn't getting far with this witness. She didn't seem hostile, and yet she was telling him nothing. How to bring her out? "It's quite a coincidence," he remarked conversationally, "your working here. I mean, this is where Dr. Jones buys his garden supplies, I've heard."

"Not coincidence at all," she corrected. "I used to work at Ac-Me. I guess you knew that already. So, when I said something about being sick of the smell, Martin said, why don't I get a job in a garden store? Just kind of kidding, you know. He said, it smells like flowers. And he happened to know this place was looking for a secretary. So I applied, and that's all there was to it."

"Of course," Sims agreed. "Then you know Dr. Jones quite well?"

"Sure, I used to. Not since I left, though - David doesn't hang out with the older people at the plant."

"Of course," he repeated, wondering what made Jones, his contemporary, or near enough, 'older people'. Where was the line? Thirty, thirty-five? Don't trust anyone over? He said, "That makes sense. Whom does he hang out with? Ferdy Arnott, I should think."

"Yes, Ferdy is a good friend. A bit juvenile, you know, but he's a lot of fun."

"Did you see him on that weekend?"

"Sure. Well, we were supposed to do something fun together, all three of us. So when David got sick, I wanted to stay with him, but he said why don't I go with Ferdy anyway. I wouldn't have except David practically shoved us out the door. Said he just wanted to sleep. I guess he was right, because he was all better on Monday when I called him."

"It must have been a 24-hour flu," Sim remarked, "if he was feeling fine on Saturday," Sims prompted.

"Well, not exactly fine," the girl said. "When he got to my place, he was tired and out of sorts. I figured, too much working out - he overdoes it sometimes. After a workout, he's usually starved, but he had hardly anything for lunch. So I said, maybe we should forget about shopping, but he said, no, he promised and anyway, he had errands to run. Well, that was prob'ly just to make me feel better, because, really, he only wanted to drop his jacket off at the cleaners. I didn't see that was so urgent. And then he came along

180

like an angel, looking at bedroom suites all afternoon. He didn't like anything, though - I guess I should have noticed something was wrong."

"Oh, I don't know," said Sims. "Men hide these things - they think it's weak or something to admit they're sick."

She smiled gratefully. I must have hit a right note somewhere, he thought; she's coming along nicely now. She was a pretty girl at any time; extremely so, when she smiled. And yet he was oddly detached. Because she's only 22, because she's engaged to a man I find unsympathetic? he wondered, or is it something about her?

"Well, he did admit it, though," said Roberta Farrell. "When we got back to my apartment. I got dinner ready while David watched some of the 6 o'clock news, but then he didn't have any appetite. That's when he finally said he wasn't feeling too good, and went home early."

"He must be very devoted to you. Of course, that isn't at all surprising," Sims added gallantly. It had its effect: she blushed prettily, with no effect on Sims.

"Oh, isn't it?!" she protested. "Well, it still surprises me. I mean, David could have any girl he wanted, he's so smart and good-looking and a real go-getter, you know? He's going to be famous one day. Not all that far away, either," she smiled knowingly.

"I've heard something about an invention," Sims remarked, without so much as a hint of eye-roll.

"It's called SuperFoam," she reported earnestly. "It's terrific. But that's all I can say, because it's still a secret. I guess you know there's, like industrial spies and things, and this is so big, people would kill for it..." She stared up at him with great round eyes that did nothing to his blood-pressure. "You don't think? I mean, David's boss knew about SuperFoam... Oh, my God! David might be in danger!"

"I wouldn't say that," the detective soothed. "After all, everyone at Ac-Me knows about it, don't they?"

"I guess," she conceded, "but not as much as David."

"Well," he said, "it never hurts to be careful. I suppose, he *is* careful? I mean, he doesn't go around telling everyone?"

"Of course not. Even Ferdy hasn't got the formula, and

they work together. He didn't even tell me all that much - just that this is going to make us rich some day. Anyway, I wouldn't understand."

"A lot of specialists don't confide in their loved ones for that reason," Sims put in.

"That's right," said Roberta. "Though sometimes I wish he would. I mean, I did work at Ac-Me for nearly a year, I know something about the place. David gets funny sometimes; it goes with being a genius, I guess. I mean, he can be real moody, impatient, sort of. Like with the news that day we're talking about. He got all grumpy because there was nothing going on in the world. Of course," she reconsidered, "that could have been just because he was coming down with flu. Still, you know, sometimes I wish he could be a bit more like Ferdy, not so serious."

"Perhaps when you're married, you can help him to lighten up," Sims suggested.

"I hope so," she agreed. "And it's good for him to have a friend like Ferdy, too, somebody to make him laugh."

"Yes, Mr. Arnott is a likeable young man," Sims led on. "You seem quite fond of him."

Roberta looked startled for a second, blushed again. Unusual, and rather attractive, in a girl of her colouring. "Oh, not like that," she protested. "I mean, not like being *interested* in him. He's just a good friend of David's. Besides, Ferdy couldn't be interested in me."

"Why ever not? You are very attractive, his own age - no, no, I'm not suggesting anything improper - but it would be only natural if he perhaps envied his friend just a little bit?"

"No," she said, very firmly. "Nothing like that. Ferdy admires David so much... sometimes, I almost think, too much, even..."

"Do you mean, more than friendship?"

"Not like that!" She blushed furiously. Her eyes became very bright and her mouth set in a straight line. Then, seeing no judgment in the policeman's face, she relaxed somewhat. "No, I mean, just like, hero-worship. But he's, you know, hanging around all the time. And, well, sometimes, feel kind of, you know, left out. A little bit jealous."

182

"That's not unusual," Sims told her. "Working together, they have a lot in common. It's you David is going to marry. Ferdy will find a girl of his own, some day."

"Maybe," she said. "I hope so. I hope it happens before they go into business together."

"Business?"

"Well, sure," she said with mild scorn. "You don't think David's going to waste his talent working for Mr. Meyer all his life? After SuperFoam, all the big companies will want him. But he's going to tell them no. With the royalties, and the fame, and Ferdy's got a real old grandfather with money, when he sees what a good investment it is, they plan to start their own company. I'll run the office, until we have a baby. David's got it all worked out."

"It sounds wonderful" said Sims, "I wish you luck."

Glancing at his watch, he realized the interview had better come to an end. He thanked her warmly and made his way down to the main floor, where he bought a big pot of pink geraniums, as cover. Petersen, of course, laughed. "Darling! It's just your colour! Brings out your eyes."

Sims didn't care: he thought it would be perfect in Amanda Morley's workroom. He also thought it was time, instead of imposing any more on her hospitality, to take her out for a change. Where? He had no idea what would appeal to her, but it should be nice - something with more tone than a highway diner. The Mermaid? He had seen her enjoy a grilled trout; seafood looked like a good bet. But would she accept? Well, what had he to lose? Face. She wouldn't laugh, anyway; she would say no with grace and charm. Or yes, also with grace and charm. And that would make this, their last evening before the dreaded inquest, a pleasant one. Afterwards, tomorrow, he might have to keep his distance: it is not done to fraternize with the witnesses in a murder investigation. And that, he reflected, was one more reason to wind this up quickly: he didn't want to be deprived of her company any longer than was absolutely necessary.

"Two bits for your thoughts," said Petersen behind the wheel. He'd just run a very dark yellow light and swerved around a delivery van making a right turn.

"I wish you'd drive more carefully," Sims told him. "After what nearly happened a couple of weeks ago."

"That's not worth two bits," said Petersen, less cheerfully than his usual tone. "I'm an excellent driver. That was Gloria's fault, that time. Would you believe the stupid bitch grabbed the wheel? Anyways, it's all over and done with." When Sims didn't reply, he added: "You're a real drip today, you know that? What's your problem, anyway? Girl turn you down?"

The rest of the ride to division was relatively silent. I need to get away from this man, Sims thought - I am not reacting well to him. He could almost see the primitive mechanism behind Petersen's frowning profile, processing very similar thoughts.

Tuesday morning began with a breakfast-table argument, in the course of which a husband broke a plate over his wife's head. She had just received eighteen stitches at East General emergency, when Sims and Petersen arrived to take her statement. She claimed not to remember anything. Perhaps so; there was a possibility of concussion - they would have to come back in 24 hours. They interviewed the neighbour who had called the police, added her signed statement to the constable's report. The husband was in custody... for a few hours, anyway. The three children had been placed in temporary care. And there, the police had to leave it. According to pattern, the man would eventually kill, or seriously injure, one or more of his dependents. Then, and only then, would he go to prison.

The only good thing about the inquest was that it was held downtown, in the afternoon, and attending it saved Sims from Petersen's company, while nominally on duty. He was allowed to give a description of the scene but not to comment at any length. In contrast, a technician from Bio-Tech, who barely looked old enough to shave, was questioned extensively about the safety systems. The pathologist recited his findings without editorializing. Mrs. Dumont, severely elegant in a grey suit, was composed, unemotional: she told her part coherently and well. Paul Ferdinand Arnott was present, for no reason Sims could think of. His intelligent dark eyes were everywhere, drinking in the exotic scene, but he kept a discreet silence; not a single wise-crack all through the proceedings. That would leave David Frayne alone in the laboratory today - perhaps working on his wonderful invention?

The proceedings moved along quickly. The verdict was 'death by misadventure', and no blame attached to Ac-Me Plastics. Mr. Quick appeared satisfied by this part, at least. Mr. Meyer shook his sleek silver head and scowled unbecomingly. From the research department, Dr. Jones, who had given his brief statement in a voice so subdued that the coroner had had to tell him, twice, to speak up, now looked solemn but relieved.

Outside the building, Dr. Cates used up three matches to get his pipe going. "Benson was being kind," he said. "He's pretty much convinced it was a suicide, but there wasn't enough evidence to force him to say so. And what he thinks, the jury thinks, perforce."

"What do you think?" Sims asked him.

"I didn't know the man... On the whole, I'm inclined to agree with you. But I couldn't very well testify to conjecture. What now? Leave it lay?"

"I can't."

"Stubborn cuss."

"No, there is more to it than ego. More, even than letting a killer go free - with the possibility of doing it again, don't forget. It also leaves the family in doubt; leaves them wondering whether their husband and father was irresponsible or cowardly; whether the justice system works... It leaves a mess."

"Doesn't it always?" the pathologist asked mildly. "Death is a messy business, Sergeant." Puffing thoughtfully, he added: "Look here. Once the case is closed, I can't let you have official documents - but I can lend you my informal notes, for what that's worth."

Sims talked briefly with the widow, surrounded by her family. She was brave and silent. Louise was pale and stoical. Her husband said: "Well, I'm glad that's over." Sims would have liked a private word with Amanda, and perhaps with Brian, but circumstance did not permit, at the moment. He told them: "I'll drop by tonight, if I may."

As he had half expected, back at Division, Inspector MacDonald was waiting for him. "Well, Sims, what's the good word?"

Sims told him. The inspector nodded three times, each

nod rucking up more rolls at his neck; four would have been a physical impossibility. "Right. Okay. File and forget." With that, he rotated his bulk 180 degrees, in the direction of his office, allowing no opportunity for remonstrations.

CHAPTER 22

"As far as the Department is concerned, the case is closed," he told the Morleys that evening.

Andrew Whitlock was not, but the two small Whitlocks were, present - the baby in his cot; the toddler, at this moment, pulling himself to a standing position with the aid of Lancelot's ears. To look at the dog's face, one would suppose that having one's ears pulled was the greatest bliss imaginable. When the child finally succeeded, Lance gave him a huge lick across the face, which sent him sprawling again; the process, with different handholds, had been repeated several times already, to the delight of both parties. If Louise noticed, she did not object.

She said: "Well, all right, then. We can put this terrible business behind us."

Brian disagreed: "And then we'll never know what really happened."

"What difference does it make!?" his sister demanded. "Our father is dead, and we'll never get him back. Why can't you let him rest in peace?"

"Because somebody murdered him! Don't you understand anything? Somebody is out there, better off because he's gone! Somebody is getting away with it!"

"Children," Amanda put in mildly. They stopped arguing but continued to glare at each other.

After a few seconds' silence, Brian quietly said: "You believe it, too, what nobody will say? Lou? You think Dad killed himself?"

With a surreptitious glance at her mother, Louise nodded very slightly. "Maybe. I don't know." She looked miserable - sad and embarrassed. She appealed to Sims, "I don't know! I want it to be an accident."

"Alec," said Amanda, "please tell Louise why you think what you think."

"All of it?"

"Please."

He took a deep breath, addressed the young woman as he would have liked, earlier, to address the coroner's court. "Dr. Morley was found on Monday morning, May fourteenth, in the Ac-Me laboratory, dead of cyanide poisoning. We now know that he had gone there at about nine-thirty on Saturday morning. He had left the house in a hurry, without changing the clothes in which he'd washed his car, merely putting on a jacket - which didn't match. In his pocket was an *unopened* pack of cigarettes. He had on a lab coat - over his jacket. He was wearing rubber gloves, the right one with a rip on the *outside* of the cuff. A flask of some plastic substance on a retort stand, was set up on his bench - not in the fume hood. There were no jars, instruments, or containers on the bench. The material in the flask, which had been knocked over, was spilled on the back of his coat and pants - not on the front. There were almost no fingerprints in the room.

"All of this seems to me unlikely - unreal - and, as I've since learned, out of character. His calendar had not been changed from Friday's date, and his notebook was inside the desk drawer – with at least one page is missing from it. The wedge which props open the fire exit in good weather was outside. A man was seen, at about ten o'clock, hurrying away and ducking through the hedge, holding something in front of his mouth." He stopped to draw breath and assess the effect of this speech.

The audience, all three adults, even the child and dog, who had tired of their game and were sitting quietly side by side on the carpet, was attentive, waiting. So many eyes made him nervous but he must continue. He took a sip of coffee. "This is what I believe happened. Someone from Ac-Me phoned Dr. Morley that morning, probably saying there was an emergency of some kind. He rushed right over. The bench was already set up, and the caller was hiding in the fume room. That person, wearing a gas mask, jumped him from behind, and broke a capsule of potassium cyanide, probably into the boiling plastic. It would take only a second or two for the victim to lose consciousness; he would be dead within a few minutes. If this is any comfort at all, he really couldn't have felt any pain. Then the killer, who had been wearing Dr. Morley's lab coat, transferred it and the gloves, onto the victim, knocked over the retort stand - either by accident or deliberately - and stepped back into the fume room. He ran water on some paper towels to put over his face, hung up the gas mask, and ran out of the building, hurried across the back lawn and ducked through the hedge."

There was a silence. Then Louise asked: "But, why?"

"I can only guess at the reason," Sims told her. "Possibly because he was standing between someone and a lot of money. Lately, Dr. Morley has been very concerned about the environmental damage done by Ac-Me products - perhaps you knew?" They all nodded, except the little boy, who had fallen asleep with his head against Lancelot's side. "He'd been working on means to recycle used plastics - this is pretty expensive. He opposed at least one potentially lucrative product in the last few months. Whereas in the past, he had made a great deal of money for Ac-Me Plastics, lately, he's been cutting into their profits."

"That," said Brian, "would make it Mr. Meyer or Mr. Quick. Who else would have gained?"

"Every employee in a supervisory position and had been with the company ten years or more, has a share in the profits. The other chemists would earn royalties on substances they developed. And, of course," he looked around the circle, "you all gain."

The murmur of disavowal made barely a ripple; none of them seemed concerned about suspicion falling on him or herself.

"What about personal reasons?" Louise asked timidly.

"Personal?"

Brian waved an impatient hand. "Let's stop pretending we don't all know what we know. This is too serious for pussyfooting around delicate issues."

Louise nodded energetically and then, as both young people turned expectant eyes on their mother, Amanda, too, inclined her head. "I wasn't sure you knew," she told Louise.

"Come on, Mom," Brian said. "When did she not know anything that was bothering Dad? I only guessed... he never told me the woman's name."

"You discussed it with him?" Amanda asked incredulously.

The boy looked at the floor. "Discussed isn't quite it," he said. "I sort of had a fight with him. I started it," he added. "I wanted to know if it was true, and he said yes, and then he told me some other stuff I didn't like... I was just a kid then. Stupid."

He had been seventeen. Sims could visualize the scene between accused father and self-righteous son - it troubled him profoundly. Brian, too, was embarrassed but determined to get it all out into the open. Sims felt he ought not to be present, and yet he was an essential part of this scene. Nobody else could narrate. He sighed. "It seems that Dr. Morley had an... a relationship... with a lady colleague, some time ago. Two years ago. It ended. As far as I can determine, there was no residual hostility. If there is a personal motive, I don't believe it relates to that incident."

There was a general soft expulsion of breath, followed by another silence. Then Brian said: "Okay. What about professional jealousy?"

"It's not impossible," said Sims. "If so, it would have to be one of two people: the one who inherited his job and the one whose invention Dr. Morley vetoed. The first has no very strong alibi. The second, I'm not sure. It doesn't seem to me as good a motive as money."

"It would be both, wouldn't it? In either case," said Brian.

Louise had not been attentive during this last exchange; little Edward had begun to whimper and she was rearranging his covers. Amanda, to whom this was old news, was also somewhat distracted, but it now appeared why.

"So," she said thoughtfully, "there was cyanide gas in the lab. And he... the... killer," she pronounced resolutely, "had to go, from the fume room, through the laboratory to the exit. Four, five seconds? With just wet towels over his nose? Wouldn't he get sick?"

"Two seconds," Sims corrected, "at a run, with both doors propped open. And by this time the extractor had been on for several minutes. Still, you're right. And one person did feel sick that day. Or, anyway, only one said so. Anyone could have, and not mentioned it."

"That's true," she said, still with the far-away look in her eyes. "Only, I can't see Charlie Quick jumping into his car and driving to Elmvale in a hundred minutes, if he were even a little bit poisoned."

"Point," he said. "And Mr. Meyer was with his family, that's confirmed. Jones? Barbecuing in the back yard all afternoon. He'd have to be pretty tough to cover up dizziness and nausea... but he's a large, physically robust man. When something is important enough, people find unexpected resources."

"Two?" she asked softly.

"Two," Sims nodded. "Wait. Maybe three: Ferdy Arnott."

"Why?"

Sims told her about the plans of the two youngest researchers to set up in business for themselves. "I haven't checked on it yet, but I can't altogether dismiss it. He's been flippant about the investigation from the start, making a mockery of it... maybe deflecting,"

"Conspiracy?"

"It's possible."

"Other executives? Foreman and so on?"

"Not likely; none of them could easily obtain the poison, or get him there without arousing suspicion."

The other two people in the room, forgotten, were following this exchange as if it were a tennis match, eyes swivelling from speaker to speaker.

Amanda said: "What's next?"

"Frayne's apartment building. Jones' neighbour or neighbours. Arnott's parents and grandfather. The actual content of that last meeting."

"I can talk to Charlie, if you like," she volunteered. "If he's not a suspect anymore."

"Good idea."

"I'll do it tomorrow and go north on Thursday. Can't put it off, the babies have begun to fledge."

"They must be a sight. I wish I didn't have to work," Sims remarked wistfully. "I've never seen baby grebes. As for the gum-shoe work, I'll have to fit it into lunch-hours and evenings. That's when people will be at home, anyway."

"Whom do you like?"

"Frayne. Or rather, him I most *dis*like. Of course, that's neither here nor there. I'll have to get back to the girl I told you about last night; she ought to be good for a few more questions."

"Be diplomatic. Remember it's not official now."

"That's a problem. I could use good pictures of these people, which I can't get without alerting them."

Brian looked at his sister. "Holmes and Watson," he said. She laughed, "Wimsey and Harriet." Sims felt horribly self-conscious; Amanda blushed. Louise said, "Well, I think it's nice." "Yeah," said Brian. "Anyone need a refill? Lou, did you hide the rest of those chocolate wafers?" They left the room, chatting amiably together, an air of relief enveloping them like a warm shared cloak. Lancelot yawned, shifted position slowly, carefully, so as not to disturb Andrew Jr., and went back to sleep.

Sims turned to Amanda. "Is it just my imagination, or have I earned a seal of approval?"

"Edward and I must have done one thing right together, after all," she said. "We have nice children." She reached across the coffee table and he took her hand for a brief, congratulatory clasp.

It was this tender domestic scene he tried to keep before his mind's eye while Petersen talked. Petersen had a new girl-friend and Sims most particularly did not want to register all the details. Gloria Venables was out of hospital and would be back on duty within the week; this knowledge kept him from requesting a change of partners. DiMarco had not yet received his test results: the mill of the Department produces grist more slowly, even, than the gods'.

While the day could hardly get much worse, it showed no sign, by noon, of getting better. The Sims who went on his lunch hour to the Arnott residence was not his most optimistic self.

"But I already told you, Officer," said Ferdy's mother in a high, irritated tone. "My son was in bed, in his room, in this house. All morning. Every Saturday and Sunday morning, for the past ten years. What more do you want?"

"I'd like to know," he explained again, patiently, "whether you, or anyone else, actually saw him during the morning."

"What do you think, I go barging into his room? Paul got up at noon or one, or whenever he got up. I saw him then. Of course he was grumpy and dozy - he just woke up, for Heavens' sakes. Anyway, what difference does it make? Paul told us his boss died of an accident."

"Did he appear to be well, physically?" Sims persisted.

"Sure. That boy hasn't been sick a day in his life. Except

for chicken pox, when he was three. All right?"

"I heard - and I would like to confirm or deny this - that Paul has certain financial expectations."

The chunky, somewhat florid woman stared at him. "Well! What has the boy been saying again!? For your information, my father-in-law, at seventy, is enjoying perfect health. Like all that family."

"So was Edward Morley," Sims muttered under his breath. As soon as it was out, he knew he'd gone too far. Mrs. Arnott refused to talk any further with him, and he couldn't, in all fairness, blame her.

But, having an empty half hour left, he looked up Arnott in the telephone book. Two F.'s, besides the commercial one. Petersen was lunching at his girl's house; he wouldn't mind being picked up a little late.

Arnott's Fine Foods occupied one section of a flat, unimaginative building in the commercial wilderness of Steeles Avenue. He flashed his badge at the receptionist and was shown into the back regions. He had expected to find kitchens, ovens, intriguing smells, but there were only more offices, carpeted in maroon, with rose pink walls adorned by prints - all depicting bread, fruit and dead fish. To the secretary in the farthest vestibule, he had to show his badge again. At last, he was admitted to the office of Ferdinand Arnott.

He knew at once that his hunch had been correct. The man who lifted himself one inch off his chair, while indicating another for him to take, was tall, spare, saturnine, with a full head of steel-coloured hair: a finished, but not over-polished, version of young Ferdy. "What can I do for you, Sergeant? In two minutes or less - I have a meeting."

Sims wondered whether businessmen really spent most of their time in meetings or whether they only said it, to show how busy and important they were. "I'd like to ask one or two questions about your grandson."

"Ferdy? What about him?" He added threateningly, as if Sims were responsible: "He better not be in trouble."

"Well, actually, it's in connection with the death of Dr. Morley. You have heard?"

The man inclined his head. "I heard. What's it got to do with me? Or my grandson?"

"Possibly nothing," Sims told him. "But I need to complete my notes, including the backgrounds of all the people associated with the victim. I understand the younger Mr. Arnott is planning to go into partnership with a colleague who has a certain invention. Do you know much about this?"

"Moonshine," pronounced Mr. Arnott. "I'm not lending him another penny. I put the kid through university, on the understanding that he would come to work for me. He thought there was more future in plastics than imported herring. So, okay. He's on his own."

Sims nodded. "I see. And he has no access to funds elsewhere?"

"Of course not. He barely makes enough to buy clothes and gas. Still living with his parents. At twenty-three!" he concluded with an implied, if not pronounced, snort.

"I see," the detective repeated. "So we can discount that rumour."

"You can discount ninety percent of what Ferdy says. He'll get something when I cash in my chips - maybe. But I'm in no hurry. Well, if there's nothing more..."

Sims let himself be dismissed. This detour might not have been productive but it was interesting. Moonshine? Ferdy spinning tales to impress his friends? Probably. On the other hand, a sinister long-term plan, which might require the removal not only of Dr. Morley, but of Mr. Arnott the first, was not beyond the realm of possibility.

CHAPTER 23

The afternoon dragged. Sims organized the papers on his desk, and then reorganized them. He ignored rumours of yet another drug bust: even if it should materialize, it would take weeks to set up. He paid more attention to a rumour about some scandal in the department; a bribery and corruption charge - already laid or pending or threatened, depending on the source - in one of the west end divisions. Safely remote and probably unfounded. Just before quitting time, Inspector MacDonald called a full Division meeting, sergeants and up, for next morning - subject unspecified. It might be to announce the raise they had been negotiating for five months... or to deny the rumour about bribes - in which case, it might be true, after all. Sims was in a foul mood by the time he got home.

Lancelot leapt from a prone position in the middle of the room, directly on his chest. He staggered, almost fell, pushed the dog off and yelled at him. Lance cowered at his feet, whining softly, which didn't make him feel better about anything.

"What is the matter with you? Been in the house too long?" Of course, Mrs. Field would not have let him out; her garden was in full bloom now. "All right, let's go for a fast walk. But then I really need to eat something before I faint." He kept up a reassuring patter all the way down the block, recounting his rotten day, then his whole week. "It's this crazy business of working shifts," he explained. "I go on nights; you get used to going out during the day, then you can't get used to being locked up again."

He could not face driving any more that day, so he took a long way around the neighbourhood, through several alleys, where nobody was likely to see him use the double plastic bag - a humiliating exercise, even without witnesses. But there was no place along this route to let the dog run free. "More exercise tomorrow, I promise."

When, upon their return, he caught sight of Mrs. Field in her front window, he signalled her to wait; he'd be right up. Then he wrote a cheque, dated Monday. As an afterthought, he picked up the pink geranium he had forgotten to water - he would get another one for Amanda.

"I didn't like to disturb you last night," he said. "Here is the rent."

"You don't like to disturb me?" she repeated. "This kind of disturbance, I don't mind. It's the other kind I could do without. You know what I mean. What that animal does all day long. Yesterday, and again today, it kept on whining and howling, fit to wake the dead."

Sims reprimanded Lancelot but his heart wasn't in it. She noticed. "That dog is just plain spoilt," she said. "You shouldn't spoil it so."

She accepted the flower with the curtest of thanks. Having made good his escape, Sims told the subject of contention: "We definitely have to move. But where? Maybe we can find a place where they already have a dog. You'd like that... but would the other dog?" Lance was paying more attention to the food landing in his dish. "You're a problem. And spoilt, to boot. And there isn't a drop of beer in the place."

"I don't know," he kept musing while he heated left-overs for himself, "Father Mike may be right. I'm not having much fun as a cop - and I'm not very good at it. Here is a case in point. A decent, unhappy man is foully murdered. And here am I, the only detective on the scene... Nobody messed it up, no-one made a mistake. The constables were superb; the ident team was professional; the pathologist was helpful; the crime lab was amazingly efficient. And I can't make an arrest. Hell, I can't even make a case. I ask you, what kind of cop is that? Pete Saunders would be ashamed of me."

Lance looked up from polishing the dish cradled between his paws. Sims stepped carefully over him to the stove. "Well," he said, emptying the pot into a plate, "let's see how the rest of mankind is screwing up today." He took his dinner to the couch and turned on the news. Half the developing world seemed to be on the brink of war, if not already at it; the so-called developed world wasn't doing much better.

He would have preferred to see Martin Jones at Ac-Me, but it was not to be. The meeting - about both the raise (they had won a barely noticeable four percent, retroactive to January first) and the rumours (a full internal investigation was being conducted, and it would be appreciated if they all refrained from speculation and 'loose talk' until it was finished) - didn't break up till almost eleven. There followed a half hour of speculation and loose talk; people were feverishly scribbling figures on scratch pads. "Where do you sign up for a bribe?" asked one sergeant. "This raise sure ain't gonna cover the new interest rate on my mortgage." Finally, everyone who wasn't due in court or already late for assignments, drifted off to lunch.

Sims was unable to shake Petersen; had to eat with him and learn more about the wonders of carnal indulgence. He could have been rude, but in the next few days, he might need Petersen's cooperation. During the afternoon, they apprehended a habitual vandal. On their return, Sims had to face the irate father of the foul-mouthed little boy he had reprimanded for trespassing. Apparently, the child remembered, after a week's delay, that he had been handled roughly. Inspector MacDonald apologized and invited Sims to follow suit.

"I didn't do anything to him. Constable Burnside and I merely escorted all three children from the premises and explained to them how dangerous a warehouse can be."

"My boy says you pushed him around and threatened him," the father insisted.

"Well, I didn't," Sims replied.

"It don't matter," said MacDonald. "Just say you're sorry."

"All right." He turned to the man, "I'm sorry your son got into mischief. I regret having had to answer the call."

"Be sorry you pushed him around," said the father, and to the inspector: "I want to register a complaint against this officer."

MacDonald tried to smooth it over but the man wouldn't budge, and neither would Sims. "The child is abusive, uncontrolled and a destructive. One day soon, he'll get into real trouble. I did not push him - but somebody will, and much worse, if he isn't disciplined at home."

After the father had filled out the appropriate forms and gone, MacDonald came to Sims' desk. "What you hafta be like that for, boy? The guy woulda went away happy, if you just said what he wanted to hear."

"I told the truth," answered the mule who had, half an hour ago, taken over Sims' body. He wished it hadn't;

things were simpler when he could back down from
something so petty. "The kid needs a spanking - not to
mention having his mouth washed out with soap - and I
was certainly tempted. But I didn't touch him."

His superior stood, perplexed. He moved his head in a
small arc, from side to side, four times. He scratched his
belly. He sighed hugely. "I don't know what's got into you
lately, Sims. You're on warning, as of now: watch your
step, boy."

Therefore, he had to postpone his visit until evening.
Lancelot was napping on the muddy back seat after his run
in and out of Toogood Pond: he would be all right for an
hour. All the Joneses were at home. Martin answered the
door, in designer jeans, a sweatshirt named after a boat,
and sneakers. Probably expensive ones that anyone other
than Sims could identify.

"Sergeant. I didn't expect to see you again, after the
inquest."

"I wasn't altogether satisfied by the verdict," Sims told
him. "Some unanswered questions are still bothering me.
May I come in for a few minutes?"

Jones led the way to his sombre, monochromatic -
Ridley's or Beverly's idea of masculine? - study. "My wife is
putting Courtney to bed - she'll be down in a little while."

Sims declined refreshment but accepted a chair - black
leather slung over metal tubing - that was as
uncomfortable as it looked, and took out his notebook.
Jones perched uneasily on the edge of another chrome
and leather contraption, holding the frame with both hands
between his spread knees. "Do you still recall that
Saturday, Dr. Jones?"

"Sure. What about it?" He leaned forward, all attention.

"You said," Sims pretended to consult his notes, "that
you were working in your garden all morning."

"That's so. I cut the grass, like I do every weekend, and
trimmed the hedge."

"Did you go out at all? During the morning?"

Jones closed his eyes in concentration, so like an
overgrown child that the detective half expected to see the
tip of his tongue. "Yeah," he said after a while. "Yes. I went
out to buy some lawn food. The grass was sort of patchy.
It's all right now."

198

"Where did you go?"

"Where I always go, to Summer Place Nurseries, at Birchmount and Denison."

"And how long were you gone?"

The chemist gazed at him as if he'd never seen anything like Sims before. "Hey, hold on a minute," he said, adjusting his eyeglasses while he teetered on the edge of his chair, then quickly replacing the steadying hands. "Why's it matter?"

"Because you left it out of your original statement, for one thing."

"Oh. Well, I forgot. Anyway, I was probably gone about an hour. It takes maybe twenty minutes to get there, and I looked around for a while and it was a Saturday in spring, so everybody and his uncle was there, I had to stand in line. Make it more than an hour, even."

"Two hours?"

"I don't think as much as that. Let's say I left at half past nine; I was back by eleven, because Bev and Courtney weren't home yet."

"And the fertilizer you bought, did you use it right away?"

"Don't be silly," Jones admonished. "You can't apply NPK in the middle of the day, with the sun shining. Sunday it rained, that's when I spread it."

"I see," Sims made a note in his book. "So, nobody saw you outside after about nine thirty."

"Guess not. I finished clipping, but I didn't notice anyone. At least, not till we had our barbecue in the back yard. The neighbours - the Butterworths, next door," he waved a large pale left hand, "were outside, too, with company, the daughter and her family. They have a boy around Justin's age, Christopher. A little cry-baby." He shook his head, more in sorrow than anger, at the frailties of other people. "They're raising him up to be a wimp. Justin is only a few months older, but he's years and years ahead of that kid."

Sims gave a small shrug to indicate his own lack of expertise on the subject of child-rearing. "One other thing. On that day, did you feel at all sick, at any time?"

"No. Why?" Jones' pale blue eyes behind their lenses were innocent and round as a baby's. "Wait a minute.

Dave was sick that weekend, and Eve mentioned something... Couldn't be. They said at the inquest there was nothing wrong with the safety system. Anyway, I felt all right. Well, maybe just a bit hung over, which is most likely what the Dumonts had, too. Dan Ferris," he grinned a very small but - for him - wickedly satisfied grin, "must have felt like hell."

At this opportune moment, possibly by design, possibly having waited outside the door for a pause in the conversation, Beverly Jones entered and knocked, in that order. "Can I come in?" she asked. That, too, was irritating. "Oh, it's the policeman. I thought you said," she addressed her husband, who slid back into the seat of his chair and tried to sit up straight, "that business was all over."

Jones gave one his understated shrugs. "Just some odds and ends, you know. Sergeant Sims wants to leave everything tidy."

"Can I help at all?" she asked Sims with a lips-only smile that would cool coffee.

"As a matter of fact, yes," he said, smiling equally insincerely. "Could you tell me again what time you got home from the little girl's dancing lesson?"

"It ends at half past ten. We're usually home in half an hour. Unless we have errands or something."

"On the day Dr. Morley was killed, did you have errands?"

Jones was following this exchange closely with his eyes, but remained silent. She said: "Let me think," and laid two perfect pink fingernails at the corner of her perfect pink mouth to simulate a frown of concentration which did not appear on her face: it would cause wrinkles. "Yes, we bought some shoes for Courtney."

"And how long did that take?"

"I don't know," she said. "Too long. I remember the clerk was not very efficient. And of course Courtney was tired and just that bit less cooperative than she usually is. As long as we were at Holt's, I tried on a few things..." Sims was watching, not her face, which didn't change expression, but Martin's. It did change - to something like dismay, perhaps his diminished version of anger. "Traffic was terrible. I really don't know."

Sims made a note, but no comment. This woman was

either uncommonly dense, or not very eager to supply her husband with an alibi. Or sure he didn't need one? "On that day, do you recall anyone in your family being ill?"

"Ill? No, we were all fine. Well," she smiled deprecatingly at her husband, "Martin was a teensy bit under the weather. We had a dinner party the night before, and he *will* drink red wine."

Jones walked him to the front door. "That wasn't very nice," he remarked softly, glancing over his shoulder. "I was perfectly frank with you."

"Yes," the detective agreed, "and I'm sorry. It's part of the job."

"You still think Edward was murdered, even though the coroner said not. Okay. But I haven't got anything to hide."

Sims would prefer to believe him. "You've been very cooperative. I do appreciate it. Good night, Dr. Jones."

CHAPTER 24

During the night, an elderly man crossing Kennedy Road had been struck and killed by a car. The driver had fled. There were no witnesses. Sims, if it were possible to like some kinds of tragedy more than others, preferred a hit-and-run case to most. He was known to have the eye for detail and sheer, dogged persistence it takes to solve one. Inspector MacDonald assigned Steig, fresh from his vacation, with DiMarco and, for good measure, pulled two men off the Mason Street bank robbery. But he couldn't leave it that; he had to stop by Sims' desk to rub it in.

"Steig's a good cop," he mused. Sims agreed with this assessment, and mentally threw in nice guy - he would happily accept Steig for a partner; therefore couldn't begrudge him DiMarco. They would work well together. "You and Petersen got court today?"

Sims nodded dumbly. It would take less than ten minutes to recount how they had caught Tony Whitehead spray-painting swastikas on a factory wall - and Petersen could perfectly well do that alone. MacDonald stretched, lumbered off to get a cup of coffee. All right, he thought, so I'm in the dog-house. What else is new? His phone rang.

"Detective-sergeant Sims."

"Abe Meyer here. I've been trying to get hold of you, but they wouldn't give out your home number. I suppose that makes sense."

"What can I do for you?"

"You know what happened at the inquest," Mr. Meyer came right to the point. "I'm not happy with it. I'd like to discuss it with you - in private. Any chance of getting away for lunch?"

Sims considered the logistics. "I have to be downtown till eleven or so. I can try to get free after that. Where?"

They agreed on a restaurant on a busy corner, not so near 43 Division that they were likely to run into other policemen, but not too much out of the way. "I'll be there about half past, and wait for you," said Mr. Meyer.

Petersen wasn't hard to shake. He made it all too graphically clear that he wanted to meet a girl other than the girl he had been seeing these past weeks. "Never rains but pours, eh?"

202

The place was tiled in green and white and dripping with artificial plants. The menu was heavy on things raw, green, fibrous and healthful.

"I've got to watch my cholesterol," Abe Meyer half-apologised, "but there must be some real food on these four big pages. Beer? Is it allowed?"

"If it's allowed for my boss," said rebellious Sims. "Yes, please." However, out of courtesy as well as personal considerations, he also ordered the apricot and beet salad with chicken. It tasted much better than it read.

"Tell me," his host leaned across the table confidentially. "How did you feel about the verdict?"

"Not great," Sims admitted. "The coroner was being generous: apparently he thinks Dr. Morley committed suicide."

Meyer shook his head, poured wine cooler into his glass, and sighed. "That's how it seemed to me, as well. But he's wrong. So, the case is closed?"

"As far as the police are concerned, yes."

"And you?"

"I haven't closed it."

"Neither have I." Meyer laid his knife and fork neatly, deliberately across the plate and regarded Sims for two silent seconds. "I'm prepared to - no, I'm *bound* to - do something about it. Look, I don't know how these things work. Would it be unethical for you to take it on, in a - um - an unofficial capacity?"

"I already have," Sims told him. "That is, I'm still working on my own time - and, to be frank, in any time I can steal from the Department."

Meyer nodded, picked up his utensils but did not use them, put them down again. "I was going to ask you for the name of a good private investigator... But I don't mind admitting, I'd rather have you on the case. You seem to me the kind of man who takes things seriously - and personally."

Sims applied his napkin to an imaginary dab of mayonnaise on his moustache, in case his expression gave something away. Mr. Meyer continued earnestly. "Look, this is important to me. Edward was a friend as well as a colleague. I want his killer caught. If you should incur any expenses... or, if you need any help - financial, or otherwise... Well, I'm here. Okay?"

Sims, not yet entirely trusting his voice, nodded soberly. Then he said: "Does that mean I still have access to the Ac-Me premises? Records? I can talk to people?"

"Absolutely. Well, the records, any time - evenings and weekends, if you like. Charlie Quick is at your disposal - we already discussed it. Discussed!" He smiled and picked up his glass. "We were up half the night, going over the facts, finger by finger. By the way, I'd appreciate any suggestions to improve security. As for the other people, I can't order them to talk to you. Tell me, do you think it's someone at the company?"

"Yes, I do."

"I was afraid of that. What position should we start advertising?" he added with forced lightness.

"I wish I could tell you that," said Sims.

"Did you know Amanda Morley was at the plant yesterday? No? I'm not sure why; Charlie would have taken Edward's things to her - sort of a sentimental journey, I guess, a last look around." He sighed. "That probably means we won't see her again. Too bad - Gracie likes her a lot. Terrible bridge player, but a really nice lady. She was always kind of shy, though, a very private person. I'm only babbling," he added, refilling his glass, "because I know why she doesn't want to have anything to do with us. Charlie told me. It's damned embarrassing. Anyway," he sighed again, "you didn't come here to gossip. Well." He concluded firmly, "anything Ac-Me can do to help is at your service. There is one more, sort of a delicate thing..."

"Yes?"

"You haven't said whether you're willing to take this as a contract." Sims firmly shook his head. "Then you have no obligation to report to me. Fair enough. But, as a favour, will you let me know, from time to time, how it's going?"

Sims choked down a lump of arrogance he hadn't known was in him, and said: "Yes, I will."

Abe Meyer thanked him and picked up the check. In the parking lot, they shook hands. Chalk up another one for that frighteningly perceptive old priest.

"I didn't know what to say," he told Amanda that evening. "You should have taken the job," she said. "He can certainly afford it, and it would make him feel better."

"It wouldn't be fair. Or right," he said. "I've been doing it anyway - but not for Mr. Meyer." He watched Lancelot making himself comfortable in the now familiar living room. "He's shedding, you know; maybe we should put him in the yard. Anyway, tell me what you were doing at Ac-Me yesterday."

Amanda smiled broadly. "Guess. No? Well, besides pumping poor old Charlie Quick for all he's worth, I was taking pictures."

"Of what?"

"Aha! Of everything. For a sort of memorial album... You know, I might even do that, sometime. The idea just came to me. What I did was photograph the building, inside and out, with special attention to the laboratory... and, as an afterthought, I took close-ups of all the people I could corner. Was that terribly underhanded?"

"Amanda! Do you mean you have pictures of the suspects, and they have no idea...? Let me see."

She produced a dozen five by seven prints of admirable quality. "I thought this would be a convenient size, but I can blow them up, if you like."

Sims was flipping through the likenesses of Martin Jones, Paul Arnott, David Frayne, Mrs. Benz, Mr. Burgess and Ernie Draper. "Who is this?"

"Barney White, the sales manager. He was there... and, who knows?"

"Lady," said Sims, "you are a genius. Tomorrow, with any luck, I'll be knocking on doors all over town with these. If I ever set up as a private detective, I'll put you on the payroll." He made no comment on the one person missing from the set; it didn't surprise him.

"So, what do we do next? Besides knocking on doors, I mean - that somehow doesn't appeal to me."

"Tell me everything you found out from Mr. Quick."

She did, and it amounted to little more than he had already learned. "I brought Edward's things home. I don't see anything useful, but you're welcome to go through them. The calendar had Friday's date - he always changed it in the morning. I suppose that means you were right; it happened very quickly." A sad, reflective expression settled on her face. "Everything else was tidy, so impersonal it could have belonged to anyone. They wouldn't let me have any old notebooks... I did look through the ones he had at home. You've seen them; there is nothing there. I put everything in a box." She released a little sigh. "Well, it had to be done."

"How," Sims began to ask, and found he had to clear his throat. "How are the grebes?"

"Fine," she dismissed the alternate subject. "Who... whom are you going after first?"

"I think Frayne," he replied. "Would you like to come along for a walk with Lance?"

Amanda shook her head, but it was already too late; the dog had heard the magic words and was clambering onto his feet, one at a time, tongue lolling, eyes alight. "I suppose we'll have to, now. You shouldn't do that," she admonished while getting a raincoat from the hall closet. "He was perfectly content till you put ideas into his head. And you just wanted to distract me. Alec," she stopped him at the door, in spite of the dog tugging on his arm, "once and for all: I'm concerned with bringing Edward's killer to justice. I don't feel happy about it all the time - I'm not supposed to - but I can cope. Give me some credit."

"All right," he said. "It's just that... well, I hate to see you unhappy. But I think I can cope."

It was a short walk; none of them, including Lancelot, enjoyed being out it in the chilly rain. Somewhere along the way, Sims told Amanda: "You might call Grace Meyer sometime. It seems she cares about you. I don't mean socialize, necessarily - just let them know you're all right."

"I will," she said. "Tomorrow. Then, if you don't want me around, I'll go up north for a couple of days. I have to start writing the text for that book and I can't seem to get down to it, here." She went on, quite cheerfully, about the book and its problems, giving him no opportunity to comment on that crack about not wanting her around. In fact, he reflected, he could no longer easily imagine a reality from which Amanda was absent for more than a day or two.

"Let me know when you get back," was all he said. "And how it's going."

He spent the rest of the week almost entirely on foot. In the daytime, questioning possible witnesses to a petty burglary, and then - rather more interestingly - an armoured car hold-up. The vehicle had been stopped by a traffic accident (staged?) and the driver had stepped down to see if he could help, whereupon someone had hit him and three men in black overalls, wearing ski masks and armed with rifles, had boarded the truck. This all took place at rush-hour, in the presence of drivers and pedestrians in the resultant traffic-jam, most of whom were confused as to what they had seen. The robbery itself took only a few seconds. The driver was left unconscious on the road and the truck, driven off along a (too convenient?) side street. It was discovered two hours later in an industrial parking lot; money gone, both guards in the back, securely tied and gagged.

In the evening, Sims revisited David Frayne's apartment building. Mr. and Mrs. Bidwell in Apt. 505 identified Frayne's picture as a member of the fitness club but didn't recall ever having seen him in the sauna. Miss Petrovich in 1402 said she had seen "that cute guy" in the hall, and sometimes in the pool, but not on the morning of May 12. Mrs. Simcoe in 1722 had seen him many times, but the date meant nothing to her. "I take my little Sparky," she indicated an apparently comatose lump of brown fur, "out for his walk every morning and evening. There is always somebody in the elevator."

Mr. Fisk in 612, a man of 28 or 30, bearing a marked resemblance to the photograph, said he often worked out on Saturday mornings and usually did see David Frayne in the gym, but had been out of town on that weekend. "That's when I see my little girl," he told Sims. "Ingrid - my ex? - she moved back to Bellville. Back to her folks? So I only get to see the kiddie once a month. I make the most of it. Drive down Friday and back Sunday night. So what's your beef with Dave, anyway?"

"Do you know Mr. Frayne well?" asked Sims.

"Sure, I know him. Not real well, just, we play squash once in a while? So, what's the problem?"

"No problem," said Sims. "I'd like to know where he was that morning."

The young man shrugged. "Can't help you out. Like I said."

"Is your visit to Bellville a regular thing?"

"Yeah. It's all in the agreement. Settlement? When she's bigger, she can come stay with me. This year, I got to go there. Doesn't seem, you know, fair? I have to do all the travelling."

"I wonder," the detective asked quickly, noting his impatience, "did you ever discuss this arrangement with Mr. Frayne?"

"We don't talk all that much... we play squash is about it. He mostly clobbers me. Real competitive guy, know what I mean? Yeah, I guess I might of mentioned it."

"Thank you, Mr. Fisk."

"Yeah, sure," said that young man. "No problem."

The parking lot attendant could match the face in the photograph with a blue Trans-Am. "Sloppy driver," he volunteered. "Goes into his space all anyhow, had to call him a couple of times - 1723, right? - to move it so other tenants could get in their space." He didn't remember seeing either car or driver on the Saturday in question. "Sorry," he said, without sounding especially regretful. "People go in and out all the time."

Sims went through the same routine in the Joneses' neighbourhood and, except for Mrs. Butterworth, nobody could tell him anything useful. "Yeah, he's out cutting that little bitty lawn every blessed Saturday, rain or shine," was a representative answer.

Young Justin's karate instructor could only say that class ended at noon and that Martin Jones had never, to his knowledge, been late in picking up the boy. "A little scrapper. Hard to discipline," was his comment on the Jones child. "But he's never missed a class, never been late, I'll say that for him."

At Summer Place Nursery and Garden Supply, the clerk was brusque and the manager, barely this side of rude. It was their busiest time of year; while the man's face looked vaguely familiar, there were hundreds just like it, in and out of the store all day, every day.

"It's cold," he told Amanda. "Even while the event is fresh, hardly anyone can give an accurate account of what they saw and heard. After three weeks, unless it had personal significance for them, people forget details - or whole days."

CHAPTER 25

Instead of concentrating on where they all were on that morning, which was getting him nowhere, Sims decided to pay more attention to where the main players always were. He was convinced, without being able to explain it, that the key had to be at Ac-Me Plastics. In the middle of a day spent fruitlessly questioning thirty-six eye witnesses to the armoured car holdup, he made a call to Mr. Quick, who readily agreed to meet him in the office that evening.

"I've taken the liberty of preparing a little summary," said the old man, handing him twenty-one pages of computer printout. "Much faster than going through the actual books." There was a page for each year of the company's existence, showing expenditures and profits, listing the products developed and to whom each was sold. "I found it very edifying myself. You see? In the past year, we're looking much healthier. There is another lot here," he added helpfully. This 'lot' detailed staff turnover for the entire period, and was fifteen pages long.

"Have you decided on a project yet?" Sims asked, just to be sociable.

"Oh, yes. Yes, indeed. We couldn't very well keep the laboratory idle all this time..."

"May I know what the product is?"

"Why, of course. In fact, there are two projects. Mr. Meyer and I put our heads together and we consulted with Dr. Jones. Well, the long and short of it is that we have a new policy. Ac-Me will not release any product that cannot be recycled or harmlessly disposed-of. I do suspect that this will result in a sad little figure at the bottom of the next page... However," he brightened, "Mr. Meredith, of Meredith and Lackey - our advertising agency, you know... Mr. Meredith assures us that the public is now ready to support such a policy; support it, moreover, with their - what is his quaint expression? - with environmentally aware consumer dollars. He means that people will buy our products because they approve of us. Isn't that nice?"

"What are the products? The new projects, I mean?"

"Oh, you'll like this, Sergeant. We are going to make a

container for liquid detergent, which, when it is empty, can be turned into a bird-feeder! You won't tell anyone? Of course not. The bottle will have perforated circles, you see, that people can simply punch out, to form little doors for the birds. We may even put loops around the outside, with a cord already attached, by which to hang it up. And - this is the best part - these are disposable bird-feeders. What have we accomplished, you ask? Simply this: the container is made of a material that slowly breaks down in sunlight! While serving our feathered friends, the plastic is exposed to sunlight! You see? After a season or so, it can be safely thrown away! Isn't that clever? Do you know who submitted this idea? Young Arnott! Really, you could have knocked me over with the proverbial wet noodle."

Sims allowed that this did sound like a good idea. "And the other project?"

"The other is not expected to yield results for some considerable time," said Mr. Quick. "It is the last thing Edward worked on, however, and we decided to continue - partly in his honour, of course, and also because - well, because we have always trusted his judgement. This would be a product that can be burned safely. So far, he had not had very much success, but we turned it over to Dr. Jones."

"You have decided, then, to keep Dr. Jones on as head of the research department?"

"Oh, yes. He certainly deserves the opportunity. I believe he is quite a capable young man. Perhaps the increased responsibility will help him to bring forth hidden resources." Mr. Quick looked right and left; Sims expected him, almost, to look over his shoulder as well. In a near-whisper, he said: "He really has not been very... um... assertive, for want of a better word. I have reason to believe that Martin does not wear the pants in his house. Have you seen his house?"

Sims nodded. "Very impressive."

"Impressive? My dear Sergeant, a home is not meant to be impressive; it is meant to be a haven. A man should be able to go home and feel as if he has come in from the cold. It should reaffirm his values, rejuvenate his spirit, restore his self-esteem, which the outside world tends to erode. He should come out of it every morning, prepared to

210

slay a dragon or two. An impressive house - especially one which he neither built nor furnished for his convenience - belittles the man who lives in it. The ladies have a more highly developed aesthetic sense than we do...
unfortunately, in their zeal to civilize us, they sometimes neglect the fundamental requirements of the more primitive sex."

Sims, who thought this was worth filing for future consideration, said: "Mr. Meyer has an even more impressive home,"

"Yes, yes, indeed, he does. Personally, I find it somewhat intimidating. However, he does seem happy enough to spend most of his time there. Of course, Mr. Meyer's house is full of Mr. Meyer's flowers and hat collection... He didn't insist on showing it to you? Well," Mr. Quick chuckled, "perhaps because you are in a position to offer armed resistance... Yes, he collects ceremonial headgear from all over the world... fascinating, if one is of a temperament to appreciate that sort of thing. Please don't quote me. Really, what I mean to say is that Mr. Meyer's house is very much a reflection of the man. And of Mrs. Meyer, naturally. Beautiful woman, Grace - and aptly named, don't you agree?"

Sims agreed, but something else was on his mind. "So, then, you do see Martin Jones socially?"

"Oh, I wouldn't quite go so far as to say that. One takes an interest, of course... Oh, I see what you mean. Actually, I have only been in the Jones house once - shortly after the decorators finished with it. We all were invited to warm it, you see. I'm afraid we failed."

"It must have cost quite a lot," Sims remarked.

Mr. Quick glanced up from under his eyebrows, a look Sims had come to categorize privately as his shrewd look; there was nothing vague or senile about the old man. "Yes, it must have done."

"Can the Joneses afford it?"

"Candidly? No. I venture to suppose, without having in any way pried into his financial affairs, that Dr. Jones lives far beyond his income. However, with his promotion there will be a substantial salary increase. And next year, he will be sharing our profits - assuming, of course, that we have any... His burden of debt will lighten somewhat."

"In view of this circumstance, how did Dr. Jones react to your policy decision? The one about bird-feeders, and so forth?"

"Rather well, all things considered. Surprisingly well. I had imagined we would have more difficulty dissuading him from the Superfoam project... Yes, Dr. Jones did advocate pursuing it, at first - that being by far the most potentially saleable product under consideration. But, you see, we were able to show him Edward's calculations of the probable cost of perfecting the substance. Why, we could lose money, for a year or more, before we made any at all!"

"Then, you have decided against Superfoam? Once and for all?"

"We have. I don't think Young Frayne has, however. Well, in two years... that is, to be precise, twenty months... he will be able to do as he pleases with it."

"Would you mind clarifying that statement?" asked Sims.

"Of course. You see, any invention or patentable modification developed in our laboratory by any employee becomes the property of Ac-Me for a period of three years. If, at the end of that time, we have not exercised the option to produce and market the substance, all rights revert to the inventor: he is then free to sell it to one of our competitors."

"You mean that, if David Frayne were to quit Ac-Me and go to work for another company now, he couldn't take this Superfoam with him?"

"Certainly not. If he tried, we could sue him - and the other firm, as well. In this sort of case, we would not hesitate to do so. I believe it's a fairly common precaution. And as every other firm does likewise, none would be so unwise as to buy it without due diligence."

"So then, if you decide not to market his invention, there is nothing he can do about it?"

"That's right. Does it seem to you unfair? It does to me, sometimes - and yet, you see, we do have to protect the company's interests. After all, the initial work on the substance was done under Ac-Me's auspices, in Ac-Me facilities, at Ac-Me expense... There is yet another consideration, which puts my own mind at ease. It is not inconceivable that, were he free to do so, Young Frayne might take this idea to some concern with a less keen sense of responsibility to the public. In our files, it can't hurt anyone."

"I understand," said Sims. "But, in less than two years, that will no longer be the case."

"True. However, much can happen in that time. Much can change. Who knows, perhaps Brass himself will have found a way to make it safe... in which eventuality, we should be pleased to take up the option. Incidentally, the financial reward we offer to inventors is highly competitive. Oh yes, he could do very much worse. So, you see, I assure myself that we are not mistreating this young man."

"Did anyone suggest that you might be?"

Mr. Quick raised his eyes heavenward. "Not many days ago, in this very room. Mr. Frayne appears to feel that he is exploited."

"But you stood firm." Sims tried and failed to imagine a confrontation between the two men: tall, brisk, handsome Frayne with a grievance must be formidable, indeed. But slight, verbose Mr. Quick had something even stronger on his side - something like the ghost of Robert Acton, now joined by that of Edward Morley. He was invincible.

"In point of fact," the old man smiled - in combination with the shrewd look, the effect was very nearly diabolical, "I sat firm. I have not what one could call a highly compelling physical presence; whereas, Young Frayne is, um, an admirable specimen. Therefore, I must enlist what props are available to me. In the case under discussion, the window at my back, and this abominable antique," he patted the surface of his enormous desk fondly. "It rather constrains the person on the other side to put himself on exhibit, as it were, while I remain in shadow, fortified... A useful, if somewhat underhanded tactic."

Sims could visualize the scene; it made him laugh in spite of himself. "I see," he said truthfully.

"I have to interview two people tomorrow," Mr. Quick changed the subject, "for a junior position on the research team. I shall sit over there in the brown chair, and look benign."

"Life must go on," said Sims. "And you would like to get home. If I promise not to show them to anyone, may I take the printouts?"

"Certainly you may, Sergeant. I have come to rely upon your discretion."

The four-door sedan used by the hold-up men to stage their accident — no question about that now - had been stolen from a parking lot on Ellesmere Avenue and reported an hour after the other crime. It was abandoned at the scene, as clean and shiny as a new penny, except for a crushed rear bumper. The owner, a Miss Melodie Hopkins, had no further information. Nor had the parking attendant. Patient tracking-down and questioning of people who regularly used the lot and departed between 4:00 and 6:00 p.m. took up the whole afternoon without yielding one single lead. Sims had no objection to this routine - it was simply police work. Petersen had no end of complaints.

Nevertheless, Sims found half an hour to make some telephone calls on a quite different matter. Martin Jones had a solid, if undistinguished, record at AllComp Chemicals Inc. in Detroit, his only previous work experience. He had moved to Ac-Me at a much reduced salary - a loss that had taken all of this time to make up. How had Beverly felt about that? Sims wondered. These were ten-year-old files, probably of little or no use. David Frayne's career was shorter and equally unrevealing: he had been recruited by Ac-Me while still working on his Master's degree. Paul Ferdinand Arnott had yet to complete his thesis.

"A very bright boy," said Ferdy Arnott's old tutor that evening over a drink. "A real cut-up, always in some kind of scrape, but bright. If he ever settled to anything, he could go far. The trouble was, he couldn't wait to start making money."

"I've been given to understand that he didn't lack for financial assistance," said Sims.

"Oh, the rich grandfather story. Yes, I heard that one often. The truth is - at least, I think it is, that Grandpa kept him on a pretty tight leash. And the boy always had something to prove, always had to show off. You know, I don't think he ever will complete that thesis, especially if he's still under Frayne's influence."

The detective became fully alert. "You know David

214

Frayne?"

"Not personally," the other man replied. "Only by reputation. And by sight, of course. He's supposed to have a lot of potential," Dr. Frankl added noncommittally.

"But?"

His guest regretfully put down his empty glass. Sims signalled the waiter for a refill.

"But." Dr. Frankl sighed, arranged his chin and knuckles in a stylized Thinker pose. "There is one of those in every class," he said with a deprecatory pursing of his lips, "all flash and no substance. No patience for doing things consequentially. In a great tearing hurry all the time." He discovered the full glass before him and his neatly manicured left hand curled around it possessively. "Of course, Paul was ready and willing to be influenced. When he came back from his first term in that place, I knew he'd found a new mentor. His work suffered, naturally." He took up the glass, sipped delicately. "His attitude suffered, too. He lost... something."

"How do you know the influence was David Frayne, and not one of the older chemists? His boss, for example, Dr. Morley?"

"Don't be silly," Frankl dismissed the idea. "To judge by Paul's bitching about him, this Morley person didn't have the... charisma. And I have observed Frayne around campus. He looks like a movie star, for Chrissake. Never without some silly young ass following him around. Boy, girl, he doesn't care, just so they're slavishly adoring... Paul's only the latest in a series of conquests." He put down the glass and continued to caress it with two fingers. It was empty again. "And he has the style Paul would fall for... all flash and no substance."

"What makes you say that?" asked Sims, ordering one more gin and tonic, thinking it had better be the last.

"Can I prove it, you mean? No, I can't. It's all scuttlebutt and conjecture. Still, where there's smoke, there usually is some dirty little rag on the fire."

"Conjecture?" Sims prompted.

"There were some experiment results that may or may not have been fudged. There was a paper that may or may not have been a collaboration - to put it diplomatically. Nothing was ever proved, you understand. And suddenly, I catch Paul taking short-cuts - guessing, for Chrissake. I never taught him that. Suddenly his name isn't Paul anymore, but Ferdinand, after the rich grandfather, and he's dressing like a preppie, way above his means. No more tight jeans and floppy sweatshirts, hair all cut off short... I know he's imitating Frayne." Dr. Frankl sighed deeply and drained his third glass. "He had a lot of promise, the little smart-ass - and he could be very, very amusing."

There are too many kinds of pain in this world, Sims reflected.

"It's completely impossible," he told Amanda. "I don't get home till 'all hours', as Mrs. Field puts it. I walk him every chance I get but, in between, he howls. It's driving her crazy, she says - and there was a kind of distracted look about her tonight - a touch of the weird. On the other hand, I can't pass up any chances to meet possible witnesses, leads - whatever I can find. When do I look for an apartment?" The object of grave concern was currently dozing with his head under the coffee table, making faint snuffling noises, while his toes twitched. "He's chasing something again. What am I going to do with him?"

"Get him a babysitter," Amanda replied.

"Sure," he laughed.

"I'm perfectly serious. In fact, that was an offer. Leave him with me. The yard is fenced; I don't have any flowers; he can stay outside all day, if he wants. Besides," she added wistfully, "it gets awfully quiet here."

"What about," Sims objected, "when you go up north?"

"On those days, he can stay home and drive Mrs. Field crazy. Or, he could come with me, but I'd have to lock him in the cottage."

It would be a huge imposition, one he didn't know how to repay. Worse: he was assailed once again by a nagging worry. Suppose Lancelot became even more attached than he already was, to Amanda. Sims could not accept this generous offer - yet, to reject it would be churlish. He pushed it aside for the moment.

"By the way, how is the book coming?" She had been gone for three days - longer than he would want to be parted from both her and Lance at the same time.

She made a sour face. "Who knows? I wrote pages and pages... I probably have two paragraphs worth keeping. But the pictures are fine. How is the investigation?"

"Who knows? Probably two facts worth keeping. Did you know that Ac-Me hangs on to any invention for three years, whether it's used or not?"

"Of course I did."

"Of course you did. It never occurred to me to ask. That must be tough on a young man in a hurry."

"Which one do you mean?"

"Frayne. I like him more and more."

"Is it time to see his girlfriend again?"

"Not yet. I think I'll talk to Ferdy Arnott some more. It seems they're very close."

Amanda got up to refill the dessert plate; Lance followed her with his eyes. As soon as she sat down again, he accepted the single cookie he was entitled to, licked the very last crumb from the carpet, heaved a great contented sigh, and went back to sleep. Perhaps it wasn't such a bad idea... It would get Mrs. Field off their case for a while, and there was no doubt it would make the dog happy. What's more important, Sims asked himself, Lancelot's welfare or your jealous qualms? "When do you go to Sculpin Lake again?" he asked.

"Not this week. You can drop him by in the morning."

CHAPTER 26

"*All* the goddamn carwashes in the area?" exclaimed Petersen, "You know how many there are?"

"No. How many?" asked Sims.

"How should I know?"

"One way," Sims told him patiently, laying out the city map, on which he had marked the parking lot from where the accident car had been taken and the intersection where the holdup occurred. He drew a line between those points, "is to look in the phone book, for anything on these streets. They only had the car for half an hour, forty-five minutes at most; they had no time to wash it themselves, or to go very far out of their way."

"You want me to look up carwashes in the phonebook."

"Yes, and mark them on this map. There won't be many. Or, you can try the licensing office, but that would take longer." Not waiting for further argument, he dropped the big yellow book on Petersen's desk, and returned to his own.

Inspector MacDonald was waiting for him. In his hand was a sheaf of familiar papers, which he now deposited on Sims' desk with a plop that would put a telephone book to shame. "Look at this garbage," he commanded. Sims looked at the uppermost sheet: Petersen's report on their interview with one of the Knox security guards. It wasn't a very good report and he admitted as much. MacDonald said: "You let that nincompoop take notes? From now on, I want all reports on this case done by somebody that can spell his own name. I want *you* to write them. Clear?"

"Clear enough," Sims nodded, "but hardly equitable."

"Equi-shit. Just do it. Redo these while you're at it."

"And when," Sims enquired mildly, "is this wholly unearned pleasure to be mine?"

"Huh?" The inspector tucked all of his chins into an amazingly compact package in order to glare down at him. "When? Give you to Monday. And don't say I wasn't generous."

Sims flipped through the twenty-odd pages as his superior departed, then put them down on the exact centre of his desk, squared all the corners neatly, and left.

He was at the fire door by 5:15. At 5:28, Eve Dumont came out. She looked fresh and cool in a pink striped cotton dress.

"Sergeant... Sims, is it?" So much for making an impression. "What are you doing here?

"Oh, same old thing, you know." Too elaborately casual? Try again. "Actually, I was waiting for Ferdy Arnott."

She laughed, a delightfully musical sound. "You've missed him by half an hour... Ferdy always leaves early on Fridays."

"Oh," he said. Now what? He had wasted a rather clever ploy to shake Petersen before their usual quitting time, but it had left him stranded, on foot. "Well, would you have a few minutes to spare?"

Mrs. Dumont looked at her watch. "A few minutes, possibly," she said, and added with a faint but extremely charming smile: "Though I hardly think I could take Ferdy's place. Why do you want him, by the way?"

"I'm looking for any sort of background information on the research staff - relationships, problems, that sort of thing," he lied like a pro. "I thought Mr. Arnott might be the most... forthcoming?"

"Yes," she agreed and laughed again, "he very well might be." Having paced her, Sims now found himself standing next to a white foreign sub-compact. His companion had the keys in her hand and, pausing, said: "I don't understand, Sergeant. Please explain." Her face was as lovely as ever, but the clear voice had a touch of frost in it.

"About still being around here?" She nodded once. "You see, I don't happen to agree with the coroner's verdict."

"You mean that Edward died by accident. I found it difficult to believe, too. But I did accept it."

"Is that," he asked as nonchalantly as he could manage, while leaning on the roof of a sun-heated car - he had removed his jacket and his arm was bare. He eased away from the offending surface unobtrusively, never taking his eyes from her face, "because you think it may have been suicide?"

She was gratifyingly startled. "I would never suggest such a thing!" she protested.

"It's what the coroner really thought, apparently. Look, Mrs. Dumont." Surprisingly, it cost him very little to call her by name. "I understand you knew him better than most people did. Is it likely?"

She didn't answer right away. She looked at Sims, then at the keys in her hand, and sighed. "I do have a few minutes," she finally said. "There is a restaurant in the plaza over there..." she made a light, neat gesture westward. "Do you want to get your car?"

"I'll ride with you, if it's all right."

Red walls, bamboo curtains, dusty paper lanterns. There were tablecloths, if not especially clean ones, were protected by paper placemats with colourful pictures depicting exotic - none of them Oriental - drinks. Only one table was occupied, by four men in blue denim shirts, around a jug of beer, engaged in lively political debate.

"I don't think they sell very much food past lunch-time," Eve Dumont remarked. "It's the only handy place for many people to drop in after work."

Nevertheless, Sims ordered a couple of eggrolls with his beer and her Bloody Mary. "Well?" he asked when they were alone again.

"Well," she said. "All right, yes, I was relieved by the verdict, even though I can't imagine Edward being careless. I did think he might possibly have been careless under the influence, or maybe even... I'm not sure."

"Why?"

She picked up the pair of chopsticks in cellophane wrap, used it to trace one of the pictures on her placemat. Sims had no mental image of her as a doodler, or any kind of fidgeter; it made him vaguely insecure. When she put it down again and folded her hands, he felt better. "Edward was not a happy man," she finally said. He had known this; he waited. "So, you found out?"

"Yes," he replied. "I was bound to, you know."

"Of course. No secrets in the great big happy Ac-Me family." Her brows had drawn together fetchingly but there was a smaller trace of bitterness in her voice than the words implied. "Of course. I didn't have any reason to make a secret of it at the time. And Edward wasn't one to sneak around. I quite miss him, you know. Even though we had no... personal... relations in a long time, I did like him.

Very much."

Their drinks arrived. The waiter withdrew. Two young women joined the group near the door; much commotion was made over pulling over another table to accommodate them.

"He was an unhappy man," Sims repeated.

"Yes. I suppose that's what attracted me..." She tasted her drink and turned her perfect mouth down at the corners. "Why do they always use vegetable juice? It should be plain tomato. All right. Here is the story you want. Two and a half years ago, my husband - we weren't married then, just cohabiting - and I had a fight, and he left. I was miserable, lonely – all the things one usually is. Edward was there. He had an unsuccessful marriage - I suppose you know this? He was full of doubt about his work, his career...

"For the record," she raised her eyes briefly, in an earnest, level stare, "and would have been better in the next few years. His death is a terrible waste. But he didn't see it that way. He was going through a period... to call it a mid-life crisis would be to make it sound routine and trivial. Still, it was something like that. He needed someone to talk to. We drifted together. We had some background in common, some interests. He was good company - intelligent, well-read, decisive. He was kind. And," she looked up at Sims, "that's about all. We spent time together for a few months, then parted."

"Because?"

"Oh, you are ruthless," she said, not angrily, merely as an observation. All the same, he felt somewhat abashed: ruthlessness had never been one of the qualities he meant to cultivate. "Because Yves came back. He changed his mind, you see. That cost him six month residency."

The waiter put eggrolls and plum sauce before them. The other group had launched happily into religious differences, over a giant shared plate of fried won ton.

"They do sell food," he pointed out.

"Their won ton is excellent. So is the chicken liver with garlic."

Sims was not deflected. "Why should he kill himself?"

"He shouldn't!" Eve Dumont picked up her eggroll, turned it over and put it back on the plate. Then she carefully wiped three fingers on a paper napkin. "All his problems were capable of solution. And yet, lately, I've thought..."

"Yes?"

"Lately, I've thought he wasn't trying to solve them. I don't know why. He just seemed to lose interest."

"Would that have anything to do with you?" Sims asked as gently as it is possible to ask a question so brutal.

"How could it? I just told you. There never was very much between us... We each had our own problems. I was in love with someone else; Edward was preoccupied by what he saw as his failures. We really were not able to help one another." She paused to consider. "No, that isn't fair. Edward did help me. But he was always so reticent... I didn't get to know him as well as you seem to think."

Sims discovered that his plate was empty. "Suicide?" he prompted.

She sighed, turned her eggroll over again, and left it. "No, I suppose not. I was willing to accept the verdict... even with the suspicions I had. But now you've made me question it, I don't know what to think."

"Are you going to eat that, or just play with it?"

"Neither," she said. "Do you want it?" He did; he was hungry. There was a dire shortage of decent meals in his life these days. He wondered idly whether Amanda was cooking tonight. "So," said Eve Dumont, "you don't like the verdict. You don't like accident - neither do I - or suicide. That leaves murder."

"Right."

"Do you suspect me?"

"Not anymore."

"Well, that's something." Her usually fine, gentle voice was sharp. "Then, why?"

He finished sopping up the plum sauce. "I think maybe because he got between somebody and their heart's desire."

"That's cryptic. Heart's desire? Do you mean a woman? Because I'm not aware of Edward having any other... I mean, I know he was not well controlled at the last couple of parties... but..."

"I don't mean a woman," he said, wiping all of his fingers and getting shreds of paper stuck to them. "I mean something important."

Now, what made you say a thing as nasty as that? he asked himself. What's your problem with her, anyway? Isn't she just as gorgeous as the first time you saw her? Yes - maybe more so. Definitely more; there is a serenity that wasn't there before. Then, what? She doesn't care as much as she ought to... Why ought she to? I don't know. She just should: she's cold. Or self-centred, or something. She didn't love him. So what? But he did love her... and she doesn't even know it. *That's* the problem. It happens, Sims. It happened. Not her fault.

"Like what?" she asked, without any sign of having noticed the barb. "Money?"

"Money, ambition... yes, that kind of thing. Who springs to mind?"

"David," she said thoughtfully. "Martin, too, but I can't imagine him taking any kind of drastic action, let alone... I do know Martin fairly well," she added, "and he's not a good candidate."

"And David Frayne is?"

"Possibly. David is..."

The waiter wanted to know if they were ready for another round. Eve Dumont shook her head; her glass was half full. "I have to go. Yves will be worried."

Sims asked for the bill. "David is?"

"Cool," she finished. "Slick. He's always seemed to me a little calculating. Even in his relationship with Ferdy... You see, Ferdy is awfully young for his age. Impressionable. He thinks David is the greatest thing since sliced bread..."

"He isn't?"

"He's clever," she admitted, "but conceited and impatient. That SuperFoam project could have been interesting. But he should have seen the problem with it long ago; he should have taken a different tack. He won't; it's too much painstaking work. Maybe he can't admit he made a mistake."

"And Ferdy?"

"He's impatient, too, only it's more from over-eagerness than overestimation of his own ability. Given a steady, positive influence, Ferdy could be very good at his job. He has brains and, more important, his heart is in the right place, really. I don't think David cares much - he just enjoys being admired."

Sims privately forgave her the sliced bread clichee. She was back in his good books. As if anyone were keeping track. He paid the bill and let her go: it wouldn't kill him to take the bus, this once.

Saturday morning is a good time to find people at home. By noon, Sims and Petersen had covered the apartments that overlooked the armoured car robbery. Those who had been interviewed before expressed a certain irritation but all were, on the whole, cooperative. Only a handful of housewives and one retiree had been at home, and their superior perspective could add nothing to the account of bystanders at street-level. A loud crash had brought almost everyone to their windows. A grey car stood an angle in the middle of the road, its horn blaring continuously. Behind it was a big grey truck. Traffic halted, people on the sidewalk stopped to stare, some rushed to the accident. The horn stopped. Then some men in dark clothing - variously reported as four, five, and several - jumped into the Knox truck and drove off. All the witnesses agreed that the whole thing had been over in a minute. No description of the robbers beyond: wearing dark hoods, carrying rifles, moving fast and purposefully.

There were only three carwashes worth considering; two of them automated, attached to gas stations. None of the attendants paid attention to what cars went through. Sims drove Petersen back to Division and sat him down in front of a typewriter. He put Petersen's reports next to the original notes they had taken. "The inspector is not satisfied with these. See if you can improve them, will you?"

"What?"

"It's all right; you're on overtime. Inspector MacDonald would like to have good copies by Monday."

"What? Are you crazy?"

Sims put a pocket dictionary next to the notes, signed out, and left in his own car.

224

CHAPTER 27

"I would like to speak with your son, if he's at home."

Mrs. Arnott reluctantly stepped aside. "I guess he's up by now. Paul! Someone to see you! Pau-lie!"

There was an answering shout from the upper regions of the house; in a minute, young Arnott bounded down the stairs. His hair stood up in wet spikes, fresh from the shower, but he was dressed. "Hey, what's going on here? I never figured to see you again."

"Just a few more questions," Sims told him. "Is there some place where we can talk?"

Ferdy followed his glance to the ostentatiously busy Mrs. Arnott, dusting furniture with her back to them. "Well, I haven't got any gas taps, but I have a closet in my room. And a window we can practice opening..."

Sims followed him upstairs to a sunny bedroom. The walls and ceiling were covered with posters of sport-cars, heavy on chrome, all in the over fifty thousand dollar range. The bed was made; no clothes lay on the floor. On the bedside table were some paperbacks and a framed photograph of Ferdy with David Frayne, leaning on the metallic blue Trans-Am, squinting into the sun.

"Nice room," he said. "You seem to like cars."

"Yeah. That's the baby I want," the boy pointed out a vehicle which looked to Sims exactly like all of the others: too many lights, not enough road-clearance. "One of these days... Have you seen the cracker box I'm driving now? I wear a paper bag over my head. Poor peripheral vision; can't see the copper trying to stop me for a routine fire-arms search. But at least no-one will recognise me. So, make yourself at home, Sergeant. Isn't this cozy? Shall I ring for tea? Somehow I'd got this crazy idea that the investigation was over."

"Not quite yet," said Sims, who was patiently waiting for the performance to wind down. "I'm not happy."

"Oh, we can't have that! The thought of my dear Sergeant being unhappy keeps me up nights. How can I make you happy?" he added with an obsequious bow and tug at a non-existent forelock.

"Cut the clowning, for a start." Sims decided on his approach; he would be direct and refuse to be drawn into charades. "Did you kill Dr. Morley?"

Ferdy looked startled. No, stricken: colour drained from his face, even as the mocking expression faded. "No," he said, "*No*, I didn't!" .

"Do you know who did?"

"Sure. He killed himself. It sticks out like a sore thumb - I guess even the coroner figured it out, he just didn't say. And he had that jury practically licking his hand, so *they* wouldn't say..." Sims was shaking his head. "No, huh?"

"No. It was homicide."

"Well," Ferdy squared his chin defiantly, "I didn't do it. Sure, I felt like it a couple of times... I mean, I was mad at him sometimes, the way he pushed people around. But, anyway, I would have clobbered him with a blunt instrument - the blunter the better. I wouldn't have snuck up on him... that's not my... idiom."

"I believe you," Sims said quietly. "What other people did he push around?"

"Everybody. Everybody except Eve - he was sweet as pie to her. But we all know why that was..."

Sims closed and opened his eyes in a minimal gesture of assent. "I know a lot of things." His deliberate stillness seemed to have a steadying effect on the boy; he would keep it up.

"He didn't have the time of day for anybody else. Marty couldn't stand up to him, that's for sure. Even Quick-like-a-bunny did whatever Morley wanted. The Big Man, I'm not so sure about."

"The big man?"

"Mr. Meyer, the absentee landlord. Maybe *he* did it. Because the old man was losing him a ton of dough. Did you know? Trying to make a plastic that'll burn clean. Be nice if you could do it, only nobody has – like, ever. He didn't care how much that cost, no sir."

"I hear you had a good idea, yourself."

Ferdy's whole face lit up with the happy grin of a child who has just found the prize in a cereal box. "Yeah! Ain't that something? Guess there'll be few bucks in it. Well," he reflected more soberly, "it's not all that much of a much..."

"I thought it very clever,"

"I mean, we used to make little bird feeders from bleach bottles in school. It's not exactly new. Not in the same class with SuperFoam, or anything."

"Yes, that was an intriguing idea," Sims replied with studied indifference. "Too bad it didn't work out."

"Didn't work out!?" the young man flared. "Didn't get a chance, you mean. Classic Morley. He figures, if his own pet project takes forever and costs a fortune, so what? Somebody else's takes a couple months longer than he thinks it should - squash it. Dave even went and talked to the Big Man... and he was interested. I think Quicky was interested, too."

"Then it must be back on track, now that Dr. Morley's not around to oppose it?"

"Should have been," said Ferdy. "We thought sure it would be. Marty was supposed to push for it; he's up for profit sharing next year, could use the money. But I guess he washed out. What a wimp! Like Dave says, if you want something done right, do it yourself."

Sims kept his face impassive. "And did he?"

Ferdy shrugged. "He went to see Quicky the other day. No dice. Who'd have thought the old boy could be so tough, eh? They won't promote it and they won't release it. Rip-off city. Well, anyway, even if they don't come around, if we have to wait a couple of years, we can still do it."

"We?"

"Dave and me. See, he's got the formula - it's big, that's a gold-plated guarantee. And he's gonna let me in on it."

"Won't it require funding?"

"Oh, that's no problem. I've got this rich grandfather, and I'm his favourite relative. Named after him, and all."

"Your grandfather has agreed to finance the project? He must believe it's a good investment."

Ferdy looked sheepish for a moment. "I'm still working on that. But he's like seventy... what's he need so much money for? I'll get it anyway - why shouldn't he give me an advance?"

"Ah, so you've got it covered," said Sims without a hint of sarcasm. "Starting your own company?"

"Yeah. Just me and Dave, like Acton and Meyer. Dave wants to let Bobbie in... I guess it's okay - she can keep the books."

"Bobby?"

"Roberta Farrell. Dave's fiancee? She's not a bad kid, if you like them dumb."

True, Sims had not formed a high opinion of Roberta's intellect, yet he winced at the dismissive remark. He concealed it, and Ferdy barged ahead: "I can see why she's crazy about Dave, but I can't figure what he sees in her..."

"Does love need a reason?"

"Love!" Ferdy's voice dripped with scorn. "Love is a con-job. It's something women use to get a hold on you. They get all sucky and clingy, and next thing you know, you haven't got a minute to yourself. You got to call them, got to be with them all the time, go shopping for furniture with a temperature of 102."

"You think Bobbie was responsible for Dave's illness?"

"Aw, no, I guess not."

"But you were disappointed that he couldn't go out with you on Sunday."

"Yeah, some."

"So you're not too crazy about Bobbie Farrell. I think she likes you, though."

"She's all right." The boy was closing up like an armadillo. But not a very sleepy one: "Hey, how would you know that? You talked to her?"

Sims nodded. "I know a lot of things," he repeated. He pulled a notebook from his pocket, began to leaf through it thoughtfully. "Dave arrived at Bobbie's, on that Saturday at 11:30. Before that, he was in the gym. Everybody else is accounted for... except yourself, of course."

"I was right here. In bed. Until noon."

"Oh, yes," Sims made a note. "You have said so."

When not allowed to perform, Ferdy tended to become a petulant - and uninformative - child. Perhaps it was time to ease up. "Well," the detective closed and put away his book, "that's one loose end tied up. By the way, Dr. Frankl seems to think you have potential. It might be a good idea to submit your thesis before setting up in business. Afterward, you won't have much time."

"Who cares?" said Ferdy. "Dave's going to run the lab; I'll be in charge of the business end. I'm the money man. Bruce Frankl's an academic... and an old fuddy-duddy. He thinks small."

228

"It must be nice, then, to have a grandfather who can teach you all about running a business."

"Yeah, he's a good old guy. Put me through school and everything. Wanted me to work for him, one time, in the food import business. Maybe I will - anyway, while we wait for Ac-Me to release the patent rights... He'd like that. Yeah."

"So, you're all set. Only two years to wait."

The boy's face clouded over. "Yeah," he said sourly. "Two years. Only." He glanced at the car poster. "Grandfather might pay better than Ac-Me..."

"Lunch!" came a shrill cry from downstairs. "Paul! Pau-lie! Lunch!"

"I'd better go," said Sims. "Good luck to you."

"I don't think he knows anything," Sims explained to Amanda. "About anything. For a bright kid, he's really a dunce. And an emotional quagmire into the bargain. Jealous of the girl, insecure... I'm certain Frayne is only cultivating him for the money - *if* he gets any, which isn't guaranteed. In Frayne's place, I certainly wouldn't tell him anything; he has a mouth like a faucet. It's terribly unfair that you feed me all the time," he took another sandwich from the bag she had brought. Lancelot was somewhere in the underbrush, trying to flush out wildlife that he hoped was there. They heard his questing bark, off and on. "Would you come for dinner tomorrow? You and Brian? I haven't seen him in a while. How is he?"

"He's well. Busy. Terribly excited about this course he's going on at the end of the month. Becoming involved in the youth program has been very good for him."

"You should meet Father Mike. I'll ask him to come, too. He'll make fun of my spaghetti, but it's actually not bad. Just say yes."

"All right, yes. I like spaghetti, anyway." Lance came charging out of the ravine, circled the bench three times and dropped at their feet, where he began busily chewing on a stick he had fetched, unsolicited. Amanda poked him with her foot; Lance gave two absent-minded tail thumps without interrupting his work. "He's a nice dog - no trouble at all. I don't understand your Mrs. Field. So, we've given up on Ferdy Arnott as a suspect?"

"I think so. We'll just keep an eye on him."

"It looks as if we're left with David Frayne, then. You preferred him all along... Why?"

He said: "I'm not sure. Something about his manner made my throat itch. That first day, when everyone else was tied up in knots - trying to protect themselves, in their various ways, from the shock of it all - he was an ice-cube. I know, that's how some people do handle stress. But there was more to it; there was a sort of challenge in his manner - not hostility, not fear. I couldn't define it as anything, except maybe a sort of rivalry - with me. There was no call for it. I have thought, you know, that I might resent him for being so attractive and confident. But why should *he* resent *me*?"

"Father issues?" she suggested. "Of course, some young men automatically oppose any authority figure. You're The Man."

"That might be it," he allowed. "Didn't I cover the other possibles fairly?"

"Yes, I think you did. Have you exhausted them?"

"Pretty much. Besides, he's shaping up to have a real motive. Or, rather, to have *had* one. He expected to push his invention through. It didn't turn out that way."

"The missing notebook page," she said thoughtfully, "what would be on it? Negative comments?"

"More likely calculations - cost of perfecting his wretched insulation material, or the risk it involved. He didn't know Edward had already given the figures to Charlie Quick."

She nodded. "Yes, all right. He thinks, with Edward out of the way, he can manipulate Martin Jones, who isn't very tough, and Charlie, who doesn't look half as tough as he is, into developing his invention. Then, he would get Young Arnott to finance a business venture... But, if Ac-Me took up the option, he still couldn't manufacture the stuff himself."

"That bothered me, too. As Roberta Farrell understood it, he meant to use the accomplishment to further his career, and the royalties to help finance new projects. Going into business for himself may be an alternate plan... He may not have worked it out in advance - several people have described him as impatient and sloppy..."

"Edward's murder wasn't sloppy," she remarked softly.

"No, but it was impatient. The smart thing would have been to confuse the evidence with some kind of mess - a lot more than some spilled muck."

"Like a fire?"

"Yes." He stared in her direction, without seeing her at all. "Like a fire. You think...?"

"It's possible: spilled plastic, gas flame left on... burning plastic releases cyanide. He hadn't much time, if you recall."

"Could be. But wait. If he wanted Ac-Me to develop his invention, burning down the lab wouldn't be very smart."

"It wouldn't burn down. It might be damaged a little bit before the safety systems took over. The alarm would go off; the firemen would come, break down the door, cover everything with extinguisher foam, tramp around in rubber boots... Voila: big mess. But temporary mess; nothing the janitor couldn't cope with."

"I think," said Sims, taking up her hand and kissing it, "that you are a solid gold, honest-to-God genius." He ignored her feeble attempt to pull away, found it harder to ignore her face turning an unbecoming beet red. So what? Not every emotion needs to be pretty. Amanda was attractive, even so. "That's exactly what he was trying to do, when he knocked over that flask. Not only to make a mess, but also to fix the time. The firemen should have been at Ac-Me at about the time Frayne was seen in the gym at his apartment building. He drew attention to himself at 10:45. What would be the point, if it wasn't known to be the critical time? There is something else, something Roberta Farrell said. Frayne watched the six o'clock news..."

"...and he was annoyed that nothing interesting was going on in the world," Amanda concluded. She had totally regained her composure; her cheeks were slightly flushed - a nice, healthy colour - but her eyes were bright with discovery. "Three wars and five revolutions, or whatever the count was that week, ought to be interesting enough for anyone... anyone who isn't waiting for news he's made himself. Can I have my hand back?"

"What for?"

"To open the thermos. I need some coffee."

"What are you staring at?" Sims asked Lancelot in a friendly tone. The dog was sitting up straight, all senses alert, antennae swivelling from Amanda to himself and back again. "Haven't you ever seen super sleuths at work? Now," he concluded, accepting a plastic cup with one hand, while digging in his pocket with the other, "all we have to do is find some proof. I'm not greedy - an eye witness will do." He found his cigarettes, but spilled hot coffee on his wrist. Amanda took the cup from his hand and put it down on the bench. He fished out his father's old Ronson lighter and turned its familiar weight over in his palm. "Why disposable? Why didn't he have one that can be refilled, or use matches?"

"He liked things colour co-ordinated." She shrugged. "Well, nobody's perfect."

CHAPTER 28

The second half of Sunday had gone well. His guests enjoyed their meal and one another's company. He really thought Amanda was reassured about Brian's future, having met Father Mike. On the other hand, the morning had been fruitless: both the apartments he had looked at were smaller and more expensive than where he lived now; the other three he'd called did not allow pets. A high-rise was out of the question because of Lancelot; a house was impossible because of price. Yet, he must find a solution soon; Mrs. Field was grudging - as she had never been before - of his use of the laundry, and this morning, she complained about his "party" – four calm adults, talking until 10:30. He was definitely out of favour.

The driver of the Knox armoured truck had been discharged from hospital; they found him at home, with an attractive young wife hovering solicitously throughout the interview. The victim's account was short and simple. In heavy traffic, the car ahead braked unexpectedly. There was a loud crash, that's when he realized that he'd rear-ended the car ahead, which had braked unexpectedly.

"For no reason! His horn was going, so I thinks prob'ly he's hurt or had a heart attack or sumpin. So I gets down to see. Guy's flopped the wheel," he buried his face in his the crook of an elbow, "an that's it. Somebody hits me on the head and the nex' thing, I'm in a ambulance."

How, Sims wondered, could anyone mess up taking a statement so straightforward? Petersen, somehow, had failed to mention the horn.

"How many people were in the car you hit?"

"Just the driver, I guess. Din't see nobody else."

The front security guard's story was identical up to this point. He had seen his partner get out, go to the damaged car, lean in the window and just disappear.

" Couldn't see what he was doing, I figured somebody was trapped in behind that horn. Went to help Mike."

Then a dark figure jumped him. The man had on ski masks and some kind of loose black top – maybe a sweatshirt or hoodie. He held a rifle to the guard's head and told him to call the guard in back. As soon as the cargo door was open, two more gun-men had come out of nowhere, bundled him and his partner inside; tied, gagged and blindfolded them. The truck had then been driven away. He didn't think it was very far, in hindsight. At the time, being frightened, it had seemed a long ride.

He had only heard the one robber speak and that, briefly; he had an impression of an accent, maybe West Indian. The robbers had never spoken at all after that. The man who tied him had been tall, slim, strong, very quick; a young man, he thought. The guard never had a good look at the other two, but thought they moved like athletes or soldiers. All three had carried rifles. He was relieved to learn that the Knox driver was all right.

The second guard, who had been riding in back with the money, had not known what was going on - only that they stopped after a loud crash, a car horn was going and his buddy asked him to come out. Next thing he knew, two burly guys in black had jumped him, thrown him on the floor of the armoured truck and tied him up. He had not heard any of them speak. He thought the little bit of skin showing in the eyeholes of their masks was dark, but he couldn't be sure. His wife wanted him to quit Knox and find safer employment. Sims could hardly blame her.

"Sounds like terrorists," said Petersen. "Regular hold-up men would use handguns - they're easier to hide."

"You may be right," Sims half-agreed. "It's odd that there were only three, for a job this big - and in the knowledge that they would be facing armed men. I should imagine they would prefer to outnumber the guards, at least two to one." He added thoughtfully: "Funny, how fear affects a person, isn't it? The guards remember the robbers as large men - yet most of the witnesses said they were average, even small... One lady close to the scene was sure they must have been teenagers."

"So they're young terrorists. Or maybe gooks. Tell you one thing for free - Knox ain't gonna see a dime of the loot again. That load of cash'll buy a helluva lot of guns." Petersen sighed. "What a waste, eh? It'd buy a lot of women, too. Yes sir, a guy could have a real good time with four mil."

Should he try to get away early and catch Roberta

Farrell at her work, or see her later at home? He opted for the nursery: Frayne might be with her later - and Sims was not yet ready to talk to Frayne.

She was tidying her desk, preparing to leave. "Can I walk you to your car?" asked Sims.

"I don't have one," she said. "I take the bus."

"In that case, can I give you a lift?"

She hesitated. "Yes, all right. But what do you want to see me for? David said it's all over."

"Not quite yet," Sims told her. "There are some things I still need to clear up."

"Like what?"

"Do you remember that Saturday well?"

"Pretty well, yeah. Why?"

"What time did Mr. Frayne arrive at your place? Exactly, if possible. You see, I want to be quite sure of his alibi for the whole day - I mean, every minute."

"Why? David couldn't have had anything to do with Dr. Morley's death."

"Probably not," he prevaricated, "but he has an awfully good motive, so we want to be absolutely certain. You could help to clear him."

"Oh, sure," said the girl. "Not that he deserves it..." she pouted. Then, reflecting on how this might have sounded, she hastened to add, "I didn't mean that. I'm just mad at David today."

"What has he done?"

"Oh, nothing much. Just postponed the wedding, that's all. That's the second time, too. I had it all planned - told my parents, and everything."

"He must have a good reason," Sims fished.

"Sure. Money. That's always the excuse. We've got almost enough saved for a down payment on a house, and I'd be willing to put off having a lot of other things..."

"He must have been disappointed when his invention was turned down,"

"Well, so am I disappointed! Anyway, he can still go into business with Ferdy, and in a couple of years, they can make the stupid insulation stuff themselves. It's not like the end of the world. But try telling David... Oh, don't mind me. Turn left at the next light."

When they arrived at Roberta's apartment, Sims

accompanied her to the elevator. There was no doorman here; it was altogether a less lavish building than Frayne's. "You had to buzz him in, did you?"

"Right," she said.

"Let me just see how long it takes to get upstairs." He looked at his watch.

"About two minutes," she said. "I don't see how it matters."

"Well, there are some small discrepancies. I want to get everything timed, for the record."

"For the record," said Roberta Farrell, "it takes maybe twenty minutes to get from his place to here, two or three minutes to get from here to my door. And, anyway, David told me that the... you know... accident... happened a lot earlier. While he was in the gym."

"Now, I wonder where he picked that up?" Sims mused. "All we know is that Dr. Morley got to Ac-Me shortly after 9:30. He could have died any time after that. Please try to remember."

They were standing outside her door and she had the key ready; she had little choice but to ask him in. It was a small apartment, sunny and bright, prettily decorated on a modest scale, with flowers on every possible surface. Sims, naturally, remarked upon it. The girl, just as naturally, metamorphosed into a hostess.

"I usually have a cup of coffee when I get home," said Roberta. "Would you like one? Or wine? I always keep some in the fridge, for David."

"Thank you; coffee would be good." He followed her and stood leaning on the doorframe companionably, while she put water on to boil. "It's a nicer kitchen than mine; very compact and efficient."

"It's terribly small," she said. "I want a house with a big kitchen. This is all right for a single person, I guess, but you really can't do any proper cooking."

"I see what you mean. Not too much counter space."

"On second thoughts," she said, reaching for the kettle, "It's too warm for coffee. I'm going to have wine. You?"

Sims acquiesced. They were getting along just fine now; he had better be careful not to spoil it by questioning her too sharply. But when they returned to the living room with their glasses, under which Roberta put cork circles, and sat on the chintz-covered sofa, she brought up the original subject. "I've thought some more about it. I'm sure David was here by 11:30. He left the gym at quarter to - he told me. He noticed the clock over the pool, didn't realize it was so late, so he rushed upstairs to change, because he didn't want to keep me waiting. He's really so sweet, I shouldn't be mad... I guess he just wants to start off right. I wish I could make him understand..."

"It's quite reasonable, a young man wanting all the best for the woman he loves," Sims put in.

"Yeah, I guess. Except things - owning stuff - isn't all that important to me. Like that day we're talking about. I don't care that much what kind of bedroom furniture we get - and the ones we looked at were way overpriced. Even still, none of them were good enough for David. Maybe it's because his folks are better off than mine - he got used to having nice things, I guess. I keep telling him we could save more... but he does enjoy spending money."

"Give him time," said Sims. "Most bachelors like to have a sporty car, good clothes, that sort of thing,"

"You don't," she pointed out.

Sims wondered how she knew he was a bachelor. Did it show? Was it a sort of stigma, a brand on his forehead, obvious to all women? Or was it just his general appearance - did he carry about the neglected air of an untenanted house?

"I can't afford to. David's car has to cost five times what mine does, to run. And what I've seen of his wardrobe, well, it would take some heavy corruption."

Roberta giggled. She seemed younger at this moment, more vulnerable. He felt deeply sorry for her. "You have to admit, though," she said, "it's quite a car. And he does look nice when we go out."

Sims admitted that. "By the way, what was David wearing that Saturday?"

"Let me think. Nothing very dressy - we were only going shopping... His Harris tweed. Yes, and matching pants, and the shirt I gave him last birthday - I call it his Neapolitan shirt: it's got vanilla, strawberry and chocolate stripes. It really sets off his colouring. I remember because, after we dropped the jacket off, I thought he'd catch cold... But I guess he must have already had the cold..." She kept reminiscing, and Sims did nothing to break the mood. "The weather was quite nice that day."

"Would you describe the jacket?" She was instantly wary, so he added, not untruthfully but feeling like a con man all the same: "We have a witness who may have seen David; if the description matches, we may be able to fill in one little gap in the time."

"Okay. It's wool, a sort of dark chocolaty brown, like," she cast her eyes about the room, "sort of like the border in the rug there, almost the same colour as David's hair, and it's got nubbly bits of taupe and lavender, and leather patches on the elbows. Really smart - distinguished, you know?"

Sims nodded. "Yes, it sounds fine. I'll have to let our witness take a look at it sometime." Indeed, he would love to show the garment to Marcie. An all-brown man, was it? "So, he dropped it off at the cleaners. I hope they did a good job."

"Actually," she said, "maybe not. At least, I guess he wasn't satisfied because last week, when I picked up his cleaning, he told me to take it to Sparkle, and they're more expensive than the Jiffy we always used before, not to mention, out of my way. The Jiffy's only two blocks from here. Anyway, he hasn't worn it, since."

"Maybe they couldn't get the stain out?"

"It wasn't serious, I don't think - just a wet patch around the pocket... or maybe it was oil? David's so fussy about his clothes. Of course, there was that plasticky smell... All my clothes used to pick it up when I worked at Ac-Me. But that airs out in a day or two, if you don't jam things in a closet. I used to hang my stuff out on the balcony." Her round face looked very pretty with a mischievous smile. "I used to wonder what the neighbours thought. David wouldn't do anything like that. David can be a bit stuffy sometimes..."

Trouble in paradise? Sims asked himself, and got a mental kick from the ghost of Mrs. Whittaker in twelfth grade: avoid clichés! Whatever; she's not terribly keen on our friend right now - that was the third or fourth criticism of him in a very short time. And to a stranger. Maybe, precisely *because* I'm a stranger; maybe she wouldn't voice these negative sentiments to anyone whom she and precious David know well. Most people find it a relief to confide in a stranger when they've had a fight with the loved one... and a serious fight it must have been, given the nature of the man's offense. Worse: he makes her pick up his cleaning, and they're not even married yet. How will he treat her, when they are? If... You see, he told the other half of himself, why I don't like the so-and-so? Quite apart from the probability of his being a murderer.

"You didn't like working at Ac-Me?"

"Oh, it's not that; it's really a pretty good place to work, except for the smell. And Mr. Quick is a pussycat, really nice. It's just... well, I do like flowers."

"I can tell," he glanced around. "But I suppose it was convenient, you and David working at the same place - to have lunch together - that kind of thing?"

"That's what he said, too. Except we hardly ever did, or anyway, not alone, because of Ferdy being around all the time..." With a devil-may-care flourish, she refilled her own glass when Sims declined. "He won't come over tonight, anyway. I'll get some more tomorrow. I guess, really, he wasn't too crazy about me taking a cut in pay."

"A big one?"

"No, hardly any difference. The fringe benefits at Ac-Me are a lot better, though. Still, that won't make any difference, once we're married; I'll get all the Ac-Me benefits just the same. At least, until David goes into business. Did you hear Ferdy quit?"

"I hadn't heard," said Sims, who was surprised the boy had acted so quickly. "How does David feel about that?"

She shrugged. "He doesn't mind. Or, anyway, he didn't make a fuss, like when I left. Ferdy wants to work for his grandfather. In the imported food business? I guess that's all right, because he has all the money." She swung her glass in an arc and put it down. "As long as somebody has."

In spite of a strong temptation to lead her on in this vein, Sims changed the subject. "So, David got here at about 11:30. That would have given him no more than twenty minutes to go up to his apartment, shower and change. He couldn't possibly have gone anywhere else in between."

"No, of course not. He even dried his hair."

"Good. And then you were together all the time, eating lunch, shopping..."

"Except," she giggled, "when he took out the garbage. That was funny... He had to ask where it was, he's never done it before, and even then, he must have got lost because it took forever. Well, maybe five minutes... I asked him if he fell in."

"Five minutes isn't long. We can put that down as being together for most of the time. Where is the incinerator chute?"

"Just down the hall, left, the fourth door." She would have said more; something else amusing seemed to have occurred to her, by the way her lips began to curl up preparatory to another giggle, but the telephone rang.

"David!" she exclaimed. "I didn't think you'd call. Guess who's here! That's amazing! Yes." The smile died on her face, quickly, but not quite painlessly. "All right," she said, and hung up the receiver. "Sergeant, you have to go now. I'm sorry."

"It's perfectly all right," Sims told her. "I should have left by now. I hope I haven't caused any problem?"

"No problem," Roberta shook her head, but her voice was faint, unconvincing. "Only, David says you've got no right to question people. He says the case is closed. Is that true?"

"Yes and no," he said. "Thanks for the hospitality."

She chained the door behind him. Instead of heading for the elevator, he looked into the incinerator room - not so much a room as a deep, evil-smelling closet. It took twenty seconds to walk there from Roberta's door; he went through the motions of emptying a container down the chute - say, two minutes altogether, if one had missed it the first time and gone past. Why the delay? It wasn't long enough to do anything significant.

"He might have been sick," Amanda suggested when Sims had told her. "He might have needed time to collect himself. Or even to throw up."

This had become a ritual in the evenings. He came to pick up Lance and to make his report. He needed, always, to talk new information through aloud - to evaluate and sift it. And, whereas in the past, he would recount the day's

240

findings to Lancelot - really, to himself, with the dog for an audience - now he had someone interested, someone quick and observant, who could catch whatever he had missed and make helpful suggestions. Not only was it pleasant and productive, he suspected it might account for his having very few disturbing dreams, lately.

"And he probably ditched the paper towels or handkerchief, or whatever. Of course, that explains the water stain... Marcie had seen him stuff something in the pocket. I'd love to get a hold of this jacket... but a search warrant is out of the question. Or is it? We've got a lot more than we did two weeks ago. Not enough to arrest, but maybe enough to investigate further. I'll try it on Inspector MacDonald in the morning."

"If it's been dry-cleaned, there won't be anything useful, though. Unless the girl can identify it positively. Is that likely?"

"It's worth a try. Of course, we only get one try, so we have to make it convincing. In the presence of police officers."

"Maybe you should get some other brown jackets, like a regular line-up."

"Good idea."

Inspector MacDonald disagreed. "I've already had one complaint about you this month. I don't need any more. You're supposed to be working on an armoured car heist - or ain't four million and aggravated assault important enough for you?"

Sims protested that he was, indeed, working on the Knox case. He had voluminous reports to prove it. Some of the notes Petersen had re-typed were not dramatically better than the originals, but they were better - at least more complete, since the second interview with the victims. All three men had recalled a little more than the first time. Some witnesses had used different words, which might be revealing on closer study.

"That Miss whatsaname, Melanie Something," MacDonald began, and Sims supplied the name of the woman whose car had been stolen: Hopkins, Melodie. "Yeah, her. She called, wants her car back. Find out if they're through with it."

Sims assented. "Now, about this murder,"

"I don't know about any murder. I heard accident."

"Will you read over my report, at least?"

"Yeah, sure, I'll do that. When I get time. Look," MacDonald turned back to Sims. "You get crazy sometimes, but you done some okay work before. I got to deal with some crap - Departmental business. Internal's gone nuts over this west end thing; they wanna have a witch-hunt. You know what kind of bribes they're in-qui-er-ing into? Couple cruisers took a few free meals at some all-night diner. Lousy neighbourhood, right? Owner likes having uniforms around, scare off the punks, right? No big deal. Some ass yells bribery: all of a sudden, Internal's on it like flies on dog-turds.

"There ain't much goin on, they don't wanna look like idiots - got to find something. So now they're all over the place. Where did this man's shoes come from? How come that one's got a snazzy car? That's the kinda crap I have to deal with." The massive head swung back and forth on its buttressed foundation, reminding Sims of a bull elephant trying to shake a clod loose from his tusk. He wouldn't like MacDonald's job, no. "Anyhoo," the inspector concluded, "I'll get to your stuff. See what you're all fired up over. See if the case is worth reopening. Okay?"

"It'll have to do," said ungrateful Sims.

CHAPTER 29

He was at the police garage when Miss Hopkins arrived. He led her gently through her statement all over again, in case, like some other witnesses, she might recall more than she had before. The exact location of the car in the lot? Far back, behind the attendant's booth, behind at least a dozen other vehicles. That was where she had found a space. She had been late that morning; her usual parking lot, two blocks nearer the office, had been full. She had returned to collect the car at five-thirty, maybe a quarter to six. She stayed a bit longer to make up for the morning. Yet she had not reported the theft immediately. That was because she had doubted her own memory and gone back to check the other lot, before calling the police. By that time, the armoured truck had been unloaded and abandoned; the robbers, far away. In what? he wondered. Their own car? Or had they stolen another vehicle? It was worth checking.

"Earlier," he told Petersen. "They'd have left it in the lot where they meant to bring the Knox truck. Not too much earlier, and from another part of town. Let's see if anything was reported stolen from all-day parking lots or garages. They'd run it through a wash, as well, once they were done. Let's see if any clean abandoned cars have been spotted."

Computers make this kind of search a piece of cake, instead of the nightmare it once was. In this case, they didn't help at all. There had been only one other auto theft on that day - a snappy red sports job, hardly suited for transporting three men and forty-six bags of cash. Besides, 28 Division was morally certain they knew where it had gone: they had surveillance set up outside the shop to catch it coming out again - green, or black or gold - on its way to market. "You better not poke your big noses in here and mess things up," the sergeant warned. "We been trying to set this up for weeks." Sims assured him that 43 Division would do no such thing.

"What we want is a truck or van. Something sturdy but inconspicuous." Nothing like that had been found; nothing like it had gone missing. Dead end.

"Sergeant Sims?" The man was of average size, balding, possibly in his early fifties, wearing a nondescript light-coloured suit. He looked vaguely familiar, yet Sims could not associate the face with any recent cases. Could he be one of those Internal Affairs people that Inspector MacDonald had been ranting about? The interruption was especially unwelcome at this moment: Sims had been poring over records, trying to match the armoured car holdup with the methods of men previously arrested for armed robbery. The simplicity and efficiency of the operation did not point to any of them. More like terrorists... But wouldn't terrorists have taken credit by now? Not if they only wanted the money.

The man stood waiting patiently for him to change gears. "I was told to see you about this Knox thing... My name is Saunders."

When the coin finally dropped, it was at least a quarter. "Not Pete Saunders?"

"Yes. So they did tell you?"

"Nobody told me anything... That's hardly unique in the annals of police procedure," Sims babbled to cover his surprise. "Sit down, will you?" He extended a hand belatedly, just as Saunders was occupied in pulling up a chair; there followed a polite and very awkward skirmish, at last resolved by the meeting of palms. "Pete Saunders," he repeated. "I remember you. From Norris."

The other man's face went through all the motions of replaying old, faded motion picture films. The last reel seemed to do the trick. "You're not Alec? Mary Sims' kid brother? So you did mean it about being a cop."

They looked at each other for a while, assessing the changes. Finally, Sims asked: "Are you still with the OPP? Have you guys tracked down our getaway car?"

"Nothing so useful, I'm afraid. In fact, I left the police a long time ago. I'm a private investigator now - at the moment, looking into this case for the Knox company... Actually, I came to *ask* for help, not to offer it. Sorry."

Having digested all this and successfully forestalled another fit of babbling, Sims returned to business. "What can I do for you?"

"You can save me a lot of time. Of course, I could go around, tracing witnesses - and Knox can certainly afford

244

the hours it would take. But I surmise that your boys have done most of it already. Duplicating work is inefficient, and inefficiency galls me. Therefore, I was hoping you would give me the names."

"Sure, no problem. Who sent you to me?"

Saunders looked down at his hands, reflected, and then smiled into Sims' eyes. "Nobody. It's a PI trick, the nameless 'They'. It nearly always works. What I had from Knox was a list of the police officers on the case. First, I approached a constable called Peebles. He didn't appear to know very much. Then I spoke to a Detective Sucks - can that be a real name?"

"It's pronounced Sooch, or something like – Hungarian. Stubborn cuss refuses to Anglicize the spelling."

"Oh. He told me you were co-ordinating officer... So, here I am. Look, my interest - my client's interest - is legitimate. My tactics are unorthodox, but that's only because going through channels takes such an unconscionable amount of time."

"You still talk like a sissy," remarked Sims.

Saunders looked startled for a second and then burst out laughing. "Norris had its limitations." Saunders had been the object of much derision for what was considered an affected mode of speech. Having grown up in the north-western part of Ontario, he was perfectly competent in the local idiom, but obstinate enough to use the words and constructions he picked up from books. "I always intended to find something better."

"And have you?"

"Unequivocally."

"All right," said Sims. "I'll get somebody - PC Browning, for choice: she's handy with the computer - to make a printout for you. List of witnesses, diagram of scene, summary of events... What else?"

"Lab findings?"

Sims shook his head. "There aren't any. I mean, zero trace. No hairs, no fibres, no prints of hand or foot. And I've just been busy drawing a blank on the MO's of known felons. What exactly does Knox expect from you?"

"Several things. Recovering the assets tops the list. Next, they want to cover their own ass," he smiled at the eyebrow Sims raised at this expression, "in case the insurance company makes difficulties. Which it indubitably will, for this much money. Then there is the question of security, tightening thereof. Last come the employees. All three guards acted against approved procedure, by the sound of it, and Knox wants to fire them, but does not want a wrongful dismissal suit."

Sims thought this last a contemptible motive. "Punishing the victims?"

Saunders shrugged. "Depends on how you look at it. *Their* job was to protect other people's money. For some reason, they failed. *My* job is to find out whether they were at fault. If so, you and other honest citizens should not be expected to trust them with your savings. That this happened at all is going to cost Knox considerable revenue; they have to do, and be seen doing, something to prevent a recurrence."

"Okay, I accept that reasoning."

While waiting for the printouts, Sims briefly recounted what the police had learned so far.

"Black men?" Saunders asked. "Or brown, or just swarthy?"

"Not necessarily any of those. It could as easily have been makeup. What do you think of the terrorist idea?"

Saunders frowned. "Not a lot. They like to brag - and these guys haven't, so far. Besides, there would have been at least six of them."

"One of the witnesses thinks they might have been teenagers. But it was all too business-like, too neat."

"Yes, that aspect piques my curiosity, also."

"You switch back and forth at will, don't you?"

Saunders grinned. "I can afford to, now. Back in Hicksville, I had something to prove. Really, I harbour no grudge against Norris. My mother-in-law lives there. I still keep in touch with some of the old colleagues. Stuyvesant is in charge of the district now - do you remember him?" Sims shook his head. "He had a rough time; the only Dutchman in a sea of Scots. He transferred out. Then, ten years later, with enough seniority to go anywhere he wanted, he transferred back in. People are simply unfathomable. But never boring."

Armed with a ream of paper, Pete Saunders left the office to retrace the steps of Sims, Petersen, Szucs,

246

Peebles, at al, but not before he had promised a social visit. Amanda was at the lake with Lance; Sims had no pressing agenda. Well, he would have to go from house to house in the environs of Ac-Me with Frayne's picture: a very tall order, that would take more than one evening to complete. He had yet to hear from MacDonald, and it was too soon to remind him again. Meanwhile, why not relive times gone by?

As it happened, Saunders was much more interested in discussing the case at hand than the characters of their shared past. He arrived at the apartment, carrying a briefcase: the volume of paper had doubled since morning. He was preoccupied.

"Bugs me no end," he remarked, "how fast and tidy it all was. It shouldn't have been so easy."

"You're bugged!" exclaimed Sims. "I've got this on top of a murder that was even tidier. No weapon, no trace – lots of nothing."

"No suspect?"

"Yes, but no official sanction to investigate him."

"Welcome to the club," said Saunders. "I manage without official sanction all the time."

"But I still have the Knox case, too."

"Okay," the older man laughed. Sims didn't recall him ever laughing aloud in his previous incarnation. He seemed altogether more relaxed and confident than the young OPP officer of memory. "you win the misery contest." Looking around, he added: "It appears that I'm doing better in many ways."

"It doesn't show," Sims pointed out.

"Oh, these are working clothes. In my line, one prefers to be as inconspicuous as possible. I make quite a decent living, actually. And decent, by the way, is the operative word. Contrary to popular misinformation, it is possible to choose one's cases - and clients - in such a way as to avoid unsavoury activities, and to a large extent, physical danger - though not discomfort."

"What kind of cases do you work on?"

"Whatever kind appeals to me. At first, I had to take pretty much what was offered – divorces and insurance scams, mainly. But now I'm well enough established... one might go so far as to say famous, in a discreet way - that I can reject any case at will. Fraud and embezzlement can be fun. What I especially like to find missing people. Right now, I have this intriguing armoured car heist. If I buy you dinner at Pierrot's, will you go over it again?"

"Done. You may have information I can use. From the other angle, as it were."

It was the best meal he'd had in weeks, including Amanda's: she was a good cook, not a gourmet chef. Sims made a mental note to bring her here sometime, perhaps to celebrate the arrest of David Frayne. Buoyed by good wine, rich food and an atmosphere of relaxed elegance, he dared to anticipate such a conclusion. Nor, except for his obsession with the Knox case, was Saunders bad company. He could be amusing and disturbingly easy to talk to.

Perhaps it was the face: almost anonymous in its blandness. A still wakeful analytical part of Sims' mind noted fair skin, slightly sunburnt, the advancing forehead peeling a little at the retreating hairline, pale grey eyes, regular features: nothing memorable. Or perhaps it was the intelligent attention with which Saunders followed every word, however banal: he gave the impression of being sincerely interested. There was something attractive, too, in the way he alternated vernacular with precise Oxford English. Or, the attraction might lie in the fact that he never forgot anything.

"You used to talk like a sissy, too," Saunders recalled. "Weren't you planning to be a writer or something, before all that nonsense about joining the police?"

"As you see, not so much nonsense," Sims reminded him. "And? Is it everything you hoped, being a big-city police detective? Is it fun? "

"Maybe not quite everything," Sims wrestled with the urge to confide and lost on points. "It's an acute discomfort in the antipodal regions, on occasion," - 'so there, nyah,' added the ten-year-old from Norris, and received his inevitable cuff on the ears. "But it's been rewarding, over all. I haven't regretted the decision. Only,"

"Yes?"

"Lately, I've been dissatisfied... I'm not crazy about the partner they assigned me." He chuckled. "The unnamed 'they'... Actually, it was my inspector, and I'm not crazy about him either. The worst thing is this murder case. It's frustrating. You see, I've known from first sight that this man was murdered, and the only people who agree with me are his family and his boss - the people who knew him best. Their opinion doesn't count. Nor does mine. The inquest came up with 'misadventure', which was a polite verdict of suicide, and the department was content to leave it at that. Who needs another homicide, right? Which leaves the family up in the air. Who cares, right?"

"You do," said Saunders, "obviously. Do I take it you've become personally involved with the family?"

"I guess so. No guess about it; yes, I have. You know what else is funny?"

"What?"

"Mr. Meyer, the victim's boss, offered to pay me to do exactly what I'm doing already."

"Did you accept?"

"Of course not. It wouldn't be ethical."

"I would have."

"That's different."

"What's different? You want to solve the case; the man wants the case solved: he's willing to finance the investigation; you need to make a living. Perfect congruence of interests. I use half a dozen operatives, full and part time, as required. Two of them are cops - yes, moonlighting. It doesn't hurt that they have access to police files, though I prefer to go in the front door. But the best thing about them is that they're trained, experienced, reliable men. Their incentive, besides the extra money - which, God knows, they can use - is the opportunity to work outside of departmental constraints. I choose them carefully: hire each for the kind of investigation for which his particular talents are best suited - which, not coincidentally, they most enjoy. We're not doing anything unethical; we're taking up the slack. After all, the police can't cope with all the beating, cheating and dirty tricks in the world - especially not with one hand tied behind their backs." This last was delivered with a hint of bitterness Sims had not suspected.

"Why did you quit?"

"Personal reasons," Saunders answered. "Maybe another time, I'll tell you at bum-numbing length."

CHAPTER 30

They returned to Sims' apartment. It was strange, almost eerie, to open the door on silence: no scrabbling feet launching no dog into the air; no bowls to fill; no walk that couldn't wait ten more seconds.

"I can't imagine living alone," remarked the visitor.

"I don't," he said. "I have a dog, but he's on vacation in the country, with a friend."

"Dogs are all right, too," Saunders allowed. "We've got three cats. And my youngest son is heavily into reptiles, which, quite honestly, don't arouse my most tender sentiments. But what I meant was family. You know - the little woman keeping dinner warm, kids jumping on your neck... that stuff. How come?"

"Personal reasons," Sims told him. "Maybe another time."

The Knox material was spread out on the table from which all unwashed dishes and unemptied ashtrays, all newspapers and books had been removed. To the police material, Saunders had added profiles of the Knox employees, notes of his interviews from this afternoon and a dozen eight-by-ten photographs: of the scene, of the recovered armoured vehicle, inside and out, of the guards and driver, of the parking lot from which the 'accident' car had been stolen.

"That's a lot for one day."

"Oh, I didn't do it all myself. This job is far too big for one man - though I personally handle all the critical interviews. You like the pictures? My photographer is an ex-OPP crime scenes man; he does all the fingerprint and handwriting stuff, too. Someday, I'd like to have a little forensic lab of my own. Your people are good, but not enthusiastically forthcoming, vis-a-vis the private sector."

Sims compared the photos of the scene with his own diagrams. "We've made a little model," he said. "Or, rather, Szuch and Browning have, from the scene photos. I keep bumping into the same problem: placing the armoured car in the right position to account for everything that happened. The Knox truck hit the stolen car – Why? Presumably it stopped just then, by design. One taillight was broken in the accident, but they both worked; he should have had warning. The car was pushed against the parked van at an angle. Okay. It's sitting like this." He drew a series of three oblongs, accordioned together. "The Knox driver runs to the driver's side of the stolen car... and gets coshed. He's out of the picture. But the Knox truck is higher than the stolen car; the guard should have been able to see what happened. Unless the assailant was waiting behind the van... References to all these vehicles is giving me a headache."

"Why not call them vehicle A, B and so on?"

"We do, hanging around the model table at Division, but it's no better. Anyway, the armoured truck's schedule isn't published; they couldn't possibly know the route or time. Why didn't anyone see this hooded man lurking behind the van? And, how could they know it would be there? We've checked it out, by the way; it was on a legitimate food delivery. The driver is clean; accounted for."

"I have another problem." Saunders said. "How does the guard, who says he jumped out to help his buddy, intend to get from his side of the truck to the other side of the car? They're touching, right? Is he going to climb over? Maybe he doesn't think about it, or maybe he gets out the driver's side, having had to slide under the steering wheel. No mention of this in any of the reports."

"I don't think we asked."

"Therefore," Saunders noted in his pocket pad, "that's one thing to be followed up. The parked van is another. Did they know it would be there? Was it always there at the same time of day?"

"Yes, the delivery man says, he always makes that bakery his last stop, so that he arrives at closing time, to pick up donations of bread for a hostel."

"So maybe he stops to chat, takes his time. If the robbers knew, they may have chosen the spot with that in mind. Plus the side street, just there – he poked at the map – Hickory? - is convenient. This was one well-planned heist! In heavy traffic, how did they know they wouldn't be bottled in?"

"They grazed two cars and pushed another onto the sidewalk. I think they were pretty sure that tank could get through."

Saunders nodded. "Another thing. Not only is the

schedule not published; Knox varies the route, too. Somebody, somewhere, talked. That doesn't make it an inside job, you understand: at least five people had to know, and if just one of them mentioned the current route to a wife, a girlfriend, a good buddy... you see how that can snowball. Yet, I believe these people would have needed something more reliable than hear-say."

"Hear-say might be enough to give somebody an idea. That somebody might then cultivate one of the people who need to know, with the specific object of getting more reliable information."

Saunders scratched the flaking line on his head. "Yeah. The whole thing could have started right there. The dispatcher, or some other Knox employee, having a couple of beers in mixed company... Well, that's an awfully long avenue - not one I wish to travel at this time. Let's try the other end. Where the truck was recovered. It must have been chosen with care, as well. The timing called for a deserted lot; they knew when the factory closed. That's easy. They also had to have another vehicle, a truck, or maybe three separate cars, waiting. There may have been an accomplice, cruising the area."

"I hadn't thought of that one. A driver, hired for the purpose, maybe not in on the whole plan? Because, otherwise, it's hard to imagine them wasting the manpower."

"You're probably right. The first scenario is the most likely. Have you exhausted all possible witnesses?"

"You mean, anyone who might have seen them in the factory lot? We're plugging away... It's unlikely; there was only about forty minutes leeway."

"Cutting it damn fine, weren't they?"

"Not really," said Sims thoughtfully. "If they spotted a potential threat, they could always keep going, maybe to a secondary location. They could park the getaway car along their intended route, drop off one of the gunmen - who removes his mask and is unremarkable - and have him follow the truck, till an opportunity presented itself. That's how I'd do it."

Saunders shook his head. "Kid, you are not making me happy. Do you know how big that theory makes the house-to-house?"

252

"Yes. And we're working on that, too. What we need," he added, "is a more precise estimate of the time of travel - and to know whether they stopped or even significantly slowed, at any time, and if so, when. Only the Knox men can tell us that. They both say they can't remember, and neither will consent to hypnosis."

"You can't force them... But you can harass them a bit. Anyway, more than I can. Come along tomorrow when I talk to them - lend a touch of authority."

"Yes, I'd like that. I wonder if I can shake off Petersen for an hour or two..."

"The unwanted partner?" When Sims nodded, he said: "Send him off to interview somebody on his own. Any nice-looking young women on this list?"

"Melodie Hopkins, the owner of the stolen car. But she's suffered enough. It would be more just to give him paperwork. I'll think of something."

They continued thrashing over the case until after midnight. "Beryl expects me when she sees me," Saunders reassured him.

"MacDonald expects me at half past eight," countered Sims. "And I got nothing done on my murder case. Oh well...the sooner this is cleared up, the sooner I can get back to it."

The rear guard was in his yard, mowing the lawn. He consented grudgingly to stop and talk with them. "I don't see what's the use," he grumbled. "I already told you everything twice. Anyways, I quit Knox."

"I'm sorry to hear that," said Saunders gently, "I really am. Might one ask why?"

"The wife," said the man, indicating with a slight motion of his head, a tall, energetic lady in the background, weeding flowerbeds. "She worries about me. She's right, too. That little adventure is as close as I wanna get to dyin, for a very long time."

"What will you do now?" Saunders asked.

The ex-guard shrugged. "Don't know yet. Leave town probably; look for someplace cheaper, with less crime. Maybe bum around in the camper for a while, first."

"A wise decision," pronounced the detective. Small-talk finished, he put the guard through the entire experience one more time, with no interference from Sims. Nothing new developed. The man was quite certain that the truck had never stopped along the way. "Course, I might've passed out once or twice. No air in there, and they had my nose and mouth bandaged up, so's I thought I'd choke." This was an exaggeration, Sims knew; the gag had been tight, but not dangerously so. "Never much liked riding in back, even when I was the one had the gun."

Afterward, Saunders addressed a question to his notes: "Not even a traffic light?"

Sims answered: "They headed generally north - perhaps on residential streets... No, too many intersections with stop signs. An armoured truck on residential streets would attract attention... No, they couldn't avoid traffic lights altogether, by any route, and running them would be too great a risk. He's got it wrong."

They hoped for more from the front guard; he, at least had seen something of the action before being bundled in with the money. He, too, was outdoors - as who wouldn't be, on a perfect June day? He sat on the porch of his rooming house, shirt sleeves rolled up, feet in a second chair, sipping a beer and listening to the radio.

"You're from Knox," he told Saunders. "I don't want to talk to anybody from Knox."

"Why is that?" asked Sims, assuming that he, as regular police, was not in the man's bad books.

"They're going to fire me. It's not official, but I'm on suspension, as of today. They should be paying me compensation," he added, "I've had a rough time."

He had not seemed like a whiner in the previous two interviews. Perhaps he had some cause for resentment. Sims asked the questions this time and Saunders held back, making himself invisible.

The guard had no more information than before. No, he couldn't recall stopping or slowing down. No, he couldn't estimate the duration of the journey. No, he had not seen who hit the Knox driver, only that the driver had been there, leaning into the crashed car, and then disappeared. He, the guard, had jumped out on his own side, and been about to hop over the bumper, when he was attacked. No, he would not submit to hypnosis; his brain wasn't open to the public. In the course of the conversation he grew

254

increasingly hostile. At last Sims gave up, leaving open the possibility of a fourth interview, perhaps on a more propitious day.

On the way back to Division, he apologized. "I didn't make a big hit with that man. Odd that neither one can recall any stops. The getaway driver must have timed the lights. If he knows anything useful, he's not telling."

"Could have been worse," said Saunders. "He was belligerent when we arrived. My fault, probably - or Knox's. Did you get a load of that tattoo?"

"The rose on his arm? I caught a glimpse of it, before he turned away."

"Interesting," said the other man. "It said, 'O, my Luv's like a Melodie'." He printed it out in his notebook. "Now, what are the odds against a victim having on his arm the name of another, unrelated, victim of the same crime?"

"Melodie Hopkins..." Sims wondered aloud. "It's worth looking into, isn't it?"

While there was a modicum of satisfaction in seeing the Knox investigation move forward again, Sims could not give it his undivided attention. The murder of Edward Morley was still his primary concern. In the hours spent waiting for reports, and in the evening, he doggedly followed up even the least promising lines of inquiry.

After so long an interval, none of the bus drivers on the Steeles Avenue route remembered David Frayne as a passenger. "They're all a blur, anyway," said one. "Ask me what the drunk that gave me a hard time last night looked like, and I couldn't tell you."

Just as predictably, the residents of Galway Street noticed the suspect - or anyone - come through the Ac-Me hedge, though several thought he looked familiar from someplace. Nor could anyone recall a strange car being parked there, at the critical time. "Somebody's forever blocking driveways," said one irate householder. "Too many cars, not enough spaces." All this futility cost nothing but time.

On the other hand, he was able to tell Saunders the very next day, that the Knox guard had been seen at Miss Hopkins' apartment on several occasions. Saunders was able to reciprocate with the information that people in the guard's favourite local had noticed the man in the company of a young lady who fit Miss Hopkins' description. Sergeant Szucs learned that Miss Hopkins had been left alone in her office at 4:00 p.m.

After that, rolling up the case was a matter of painstaking routine. The second guard had purchased his camper only a few months before, with the aid of loans from the other two men.

"You tryin to tell me," Petersen demanded, "these gunmen were women?"

"That's what I'm telling you."

"So, who bashed the driver in the head?"

"His own wife, most likely - I doubt if she would trust any of the others to do it."

The police still needed witnesses to the movements of the other two women, to the whereabouts of the camper during the robbery... And to discover where the money was hidden. All of this ought to be simple leg-work, once the first, vital connection had been made.

CHAPTER 31

"All because of a tattoo," he mused at supper. "If Saunders hadn't spotted it, we might very well have bungled the case."

"Nonsense," Amanda said. "The deus ex machina isn't necessary. If Saunders had never shown up, there would have been some other break."

"I don't know,"

"Of course you do. How many crimes have you solved, without the legendary Saunders?"

"Some," he allowed. "Well, quite a few."

"And now, are you going to depend on him to solve the next one, and the one after that?"

"Of course not. All right, I get the point. One fluke will do as well as another. But the man is *good*."

It was nice to be here again, with Lancelot, who had put on a very gratifying show of hysterical joy at their reunion, sleeping on his feet. Brian would return from the Second Chance open house any minute now and tell them, with shining eyes, about every scruffy kid he met during the evening. They had eaten well. Amanda had shown him the latest series of pictures, and complained about her difficulties with the text. The lilacs outside were faded brown, finished for the year. Saunders was right, of course; it's not good for a man to be alone. But if one had no 'little woman' to keep dinner warm, or kiddies to jump on his neck, this one, anyway, had the next best thing. Sims was not complaining.

While Amanda had been up north with Lancelot - only two days, he realized; it seemed so much longer - he had been in a sort of limbo. His apartment did not feel like a home, without the dog. And this blue and grey room... did. It troubled him not all that Edward Morley had so recently occupied this place. He felt that they were friends of a sort, allies, at the very least: if this house was haunted, it was by an approving ghost.

"I'll tell you another thing," he said. "Saunders has a trained crime photographer and his pictures are pretty good. Yours are better."

She smiled and blushed, but very faintly; she was learning to take a compliment. "And a lot of good it's doing us," she said.

"I'm plugging away... If Frayne wasn't where he said - and he wasn't - he must have been someplace else. And if he was someplace, somebody must have seen him. I just have to find that somebody."

"You've tried Galway Street. You've tried his building. Where else was he, besides Ac-Me?"

"My guess is, he slipped out the back door of the garage, into the visitors' parking lot. Three buildings overlook that lot: one of the tenants may have noticed him, but it will take some time to see them all. I think he changed his clothes in the stairwell."

"The gym bag!" said Amanda. "Of course. I wondered why he should carry a bag when he was already wearing a sweat-suit."

"Right. The elusive brown jacket. I haven't checked the logs of all the taxi services..."

"He wouldn't take a chance on calling a cab to his own address, but to another of the buildings - or he'd catch one in the street. Want me to try?"

"Are you serious?"

She nodded energetically. "There are only three companies serving the area. Suppose I went to them with a story... Let me see... nice little suburban housewife... what would she want to locate a particular cab for? Maybe she lost a piece of jewellery - something small, not too valuable, or I'd have looked sooner."

"What will that get you?"

"With any luck, the numbers of the cars that were on Steeles at around nine a.m. on that day. How many could there be? And that, in turn, will give me a crack at the drivers."

"Not bad," Sims admitted. "It's a long shot, though; don't be surprised if it turns out to be a waste of time."

"I have time," she pointed out, "you don't. And we are pretty well down to long-shots. But how did he return? He certainly wouldn't stand on the corner of Birchmount and Steeles, waiting for a taxi..."

"No... My guess would have been bus: one stops there

at 10:05 - if it's on schedule. But that washed out... He might have rented a car - that's risky. Or he could have someone else do it for him. I'd like another talk with young Ferdy Arnott."

Sims had to wait until evening: the day was fully occupied by Knox business. Reports kept coming in from officers all over the city. The rear security guard, he of the camper, had joined Knox only two years before and worked on four different crews in that time. The dispatcher had been fed up with him; he seemed unable to get along with anybody... until five months ago, when he had been assigned to the present driver and guard. After that, no more trouble. The driver had a hobby: collecting antique weapons. Expensive ones... he was chronically in debt, and yet had managed to swing one more loan, for the security guard he barely knew. Though they had no children, his wife had quit her job at a down-town department store, only last month. Nobody had yet been found who could recall seeing her on the day of the robbery. It was all coming together.

"Hello Sergeant," said Ferdy wearily. What, no wise-cracks? No clowning? "What is it this time?"

"I hear," said Sims in as friendly a tone as he could muster, "you've quit Ac-Me. Giving up plastics?"

"Yeah. My grandfather is giving me a job." He did not appear excited at the prospect. "I start next Monday."

"Congratulations," said the detective.

Ferdy shrugged. "Yeah."

"Something wrong?"

"The pay ain't all it could be, and the job is crummy and boring. Otherwise, except for getting lectured and pushed around, it's just the biggest thrill of my young life." This was such a wan shadow of his customary style, Sims almost felt sorry for him.

"Then, why take it?"

Again, Ferdy shrugged. "I took it, all right? Anyway, I don't have to talk to you."

"Of course you don't," Sims agreed. "I'm only interested, that's all."

A look of petulant obstinacy, reminiscent of nothing so much as a two-year-old saying no, settled on Ferdy

Arnott's handsome face. "I don't have to talk to you, and I won't."

"Did Frayne tell you not to?" Sims asked softly. Ferdy's eyes met his in a fleeting glance of surprise, apology, appeal for sympathy, all come and gone in a moment, then he cast them down and shrugged once more, keeping silence. "Yes, I see. You don't have to talk to me, but I can talk to you. I know that David Frayne killed Dr. Morley,"

"No!" the boy protested. "It was an accident. The coroner said so, didn't he?"

"What I don't know," Sims continued as if the outburst had not occurred, "is whether you were an accessory." Ferdy was now staring at him with open mouth; Sims ignored this, too. "We're checking with the car rental agencies now." The boy's face did not change. No, he probably had not been involved; at least not in that way - Ferdy had never yet been able to hide his feelings. "My guess is that you didn't have anything to do with it. Maybe you didn't even know. I think he's been using you, and is still using you, and you're starting to catch on, but you don't want to face it. I think, too, Dave wants you to take this job, to get back into favour with your grandfather, for his money."

"No," the boy mumbled, without conviction; it didn't really matter, in response to which statement.

"And now," Sims went on inexorably, "he will start pumping you for information about Grandfather's habits, finances, anything useful. Mr. Arnott senior impressed me as a man who knows his own mind. He's not likely to invest in Superfoam, is he?"

The stricken look on the kid's face was quickly replaced by defensive anger. He closed up like a clam: utterly still and stony. In another minute, he might cry. Sims felt like a bully, picking on somebody so much smaller and weaker. He'd also shot his bolt and wondered briefly whether this had been wise: he had planned to keep his suspicions from David Frayne as long as possible - circle him like a buzzard, not swoop down like a hawk... It had been a snap decision to abandon caution - and now it was too late to reconsider; now he must follow through.

"What, then? Is Grandpa next to die? Just to be on the safe side, I'll warn him to write you out of his will. Pass that on to your *friend*, and see how fast he drops you." Sims turned neatly on his heel, leaving Ferdy Arnott to his own devices.

Now Sims must get to the girl, quickly. But it was already too late. She refused to admit him, or even to unhook the chain on her door.

"I don't have to talk to you," she said.

"That's true," replied Sims, "but it would be in your best interests to do so."

"I haven't done anything," she said.

"What about renting a car on that weekend?"

"What car?" There was no dramatic reaction of voice or movement. Then she repeated, "I haven't done anything."

"Maybe not, but what about your boyfriend?"

"David hasn't done anything either," she insisted.

"Are you really sure of that?"

The girl's expression was difficult to read, with only one third of her face showing through the crack of the door. However, he did notice the one visible eye roll to the side, as if looking over her shoulder... and he was positive that this minimal gesture denoted fear. Frayne must be here, keeping still, listening. Moreover, Bobbie was afraid of his reaction. Afraid of saying the wrong thing and losing him? Or afraid for her safety? He could not know. And, having put her in possible danger, he could not protect her. Would Frayne dare take violent action while under suspicion? Would he take a chance on alienating his alibi? Probably not, but Sims could not risk the girl on mere probability.

He had lost two witnesses in an hour. He had alerted Frayne. He had spoken aloud his belief in Frayne's guilt. All the buzzard airways were now closed: he had left himself no choice but to be a hawk. Inspector MacDonald had better come through with official approval of this case, by tomorrow morning, or else... Or else, what? Trouble, big trouble; Sims didn't know what form it would take.

He slept fitfully. Each time he awoke from a dream of someone else being killed - and none of these killings were like the tidy, quiet death of Edward Morley - he turned on the light, and lit a cigarette. Lancelot, puzzled and concerned, stayed close, butting him with his hard bristly muzzle. "It's all right, kid," Sims told him. "I'm not sick, just a little worried. I may have made a very big mistake today. I may have let impatience ruin a case..." There was no late movie on any channel that didn't feature violent death and loud screaming. There was nothing at hand to read that would take his mind off the problem...

Yes, there was. Amanda had given him a working copy of her grebe book text, days ago. He started reading that. Without the pictures, it was pretty flat. Where was the excitement she had shown when talking about these birds? Where was the enthusiasm for their possible rehabitation of the northern marshes? Where was the fiery-eyed champion of waterfowl who had so charmed him at Sculpin Lake? This text was written by an inarticulate college girl with no confidence in herself or in her subject. He kept drifting off to sleep over it, only to be startled awake by another bout of violence. Thus passed the whole night. At last, more tired than he'd gone to bed, he gratefully got up.

There was one more long-shot to play. At opening time, nine a.m., he was at the door of Jiffy Cleaners, on the corner of Copernicus Crescent and Steeles Avenue. The overweight young woman behind the counter had no reaction to David Frayne's photograph, except, "Cute," which judgement having delivered, she continued placidly to chew gum.

"Is there anyone else here?"

She thought long and hard about this, her white, beringed hand slowly twisting a lock of bright red hair. She finally came up with: "Yeah, sure,"

"Would you call them, please?" asked Sims, with the patience of a seasoned policeman - not even sighing.

The girl turned the pink wad over in her mouth, gave it two or three considering chews and said: "Yeah, sure." Then she turned and sauntered off into the forest of plastic-sheathed garments. Eventually, there came forth a lady of more advanced years and vaster proportions but similar features, moving just as slowly. Her hair was a lighter shade of orange, her eyes, almost as vacant, but at least her mouth was empty.

"Have you ever seen this man?" asked Sims, after the

customary introduction and showing of badge.

The woman considered David Frayne, "Cute," she pronounced.

"Have you seen him before?" persisted the detective.

"Yeah, sure."

"In here?"

"Where else? Yeah."

Sims gave himself a mental pat on the back for keeping his voice level and mild. "Can you possibly recall when you last saw him?"

"A long time ago," she said, after reflection. "Weeks."

"Do you work on Saturdays?"

"Yeah."

"Did you see this man on a Saturday?"

More reflection, then: "Yeah, could of been."

"Did you see him in the evening, at any time?"

"Don't think so,"

This time, he did heave a sigh, but only a small, quiet one. "The last time you saw him," he ploughed on. "Now, think very hard. The last time you saw him, did he pick anything up?"

"Like what?"

He wanted to say, like firewood, or a truck-load of turnips, but settled for: "Clean clothes."

The younger version appeared behind his witness and stood, masticating, her gaze lost in the street behind Sims. The older woman gave a soft moaning sound: she was making an effort.

"I donno," she finally said. "It'd be in the book, I guess."

This feat of rhetoric must have cost her dearly; her whole body sagged in exhaustion. Sims felt as if he'd been awakened, only now realizing how the somnolence of the place was affecting him. "May I see that book, please?" he asked, trying to keep urgency out of his voice. He felt an irrational fear that anything sudden or startling would frighten them into a collective coma. Mutual? What is the proper term for two?

The woman said nothing but leisurely reached under the counter, brought out a thick pad of carbon invoices and laid it on the counter. Somewhere, a fly buzzed fitfully. Sims, waiting with difficulty until she had withdrawn her hands, turned the pad toward him. Less than half of it was used, three sheets for each transaction. Leafing back toward the front, he came to May eighteenth. "Do you have the book before this one?" he asked.

"Yeah, sure," said she, making no move.

"May I look at it, please?"

The woman sank deep into thought, for what felt like several hours. The fly gave up its struggle. Then she turned slowly to the girl: "Honey, get the last book, will you?"

Honey wandered off among the garments. An eon passed. Nothing moved; no-one spoke. Sims, barely able to keep his eyes open, gripped the counter to steady himself and concentrated on a long jagged scratch on its surface. The girl returned and placed another invoice pad before him. This was thinner than the current one; when she finally relinquished it, Sims could see why: two of the three sheets for each transaction were gone. Near the end, he found May twelfth, and Frayne's jacket.

How to ask this next question? As simply as possible. "How do you know if something..." No, he must be more concrete, must not strain their capacities. "How do you tell when this jacket was claimed?"

He waited for the information to filter through. When it came, he realized he'd been holding his breath, which now escaped in a sigh that sounded explosive in that sleeping place. "Pink slips..."

Yes, the middle sheet of each invoice was pink. So were the slips of paper stapled to the plastic wrap on each clean garment on the racks before him. "Yes? When somebody gets his coat, and pays for it, what happens to the pink slip?"

Honey, thinking fast - perhaps the rhythmic working of her jaws sends extra blood to her brain, Sims thought wildly - volunteered: "In the box. We take it off and put it in the box." She actually reached under the counter without being asked, and pulled out a shoebox full of pink slips.

Sims didn't grab for it; he was too overwhelmed by this unprecedented activity. He reached for it slowly, carefully. He searched through the contents methodically. Twice. There were a number of clothes brought in on May twelfth, none by Frayne.

"It isn't here," he said to the women. Not that this made

264

very much difference, he thought, since no second date was on any of the papers.

"Hasn't picked it up, I guess," said the older woman. "He better get it this week," she added, "or he won't."

A dawn of great splendour broke over Sims' mind. "You mean it's still here?"

Both women shrugged in unison; soft mounds of white flesh and blue cotton, rising and gently falling. The daughter said, "Yeah, I guess."

Sims was tempted, only very briefly, to kiss her. He held down his excitement. "Can I have it?"

Both curly red heads began to rotate slowly in the negative. He rephrased the request. "I'll take it. I'll give you an official police receipt. And," he added, "I'll pay for the cleaning."

CHAPTER 32

So this, he thought, is how it feels to climb Mount Ararat and recover the remnants of Noah's Ark. He had prevented, by virtue of greater speed, the removal of the pink slip. He had asked for a second plastic bag in which to encase the relic, and carried it directly to the forensic lab. Not very much could be expected of it after cleaning... Still, the fact that Frayne had not claimed it in all this time was indicative of something, such as a reluctance to be associated with the garment. And the fibres could perhaps be matched to those on the back of Dr. Morley's lab coat. And if Marcie would identify it... I've got him, Sims told himself happily, I've got him now!

"You've got no authority to order any tests in this case," said the forensic technologist.

As he had not kissed Honey, so now Sims did not hit the man. He said: "That's all right. You hold it, and I'll get the authorization."

"Okay, sign here," the technician tagged the item.

Amanda didn't answer. Of course not; she was out hunting taxicabs. Sims's mind said that was good; the more could get done in the shortest possible time, the better. But his heart sank in disappointment; he had so much wanted to share this accomplishment - well, all right, piece of luck - with her. If it's not one fluke, it's another, and Saunders had nothing to do with this one. He would try again from his desk at Division.

"We had another customer complaint about you, Sims," Inspector MacDonald greeted him. "Where the hell you been, boy?"

"I," he said portentously, "have been collecting evidence. You can't tell me anymore that this isn't a case. I've got a case, all right. What customer?"

"One David Frayne," said MacDonald calmly. "Skinny snot in expensive duds. Know him?"

"Sure I know him. He killed Edward Morley."

"That's what I hear you been saying about him," MacDonald scratched his midriff where the shirt did not quite meet. "Can't do that, boy. Anyhoo, not unless you can prove it. Can you?"

"I think so. Maybe not enough to arrest, not yet... But enough to merit official investigation. Motive, means, opportunity, circumstance, maybe a witness at the scene."

The big pink head came forward to rest on its chins; the always unexpectedly alert little eyes fixed Sims for three or four seconds. "You sure?"

"I'm sure," he asserted.

MacDonald gave one of his ponderous double nods. "Okay, I'll look into it. Where's your report?"

"On your desk," Sims told him, not trying very hard to hide his exasperation, "for the past five days."

"I been busy," Inspector MacDonald smoothed down his shirt-front and turned to go. Sims took this as something on the order of an apology - and a resolve to act upon the matter.

"I'll have another item to add in five minutes," he called after the boss cheerfully. Authorization for lab-work would certainly come by this afternoon.

The other turned back, but only half way; his feet were still going toward his office. "Get back on the Knox thing. It's broke wide open. Stuff coming in from all over. Then we'll talk some more."

Indeed, there was the rear guard's wife, driving their camper out of the yard at 3:30, seen by a neighbour: "Because I always call in the kids for Polkaroo, and I saw that great big thing pulling out." A good, reliable witness, this sounded. And there was the same - or one very similar - vehicle, seen two blocks from the factory in whose lot the Knox truck had been recovered. All three residences were to be searched - might, even now, be undergoing a search - and here Sims was, sitting at his desk, missing all the action. He should get out there. If only he were less tired... Still no answer at the Morley house.

"Where were you?" Sims demanded. "I've been trying to call you all day!"

Amanda took a startled step backward. "Why," she began.

He was already in the door, still blustering: "All day! From ten in the morning, till half an hour ago! Do you have any idea how worried I was?"

She took one more step back and her half-frightened

expression began to change to one of anger. Before Sims finished realizing what an ass he was making of himself, her face had undergone yet another transformation: to something not unlike amusement. "Stop ranting and come inside, for heaven's sake," she said. "I told you exactly where I would be today. What was there to worry about?"

Having flung himself into his customary chair, Sims cooled off. Then he explained.

"Do you mean, you came right out and accused him? That wasn't wise, surely?" He shook his head ruefully. "To his face?"

"Not exactly. To his friends. But I'm virtually certain Frayne was in Miss Farrell's apartment at the time, and he must have heard, because he beat me back to Division, with a complaint."

"Poor Alec! What a terrible day you've had!"

Much as he enjoyed her sympathy, and would gladly have basked in it a bit longer, honesty compelled him to admit: "Actually, it was a quite successful day... Wait a minute." He looked around, "where is Lance?"

"Oh, dear," said Amanda, without any trace of upset in her tone. She stood up and he followed her to the back door, where a black nose was making wet patches on the glass at the level of Sims' face. "You'd better go out to him."

When the two had got their joyful cavorting safely over with outside and, calmed, returned sedately to the house, Amanda was in the kitchen, making coffee and sandwiches. "Sorry, I'm not up to cooking today," she said. "Do you mind if we sit here, to keep Lance company while he eats?"

The dog had already found his dishes and flopped down with a contented sigh to munch kibble. Sims looked around the kitchen he had only been in once before - and had not, then, really seen at all. It was spacious and bright, painted white, pale green and orange. A round pine table stood under a window onto the fenced yard (which, he noted, with a second attack of guilt, looked as if some mad contractor had begun to build a swimming pool before deciding where it should go). "This is a much happier place than the dining room. Why don't we ever eat in here?"

"We do, except when we have company."

"I'm not company,"

"I suppose not," she replied. "Guests hardly ever yell at me on the front porch."

"I'm truly sorry about that. It's just... well, it's probably foolish, but I imagined you in danger, after... well, after I blurted things all over the place... In fact, on sober reflection, I've been an all-round ass today, haven't I?"

She laughed. "Not really. I'm flattered, actually. But why would Frayne be a danger to me? He doesn't know I'm involved, does he?"

The detective shrugged. "I didn't exactly think it through that far... Besides, he might, since you took those photos at AcMe. I don't know what he knows." She poured coffee into heavy ceramic mugs, not the dainty cups she'd used on previous occasions. This was better; he wouldn't need two refills and look greedy. His was orange with a sad-eyed bloodhound on it. "I like this cup."

"It's yours. Now, tell me everything."

He did, concluding: "Inspector MacDonald called the lab this afternoon and authorized tests on the jacket. They start tomorrow morning. It might not prove useful - but, then again, it just might. Anyway, the important thing is that it's an official investigation again and he's officially a suspect. Did you get anything?"

Amanda sighed. "No, nothing. I must have spoken to two dozen cab drivers... Eleven, to be exact. I did take notes. None of them remembers David Frayne."

"Which doesn't mean very much, after so long. Neither Ferdy Arnott nor the girl reacted when I mentioned renting a car. That's how I ended up accusing him, you know - I tried to catch them off-guard with the car thing and it just got out of hand, somehow. This is good - what's in it?"

"You don't want to know. Whatever odds and ends I could find in the refrigerator, with mayonnaise... I forgot to buy groceries and ran out of almost everything. I hope they feed Brian at the Second Chance place..."

"He seems to be spending a lot of time there," Sims remarked.

"Every waking minute. Sometimes I'm surprised when he comes home at night - I forget he's not away at school. Of course, in a little while, he will be again. It's all right, really: he's making friends, doing something valuable. And he's happy."

"How is Louise? And the babies?"

"Fine, I suppose. I don't see so much of them now, either... Well, I've been busy myself. In a way, you know," she added, "I'll be sorry when Frayne is finally arrested. No, of course, that's not true. What I mean is, the children have their own lives - it's right and good they should, but, without this to keep me occupied, what will I do all day?"

"Finish the grebe book, for a start," he said, rather primly. "Then you should start another one. From what I've seen, it's very good."

"No, it isn't. The pictures are good. The text is crap."

He didn't know how to counter this, since it was true. "You've been spending too much time with cabbies."

Yet he must find a way to encourage her; she seemed more despondent now than in the weeks immediately following her husband's death. She looked weary, somehow faded, today. It made him sad - no, sad wasn't how he felt; it was more like irritation - as if someone had taken a liberty with the correct order of things. Amanda was supposed to be enthusiastic, brisk; she was supposed to have things under control. Part of Sims' ecology was out of kilter and he needed to fix it.

"I've been looking over your text," he said thoughtfully. "I haven't had time to read it through, of course, but I think I know what the problem is. You don't write the way you talk. I mean, when you told me about those birds, they were real and alive and... and I don't know... important. I'd never heard of them before, yet you made me care. That doesn't come across in the written version. You're too careful, too self-conscious... I think what you need to do is write just whatever you would say to a friend who knows nothing about the red-necked grebe. Imagine that we're sitting in the canoe, and tell me what I'm seeing."

"You think?"

He nodded. "Anyway, it's worth a try. When do you go north again?"

Amanda considered. "Well, tomorrow, or the next day. Now that the police have taken up Edward's murder, I don't suppose I'll be wanted here..." She looked unhappy over that, but instantly rebuked herself. "That's awfully childish. I'm really glad you're going to get him."

270

"There will be the trial, of course," he reminded her. "It will go on, probably for weeks; you'll want to be there?" She assented. "So, it might be a good thing to have the book finished before then."

"Yes, of course, you're right. Only..."

"What?"

"Oh, just being silly. Worse than silly. You see, I liked it. Oh no, I mean, it's horrible, Edward being killed. And I do miss him - sometimes, I miss him very much... in spite of how we were..." She sighed, shook her head as if to clear it, or to make the thoughts go away. But, as Sims continued attentive, expectant, she decided to finish the confession. "I don't know how much help I was, really - but some. Yes? And it was exciting, talking it over... I wish there were more of it."

"There *is* more," he said. "There is still the whole business of finding a witness - anybody who saw Frayne in the stairwell, in the parking lot, on the street... Trying to get Ferdy to recount whatever may have been said before... There is the question of whether Marcie actually can identify him - or his clothing... I'm waiting for a lab report... There is a *lot* more. I promise to come over every evening, and tell you every detail."

"Is that allow- What's wrong?"

"Mr. Meyer! I promised to tell him about any progress, and I've completely forgotten. I'll call him now, if it's all right?"

When he returned from the living room, trailed by a disappointed dog - in Lancelot's sphere of interest, masters suddenly getting up from chairs ought to mean a desire to go for a walk, not to sit down again someplace else and talk gibberish to inanimate objects for inordinate lengths of time - Amanda was putting away the washed plates. "More coffee?"

"Yes, please. You know what he said?"

"No. But then, I wouldn't, would I?"

"Don't be snarky - it doesn't suit you. He was glad I didn't call him until there was a real break... I forget about him, and he's grateful."

"Some people are just natural Polyannas... I didn't mean to be snarky."

"I didn't mean to call you snarky. Still feeling left out?"

"A bit. But I'll get over it."

"I expect you're too tired to take the inane quadruped for a brief perambulation?" Before she could formulate an answer, Lancelot was on his feet and bounding to the front entrance, where his leash hung. "How does he *do* that?" Sims demanded of nobody in particular. "This is an animal who doesn't understand 'get down', but if I learned to say 'walk' in Swahili, he'd understand that. On the way back, I'll stop in at that all-night supermarket. Anything you particularly need, or should I just buy generic food?"

"I'm coming along," she said. "I don't want to eat spaghetti for a week." Amanda was brisk and competent again. Her cheeks were the right colour and her eyes, bright. She even smiled, to show no offense was intended; certainly, none was taken.

In the morning, Sims was disgruntled. He was wearing a shirt for the second time, and had to keep pulling down his jacket sleeve to hide the soiled cuff. I should buy only grey shirts, he thought: a kind of slate grey, the colour of police desks, the colour of counters in civic offices. He was hot, too, and would have liked to take the jacket off. And then, the search of the Knox employees' homes had turned up nothing in evidence. Without that hard evidence, it would be difficult to make the charges stick. He could not yet start nagging the forensic lab. But the coffee was already thick and bitter.

And Petersen was hanging around with nothing to do. "Know who I talked to yesterday?"

Sims grunted; he wasn't interested.

"Little Gloria, that's who! She's back, you know. I mean, back on duty. Good as new, she says. Looks pretty good, I got to admit. Lost a couple pounds. That little piece I been hangin out with, she's all right, you know, but I mean, just all right. Gloria, now, she could give a guy a hard time, I'm the first to admit that, a real hard time, but I got ta tell ya, she wasn't boring. No, sir, she was sure never boring. I just might give her another chance, know what I mean? Sims, you're not listening."

"That's right," he said. "Where is the money?"

"Well, I haven't got it! If I did, you wouldn't see me for dust."

"Has the camper been impounded?"

"Yeah, sure, yesterday. Clean... well, pretty clean. Anyways, no money and no guns."

"Yes. Where are the guns? They're with the money, I'll bet. None of these people have anything like a cottage or cabin... Do they have any close friends or relatives with cottages? It doesn't matter; none of them was gone long enough... Besides, it's summer, and they wouldn't put it where someone else might find it..."

"Sims, you're making me crazy," said Petersen. "We'll find it, all right? Just a matter of time."

"Time!" Sims exploded. "Time! I don't have any time. I've got a murder case. According to the inspector, I have to get this Knox business wrapped up before I can go back to work on it."

"Yeah? Well, keep your shirt on. It's goin just fine."

"We've searched Miss Hopkins' apartment?"

"Sure. Nothin there."

"Have we looked in the yard?"

"What yard?"

"Mr. Emery's - the rear guard on the armoured truck. His yard. Have we dug it up?"

"Doesn't say so in the reports," said Petersen.

"Then, do it. In fact, I'll come along and we'll all do it. The warrant is still good. Get me some constables."

"Sure, Massah, whatever you say, Massah."

CHAPTER 33

The Emerys' flowerbeds went down before unenthusiastic departmental spades. The Emerys' lawn was torn up in sections, and deep holes dug beneath. "Roll that turf neatly," Sims told the constables. They swore under the scant breath left in them. The Emery's new hedges were uprooted. "Gently, now: we'll have to put them back." Sims was not one of those policemen who think a search warrant is license to devastate a premises - and MacDonald was not an inspector who enjoyed complaints from the public.

"Sergeant, hey!" exclaimed a man in blue shirtsleeves. "Check this out!"

'This' was a long burlap package, tied with new rope, laid neatly in the bottom of the trench, three feet down. The constable brought it forth with difficulty: it was evidently quite heavy, but the second uniformed man stood by, waiting for Sims to lend a hand. Inside it was a plastic bundle, taped around with care. Inside that were three rifles, from two wars and three armies. They were well greased for storage. On close examination, not one was functional. "The driver," said Sims. "They belong to the driver. He planned to come back for them."

"All we got from the witnesses," volunteered Sergeant Szucs - by virtue of his rank, like Sims and Petersen, an onlooker at the excavation - "is that they had rifles. Nobody described the guns in detail. I wonder if any witnesses can identify these?"

"Round them up - just the ones who were near enough to see clearly," said Sims. And to the uniformed men: "Keep digging."

By the end of the day, the entire Emery property had been turned upside-down, and very little of it repaired; they would have to return early tomorrow. No cash was found.

"Keep digging," Inspector MacDonald told Sims at quitting time. "If not that place, dig up the area around the other guy's rooming house. The driver lives in an apartment, so that's not much good."

"We did find the guns," Sims pointed out. "I think Sergeant Szucs is on top of the situation. He can carry it through. I'm ready to get back to the Morley homicide

274

now."

MacDonald regarded him blankly, as if he'd forgotten who Sims was. Or what he was talking about. MacDonald stretched in his huge swivel chair, scratched at his belly. He had on a pale blue undershirt. "Naw, you been doing a good job, boy," he said. "You finish it up, there's probably a commendation in it. Anyhoo," he added, almost absently, "I turned the other thing over to Homicide."

"You did what!?"

"Homicide," the inspector patiently explained, giving the word his full attention: even his right hand arrested in mid-scratch. "You know, the guys who investigate murders. They got the time, the manpower, the budget... God knows, we haven't. And they're good at it. They liked your report."

"That's nice," said the robot standing before the desk. Someone had forgotten to program it for this contingency: he couldn't move. He couldn't even decide how to feel, once he recovered from the shock. Which would be soon, he hoped, because he didn't want to spend the rest of his life standing here. "You turned it over to Homicide," he repeated.

"Well, for cryin out loud, boy, it *is* a homicide, ain't it? You chew my ear off for weeks, telling me it's a Goddamn homicide, and now you're all wrecked up, cause I agree with you. It's what you wanted, ain't it?"

"You also told me, right at the beginning, that if I turn it into a full-scale murder investigation, I'd get first crack at it. Your exact words. I've done most of the work on my own and I want to be in at the end."

"Yeah, well," said MacDonald. "See, the way it is, Homicide don't like nobody cuttin in on their action. Anyhoo, you got a real sweet case going, all I heard. Real sweet. You been co-ordinating it from the start, right? You done good. All you got to do now is find the money. Do that, and I'll see if I can't second you out to Homicide... Who knows, they might let you transfer in permanently. I wouldn't mind," he added. "You're an okay cop, but you're a pain in the butt."

Argument seemed futile. Besides, his limbs were working again; paralysing shock had given way to a rage that shook every fibre of his body. Sims looked down at his hand. It was steady; none of the internal tremor showed. He would go away, for now, and regain control. But he would be back.

First, he called Saunders on his car phone, to impart the latest news. "Where else could they have put the money?"

"I'm working on that," said Saunders. "Of course, I was working on the recovery of the weapons, too, only you boys beat me to it. I assume you did a thorough search of the dwellings in question; locker rooms, and so forth. Yes, of course you did. What about some public place? Out in the woods, for example, or in a park? I'll see if any of my sources know about a favourite picnic spot these charming people may have frequented. I'll keep in touch," he concluded. "Stay loose."

"That dates you," Sims told him, in a voice much more like his own. He was calming down, he really was. Now, he must think very hard what to do.

A transfer to Homicide? It would free him from some of the present discomforts: MacDonald and Petersen, for a start. But it would also get him into some things he didn't relish. Teamwork, with a very big T, and close supervision. The Homicide Squad carries prestige, he told himself. Yes, and you get to look at horribly mutilated people. The dilemma was not unlike that of Mr. Quick and SuperFoam. There are no petty cases on Homicide, said the first part of him - no factory break-ins, no irate fathers of sub-compact delinquents, no shouting matches over the breakfast table. Sure, he replied, but I'd get to see the remains of that poor woman, after her old man beats her to death. Well, but at least, then, you could finally put him away. I don't want to put him away. Well, yes, I do, but right now, I'm really only concerned with putting David Frayne away.

So, take the boss-man up on his offer. Recover that money, get a temporary assignment, and see if you like it. You don't have to make a final decision today... Of course, the choice may not be yours: everybody and his dog wants to be on the Homicide Squad. I don't, not really, and neither does my dog. Oh, for crying out loud, boy, said the Little Mac in his head, stop being so Goddamn wishy-washy. You can do anything you up your mind to. So make up your mind!

First, find the loot for Knox. All right, where haven't we looked? Saunders is covering the open spaces; no point in duplicating his work. We've searched the homes, the yards, the cars, the basement locker rooms. No good: for those big canvas sacks of money, they would need half a dozen lockers - or one the size of a truck... Did we search their garages? Of course we did. They didn't plan to hide it for long, not more than a couple of weeks... Short-term storage?

"Get me Detective-sergeant Sooch!" he shouted into the phone. "I mean," he told the dispatcher more quietly, "please find Detective Sooch. I need to speak to him urgently."

Sims pictured himself as some kind of Borgia, sitting in state, waiting for his spies and minions to gather in the fruit of his multifarious intrigues. He would be cold and calm, his emotions kept in iron check, impenetrable to lesser mortals. It didn't work. He merely sat behind a dented grey institutional metal desk, piled high with notes and diagrams. He had organized it, first thing, but he kept looking up this, double-checking that, mixing up the two cases, and having to sort them out again. He'd had three cups of bad coffee and eight cigarettes: twice what he normally allowed himself, before eleven in the morning. He was, in fact, fidgeting to no purpose. Waiting was not Sims' best activity, especially under the circumstances. He had lost all interest in the Knox case: it was solved, finished, but for the last detail. But for the final documentation, it was ready to be sent to the prosecutor's office. From here, even Petersen could have handled it.

And he was still angry. Normally, it would have passed overnight; normally, he would be as resigned by now as he tried to appear. He might have been on one of the searches; instead he had chosen to remain at Division, waiting. It would take time.

So would the forensic report on David Frayne's jacket. He had briefed two detectives from Homicide, had what could pass for a pleasant enough chat... After all, they were not to blame. One was a gentleman - and Sims used the term advisedly - named Dan Cryer, whom he had encountered before; a man of keen intelligence and un-coplike good manners. The other was familiar and forgettable - traits, Sims would bet much, he had cultivated through a long career. Competent men, and trustworthy. They had paid close attention to all that he said, had been respectful of his observation and experience. Perhaps they knew something of the situation and made an effort to spare his feelings. But it was now their case. Phrased more tactfully, nevertheless the message was clear: when we want your help, we'll ask for it.

All the same, at half past ten, he did telephone the forensics lab. He allowed a certain amount of good-natured ribbing to pass unchallenged: he wanted the man in a good mood. Finally, information came: "You were right about the fibres. I won't say match, at this stage, but they're consistent, all right, with the little bits of fluff we got from the back of the victim's lab-coat. Maybe the same as the victim's jacket, but my textiles guy doesn't think so... We haven't given this to Homicide yet, not till it's more conclusive - what I'm telling you here is strictly educated guess - call it gut feeling - nothing you can take to court, all right? It's been cleaned, you knew that already. Not by a top-flight cleaner, though, lucky for us. No stains, except a little oil on the leather patch at the elbow. What we have got - you'll love this - we've got some - well, actually two, so far, but we're still looking - itty-bitty fragments of glass. Consistent with - don't quote me on this, now - consistent with the bits in the plastic muck from that flask. They were embedded in the lining of the left hand outside pocket. It's not iron-clad, you understand - there is so little of the stuff, it could be trounced in court, if it gets that far. But I think we'll have something more definite by tomorrow or the next day. And then, if you can prove ownership – oh, wait you've done that with the cleaner's carbon. Just get somebody to say he was wearing it on the day, I think this jacket puts your guy at the scene, all right. Yo, Sergeant! Let's have some major gratitude here." Sims expressed all the appropriate sentiments. A week ago, even yesterday, he would have jumped for joy. Now - well, now, it wasn't his case anymore; let Homicide dance in the streets.

He stacked his informal notes tidily and placed them in the only drawer that wasn't full. His good notes had gone, through Inspector MacDonald, to Cryer and the other one, whatever his name was. That left the desk top with nothing but the current case: the Knox holdup reports. Where were the officers with that piece of paper? That key? Possibly the two items wouldn't be together: Sims' guess, based on how all incriminating evidence had been shared out, was that they would be with the front guard and the driver, respectively. Still, all the domiciles would have to be searched all over again. It could very well take all day.

The hell with it, said the new rebel Sims, whose increasingly frequent visits were making him uneasy. He would put in an appearance at Ac-Me Plastics. And what would that accomplish? At the very least, he could count on a decent cup of coffee from Mrs. Benz.

Nothing had changed. The corridor was empty at the moment, just before the lunch-time bustle started. The receptionist in the front lobby hardly glanced at him. Miss Hillyard gave him the sweet smile he had learned not to take personally. Mr. Quick was as flustered and courtly as ever.

"As you are no doubt aware," he said, after polite preliminaries, "there has been much activity. I spent upward of an hour this very morning, being subjected to the third degree by the Homicide Squad, no less. My goodness, they're formidable, are they not? Of course, having spoken to Mr. Meyer, I was prepared for something of the sort... and yet, I had rather become accustomed to your own - shall we say, low-key - style of interrogation... I do hope I made a good impression. I take this to mean there is no longer any doubt?"

"There is always some element of doubt," replied Sims cautiously. "But, on the whole, yes sir, you may take it to mean that an arrest is imminent. Perhaps it would be wise to review any applications you may have, for the position of junior chemist."

Mr. Quick's well-used face crinkled into a smile, which he prevented, just, from slipping over into laughter: the situation was too grave for that. "I must admit, I shall not mind terribly. Aside from this... this outrage that he has perpetrated - allegedly perpetrated - I have never quite warmed to that young man. We already have two new people, did you know?"

"I had heard about Mr. Arnott's resignation."

"Pity. Without the other... I rather thought young Crass might mature into a valuable member of our team... To be perfectly frank, just between us, I rather enjoyed his irreverent high spirits. And now this... With one thing and another, it seems as if the entire laboratory staff must be replaced. I do hope Martin Jones will stay with us."

"He's doing well, is he? No further misgivings?"

"Somewhat to my surprise, though not," he added ruefully, "to Mr. Meyer's - I must, as usual, bow to his superior grasp of human nature - Martin exhibits all the qualities of a leader. As he must, in order to maintain any semblance of productivity, under the circumstances,"

"Surely, Mrs. Dumont is a stabilizing influence?"

"Oh, dear me, no! Or, rather, that is yet another development which ought to have been foreseen, and was not..."

"What do you mean?" asked Sims, a touch of the alarm he felt creeping into his voice. "What's happened to her?"

This time, the old man did laugh, though very softly. "The usual sort of thing. She is ah...er... in the family way. A condition, apparently, that both Dumonts had anxiously awaited for some time. Well, you see what this means: her present working environment is not considered suitable for a mother-to-be, however safe we may attempt to make it..." He sighed. "One finds it difficult to weigh one's own loss against another's gain... I do try to rejoice for Eve and her young surgeon, but I cannot help regretting her departure...

"I have been sitting here, contemplating the past twenty years, in juxtaposition with the last two months. So much sound and fury, in so short a time! I have been feeling a little as the last Caesars must have done... The barbarians having risen, the empire can never be the same... Oh dear," he said, shaking himself as if emerging from a deep water, "I really must get hold of myself. So much to be done. First, and least onerous, is a luncheon appointment with Mr. Meyer and Dr. Jones. Would you care to join us?" Sims, thinking that the same etiquette which prompted the invitation also required that he refuse it, began to do so, when the other man added: "I do realize it's an imposition, but you are so much more abreast of these... " He waved a

280

frail brown hand vaguely in the direction of the laboratory, "these disquieting events... Perhaps you would be kind enough to - how do they put it? — brief us..."

How could he then refuse? Besides, he was ravenous.

I'm having lunch, he thought, with Claudius and Aurelian... had those two emperors been contemporaries? And who was Jones supposed to be? He now had a presence that he had previously lacked; seemed at ease in the company of his employers. Did Sims imagine it, or were his gestures somewhat looser, larger than before? A contender with barbarians... Roman history had become hazy in Sims' mind; he would have to learn it again. There was a green leather-bound copy of Gibbon in Edward Morley's room: he would consult that.

While conversing amiably, often intelligently, over the excellent food, his mind kept wandering off to impertinent topics. Why? He liked and respected these men; he did want to help them cope with the trauma of a murder in their midst. Yet he was reluctant to share his observations. It was his case, his investigation. He was involved with the murder of Edward Morley, not with them. They were suspects or witnesses or sources of information. He was uncomfortable with them as human beings in their own right. Hence the labelling; turning them into cyphers was a way of creating a barrier.

Aurelian remarked: "Sergeant, you seem abstracted. Is something wrong?"

"I'm sorry, Mr. Meyer," he replied, "I was woolgathering. Look," he addressed them all. "I have a problem with this case. I'm the one who kept pushing it, and I succeeded. Now it's an official murder investigation being conducted by the people best equipped to conduct it. I'm not really in the picture any longer. I have another case to work on. I'm not sure it's even appropriate for me to be here. Homicide is close to making an arrest, if that's any comfort. I will make one request of you, Mr. Quick."

"Name it," said Claudius with imperial, brevity.

"When Marcie is questioned - not if, but when, because she is a material witness. I wish I'd been able to find someone else, someone less vulnerable, but I haven't. Ask - demand, if necessary - that it be done by a detective named Cryer."

"Yes, all right. And I shall insist that Mr. Draper be present."

Sims nodded. "I think I'd better leave you now." He stood up to do so. "Thanks for the fine lunch. And for all your cooperation."

"Sergeant, have you another minute?" Meyer caught up with him at the door. "Outside?"

But he hesitated, unlike the smooth, confident Lucius Aurelian to whom Sims had grown accustomed. "I'd hoped to consult you, confidentially, on another matter... A friend - really, a friend, *not* myself - has a problem of... What would Charlie say? Of a delicate nature. Some valuable property gone missing, and..." He took a deep breath and finished the statement, succinctly. "He thinks his son may have taken stock certificates, not all of them his own. He wants to recover them, without involving the police, you see. In short, he needs a private detective. I thought you might know of someone reliable?"

"As a matter of fact, I do," said Sims. "And this sounds like the sort of problem he might like." He handed over the card Saunders had given him at their first meeting. Then, too late, already accepting Mr. Meyer's gratitude and hand, wondered if he had copied the phone number into his notebook, or only meant to.

Of course, there was the slight embarrassment of having to collect his car from the Ac-Me parking lot and returning the friendly greetings of employees he had interviewed. There were many: on a warm summer day, people liked to eat their sandwiches outdoors. Sims had to exchange a few words with Miss Valentine and with Mr. Draper. Eve Dumont was not in evidence, much to his relief. He did see David Frayne, returning from somewhere alone; the man turned away ostentatiously - and quite unnecessarily - snubbing him. He felt like someone making an escape. Well, that was over. Good-bye, Ac-Me Plastics. Perhaps that had been his real reason for coming.

CHAPTER 34

"Where the hell have you been again?"

"Lunch," answered Sims. "Why?"

Inspector MacDonald made a noise in his throat like distant thunder. "I'm not so crazy about your attitude lately," he said. "Anyhoo, stuff been comin in on the armoured car heist. You remember - big case? Over four mil? The one you're supposed to be in charge of? Peebles was lookin for you, yellin fit to bust."

"Yelling what, specifically?" If Sims got any cooler, they might try to ship him off to the morgue.

"Sez they found it. Found what?"

"I suppose, the receipt from a public storage locker. Or the key. Both, I hope. Where did he go?"

MacDonald shrugged, ordinarily a daunting spectacle, which would conjure for Sims the quaking of whole mountain ranges. Yet now, merely a fat man, taking a cheap shot. "Lunch," he pivoted his mass and walked, in leisurely state, away.

PC Browning gave Sims the messages without fanfare. Szucs and Peebles, Petersen, Whistler and Burnside were getting some food in the cafeteria while they waited for him. They had found a receipt from one U-Stash Storage Ltd., on which the combination of a lock was written, at the home of George Woods, the front security guard. Well, of course. He called Saunders, whose numbers, car and office both, were neatly copied into his address book. Naturally.

"I thought you might like to join us at Markham and Fourteenth Line, in about half an hour."

"You haven't found the money."

"I think we have, though."

"I'll get there," and Saunders hung up.

Then he collected his troops to move in for the payoff - the grand discovery. All the canvas bags were there, intact, neatly stacked behind some furniture. As expected. And there was much rejoicing. He thought of Ferdy Arnott, not doing a Monty Python routine, but white-faced and silent, drawn in like a little frightened tortoise. He ought to see the boy one more time, just in case he did know something and was ready to tell it. No; Homicide would question him now - maybe even at this very minute. If there was something to get, they would get it. Of course they would. If the girl, Bobbie, had anything more to say, she would say it to them. The locker was emptied into the waiting police van. He did not offer to help the constables. Pete Saunders, in the moment of jubilation, threw an arm across his shoulders.

"All right, Alec! I'll take you out for the best meal you ever had. Wine, dine and lionize you. Hell - I'll split my fee with you. Anything, man, just name it."

"Only doing my job," said Sims.

"You are not partaking of the victorious mood. You did a fine piece of detecting here. Or, rather, we all did. We deserve to be happy and proud. What's troubling you?"

Sims gave him a wan smile. "You broke the thing open. Everything after that was routine. Oh, don't mind me - it's just - something else."

"Your murder case? Come on, tell Uncle Pete."

"Sergeant, hey! We're ready to roll here."

Sims waved assent to Constable Peebles, began to move off toward his and Petersen's car. "Maybe later, okay?"

"I'll call you," Saunders said, as if he meant it.

Sims had the next day off, so he slept. Amanda was up north, but Lance had stayed at home this time, and needed to be walked and fed. He did these things conscientiously, without enthusiasm. Between walks and meals, he attempted to clean the apartment, considered washing clothes, and lay down instead. Lancelot was quiet, undemanding, as he had been while Sims had suffered a week-long illness last winter; followed him about, if not physically, then with anxious, myopic eyes. It made Sims feel vaguely guilty, but he couldn't find the energy to do anything about that, either. He tried to read Amanda's manuscript; it made him sad. Waterfowl were such hapless creatures, at everyone's mercy... Imagine sleeping out in the cold rains of early spring, with a nest full of fledglings to look after... He pulled another blanket out of the cedar chest, the only thing he had brought away from their old house in Norris, and took a nap.

Every time he dozed off, something terrible happened:

foxes raided the nest, or there was no food in the shallows - only plastic jars, filled with weed and something infinitely worse, that he didn't like to examine - or greenish frothy gunk was floating on the surface that made his feathers sticky, so that he couldn't swim. Each time, he woke more tired, colder, and tried to decide what should be done. He might cook something in the evening, if it seemed worth the bother by then. He might call Father Mike, if he could summon up the social graces needed for speaking to anyone. He could talk to Saunders or Marjory, given the same prerequisite. Why was Amanda out on some lake? She was the only one he felt like talking to. And she would be gone, at least another day.

At some time after eight in the evening, he told Lance: "Pack your kibble, we're going on a trip."

Having driven fast on the highway but very slowly on the dark gravel roads, having lost his way twice - the second time, finding himself back at Sculpin Falls - and asked directions to Jonas Thompson's place - Sims got to the cottage well after midnight. All the windows were black, as were those next door. He considered sleeping in the car, or out under the stars. It was warm and dry; he wouldn't have to share the early spring lot of red-necked grebe. On the other hand, he had brought only one blanket and his pillow, nothing remotely like a sleeping bag to soften the ground. The matter was settled by Lancelot. On his last permitted run of the day, he made for Amanda's front door, where he scratched and whined piteously.

"Lance, sweetie, what...? Oh, Alec. I wasn't expecting you." She was still half asleep, an old robe that almost certainly had belonged to Edward thrown over her shoulders. "Well, come in."

She woke up enough to make coffee for Sims - that is, enough to recognize that this was something of an emergency. He told about his day - days: the last two or three had somehow run together into one monstrously long and disagreeable day. She listened, but at several crucial points, she nodded off, barely noticed by Sims, who was preoccupied with his own problems. At last she admitted: "I don't think I can do much more of this. I was up at 5:30 this morning. It's almost four now - I've had a grand total of two hours' sleep in the last twenty-four. Why don't we go to bed and pick this up tomorrow - later today, I mean. All right?"

He let himself be tucked in and kissed good-night. He dreamed, not surprisingly, about Mary and old times. The oldest times, before anything had turned bad.

"Let's not go back," he said.

"I have to go back," answered Amanda. "I have to leave right now."

It had been a good day, considering that they had started it on so little sleep. Sims had learned, to his amazement, that Lancelot could be taken out in a canoe - he needed some help getting in, but during the ride, he could keep still. Evidently, the desire to share in human activities was stronger than the desire to jump around. He could be left on one of the small islands for a half hour or more, playing happily with the lapping wavelets. The only thing he refused to attempt was swimming.

The young grebes were spectacularly ugly in their changing plumage, but photogenic, for all that. And amusing. There was no trace of pathos about these birds, young or parents: they simply lived their lives, uncomplaining, one minute to the next. The weather continued warm and dry. Early in the morning and at sunset, mosquitoes were a nuisance. Amanda assured him that this was a blessing compared to the black flies of three weeks ago. Trees whose names he didn't know were in magnificent flower; red and white trilliums starred the hillsides. Chipmunks foraged and argued in the foliage overhead. That morning he had seen a deer. Still deaf and half blind with fatigue, he had taken Lance out for the first, most urgent walk - and there it was, standing at the edge of the forest, perfectly motionless. Lance was too much in awe, even to bark. And then the deer, having regarded man and dog as if they were the exotic beasts, rose six feet straight up into the air, effortlessly, and disappeared among the trees. Just like that, in a silent instant.

Amanda had said. "One or two come by almost every morning."

"But it was so..." He could find no words for the grace and dignity of the creature, its flawless subtlety.

"They are."

He had paddled, gazed, taken a few amateurish

286

pictures, eaten and rested. He had gone for walks, run with the dog, and sat on rocks, watching the dog run. He had exchanged brief, shouted pleasantries down the beach with Jonas Thompson. He had done nothing, really, extraordinary or adventurous. Yet his other life, in contrast, appeared both cluttered and bleak, like some musty forgotten basement storage room.

"What about your work? Shouldn't you be back tomorrow morning?"

"For what?" he asked. "To rewrite Petersen's reports? To catch some kid painting on fences? To interfere in other people's messy private lives? They don't need me - and I sure don't need them." He heard himself becoming a fretful, difficult child, and didn't know how to be otherwise.

"All right," Amanda finally said. "What if I go, and you and Lance stay here a day or two? It might be a good idea, at that, for you to spend a little time alone. There is food, and you can always go into the village for whatever you need. If you get lonely, visit Jonas. Do you want me to call the station?"

"No... I'll call them from the village. You really shouldn't let me get away with this."

"With what?"

"Being such a pain in the neck."

"It's all right," she said. "I'm quite happy now, I can afford it. Besides, everybody gets that way sometimes. Don't worry, it will pass."

"I don't see how..."

"You obviously have a decision to make. Make it, and you'll feel better. Alec?"

"Yes."

"Is it all over, really? I mean, the investigation of Edward's murder. The homicide squad will have it all cleaned up in a couple of days... David Frayne will go to prison, and it's all finished?"

"I think so. All they need is one or two more facts - a footprint or something - to prove he was near Ac-Me at the right time... Marcie can do it, I think. They have, right now, enough to indict - maybe not quite enough to convict. If it can be done, they'll get it done."

"I was just thinking. Before Brian leaves, we might go to the cemetery... I'd like to be able to tell him." It wasn't

287

clear which him she meant, Brian or Edward. Perhaps both.

"Oh. When is he going?"

"Tomorrow."

"Let's get moving."

Father Mike was there, naturally, and two other recruits with their parents. The boys shuffled nervously, eager and reluctant to be on their way, afraid their mothers would make a fuss - afraid they would not. The airport was so crowded, so many people rushed about, each intent upon his own affairs, that only the very young could possibly imagine that anyone would know or care how well they made their exit from the nest. At last, having long ago checked in their knapsacks - not one would be caught dead in a ditch with a suitcase - having eaten stale, overpriced pastries in the coffee shop, having milled about, nobody knowing what to say, Sims hanging back from the parents, it was time to go. Father Mike solemnly shook hands with each of the young men, murmured a few more admonitions and sent them off. Sims caught a glimpse of them beyond the security door, already back in their own world, mocking and bumping one another.

"Whoever he is," Amanda reflected looking at Brian's retreating back, "he's not my little boy anymore."

Father Mike accompanied them to Don Mills, where he had left his car. "Let the neighbours worry about property values," he had said. "Any year now, the diocese will see fit to budget for a new one."

As they entered the house, it seemed to echo with emptiness - surely a fancy, for Brian had spent very little time there in the past weeks. Perhaps it was only something forlorn in Amanda's bearing, in her unprecedented failure to act the gracious hostess. Sims went off in search of coffee and biscuits, leaving her to the priest. He assumed their serious conversation was about Brian, except that they fell abruptly silent upon his entrance.

"What's going on?" He put the tray down.

Father Mike said: "Sit down, Alec. I understand you're having a little crisis."

Sims aimed his darkest scowl at Amanda, which made

288

no visible impression upon her. Of course, the priest would certainly have been the next person he talked to, should he feel any more need to talk - which seemed doubtful; at the moment, his little crisis was the most wearisome topic he could imagine. But it was his prerogative, not hers.

"It's not Amanda's fault," said the priest. "I asked. Well, for Heaven's sake, man, did you expect to walk around like some depressive zombie and not have anybody notice? Sit down." When Sims obeyed, he continued in the less authoritarian of his lecturing voices. "You've just had two successes in a row. From what I hear, solving that armoured car holdup is a real feather in your cap. A few months ago, if something like that happened, you'd be walking on air - we'd have to shoot you down with a cannon. And here you are, instead, running away..."

"Not running away. Taking a day off. Besides, I didn't solve it; Pete Saunders did."

"And that's another thing," Father Mike pursued. "You have just been reunited with an old friend - at least, with someone you once admired, and he hasn't disappointed you. Yet it doesn't seem to make you happy."

"Sure it does. I'm thrilled about that."

"You don't sound it."

Amanda looked uncomfortable; she kept giving the priest sideways glances, which Sims, had he been the recipient, would interpret as "Lay off!". He probably would, too, but Father Mike seemed oblivious. Serves her right, he thought spitefully: she's gone and unleashed one of nature's inexorable forces - sown the wind, let the genie out of the bottle... A mental picture of Mike O'Connor - exceptionally (for the solemn occasion of sending three new youth counsellors off to his old school) wearing his clerical black and dog-collar - extracting his well-nourished form from a bottle, made Sims laugh quite inappropriately, surprising his companions. In the ensuing second of confusion, he also realized that the subject of Amanda's concern - both in consulting the priest and in trying, too late, to restrain him - was Sims himself. "I'm sorry," he said, to cover everything.

"Well, then," replied one of nature's inexorable forces, "explain yourself."

"I was glad to see Pete again. I do still admire him. He

seems truly satisfied with his life. Nice family, independence, plenty of money... and he enjoys making it. Next to his, my life is a shambles."

"Is that your problem? Envy?"

"Something like that..." Envy, and the concomitant shame, were simple emotions. Admitting these was easier than trying to explain all that he had been feeling.

Father Mike wouldn't buy it. "Okay, that happens. It passes in a day. So then, he also helps to solve a case with which you're having trouble, and you're a little miffed - maybe two days. And then what happened?"

"I got the credit."

"And Saunders collected the fee. Seems fair to me: everybody doing his job, everybody getting his reward. You didn't resent the other - how many? - at least seven, probably more, if I know the department - other policemen who worked on that case."

"It was a silly case."

"It was nothing of the sort, and you know it. Unusual, certainly, but never silly."

Sims wanted to get up and walk away. He wanted to tell Mike and Amanda to mind their own business. He didn't, of course, any more than he would have told one of his sisters. Because he didn't want to hurt their feelings? Because he saw Father Mike as some kind of authority figure, to whom one cannot conceivably be rude? Or because they both so obviously cared about him that being cross-examined by them was on the order of taking medicine: unpleasant at the time, but ultimately for one's own good? As a boy, whenever he was lectured, he would have hung his head, replied in monosyllables, and waited patiently for it to be over. He couldn't do that now.

"Anyway," he said, not specifically in response to the last statement, "that's over. All six people have been charged with grand theft; they'll go to jail for a few years. It was exciting as an armed robbery; it was interesting to discover what really happened... but now it's no big deal."

"Murder is a big deal," said Mike O'Connor softly.

"Yes."

"And you did solve Dr. Morley's murder single-handedly. From what I hear, you handed Homicide a pretty good case. Maybe you won't get all the credit... Is

290

that the problem?"

"No. First of all, I didn't do it alone: Amanda helped, almost from the beginning. Secondly, it isn't solved yet. That's the real problem, if you want to know. We made progress, but it wasn't finished. Oh, I have every confidence in Homicide - but I wanted to get the job done myself. Well, it's personal. I wanted to get that bastard, Frayne."

"What do you need to finish it?"

"One witness!" Sims almost shouted. "One single witness, or one solid piece of physical evidence, would wrap it up. It has to be wrapped up. I don't want him getting off on reasonable doubt; I want him packaged tight. I want him bandaged like a mummy. I want him gift-wrapped!"

The priest smiled. "You feel quite strongly about this, do you?" Sims nodded, a little ashamed of his outburst, but somewhat relieved by it, too. "Then, why don't you?"

"Why don't I what?"

"Finish the job. Gift-wrap the mummy... I like that."

"Yes," Amanda spoke to him for the first time since they had entered the house. "So, you're not officially on the case... That didn't stop you before, when there was no case, officially - why should it matter now?"

"Homicide won't like it. So what? You're right," Sims brightened. "So what? Saunders didn't stop investigating for his client, just because the police were on the case. I'll take my vacation - starting two days ago. Oh, would I love to beat them to it..."

Amanda hesitantly volunteered: "I could be your client,"

"No. You can be my partner."

"All right, then." Her voice, Sims approvingly noted, began to regain its usual no-nonsense quality. "As a partner, I propose to make Edward the client. Any expenditures will be charged to the estate, so don't worry about spending money, whenever necessary. Now, where do we start?"

The priest, whom they had all but forgotten in the excitement, said: "My work here is finished... now where did I park the Batmobile?"

CHAPTER 35

The dining table was covered in notes, diagrams and photocopies smuggled out of 43 Division; lists of names and addresses. "We need a proper filing system," Amanda remarked.

"We need a witness," repeated Sims for the umpteenth time. "By now, the real police will be canvassing all the apartment buildings overlooking Frayne's... I think Cryer would tell me if they came up with anything. I'll call him. Will they check around the neighbourhood of Ac-Me? Yes, of course. But it wouldn't hurt to check again."

"How do we go about it? In a grid or a gyre?"

Sims looked up questioningly. "I understood grid,"

"A gyre is the pattern falcons fly when hunting - a spiral. You'd probably start in close and work outward."

"Remind me never to play Scrabble with you. Yes, that one."

"We're both known at the plant... does that make any difference? Is he still there?"

"I think so... I'd have heard if he'd been arrested, and he's too cool a suspect to draw attention by staying off work. No, it doesn't matter if he sees me - let him sweat. But you'd better keep out of sight. It might be best if we split these gyres by diameter. You take the outer circles... Now, where did the map go?"

"Under the addresses. You know, we need to put that map on a wall... that wall, if I take down the painting... I never liked it very much, anyway."

By the end of the day, the dining room was transformed into a passable operations room. Amanda removed all three paintings and stood them by the door, not so much because they needed the wall space, as to create the proper atmosphere. Four of the eight chairs were stacked in the hallway, and the table moved against a wall. She liberated a filing cabinet by packing her oldest photographs away in cardboard boxes. A less organized person - such as myself, thought Sims - would have had to run out to the supermarket, only to be told there were no boxes to spare. Little could be done about the sideboard, but to move whatever was on top of it, inside. Now there was plenty of surface on which to spread papers. Amanda completed the setting with a desk lamp from her work room; it was both easier on the eyes and more in keeping with the room's new function than was the chandelier.

"Now, we'll *have* to eat in the kitchen," she said, with an unmistakable note of satisfaction.

"What happens to the stuff in the hall?"

"Oh, I suppose we can find room in the basement."

Sims followed her down the stairs, with two chairs in precarious balance. The dark-room, he knew. Next to it was an open door: a bathroom, then a closed one. Aha, so that's why Edward had the upstairs bathroom all to himself. Sims had not realized the full extent of the Morleys' separateness. Amanda came to the end of the short passage, which gave onto a larger, more basement-like space. Here was the furnace, the water heater, laundry area, and some open shelving with boxes neatly stacked underneath. "Just put them anywhere," she said.

"What was the other door?"

"My bedroom." On the way back, she pushed the door open, "See? Very convenient, especially when I came home late, or wanted to start developing early. And it's cool in the summer. I thought of moving upstairs, now that... you know. But I like it here." It was a place of clutter and warm colours; a friendly, very personal room.

"So, you're just going to leave the second floor empty?" He thought it might become a home for ghosts and unhappy reminders - not healthy, in the long run.

"I don't know," she said, already on the stairs. "It's a problem..."

After moving the chairs and the paintings, carefully wrapped in brown paper, (Who keeps a roll of brown paper on hand? Someone who has a son away from home, who remembers to send him fruitcakes and seasonal clothes; the same kind of person who has paper cartons, folded and stacked, ready to use.) and the good china and photographs, they owed themselves a rest. Over coffee, Sims picked up the house theme again.

"I don't know if it's a good idea to keep Edward's rooms like that..."

"I'm not sure I want to keep them at all. I might sell the

house, furniture and all...I may decide to winterize the cottage and live there all year."

Sims was horrified and wondered why. He could, and certainly would, visit her there. He did understand why she loved the place. But it was a two-hour drive; he couldn't very easily drop by, just on a whim. Even though that was exactly what he had done, two nights ago. And, of course, Lancelot would be, once again, be alone in the apartment all day, fretting more than ever, after his taste of the very good life.

Well, no: he and Lance would have to find new accommodations, a place where the dog could go outside during the day. Sims had very quickly come to take far too much for granted: it was selfish and presumptuous to consider her plans in terms of his own loss. But that loss could be devastating. He did not want a change in their relationship; it had become the most stable, the most important thing in his world.

"Not for a while yet," Amanda continued, "not until Brian is settled. I expect he'll go back to BC. Changing courses will cost him a year, maybe two. As much as I like this house, it would be quite ridiculous for me to live in it by myself, but I won't move as long as my son needs his safety net."

"Well, that's a relief,"

"Which is?"

"All of them. That you're not going to disappear overnight; that Brian has a home to return to... and that you don't mean to keep Edward's rooms as some kind of shrine."

"Why should I want to? I can remember him perfectly well without props - and he knows it. He wouldn't approve of the sentiment; Edward hated waste. I've already packed most of his things to give away - everything but the books. The children will want some mementoes... "

"Oh, that reminds me," said Sims. "of something I meant to look up... May I?"

There was the Gibbon, as he had remembered. There, too, was the bedroom, with its big window and heavy furniture, but without clothes, ornament or belongings. He had thought, the first time, that it looked impersonal. Now, it truly was: just a well-proportioned, vacant room. It had

294

not the feel of being haunted - or even of ever having been occupied. Amanda opened the window; a fresh, summery wind brought in the scent of gardens.

He didn't know exactly where to begin searching for Claudius and Aurelian, though he was all but certain he had used them inappropriately. The reference was hardly important; it had been the whimsy of a moment, long past. Yet, finding out was, in some little way, part of finishing this job. There must be no loose ends of any kind. He asked to borrow the book for bedtime reading.

"Of course," Amanda said. "Why don't you keep it? And any others that you like. Louise repossessed hers already."

Did he feel that taking a dead man's book was ghoulish, opportunistic? Not at all. It was more, in fact, a gesture of friendship toward someone he had come to know well - to like and respect - without ever having met. "Yes, thanks, I will." He noticed 'A Perfect Spy' in the bookcase, the bookmark gone. "Have you read this?"

"I tried," she said, "after we found it here... when I couldn't sleep one night. It was terribly sad. Why couldn't he have chosen something nice... something bright and funny... not to finish?"

"At the time, Winnie-the-Pooh would probably have made you sad. I'll keep this, in case you want to have another go at it sometime. Come on, partner," he took her hand to lead her from the room. "We have a lot more work to do."

"Cryer says they can't find anyone who will swear to seeing Frayne outside his apartment building that morning. I'm not surprised, after all this time. He's impressed with Mr. Edmundson, the doorman. He's such a dear, frail old person - the defence will be floored: he forgets nothing and doesn't get confused. But Cryer isn't sure they can use Marcie's testimony. She didn't see his face - and there may be a question of competence." Sims sighed, dropped into his usual chair. Lancelot sighed more loudly still, and dropped onto the floor. "I knocked on fifty-four doors today and got nothing. How about you?"

Amanda glanced at her notes. "Only thirty-eight doors. Also nothing. I had some second thoughts about the detective business... It's not always exciting, is it? Hard on the feet." She propped hers up on the coffee table. "Tomorrow, I wear sneakers."

"Some of the people I spoke to were annoyed - they'd already talked to the police. Did you encounter anyone who had been questioned?"

"No. I think my circle is too big, quite frankly. I don't see how people that far away could have seen anything, unless they were on their way to someplace... I would say it was a very long shot. Well, since you did more work, I'll get dinner." She shifted over to reach the phone. "What do you like on your pizza?"

"Anything but green peppers – they cut them too big and leave them raw," he said, standing up. Lancelot sprang up, too, much faster. "Not today, kid. But I'll feed you."

The partial circles they filled in with coloured markers were pathetically small on the city map. "It would look like more," Sims observed, "if we had just the relevant section - something like a page from a street-guide, enlarged."

"I'll do that... when I get time."

The next day was not any more fruitful. Rather less, in fact; it was a Friday and most houses were unoccupied during working hours. Therefore, Sims concentrated his efforts on commercial premises, of which there were many along Steeles Avenue. Unfortunately, most of them were organized into industrial plazas, built at right angles to the road. Nevertheless, he must go to each one, in case an employee should have been en route, in or out, at the critical time. This entailed a great deal more walking than canvassing the residential areas had done. Some of the people had been approached by homicide; others had not. Some of them reacted positively to the photograph of David Frayne; they had seen him before, somewhere, some time. One young salesman at an electronics outlet knew him by name, make of car, and price-range, but his memory was confined to business.

By supper time, Sims didn't think he could take one more step, until he realized that there would be no supper. He stopped at the Three Dragons for take-out. What would Amanda like? Breaded shrimp, almost certainly. Sweet and sour chicken balls - everybody likes those. He added

296

honey garlic ribs, vegetables, fried rice and egg rolls, of course. A well-balanced meal - at least by his own standards.

While waiting, he became aware of familiar sounds: cheerful, noisy argument from a group of young working-men and women at two tables pushed together near the door. The same people who had been at the same tables on the day Eve Dumont brought him here. Regulars, he had thought at the time; their presence now confirmed it. They received his intrusion with good grace, even before he ordered a pitcher of beer, and several of them recognised immediately the photograph of David Frayne.

"Where have you seen him?" Sims asked hopefully.

"He's been in here, couple times, for like dinner," one of the men replied.

"More than a couple," put in the younger of the women. "Used to be fairly often. Not lately, though."

Another young man said: "Yeah, that's right. With the gorgeous blonde - *super* legs."

"It was funny," said the second girl, "because we kind of had him figured for gay, remember?" She turned to her friend. "That time he was eating with the cute young guy? They had their heads together, real like, you know, intimate? Talking so quiet we couldn't hear a word?"

"And we said," the other girl took up the narrative, "what a waste of two hunks."

"And then the same guy - the one in the picture? - shows up with a woman?"

"You're quite sure the woman was blonde?" Sims asked the table at large. "Not dark? Not a pretty girl in her early twenties with short brown hair?"

The four men shook their heads in unison. "A blonde," the first one repeated. "Fantastic hair - you couldn't forget. Long. And legs to match."

"Way too much makeup," said one of the girls disapprovingly. She herself had confined the improvement of her buxom good looks to little more than lipstick.

"There *was* a brunette," volunteered a man who had not spoken before. "Just one time. Short hair, like you say." With two forefingers, he drew bangs on his own bare, sunburnt forehead. "Dark, short hair. Nice, except her eyes were kind of red. Like she'd been crying."

"Was this before or after you saw him with the blonde girl?"

"Before. Not long before. What I figure: he's got a new girl, younger, sexier... and he's kind of letting the old one down easy. He was all the time smiling, doing things for her, real attentive, but she's kind of like keeping her distance. I never seen her again. Too bad, I wouldn't mind catching that rebound. Ow!" He leaned down to rub his leg, while shooting a hurt glance at the girl with no makeup. "I was just talking! Anyway, it was months ago."

"And the man? You said he hasn't been in here lately. Can anyone recall the last time you saw him?"

"The last time," said the man who appeared a little older than the rest - perhaps the natural leader, "would have been in March - about when we got our January raise." There was a light scattering of laughter at this, along with unanimous agreement.

"And the young man he had been with before, you never saw him again?" Muttering and shaking of heads: not that any of them could say for sure. Sims showed them a small photo of Ferdy Arnott. Yes, both girls and one of the men agreed, that was him. The other men shrugged; it could have been: who looks at guys?

"I don't suppose any of you have seen either man on a Saturday morning?"

"Naw," said the leader, "we don't work weekends."

His order had been ready for some time, in a paper bag, under the red heat lamp. He hoped Amanda liked wilted Chinese food. This new information was interesting but not useful: Frayne had taken Miss Hillyard out after work at least twice; had possibly fought with Roberta Farrell over it. Or over something else, for that matter; it was about that time Ms. Farrell had left Ac-Me. That he'd also dined with Ferdy was no surprise. It had all taken place months before Edward Morley's death.

CHAPTER 36

"Oh, no! You've brought food," Amanda greeted him. "And I made a pot-roast. Never mind, we'll have that tomorrow. Get some plates out, would you, while I feed Lance."

Of course, the dog refused to touch his own dish until every chicken ball, every garlic rib bone, and most of the fried rice was gone. Meanwhile, Sims told of the meagre results of his day. "When did you have time to cook?" he concluded.

"Well, I did start out knocking on doors. But when three in a row didn't answer, I decided to leave it till evening. I tried something in the dark-room instead. Well," she looked at her watch, "I should be off. I walked you already," she rebuked Lancelot, who was up and heading for the door. "You stay with Alec."

"Wait a minute," Sims protested. "You're not going out now? It'll be dark in a little while."

"Nonsense. It's a quarter to seven. I have two hours of daylight, to catch people at home. I'd have left sooner, except there was no way to reach you. If I'm not home at this time tomorrow, don't start imagining things, all right? We need mobile phones or something. Oh, and we could use a computer. That is, if I knew how to... We'll talk about it later."

Sims called her back again. "Look, why don't you forget canvassing today? I'd rather hear what you did in the dark-room."

Amanda shrugged. "All right. To be honest, I'm not all that keen on canvassing." She put down her hand-bag, detached the bill from the take-out bag, and led the way to the converted dining room.

On the wall next to the city map was something new: four pages from a street guide, blown up several times their original size, neatly fitted together into one continuous detailed map and mounted on a sheet of Bristol board. She had covered it with stiff, clear plastic, on which she had drawn their proposed search pattern in yellow felt pen. The area Sims had already covered was shaded in green; hers, in orange. Sims thought this as professional a job as anything he had seen at Division, and told her so.

"Oh, that," said Amanda, scarcely glancing up from the bill she was carefully smoothing out, before she put it in a shoe box with three others. "Yes, it's all right. But that's not what I was talking about. It's not finished, but I'll show you what I've done so far." She took up a slim stack of photographs from the sideboard and spread three of them out on the table. They were of people's backs. "I had to sort through about a million old company parties and picnics to find them. I used to cover all the events for the Ac-Me newsletter until - you know. Charlie thought it would be fun to have candid shots of everybody having a good time - making fools of themselves, was what he really wanted. It turns out, they were not all that candid," she smiled ruefully. "People usually posed when they saw me coming. I blew these up from group pictures."

"That's Mr. Quick," Sims laughed, "in Bermuda shorts! And the most garish teeshirt I've ever seen. Waving a bottle of something in the air... making a toast?"

"Yes. And here is Martin Jones, umpiring a children's baseball game. He doesn't look quite so helpless as usual - I suppose the uniform boosted his ego."

"It must have... I think he doesn't need bolstering any longer. This one is our man, Frayne, deep in conversation with another man. Very nicely turned out. Coloured lights in the background... Christmas party?"

Amanda nodded. "You have no trouble recognising people, even without their faces, right?"

"Right. I see what you're driving at. Do you think Marcie could pick out the one she saw, weeks ago?"

"Maybe not from those shots, but from these, I hope so." She put another set of pictures beside the first. They were actually the same pictures, doctored. All but the central figure had been removed, as well as trees, lights and other background. And all three men were dressed in brown: slacks, sport jacket, shoes. Each had one arm down and one raised in some ambiguous gesture. "See, they don't look anything alike, even from behind. I'll do this with all the Ac-Me people I have on film. Only, it takes forever! They say a computer could have done the whole thing in ten minutes."

"That's not what I hear from PC Browning. She says it's a whole different art-form; it takes time and patience to master. Damn, I wish we had access to police facilities! This is a stroke of genius - I guess you already know that." She smiled shyly but didn't deny it. "Suppose I do the leg work from now on, while you create more masterpieces?"

"It wouldn't be fair..." Amanda protested.

"It would, though. And practical. In the police force," he lied smoothly, without batting an eyelash, "we don't waste special talents on jobs that anybody else can do just as well."

She didn't take a great deal of convincing. It occurred to Sims that, introverted as she was, approaching strangers must be hellishly difficult for Amanda. Yet she had, twice, volunteered to do so. With no tangible result to show for either time. That must have been depressing; he felt a little discouraged himself, in spite of having done house-to-house hundreds of times over the years. Before calling it a night, he dutifully coloured in another green quarter-circle on the map, and handed over his list of addresses and brief notes for Amanda to file.

The rent was paid already, and he had no recent sins to repent of; therefore he made no attempt to avoid Mrs. Field.

"Oh," she said, "I thought sure you'd got rid of the dog, it's been so quiet around here. But I see you still got it."

Lancelot sat down in front of the landlady and offered a paw - the right one. On the rare occasion when he could be coaxed to shake hands at all, he would normally give the left. Sims had heard somewhere that dogs are naturally left-handed; certainly, this one was. Had Lance made a psychological breakthrough, or had Amanda been coaching him? In either case, he must be rewarded for doing it correctly. As Mrs. Field made no move to accept the paw, Sims had to. Lance was puzzled, but triumphant in receiving his due praise. Mrs. Field only glared at him.

"Well, yes," Sims told her. "I expect to have him for a long time. A very long time. That's what I meant to talk to you about."

"It's not setting foot in my garden," she said.

"Of course not. In fact, you needn't worry about him anymore. We plan to move at the end of the month," Sims heard somebody saying. He knew there had been no such intention in his mind, but the voice sounded very like his own. "If that's agreeable."

The landlady looked as surprised as he was. "Well! Why'd you want to go and do that for? I've never done anything to offend, I'm sure."

"No, certainly not," Sims assured her, though not with any excess of warmth. "Only, I believe Lancelot would be happier somewhere else. And I'm sure you'll be pleased not to have him here anymore."

"Can't say I ever took to the creature... Still and all, you was always a pretty good tenant, Sergeant. I kind of like having a policeman in the house - makes a body feel safer in her bed, like. I don't mind the animal that much..."

"That's gratifying, Mrs. Field, but I'm afraid our plans are made. I'll pass the word to my fellow officers, if you like. I'm sure some of them have no pets or bad habits."

"That reminds me," she said. "Your phone's been ringing itself off the hook, these three days. So I answered it, finally, thinking maybe it was important police business. It was a Mr. Saunders. Nice spoken gentleman? He wants you to call him, says you have his number."

Sims quickly thanked and bade her good-night.

The apartment was relatively tidy. Since his return from Sculpin Falls, he had come here only to sleep. Tonight, he was back early - in time to read a book, to scrounge for a snack, to scatter a few clothes. But it didn't seem worth the trouble, making the place look like home again. It was not a home, in any case: he didn't even own the furniture. Well, he wouldn't be using it much longer - apparently, he had other plans. What plans? Some crazy alter ego had made up his mind, and now all of Sims was committed to moving. Perhaps I can combine house-hunting with searching for a witness, he thought - if I wanted to live close to Ac-Me Plastics. There are some quite nice neighbourhoods there... and plenty of dogs. Also squirrels and cats; Lance would love it.

What did Saunders want?

"Just wondering whether the earth had swallowed you up," that man replied. "You were in a pretty foul mood last time we met - and then you disappeared. What's going on?"

Sims told him briefly, with imperfect accuracy, about his own recent activities.

"Sounds like fun. Can I play too? No, I'm not serious. I'm so busy right now, I can't even take that rather intriguing case you apparently directed my way... Too bad; I quite liked the man, and he has a genuine dilemma. Therefore, you need waste no anxiety over any attempt on my part to butt in on your personal homicide. On the other hand, if you could use a couple more legs and ears, I'd be happy to find you an operative or two. Not my regular guys, you understand - they're pretty well tied up - but I know some good occasionals you could have... on my payroll, of course. I take my debts seriously."

"Thanks, Pete. But, actually, payroll isn't the problem."

"So, what is?"

How to explain without hurting his feelings? "I guess I'm the problem. As you said, it's a kind of personal homicide."

"Ah, a question of ego, is it? Wait a minute! Is that why you were so ticked off about the Knox case? Because you didn't solve it all by yourself? I hate to lecture..." Saunders paused for a chuckle: "No, that's a bare-faced lie: there are few things I enjoy more than lecturing. So, I shall remind you that it would be rude to hang up on an old home-boy. You've been a cop now, for how long?"

"A long time," Sims admitted. "Long enough, anyway, to learn the value of team-work, if that's what you're driving at."

"Well, that, too. It also applies in private investigation. Nobody can do everything; the man who tries, usually fails... Or, anyway, takes too long over a case to make it cost-effective. But that ain't news. What I think you're suffering from is known in professional circles as Approaching Frustration Threshold. I wish we could get together - this is a phenomenon best discussed over decent comestibles. We'll do that soon. For the time being, however, suffice it to say that every cop gets AFT, unless he's corrupt or daft. Been there myself. The solution is as various as the problem, within a few rough categories. I found mine; you'll find yours.

The first overt symptom is defiance - you've had that? Suddenly, you catch yourself saying no to things you've always accepted. Then you start getting mad at people, resenting the routine, chafing at the constraints, breaking rules... all kinds of little things. Depending on your temperament, you might slug somebody - even shoot somebody. In your case, I would expect withdrawal, moodiness, depression... Well?"

"Well, yes, more or less." Sims would have liked to deny it, but reconsidered: Saunders wouldn't believe him. He had imagined that his recent problems, large and small, were specific to himself. To have them laid out like a clinical textbook example was both disturbing and comforting: while one prefers to be unique, there is something to be said for not being alone. "What does one do about it?"

"Something that works. You've done something... see if it works. If it doesn't, try something else. Meanwhile, don't sweat, don't fret and don't worry. Also, you might try accepting help from an old friend."

"I just might," said Sims. "Really. If we get stuck, you'll be the one we turn to."

"Either way, let me know how it comes out, before I read it in the papers, okay?"

Sims watched the first ten minutes of the news on television, became despondent over the world's troubles, and turned it off. Then, recalling that he meant to spend the whole next day on foot, tuned in again, just in time to have missed the weather forecast. He read Gibbon; found all three of his references and was satisfied: the time-frame had been inaccurate, but his designation of personalities fit well enough. Did it matter? Not one iota: it was merely a minuscule and secret point to have scored - something of which he could use more these days. He kept reading at random, for pleasure, until he fell asleep.

As on every previous occasion when he had been forced by circumstance to change domicile, his dreams were all of interiors. Ranging from the benign magnificence of Abe Meyer's home to dark, threatening, warren-like

304

dreamscapes; from the over-furnished, bedoilied, polish-scented house of Mrs. Sims to vertiginous skyscrapers made of glass; from impossibly vast, sunlit greenhouses to what he imagined as the self-indulgent luxury of David Frayne's apartment; from the cold perfection of the Jones house to the soft blues and mahogany of 39 Linnet Avenue, he and Lancelot searched for their next dwelling. These dreams were always rather exciting - they bore little resemblance to the tedium and frustration of house-hunting in real life. On the whole, he slept very well.

CHAPTER 37

The second green circle coloured in, and still no miraculous witness found, Sims was despondent. Not on the order of last week's doldrums, but there was a palpable trace of AFT in the air. It was not lessened by Amanda's jubilant mood.

"We kept it all very light; it was like a game to Marcie. We took her to the cafeteria, Ernie Draper and I - Charlie looked in for a minute, but he had business to attend to. Did you know she had quit? I see you did, and never mentioned it. Our man Frayne wasn't around today, either, which is just as well - I didn't like the thought of bumping into him. I hesitated to go there at all, especially as you didn't want me to, but I couldn't see any other way to do this. And it was important, it really was."

He nodded glumly. "Go on,"

"Anyway, she's a sweet girl, not nearly so... um... damaged as she first appears. I showed her a few of the pictures - you know, the 'Before' set. She recognised Ernie right away, which made her happy. She knew Charlie, too, in his shorts. Then I gave her the brown versions, and she had no trouble with them. There were some other people that she named - including two I don't know myself - Ernie says they were both correct. She had seen Martin Jones and the Arnott boy before. I asked where, and she said, here, in the cafeteria, eating. She remembers the Saturday of the brown man, but is positive none of these are the same brown man. What do you think of that?"

"I think it's wonderful," said Sims. "Now, get to the good part. Did she identify Frayne's likeness?"

"Not yet. I didn't show it to her. Well, I don't want to waste it."

"Waste? How?"

"Remember," Amanda continued, unperturbed by the colour he was turning, "when we were talking about a line-up, and how careful we would have to be? Well, I'm convinced that Marcie is competent to identify the man she saw. I'm also convinced that man is David Frayne. We still have to convince Sergeant Cryer, correct?"

"Correct. Yes," Sims finally caught on, "and you don't want Cryer to think that she was predisposed to select the

306

suspect."

"That's why I wanted Mr. Draper present. Later on, the police can make their own set of pictures, set up a live performance - whatever they think best. The most important thing, right now, is to give them a credible witness."

"On a silver platter, with garnish," Sims laughed. He was starting to feel much better. "Have I mentioned that you are a genius? Well, have I mentioned it recently? If I don't tell you at least once a day, remind me."

"Will you arrange it? Marcie likes Sergeant Cryer, by the way. Even Ernie Draper approves, insofar as he can approve of anyone questioning his little girl. So it has to be Cryer."

"Consider it arranged. Same place? I'll get him there, if I have to drag him by the... necktie."

This was at least *something*, even if he had not brought it about himself. It should not be a question of ego: they were, by his own definition, partners - and the investigation was, after all, more personal to Amanda than it was to Sims. Marcie Bowers must be proved a credible witness. She had no reason to lie - might not even know how to lie. On the other hand, how would she fare against a clever and determined defence attorney? He wouldn't need to do much more than plant the suggestion in the jury's mind that the girl had been coached...

"We need another one."

"Another what?"

"Witness. Someone to swear that Frayne wasn't where he said he was... or someone to show previous intent."

"That would have to be one of his friends," Amanda said. "Now that he's officially a suspect..."

"...it might be worth going back to them?"

"Suppose I speak to the girl. Could it do any harm?"

Sims thought about it. "Maybe not, if you catch her at work - or someplace public, where Frayne can't suddenly turn up unexpectedly. He's dangerous, never forget."

"He couldn't do anything - not now. His only chance is to stay calm and ride it out, to hope there isn't enough evidence."

"All right. I'll go see Ferdy again."

That young man, when summoned from the nether

regions of his new place of work, had a pathetically wan look about him. "More police harassment," he said. "At least this fuzz looks familiar. What now?"

"How is the job?" asked Sims.

Ferdy Arnott shrugged. "Okay. The ancestor's being pretty decent, considering... But he won't let me near the front office... Like I was gonna steal his shipment schedules, for Pete's sake! And it doesn't smell like anything here, you know? I mean, not even fish - nothing. I got a severe case of olfactory deprivation. On the up-side, I get to count crates of canned food coming in, going out, coming in, going out... Can't complain."

"You're doing a pretty fair imitation, so far,"

"Oh, I could do much better," said Ferdy, with a spark of his old spirit. "How about this? My back is bent, my eyes are dim, my knees are... I forget what my knees are... The girls are ugly and the guys are dull... Forsaken by old friends, my unbounded youthful potential withering on the vine... No?"

Sims gave it a four out of ten. "Tell me about old friends."

"You mean Dave. I've been asked about nothing else all this week."

"Well, how is he?"

The kid flared: "How would you be? He's suspected of murder, for Pete's sake! And it's all your fault."

"You don't think he did it?"

"He did not! I mean, okay, maybe he's got a motive... The old man did everything to keep him from getting ahead. And maybe, when he was really frustrated, he said a couple of things - well, who doesn't?"

"What kind of things?"

"You're expecting me to say threats, aren't you? Well, you're wrong. He never said anything worse than, 'If Morley wasn't around, things would be different,' kind of thing. That doesn't make a guy a killer. Anyway, he didn't benefit, did he? The old man fixed it before, so they wouldn't develop SuperFoam... If Dave had done it, he'd have done it sooner, wouldn't he? I mean, he's smart, right?"

"Suppose he didn't know it was too late?" Sims asked quietly.

"But he *would* know! That's what I'm telling you: he's smart, Dave is. He would know, because he kept tabs on Quickie's office. So there."

"You mean, by cultivating Miss Farrell?"

"She doesn't work there anymore."

"And then Miss Hillyard."

"I didn't say that."

"You didn't have to; I already knew. And it's done him no good," Sims pointed out. "Miss Hillyard doesn't know what management discusses at their lunch meetings - they don't take minutes, and Mr. Quick doesn't confide in her, Paul. He did not know." The boy gaped at him; whether in response to being called by his given name, or the suggestion of David Frayne's fallibility, Sims could not tell. "He believed there was still hope for his superfoam. That's why he ripped out the pages from Dr. Morley's notebook. Oh yes, and he tossed them down the incinerator chute in Roberta's building - along with the paper towel, which didn't keep him from getting a whiff of cyanide... That's why he was sick that day."

"No," said Ferdy Arnott quite faintly. "No..."

"So," the detective was merciless, hearty, "what's this about old friends forsaking you?"

"Oh, nothing," said the boy, looking down at his shoes. He didn't actually shuffle his feet, but might have, at any moment. "Just talk."

"Right. Has he made many attempts to find out about Grandfather's business? Grandfather's will?"

"No! Anyway, I'm in the warehouse all day, haven't I said? As for the will, forget it. The venerable ancestor is good for another twenty years. He told me he hasn't made a will... which means my Dad would inherit, anyway. So, you see, I've got no axe to grind, no ulterior motive."

"I see. Yes, I do see. Well," Sims added without explanation, "that's David Frayne for you."

He left Ferdy Arnott more miserable than he had found him. And, with any luck, that half-inch closer to breaking with the villain of the piece.

"I was cruel," Sims told Amanda, "and it didn't get me any solid information. I'm more convinced than ever that he never did know anything. I only hope rubbing his nose in it will help him to get free. He's not a bad kid, you know."

"Neither is the other one," she said. "Roberta. How does he get these nice young people so attached to him? Still, I don't know... there was a hint of *something* not quite right... She told the same story, though I had to press for details. For example, she didn't mention Frayne's impatience with the evening news... And when I did, she pretended not to remember. I know, that doesn't mean much. But, when I started asking her about taking that jacket to the cleaner's, she looked frightened. There is no other word for it - the poor girl was practically rolling her eyes like a spooked horse. Now, why would that be? I mean, the police had taken her over the whole thing - it's a matter of record. If she didn't think there was something wrong about it, why should it upset her so? You know what I think? I think the man has threatened her."

"I hope so."

"Alec!"

"No, listen. It's not nice, but think about it. If he's sweet and loving and innocent, what will Roberta feel? Loyalty, right? If he's disturbed enough to get mean, she might begin to suspect the truth."

Amanda sighed. "I suppose so. It is hard, though. I'm quite sure she had nothing to do with the murder... He didn't really trust them - the kids he was using - did he? I'll tell you something else: Roberta didn't know about Miss Hillyard."

"How can you be sure?"

"Well, I hinted, you know? Did they ever have a falling out, over, say, other women, other men? She was definite about that: no - she was on safe ground there - not a blink. The police didn't know, either, or it wouldn't have been news to her."

"I haven't told them... I'm not sure it's relevant, yet. I'd like to speak to Miss Hillyard first. In fact, I was planning to do that tomorrow, when they interview Marcie. You'll be there?"

"I wouldn't miss it for the world. Is that ego?"

He laughed. "Yes, I think so. I also think it's high time you grew one."

The audience was shaping up to be quite numerous...

310

Bad, in that so many people might make the girl nervous - good, if that, in a way, it prepared her for the courtroom. There was Mr. Quick with Mr. Meyer - of course, they would both want to be present. Mr. Draper, standing beside young Franco Gionelli from the factory. This was Amanda's show; Sims positioned himself inconspicuously in the background. Cryer finally turned up with his grey partner, who, after nodding the most perfunctory of greetings, stood quietly next to Sims. There was also an ident man, introduced as Sergeant Webb, holding a large manila folder: so, the police had made their own set of pictures. Good: they were taking it seriously.

Cryer was gentle, patient, soothing; without giving a hint of what he expected, he let Marcie feel appreciated, important: just the right tone. You had to admire the man's technique. Well, of course; one doesn't become a very successful homicide detective through sloppy technique. Amanda sat close, but asked no questions. She looked more anxious than the girl. For her part, Marcie performed flawlessly. Though the photographs had been mixed together, she had no trouble picking out which ones she had already seen and which she had not; which people she recognised and which were strangers. Cryer deposited before her a group of new photographs.

"I saw him!" she cried triumphantly. "This one." She held up Amanda's doctored snapshot of David Frayne's back. "Yes I did." Her pale eyes sought out Sims among the onlookers. "Remember? We went for a walk. With Franco, because it was a nice day. And there was a brown man, and he was holding his hankie like this," she pretended to clutch something up to her face. "This is the brown man!"

He smiled and waved to her. Marcie looked around the other faces, ending with Cryer's. "I told you, too, just like I told the nice policeman. Yes, I did," she nodded emphatically.

Cryer patted her arm. "It's very clever of you to remember," he said. "Now, what about this man? Have you ever seen him?" He had placed before her the back view of Frayne from the Christmas party.

Marcie giggled. "Silly. It's the same. The man changed his clothes... I liked him better all brown."

Cryer handed her several pictures of men with hair and build similar to Frayne's, and she did not react to them. He gave her some of the Ac-Me staff, all of whom she identified without difficulty. Finally, he slid across the table a photograph of Frayne, dressed in light-coloured slacks and sweater, with both arms at his side. "And this one?" he continued in a neutral tone, without breaking rhythm.

Marcie stared at the photo, then at Cryer. Then she laughed and clapped her hands. "It's the brown man. Yes, it is. Sometimes he is all brown, but sometimes he isn't. You can't fool me," she added, with an air of having put something over on the policeman. "I like this game. Show me some more pictures."

"Well," Cryer told her seriously, "I don't have any more pictures. But," he continued as Marcie's lips turned down at the corners, "I have something just as good. Maybe better. Would you like to see some real people?"

"Real people?" she asked uncertainly, gazing around at the assembly. "I see real people."

"But the brown man isn't here, is he?"

"No, the brown man is outside. He goes in the bushes."

"Would you like to see the brown man again?"

"Oh, yes!" she said. "Can we go outside? Oh..." She looked disappointed. "We can't. He's gone, you know. He went away a long time ago. Yes, he did. I looked for him but he wasn't there anymore."

Cryer said: "I can bring him back. Would you like that? I can bring lots of brown men. Only, you have to promise that you can pick out the same one you saw that day you went for a walk with Franco. All right?"

"All right," said Marcie, giving him a warm, surprisingly flirtatious smile. "I promise," she solemnly crossed her heart. Cryer had won her fair and square, Sims had to acknowledge. Just so he doesn't push it...

He didn't. He patted her on the shoulder - a light, fatherly gesture; no lingering touch. "You did very well, Marcie. I'm proud of you. Mr. Draper is proud of you, too, and so is Franco."

"Really?" she asked, glancing uncertainly in Gionelli's direction. "Are you proud of me, Franco? You're not mad?"

"Yeah," said that young man grudgingly, shifting his glare only for the briefest instant away from Sergeant

312

Cryer. He's jealous, Sims realized. But then, receiving a squeeze on the arm from Ernie Draper, Franco added: "Sure I'm proud of you, Hon. You done real good."

"Okay," Cryer told them. "She'll do. If she's this sure about a line-up, we can use her." He sighed. "I guess we'll have to, anyway... we haven't come up with anybody else. I don't suppose you have?"

"So far, no," Sims admitted.

"Mrs. Morley," Cryer said, "I congratulate you, and thank you." He held onto the hand Amanda had offered in farewell and raised it to his lips. She blushed lightly, but made a prompt and graceful reply. Sims knew how Franco Gionelli felt. Cryer turned to him: "You, I envy."

CHAPTER 38

Miss Hillyard was at her desk, where she had been throughout the excitement. "Oh, good, it's you! I've been on the edge of my seat," she said. While the reception was gratifying, Sims could think of no way in which he had earned it. "What happened?"

Sims told her: "Marcie Bowers identified David Frayne as the man she had seen on the grounds, on the morning Dr. Morley was killed."

She drew in a long breath, shuddered. "He did do it...?"

"Certainly."

"Oh, my God," said Miss Hillyard," her voice as colourless as her face, "I went out with a... a murderer.."

"I don't think you were in any danger."

"Oh, it's not that," explained Miss Hillyard. "It's just, you know, I thought he was so nice... I mean, how can you tell? I mean, what if I go out with some other guy, and he's nice, and I like him and everything...?"

"Well," Sims tried to reassure her, "you stopped seeing him... When was it? April? You must have realized he wasn't as nice as he seemed. That suggests your judgement is pretty good, doesn't it?"

"I guess - maybe." She hesitated.

"Of course it does."

The girl shook her head. "Not really, though. I mean, I would've stopped seeing him anyway, after... when I found out he was engaged. The sneak! I never guessed..."

"What about the girl he's engaged to," said Sims. "Think how she must feel."

Miss Hillyard put her hand to her mouth prettily, only half play-acting. "The poor thing! If I'm not very smart, she must be some kind of prize dope."

"She isn't, you know. Just a nice girl who got taken in by an expert con-man. It could happen to anyone. It *does* happen, and you should be careful. Fortunately, there aren't all that many David Fraynes in the world. Why did you break up with him?"

"Well," she hesitated, then made a visible decision to level. "I really didn't. I mean, he just stopped asking me."

Sims did his best to sound surprised.

"It's okay. I mean, well, I was kind of hurt at the time,

314

sure. But... Even without me knowing about... you know, what kind of guy he was and everything, it's good, really. It wasn't getting anywhere, if you know what I mean."

"I'm not sure that I do,"

"Well, like, it's good, now that I know? But I thought it was bad, him not getting any more serious. All's he ever did was take me to a crummy Chinese restaurant down the street and talk shop. Well, I mean who cares if Mr. Q. had a meeting with Mr. M.? Or if one plastic stuff gets made and another one doesn't? Sure, I kind of knew it was important to Dave if his stuff got made... but, like, I couldn't get all worked up about it. It's not exactly romantic, you know?"

"I see what you mean." Having already worked this out, Sims was able to contain his excitement. "And that's all he wanted to talk about?"

"Practically... Oh. My. God!" The penny dropped. "That bastard was just using me! Wasn't he?"

Sims nodded. "He used everybody. He's very good at it. Would you like to get even?"

"I guess..."

"Then testify."

"You mean, stand up and admit that I fell for some guy that all he wanted from me was to find out my boss's business? In front of everybody? I'd just die!"

Sims gently pointed out: "Someone *did*."

Miss Hillyard quickly lost the colour anger and shame had given her. "Yeah. I kind of forgot." She took a breath so deep that at least one of the regulars at the Three Dragons, had he been present, would have fainted. "All right. Well, anyway," she clarified, "it's not like I married him, right? It's not like I was the only sucker on the block. Or even in this building," she added darkly. "Poor Winnie!" This afterthought was a shade less sincere. She explained: "Rowena Stenchuck. Mr. Meyer's secretary? There's another sucker for you."

Sims took down the high points of the preceding conversation and told Miss Hillyard to expect a visit from Sergeant Cryer. "I talked to him," she said, not at all unhappily. "He's nice."

Miss Stenchuck was no great surprise now: an attractive woman in her early thirties, with short dark hair cut in straight bangs. Of course. You should have known, you prize dope, Sims told himself: the man in the restaurant had all but drawn you a picture. Roberta Farrell doesn't have bangs; she has short curly hair, brushed off her face. And she's younger than Miss Hillyard, not older. There you were, with a preconceived idea, not paying attention. Dope. Miss Stenchuck had dark brown eyes and looked a little as if she had been crying. Over Frayne? Surely not - even if the word got around this fast, she had only gone out with him one time. One time, he corrected, to the Three Dragons. Suppose, being secretary to the biggest boss, Frayne had decided to cultivate her in more auspicious surroundings... Better be very tactful indeed; she might be delicate.

He introduced himself. "Is Mr. Meyer in?"

"Not exactly," she said. "He is on the premises, but he has not yet returned from a meeting. Would you like to wait, Sergeant?"

Oh, very nice. Good-looking, well-spoken... Why had Sims never met her before? He asked.

"I only work when Mr. Meyer does," she told him. "It's an unusual arrangement - one we both find convenient. Would you care for a coffee while you wait?"

"No, thank you. In fact, it was you I wanted to see."

"Oh? Why should that be?"

"I believe you must know what this meeting was about." She acknowledged it with a slight nod, offering nothing more. He explained anyway: "It was to ascertain whether a girl in the factory named Marcie Bowers could identify the man she had seen leaving Ac-Me property on the morning Dr. Morley was killed." She nodded again, never taking her pink-rimmed eyes from his face. "Do you know who the main suspect is?"

"I believe it's David Frayne. Was she able to identify him?"

"Unhesitatingly. Does it shock you?"

"Not really. There was something cold about the man. I would not have taken him for a... But then, one can't guess who might be a killer. Or, perhaps you can?"

"No, I've never noticed any one characteristic common to all killers. Not even coldness. So, you do know David Frayne personally,"

316

"Not very well. I have had dinner with him."

"Often?"

"Once."

"I see." He didn't, with any great clarity. "It was not a happy occasion?"

Miss Stenchuck lifted her shoulders slightly and let them fall. "It was no sort of occasion. Merely a casual invitation, a casual acceptance... some eggrolls, quite good won ton, adequate shrimp... and then, good night."

"No excitement?"

"No excitement," she smiled. "The little weasel only wanted information about his precious insulating material - which, incidentally, was never viable. He didn't get any."

"And that was all?"

"That," she smiled again, "was quite enough."

"But if you had no... um... feelings for him, why were you crying?" he persisted gently. "Then - or just now?"

"Crying? Oh, you misunderstood this," she waved two fingers under her own eye. "It's the price of vanity. You see, I started wearing contact lenses early this year - in spite of a known allergy. The optometrist warned me... yet I persevere. My only hope is that I'll grow accustomed to them and this unfortunate effect will disappear."

"Ah. Then, you don't care about Frayne?"

"Not in the least."

"That's wonderful!"

"I'm quite relieved myself, under the circumstances."

"And you wouldn't mind testifying against him?"

"Not at all, if it were any use. Only, aside from company events, I never saw the man socially, but that one time."

"Tell the police what you just told me. It will help to establish premeditation. You are not the only woman - person, I mean - he tried to cultivate for information."

"I didn't imagine so. Jane Hillyard? Yes, naturally. Though she's not a very sophisticated girl, I should think she had the native intelligence not to fall for his line."

"Miss Hillyard has consented to testify."

"Good," Miss Stenchuck said with every appearance of genuine approval. "I hate to see a young girl fall prey to his sort."

Now this is the kind of witness we really do dream about, Sims said internally. Where were you six weeks ago? He didn't ask and also refrained, though he was sorely tempted, from enquiring about any relations she might have had with the victim. Right after Eve Dumont, this was the woman at Ac-Me Plastics Edward should have succumbed to. Sims, too, for that matter. The young man at Three Dragons was right out of the running. And yet, the interview had been just that. No firecrackers, no sirens, no more excitement than if he had been David Frayne, seeking information... Very strange. Well, it would have been very strange, then, six weeks ago. Things change.

"You said," Miss Stenchuck remarked, "tell the police. Are you not the police?"

"Yes and no," he replied. "It's ambiguous, my present position."

"I see," she said. "None of my business."

Sims was on the point of explaining, then thought better of it. He merely smiled. "Please talk freely to Sergeant Cryer."

He spent a few more minutes, waiting for Mr. Meyer, only because it would have been rude to leave without a word. It wasn't much more than a word that they exchanged.

Amanda joined him in the hall outside Mr. Quick's office. "Well, Charlie's pleased as Punch," she said. "And you look like the proverbial cat. Lots of pretty canaries around here?"

"Dozens," Sims agreed. "But I don't stalk."

"Well, that's a relief," Amanda said, next morning, when he told her of David Frayne's arrest. "I was worried about Marcie. I didn't think he'd try anything, but you never know, do you? Were you there?"

Sims nodded. "Cryer called me at the crack of dawn."

"Cryer seems a nice man. How was he?"

"Fine... well, not very excited about the whole thing,"

Amanda interrupted: "I meant Frayne. Was he frightened, blustering, cocky - what?" There was impatience, perhaps anxiety, in her voice.

Sims reflected. "Pretty cool, on the whole. Very pale, but steady and calm. No confession... in fact, I don't think he said anything at all. They'll be questioning him all day, chalking up lots of overtime. Cryer decided on Saturday

318

morning, so as to have him for 48 hours before the legal system kicks in - his words. Good thinking, too. But I don't suppose Frayne will say anything new: he has a well-rehearsed story; he's smart enough to stick to it."

Amanda gave him a level stare. "Tell me honestly. What kind of case do we have?"

"We have a case. Cryer isn't one to jump the gun. How good? I'm not sure... Much depends on his lawyer."

They were in the late dining, now operations room, finishing a hasty cup of coffee. Sims put it down, absent-mindedly stroking the sad dog. This had become a habit with his bloodhound mug. Earlier, he had rushed over to Galileo Crescent, delaying only to let Lancelot out while he dressed. The dog hadn't had time to dig... and if Mrs. Field objected to the other thing, Sims would make it up to her later. It didn't matter - it couldn't matter, given the importance of Frayne's arrest: Sims could not allow himself to miss that. But Lance hadn't had time to exercise, which made him restless in the car and more so, on the way to Amanda's house: he had expected the ride to end at the ravine, or in some nice green park full of squirrels. Sims realized he had been neglecting the real dog and made a silent pledge to do better, once this mess was over. Now Lancelot lay quietly, with ears and eyes alert to every nuance of the conversation: should anyone mention 'quadruped', 'perambulation', or any relevant subject, he was at full readiness. But the humans paid no attention.

"I've been reading over the notes," Amanda said thoughtfully. "Motive, means, opportunity, little bits of circumstance... Too much depends on Marcie, and she's not a strong witness... Alec, I don't want him to get away with it!"

"Neither do I," he said. "That's why I'm going back on the street."

She looked up at the map. "It's three blocks out now - do you still think...?"

"I thought I'd concentrate on Steeles. He had to get there; he had to get back. Cryer's team covered car rentals and duplicated all your work on taxi drivers. Nothing. That leaves a ride from a friend - and I'm almost positive he didn't let his friends in on it. Aside from the fact that he wouldn't trust them with his life, I don't see either one as a great actor. That leaves the bus. One simply cannot ride public transit without being seen." He drew a yellow border one block south and one block north of the route from Ac-Me to Galileo Crescent. Then he extended each end another two blocks. "He wouldn't board in front of his own place, or the scene of the crime. Now, who rides the bus on a Saturday? People without cars. Mostly women." In reply to her sharp look, he added: "I talked to the drivers, remember? Mostly young women. And who notices David Frayne, wherever he shows up?"

"Young women!" they said in unison.

He continued: "We're interested in nine to 9:30 a.m., and again in some time after ten. Most people wouldn't be going to work at that hour; they would be shopping or doing errands."

"And some of them," Amanda took it up, "will be doing the same errands today..."

"...so I'd better get on my horse." He rose. "You'll let Lance out?" This, of course, was a tactical error: the dog immediately scrambled up on his long legs and was half-way to the front door.

"I'll leave him in the yard," said Amanda, without even stopping to comfort the disappointed animal. "Where do you want to start?"

"On the bus. Bayview end, south side."

"Okay," she said, all business. "I'll take the north side, from the other end. I'll get off two stops past Bayview and take the next bus going east." She riffled through the notes, found the schedule, made a quick mental calculation. "That's five rides from nine to noon. Six, to get back to my car."

"Are you sure you want to do this?" The tilt of her chin stopped him. "Sorry. Of course, you do. Suppose you make it five rides, and meet me at the Three Dragons for lunch. Say, 12:30?" She gave a smart little salute. "It's after eight now. Let's get going."

"Better take time out to dress," he gently reminded. She was in a bathrobe and barefoot, just as he'd roused her out of bed half an hour before.

CHAPTER 39

Canvassing was no less tedious on a bus than on the street, but with the added inconvenience of having to approach people cold, with little time for introduction or preamble. Sims took the precaution of identifying himself and telling his business to each driver upon boarding. The first man remembered him from their earlier, fruitless interview and mentioned that he had, ever since, kept his eyes open, and not seen the man. The route was not heavily travelled on a Saturday morning; Sims was able to note each passenger as he or she got on. In the first two blocks, he had already flashed Frayne's handsome face at the assembled riders, all of whom shook their heads in regretful negation. After that, there was silence, total attention. He felt like the leading man on a stage that would not keep still; the passengers waited with bated breath for the next performance. Some were reluctant to disembark at their stops, wanting to see an outcome; the bus was growing unusually full He took advantage of a red light to address the audience.

"Ladies and Gentlemen. There isn't going to be any drama here. If I should find the person I hope to find, all that will happen is a quiet conversation. It isn't worth missing your appointments for. And it would be a great help if I could do this as inconspicuously as possible."

The driver breathed a sigh of relief. Too soon; large numbers of people began asking for transfers before descending. Not one of them had recognised David Frayne. The return journey was similar, except in that Sims asked each person he approached to go on about their normal business, so as not to "blow my cover". This worked; while there was an unnatural hush and surreptitious glances, no crowd formed. No positive identification resulted, either. At least one person - young and female, in every case - on each trip thought she might have seen the man before; none could say where or when. By lunch-time, Sims was exhausted and discouraged. He could only hope Amanda had been more successful. If they came up with nothing by this method, there remained only to canvass all the houses and offices and factories along the route - a formidable and time-consuming task.

He could see, the minute he entered the restaurant, that she had fared no better. She was sitting by the window, her shoes kicked off under the table, looking a little dishevelled and more than a little disgruntled. An even more ominous sign: she was sipping at something golden-brown in a thick glass.

"Scotch? At lunch time?"

She nodded. "Anything?"

"No."

"No. Back to foot patrol?"

He shrugged. "I suppose so."

She sighed, picked up the menu. "We'll need our strength."

"First, I need one of those," he pointed to her glass. Looking around for the waiter, Sims reached into his pocket, came up with an empty cigarette pack. There was a vending machine, but he had used up all his change on the buses. He swore softly - not at that circumstance, specifically, so much as at things in general. "Sorry."

"It's all right; that's the way I feel, too."

"Order something, will you? Doesn't matter what - it'll all taste like ashes, anyway - just so it comes with a scotch, no water, no rocks. I have to go next door for a minute."

As it turned out, he spent more than a minute. The milk store was in the capable charge of Patti Robinson, who recognised him from their earlier interview.

"Sergeant Sims, isn't it? Are you still trying to find out about that poor man who got killed? Some other policemen asked me all the same questions you did, and now you're back again. Don't you guys trust each other?"

"Actually," he said, "I just came in to buy some cigarettes. Dunhill, I think, filter..." The girl slid a flip-top box across the counter. Sims raised it as in a toast. "To Edward Morley." While she counted out his change, he explained: "It's not a matter of trust - we just have to make sure everything is thoroughly covered. Sometimes people recall more details, once they've had time to think."

"Well, I couldn't tell them any more than I told you. Nothing much happened, you see." She looked a little disappointed.

"But what you did know was vital to establish time of death. Really. I don't think we'd have much a case without

322

you. The murderer has been arrested, by the way."

"Really? That's great! How come I haven't heard?"

"It only happened this morning. You're going to be one of the star witnesses. Don't be nervous, now," he added, seeing a look of apprehension cross her pixie face. "You have an excellent memory - you'll do just fine."

It occurred to Sims that he was talking to a very bright, alert young woman as if she were a child. Well, in a way, she was a child; possibly, she could use a little appreciation and encouragement. But was he condescending? Too paternal? Was he mistaking her for Marcie Bowers? She didn't seem insulted... He made one or two more inane remarks, then turned to leave. Almost at the door, stepping aside for an elderly woman to enter, he noticed the empty Renters News box on the corner outside, next to the bus stop, remembered that he should be looking for an apartment, and turned back to buy a newspaper.

Beside the bus stop. Well, why not start right here? He had to wait until the other customer had gathered up her purchases and gone out the door.

"There is one more thing I'd like to ask you," he said, as he returned the change Patti had just given him. He put the paper down and reached into his pocket for the well-worn photograph he'd carried next to his heart for over five weeks. "Have you ever seen this man before?"

"Sure," said Patti, "lots of times."

"He works at the same place as the man who was killed," said Sims in his steadiest, most neutral voice.

The girl paled, so that her freckles stood out individually. "The homicide people didn't say anything about him. He didn't get killed too?"

"No," said the detective. "I just want to know some things about him. When did you see him?"

"He didn't come in here much - just once in a while for, like an evening paper or a candy bar – when I was working after school. I used to see him go by - to the restaurant, I guess." She sighed. "Mostly with some nice-looking girl... He's got this great car - a blue Trans-Am, you know? It was funny, he always parked it under the light and took up two spaces. I thought he was a lousy driver - I could do better than that, and I only had my license a couple of months. But then Leroy told me, guys do that on purpose, so nobody can get close enough to scratch their paint. Well, but it's still rude, don't you think? In such a small lot?"

"Yes, it is. So, you know this man pretty well by sight. You don't know his name, by any chance?"

Patti shook her head regretfully. "I haven't got his phone number, either."

"Have you seen him at all, since you've been working weekends?"

"I don't think... wait! Yes, I have, too. Not in here, though. Outside."

With a huge effort, Sims kept his voice quiet and dead level. "Tell me about that." He felt like a hunter: if he made a sudden move now, a noise; if he sneezed or scratched or stepped on twig, the prey might get away. Another part of his mind registered how foolish this was: either she had seen Frayne that day or she had not - nothing he said or did now could change that. Nevertheless, he held his breath.

"No big deal, really," she said. "He got on a bus, that's all. He must have just crossed the street, I can't see traffic light from here, only a bit of sidewalk. He turned around, the bus came almost right away, and he got on it. What?" she added anxiously. "Is that important?"

"Miss Robinson." His teeth were clenched tightly enough to hurt. "When?"

"Why, on the same day. When the other man was here."

"What time?" His hand did start out across the counter, but he stopped it, managed to refrain from seizing the girl's wrist. She had taken a backward step and was looking decidedly apprehensive now.

"I don't know... It matters, doesn't it?" He gave one quick nod. She took a deep breath. "Okay. The other man, the one who got killed, he was in at 9:30 or so. Around that. Then this had to be at maybe ten... I can't tell you exactly... There was a lady and then a little kid - he came in for milk and he took forever deciding what candy to buy with the change... Yeah. Half an hour, maybe. How important is it?"

Sims got a grip on himself. After a while - not a whole year but something like, it seemed - he was even able to speak, rather than shout. "Important," he said. "Very, very important. Are you absolutely sure?"

The girl nodded. Her eyes were wide and serious, her arms out at her sides, elbows bent: a fight or flight stance, well out of his reach.

"Absolutely? You can identify him? You can swear he got on that bus, at that time, on that day? You can swear it in a court of law?"

She nodded again. There was a silence. Her body began to relax. Then, in a near-whisper, she asked: "He's the one? That cute guy is the one?"

"Yes! And we got him! *You* got him." She didn't look at all happy. "Patti, listen to me. This is not a cute guy. This is a cold-blooded murderer. He took the life of a decent, honest, smart, useful man, who had a wife and children and friends who cared about him. He planned it for weeks, maybe months. He did it because that decent man wouldn't let him produce a substance which might have hurt a lot of people. Those nice young women he took to dinner? He only wanted to use them. He used two other nice young people who admired and trusted him. Do you understand? It doesn't matter what he looks like - it matters what he is."

"I guess," she said, her round cat-like eyes still fixed on Sims' face. "Yeah," she repeated, dropping her gaze with a small sigh, "I guess I understand. But it's a shame,"

"It is," he agreed. "Are you all right?"

She shrugged. It was a somewhat self-conscious gesture; she was already trying on the role of star witness. "Sure. Well, it's not like I was dating him, or anything..."

"Now, I'm going to call those other policemen. From here, if I may use the phone. They'll come very soon, and ask you all the same things... probably over and over. They may want you to go to the police station. If you want, I can stay till they get here..."

"No, that's all right... I mean, I'd kind of like to be alone for a while... I better call the manager, too..."

At the restaurant he did shout - almost. "That's not enough food! We need eggrolls. Lots of them. And something sweet and sour - better make it a horse. I have to kiss somebody." To Amanda's amazement - and acute embarrassment - he did. "Well, Patti's far too young. And the waiter isn't my type. Not that that would necessarily stop me right now..."

Amanda was slowly regaining her composure. She pulled the glass away, just as he reached for it. "I don't know about that. You were gone long enough to have cleaned out a whole liquor store... Would you like to sit down and tell me about it? Please?"

He reclaimed his drink. "I'm trying to," he said. "Pay attention, will you? We've got him! We Have Got Frayne. Nailed, dead to rights. Gift-wrapped. Mummified. I can't think of any more cliches. Patti Robinson saw him get on the bus," he waved the empty glass in the direction of the street. "That bus. Westbound. On the right day, at the right hour. She knows him. She saw him. She can identify him. You think we could adopt her? No, she's got a perfectly good mother. All right then, we are going to take that girl home and put her in a glass case till the trial. Have we got a glass case? Never mind, we'll buy one on the way home... Where are my eggrolls?"

"Alec, do you know you're babbling? I don't mind, of course, but you might like to keep your voice down,"

"Yes," he said. "Yes. I'll be all right in a minute. Is there another drink someplace?"

"Here, have a glass of wine; it's cooler. And eat something before you fly through the roof. Now," she continued when he had set to work on the food, the nature and temperature of which he did not stop to question. "Do I understand this correctly? You found the witness we've been looking for?"

Sims nodded, silent at last, mouth full.

"And that it's the same girl who established the time of Edward's arrival at Ac-Me?"

"Yes. Worth her weight in gold. Double her weight - she's a little skinny thing."

Amanda nodded sagely. "That will do it. Yes, it will. We really have got him." She put down her fork, stood up. Without bothering to regain her shoes or check whether anyone was watching, she came around the table, pulled Sims to his feet and embraced him. "It really is over."

CHAPTER 40

The formal portion of the meeting did not take long. Inspector MacDonald reviewed the highlights of the case, agreed that, but for some slovenly typing on the last two or three reports, it was ready to be presented to the Attorney General's office. Cryer and the ubiquitous, invisible Fenton would do that later in the day. Sims was invited to attend.

"After all," Cryer said, "it was never our case." He held up a restraining palm and MacDonald subsided in his chair. "We should have had it immediately, or not at all. As it transpired, we had only a week to rake over cold ashes, already adequately covered... And that, if I may be candid, is a waste of departmental time and manpower that might have been far better utilized." Transpired? Utilized? Sims was surprised at Cryer using such words. Yet, the inspector was paying attention. Well, of course: this was a rebuke aimed at a superior rank - it had to be couched in officious terms. "We are cognisant of the pressures under which 43 Division has been labouring, but in future, the Squad would appreciate every effort to be apprised of homicides at the earliest possible point in the investigation."

He's mad as hell, Sims realized. And he has every right to be mad. I was so preoccupied with my own bruised pride, it never occurred to me to wonder how they felt. Would I like to be called in on an investigation near its completion? Not on your life. How had Cryer contrived to be as civil and cooperative as he had been? How had Fenton managed to utter no word of protest - or any other kind of word?

"Are you through, Sergeant?" MacDonald asked mildly. "You got it out of your system, or you want to spend more precious dee-partmental time, dressing me down in front of one of my men?" Cryer had the grace to look abashed. "Okay, look. You got a point - but, like you say, there have been ah... other pressures. This wasn't your regular homicide. And that's all I got to say about that. The guy is behind bars; justice, like they say in the movies, is served. So what do you care who brought in what little bit of evidence? Ain't we all on the same side?"

Cryer nodded and, astonishingly, smiled. Then he

extended his right hand, which MacDonald took. No hard feelings. It was Sims' turn to feel abashed: he had just been given a lesson in the conduct of officers and gentlemen, which shed a very poor light on his own recent behaviour.

The inspector heaved a super-sized sigh. "So, okay. We got a case. Put it together, take my boy Sims along like he was one of your team. Which, anyway, he might be, soon. Any comments on that?"

Cryer answered: "I, personally, would be proud to have Detective-sergeant Sims on the Homicide Squad." And turning to the man in question, he asked: "Have you put in for transfer?"

"Not yet," said Sims, "but it would be an honour to serve on your team."

Anyone overhearing this exchange, Sims thought, would be sick to his stomach. But the courtesies are necessary; egos are on the line every minute; they need to be protected. The homicide men departed, with more handshakes all around.

"Hang on, boy," MacDonald called after him. "Take a load off. We got to discuss your future... No time like the present, eh?" He snuffled into his chins: a restrained laugh at his own joke. He was exceptionally jovial, given what had just taken place, and Sims wondered if there might be some reason for this, aside from the completion of a case - in which he had not believed until almost too late. "So," the inspector leaned back, fingers interlaced behind his head. "You gonna put in for Homicide, or what?"

"I've given it some thought," Sims admitted. "But, no. On the whole, I don't think it's for me."

"You done a good job on that armoured car thing..." MacDonald broke off for a real, out-loud laugh. "Three Goddam women with antique rifles! You got to hand it to some of these criminal types. Well, some of em." His face grew sombre once again. "You hear about the drug ring? No? Dammit, boy, I don't get on the news every day of the week - least you could do is watch! We busted it, night before last. Yessiree, rounded up the scumbags. House full o shit, guns - the whole ball of wax."

"Congratulations," Sims was startled into saying. He felt he ought to say more; this was very big and very good news. But MacDonald stopped him.

"Yeah. I feel okay about it myself. Anyhoo. Seems like it's gonna get me a promotion, finally... That and my... ah... How does it go again? My expeditious and diplomatic handling of the internal investigation... You know which one, the corruption mess. Goddam stoopid business. So, okay. That's gonna leave my job up for grabs. I figure you're one of three guys in this whole place senior enough and smart enough to handle it." He leaned back even farther; Sims was worried that the chair might tip over - a breach of dignity he had often wished upon the inspector and which, at this moment, he would deeply regret. Of course, it did not happen; it never would: Big Mac had a superb sense of balance.

"Are you suggesting that I apply for it?" MacDonald inclined his head slowly, rucking up chins, while his little dark eyes remained level and fixed. Birds had that knack of keeping their eyes on the target, whatever their bodies might be doing. Amanda had explained it: they had a sort of inner gyroscope.

"With all respect, sir, I must decline."

"Yeah, that's what I figured - smart enough to do it, smart enough not to take it on toast, with marmalade. It's like any other job - some days, it stinks - some days, it ain't so bad. You got to know, though: it's about the only way up. No? Okay, I asked. So it's Steig or Curie. You gonna get along with either one better than me."

Sims turned this information over in his mind. Did it change anything? Two weeks ago, it might have changed everything - but not now. "That is no longer a factor," he said. "I intend to hand in my resignation today."

The oversized chair hit the floor with a resounding thump. There was some little satisfaction in having surprised Inspector MacDonald. "You *what*!?"

"I'm quitting, sir."

"To do what? You gonna move to the north woods and look at ducks? Course I know bout that... I'm paid to know stuff. Well?"

"Well, that, too. I have promised to help Mrs. Morley with the text of her book on the Red-necked Grebe..." Here was a perfect opportunity for a cheap shot at red necks and his experience of them, yet it cost Sims little to pass it

329

up. Today, we are all behaving like grownups. He continued: "I've decided to set up in business for myself."

"What? Open a hardware store? Or has that Saunders guy been turning your head? I hear they do okay, PI's, cash-wise."

"Yes."

MacDonald blinked several times in rapid succession. "Yes, he sez, cool as a cucumber. And here's me, short-staffed, and half of what I got, strictly light-weight in the brains department." This was a compliment and Sims accepted it in that spirit. As a description of the actual state of affairs, it was inaccurate: the division was at full complement, or better, with DiMarco's promotion.

"Surely, that will be a problem for Steig or Curie."

MacDonald grinned. "Yeah, whaddo I care? So, you got your mind all made up?"

"Yes, sir." Quite recently, he would not have uttered this many 'sirs' in a month, let alone in a single conversation. They cost nothing now.

The inspector nodded, stretched, snorted, scratched his belly - as if deliberately running through his repertoire of irritating habits to remind Sims of what he would least miss. "Okay. Well then, best thing to do is clear out your desk - I mean, right after you type up the resignation - neatly, mind. No offense, boy. It's just, we got to think of morale - y'know? Better not have you around here for two weeks, shovin all the other guys' faces in it. Eh? You still got a week an a half vacation... Date the thing back to, say, last Wednesday, that oughta do for notice. Okay?"

"Okay," said Sims. "Yes, sir, I'll do that."

The chair thumped down again. The ponderous bulk of Inspector MacDonald reared up like a whale from the deeps - and with a similar majesty. A huge hand advanced toward him and Sims took it. "Good luck to you, boy."

On that Monday, Sims turned quite a few heads at 43 Division - and not only feminine ones, although PC Browning did compliment him on looking very dapper. Dapper? That was a word for Charlie Quick. He had taken some trouble to shave and trim his moustache. He had been up early enough to walk the dog properly, eat a wholesome breakfast and dress with a great deal more care than usual. And if he looked an inch or so taller, it was because he had barely touched ground since Saturday afternoon.

Saturday evening had been spent celebrating, then talking with Amanda, late into the night. Early into the morning, actually. Sunday was truly busy. He had visited Father Mike, for a long an earnest discussion of his plans. Perhaps his blessing was not necessary, but it was comforting to have.

Then he had called on Pete Saunders at home. He met Mrs. Saunders and two of the children briefly, before retreating to the office.

"Now," his host said. "Make yourself comfortable." It would have been impossible, in that room, to do otherwise. It had more leather than Dr. Jones' study, but all of it was well padded, supple and scuffed with age. There was a necessary desk, filing cabinets and bookcases in worn oak of different hues, none matching. Saunders explained with pride that it had taken ten years of dedicated auction-going to collect the furniture. Almost as soon as he was seated, a long and narrow orange cat approached, bent its tail in a question mark and put two white paws on Sims' knee. When he patted the animal's head, he/she jumped up into his lap, and stayed there throughout the interview. "What, at long last, can I do for you?"

Sims outlined his and Amanda's plan to set up as private investigators. "You're serious? Hey, that's great! And with a partner already."

"In fact, that's the favour I came to ask," Sims told him. "You said you'd lend us one of your men... Well, we'd like to borrow a particular one, if he's willing. What I mean is, Amanda would like to spend some time with your scenes-of-crime expert. She's already an excellent photographer, but she needs the rest of the lore... dabs, casts, documents...?"

Saunders stopped laughing after a while. "Please accept my most humble apologies for that outburst," he said, wiping an eye. "It was not intended to be disparaging, believe me. I just had this picture... you ever get those? Yes? Then you know there's no defence against them. I just saw, in living colour, my ident guy, who happens to be six foot five and about 140 pounds, never without a two-day stubble - I do not know how he maintains it at exactly two days - and he prefers to work in a ratty old teeshirt and coveralls... with your sweet, neat, ever so well-bred Mrs. Morley - crawling around in the mud together, casting a tire-tread."

"Nevertheless," replied Sims coolly, "Amanda is competent to crawl around in the mud, as you put it, casting tire-treads. Or anything else that needs doing. And neatness is hardly to be considered a drawback in such work."

"All right, all right. Point taken. You needn't be so touchy; I really didn't mean to put down your ident guy. Lady. Person. As to the question of a... an apprenticeship, is it? Sure. I have no objection, and I venture to presume George will be delighted. A ray of sunshine in his hum-drum life. I'll arrange it, first thing tomorrow. Anything else?"

Sims, mollified and repentant, said: "Anything you can tell me. Or rather: I would very much appreciate the benefit of your vast and superior experience in this enterprise." He looked questioningly at Saunders.

That man grinned. "By George, I think he's got it. And, to me, 'by George' is no trivial oath... Your ident person is your single most important asset. That's thing one. Things two through fifty, you already know. I guess you'll have no problem with a license or gun permit... You'll need suitable premises... Now, I've got a classy office downtown, but I started out with a little hole of a study in my house. Not this house - this is one of the benefits. What else? A good - a really excellent - computer if you can afford it. I can recommend a man for that. You'll need cards printed... A case would be nice, too. Not a card-case, I mean, but a job. That man with the son and the stocks is still looking. Interested?"

Sims was. In fact, he was counting on it: it had been a factor, if not a major one, in his and Amanda's calculations. The cat was purring almost as loudly as Saunders talked. "He likes you. That's a good sign - Pooky doesn't thrust his attentions on just anybody. Disgusting name, ain't it? My daughter did that to him when she was eight. Pooky is nearly eight himself now, and Karen is dating." He rubbed a hand across his shiny pink forehead. "Life just keeps getting tougher." But his tone was one of profound satisfaction.

Later, he casually invited Sims to dinner with the family. It was a lively affair, in spite of the two younger children - Bruce, who looked about eleven, and Taylor, of reptile fame - having been warned not to bicker. They merely kicked each other under the table and giggled a lot. Karen was, at least for this occasion, a sophisticated young lady, making adult conversation. Pooky and two companions took it in turns to canvass the table for contraband. Mrs. Saunders, who looked strangely familiar to Sims, but whom he could not place and did not want to ask, was a cheerful, competent woman, and a warm hostess. He left, quite late in the evening, filled in about equal parts with gratitude, well-being and envy.

The crown attorney made every effort to appear objective and controlled but Sims noted, not without a certain smugness, that he was impressed. It was a good, solid case. Cryer presented it, point by point, coherently and well. Then Sims answered questions of detail and background. Fenton kept his habitual silence. They discussed the advisability of calling Paul Arnott to testify and agreed to hold off on that decision. Sims would visit him, some time in the near future - not only for the purpose of assessment, but because he wanted to know how the boy was faring. Roberta Farrell, however, was essential. It would be necessary to apprise her of certain facts concerning her fiance... Cryer took on that task, to Sims' relief. They trusted - hoped - that she would not be hostile by court-date. Sims never need see, or hear of, David Frayne again until the trial. This suited him perfectly. Cryer deposited his own reports, the lab results and the neatly-typed notes that Sims had given him. It was, by all appearances, a fine example of team-work.

Cryer was philosophical. "At least it didn't tie up the squad for two months," he said. "We do have other work. So, you're off on your own? Just as well, from everything I hear."

They shook hands. Sims estimated that by the end of the day, he must have shaken more hands than a candidate for some minor political office. He also got a few hugs and kisses from female personnel who had never before seemed inclined to demonstrations of affection. He drank a dozen cups of the nearly solid institutional coffee and lunched on doughnuts someone had brought in to make the occasion more festive. At last, desk clean for the next occupant - DiMarco, in all probability, a more than worthy successor - he was ready to leave.

"Big Mac's not in," remarked the clerk. "Hasn't been, since lunch time. He said to tell you not to forget your court schedule." She added under her breath: "Boy."

So that was that. He shook one more hand.

At the front door of the Morley house, Lancelot must have been lying in ambush: the second he opened it, the dog leapt on his chest - something he hadn't done in a long time. Amanda, not far behind, asked: "How was it?"

"Not too bad. Quite smooth, in fact. I ought to be elated."

"No, you ought not. It's bound to be painful, leaving a place - leaving an environment, a function, a whole crowd of people, you've been accustomed to for years. Wallow a little - it's normal."

"All right." He settled into his favourite chair and Lance dropped with a happy sigh onto his feet. "Can I have cocoa in the hound mug, please?"

"With marshmallows," Amanda said.

Later, having recounted the day's events as nearly word for word as he could manage, Sims started on his conversation with Saunders. That, too, she must have in all detail. She was excited and a little nervous at the prospect of studying scenes-of-crime technique. "George sounds formidable. I hope he doesn't hate me."

"You will dazzle him with your intelligence, your wit - and, if absolutely unavoidable, with your charm. How was your day?"

"I called around for someone to cut the new door," she said, referring to the dining room. As their office, it should open from the front hall, not the living room. "It won't take more than a couple of days. The same man says he can put in some shelves, but we still need to buy a table and filing cabinets. Louise wants the dining furniture, but Andy can't get hold of a truck till the weekend... We still have

334

quite a lot of work to do. Will that case wait?"

"I haven't spoken to the man yet. I must call him tonight. If he's in a hurry - and, with his problem, time might well be of the essence - I can get started on it from my place." He stopped in dismay. "I'd almost forgotten. I have to make time somehow, to look for an apartment."

"You don't need an apartment," she said complacently.

"I've given notice... I have less than three weeks left."

Amanda sighed. "Alec, don't be so dense. I've already put Edward's things into storage. You only have to tell the contractor what colour you want and they'll have the painting done by next week. You said yourself: if those rooms are haunted, it's by a ghost who has every reason to approve of you."

Sims knew he was supposed to say something. Protest, perhaps, or argue, but he could not think what the appropriate words might be.

"Oh, for Heaven's sake!" Amanda continued. "Isn't it self-evident? You're already here eight hours of every day; you eat here and relax here. Lance has been living here for weeks and he's happy. Now you'll be working here, too. Why in the world would you go somewhere else to sleep?"

He had no alternative but to agree. "One question."

"Shoot."

Now, where had she picked that up? He'd have to put a stop to it, at the earliest opportune moment. Sweet, neat and ever so well-bred, Amanda couldn't go around talking like some movie private eye. But it was a matter of lesser importance.

"Can we get a cat?"

Ordering Information

You can order a copy of this book at the following venues:

- www.amazon.ca
- www.amazon.com
- www.alibris.com
- www.abe.com
- www.montland.ca

or by sending email to the author to the following address:

books@montland.ca

I will respond to queries within 24 hours.

www.ingramcontent.com/pod-product-compliance
Lightning Source LLC
Chambersburg PA
CBHW051952060726
47506CB00011B/310